IN HER SHOES

'A witty, true-to-life tale of family ties, sibling rivalry
and the search for happiness'
COMPANY

'Weiner is a witty writer and her novels are a fine blend of
comedy and genuine darkness . . . she writes about everyday
tragedies without sentiment and with grace and
sharp humour' SUNDAY TRIBUNE

'A must-read lively comedy' SUN

'Like Helen Fielding, Weiner balances romantic formula
with fresh humour, deft characterisations
and literary sensibility' GUARDIAN

'A seriously smart and classy read. Witty and moving,
IN HER SHOES has reminded us never to judge a book
by its pink and fluffy cover' HEAT

'A funny, poignant novel about sisterhood' LUCKY BREAK!

'A good girlie read' IN STYLE

Little Earthquakes

Jennifer Weiner

POCKET
BOOKS

LONDON • SYDNEY • NEW YORK • TORONTO

First published in Great Britain by Pocket Books, 2004
This edition published by Pocket Books, 2005
An imprint of Simon & Schuster UK Ltd
A Viacom Company

Copyright © Jennifer Weiner, 2004

The right of Jennifer Weiner to be identified as author of this work has
been asserted in accordance with sections 77 and 78 of the
Copyright, Designs and Patents Act, 1988.

1 3 5 7 9 10 8 6 4 2

Simon & Schuster UK Ltd
Africa House
64–78 Kingsway
London WC2B 6AH

www.simonsays.co.uk

Simon & Schuster Australia
Sydney

A CIP catalogue record for this book is available from the British Library

ISBN 0 7434 6894 5
EAN 9780 7434 6894 7

Mr Brown Can Moo! Can You? By Dr Seuss, copyright TM and copyright by Dr
Seuss Enterprises L.P. 1970, renewed 1998, used by permission of Random
House Children's Books, a division of Random House, Inc.

'Soliloquy' copyright © 1945 by Williamson Music. Copyright renewed.
International copyright secured. All Rights Reserved. Used by permission.

This book is a work of fiction. Names, characters, places and incidents are either
a product of the author's imagination or are used fictitiously. Any resemblance to
actual people living or dead, events or locales is entirely coincidental.

Printed and bound in Great Britain by
Bookmarque Ltd, Croydon plc

For Lucy Jane

"What is REAL?" asked the Rabbit one day, when they were lying side by side near the nursery fender, before Nana came to tidy the room. "Does it mean having things that buzz inside you and a stick-out handle?"

"Real isn't how you are made," said the Skin Horse. "It's a thing that happens to you. When a child loves you for a long, long time, not just to play with, but REALLY loves you, then you become real."

"Does it hurt?" asked the Rabbit.

"Sometimes," said the Skin Horse, for he was always truthful. "When you are Real you don't mind being hurt."

—MARGERY WILLIAMS
The Velveteen Rabbit

Little
Earthquakes

April

LIA

I watched her for three days, sitting by myself in the park underneath an elm tree, beside an empty fountain with a series of uneaten sandwiches in my lap and my purse at my side.

Purse. It's not a purse, really. Before, I had purses—a fake Prada bag, a real Chanel baguette Sam had bought me for my birthday. What I have now is a gigantic, pink, floral-printed Vera Bradley bag big enough to hold a human head. If this bag were a person, it would be somebody's dowdy, gray-haired great-aunt, smelling of mothballs and butterscotch candies and insisting on pinching your cheeks. It's horrific. But nobody notices it any more than they notice me.

Once upon a time, I might have taken steps to assure that I'd be invisible: a pulled-down baseball cap or a hooded sweatshirt to help me dodge the questions that always began *Hey, aren't you?* and always ended with a name that wasn't mine. *No, wait, don't tell me. Didn't I see you in something? Don't I know who you are?*

Now, nobody stares, and nobody asks, and nobody spares me so much as a second glance. I might as well be a piece of furniture. Last week a squirrel ran over my foot.

But that's okay. That's good. I'm not here to be seen; I'm here to watch. Usually it's three o'clock or so when she shows up. I set aside my sandwich and hold the bag tightly against me like a pillow or a pet, and I stare. At first I couldn't really tell anything, but yesterday she stopped halfway past my fountain and stretched with her hands pressing the small of her back. *I did that,* I thought, feeling my throat close. *I did that, too.*

I used to love this park. Growing up in Northeast Philadelphia, my father would take me into town three times each year. We'd go to the zoo in the summer, to the flower show each spring, and to Wanamaker's for the Christmas light show in December. He'd buy me a treat—a hot chocolate, a strawberry ice cream cone—and we'd sit on a bench, and my father would make up stories about the people walking by. A teenager with a backpack was a rock star in disguise; a blue-haired lady in an ankle-length fur coat was carrying secrets for the Russians. When I was on the plane, somewhere over Virginia, I thought about this park, and the taste of strawberries and chocolate, and my father's arm around me. I thought I'd feel safe here. I was wrong. Every time I blinked, every time I breathed, I could feel the ground beneath me wobble and slide sideways. I could feel things starting to break.

It had been this way since it happened. Nothing could make me feel safe. Not my husband, Sam, holding me, not the sad-eyed, sweet-voiced therapist he'd found, the one who'd told me, "Nothing but time will really help, and you just have to get through one day at a time."

That's what we'd been doing. Getting through the days. Eating food without tasting it, throwing out the Styrofoam containers. Brushing our teeth and making the bed. On a Wednesday afternoon, three weeks after it happened, Sam had suggested a movie. He'd laid out clothes for me to wear—lime-green linen capris that I still couldn't quite zip, an ivory silk blouse with pink-ribbon embroidery, a pair of pink slides. When I'd picked up the diaper bag by the door, Sam had looked at me strangely, but he hadn't said anything. I'd been carrying it instead of a purse before, and I'd kept right on carrying it after, like a teddy bear or a well-loved blanket, like something I loved that I couldn't bring myself to let go.

I was fine getting into the car. Fine as we pulled into the parking garage and Sam held the door for me and walked me into the red-velvet lobby that smelled like popcorn and fake butter. And then I stood there, and I couldn't move another inch.

"Lia?" Sam asked me. I shook my head. I was remembering the last time we'd gone to the movies. Sam bought me malted milk balls and Gummi worms and the giant Coke I'd wanted, even though caffeine was verboten and every sip caused me to burp. When the movie ended, he had to use both hands to haul me out of my seat. *I had everything then,* I thought. My eyes started to burn, my lips started to tremble, and I could feel my knees and neck wobbling, as if they'd been packed full of grease and ball bearings. I set one hand against the wall to steady myself so I wouldn't start to slide sideways. I remembered reading somewhere about how a news crew had interviewed someone caught in the '94 Northridge earthquake. *How long did it go on?* the bland, tan newsman asked. The woman who'd lost her home and her husband had looked at him with haunted eyes and said, *It's still happening.*

"Lia?" Sam asked again. I looked at him—his blue eyes that were still bloodshot, his strong jaw, his smooth skin. *Handsome is as handsome does,* my mother used to say, but Sam had been so sweet to me, ever since I'd met him. Ever since it had happened, he'd been nothing but sweet. And I'd brought him tragedy. Every time he looked at me, he'd see what we had lost; every time I looked at him, I'd see the same thing. I couldn't stay. I couldn't stay and hurt him anymore.

"I'll be right back," I said. "I'm just going to run to the bathroom." I slung my Vera Bradley bag over my shoulder, bypassed the bathroom, and slipped out the front door.

Our apartment was as we'd left it. The couch was in the living room, the bed was in the bedroom. The room at the end of the hall was empty. Completely empty. There wasn't so much as a dust mote in the air. *Who had done it?* I wondered, as I walked into the bedroom, grabbed handfuls of underwear and T-shirts and put them into the bag. *I hadn't even noticed,* I thought. *How could I not have noticed?* One day the room had been full of toys and furniture, a crib and a rocker, and the next day, nothing. Was there some service you could call, a number you could dial, a website you could access, men who would come with garbage bags and vacuum cleaners and take everything away?

Sam, I'm so sorry, I wrote. *I can't stay here anymore. I can't watch you be so sad and know that it's my fault. Please don't look for me. I'll call when I'm ready. I'm sorry . . .* I stopped writing. There weren't even words for it. Nothing came close. *I'm sorry for everything,* I wrote, and then I ran out the door.

The cab was waiting for me outside of our apartment building's front door, and, for once, the 405 was moving. Half an hour later, I was at the airport with a stack of crisp, ATM-fresh bills in my hand. "Just one way?" the girl behind the counter had asked me.

"One way," I told her and paid for my ticket home. The place where they have to take you in. My mother hadn't seemed too happy about it, but then, she hadn't been happy about anything to do with me—or, really, anything at all—since I was a teenager and my father left. But there was a roof over my head, a bed to sleep in. She'd even given me a coat to wear on a cold day the week before.

The woman I've been watching walked across the park, reddish-gold curls piled on her head, a canvas tote bag in her hand, and I leaned forward, holding tight to the edges of the bench, trying to make the spinning stop. She set her bag down on the lip of the fountain and bent down to pet a little black-and-white-spotted dog. *Now,* I thought, and I reached into my sleepover-size sack and pulled out the silver rattle. *Should we get it monogrammed?* Sam had asked. I'd just rolled my eyes and told him that there were two kinds of people in the world, the ones who got things monogrammed at Tiffany's and the ones who didn't, and we were definitely Type Twos. One silver rattle from Tiffany's, unmonogrammed, never used. I walked carefully over to the fountain before I remembered that I'd become invisible and that nobody would look at me no matter what I did. I slid the rattle into her bag and then I slipped away.

BECKY

Her cell phone trilled as she straightened her back. The dog gave one sharp bark and trotted away, and the woman with the long blond hair in the long blue coat walked past her, stepping so close that their shoulders brushed. Becky Rothstein-Rabinowitz brushed her curls out of her eyes, pulled the phone out of her pocket, winced when she saw the number displayed on the screen, and replaced the phone without answering. "Shit," she muttered to no one in particular. That marked her mother-in-law Mimi's fifth call in the last two hours. She and Mimi had had a reasonably peaceful détente when Mimi had lived in Texas with the latest in her five-husband series, but the marriage hadn't lasted. Now Mimi was moving to Philadelphia, and she couldn't seem to grasp the simple fact that her daughter-in-law had both a job and a baby on the way and, hence, better things to do than "just drop by" the shop that Mimi's decorator had recommended and "take a l'il look" at Mimi's custom-ordered drapes. Nor did Becky have "just a quick sec" to drive half an hour to Merion and "sneak a peek" at how construction was proceeding (her mother-in-law was in the process of building a pillared, gabled, verandaed minimansion that looked, to Becky's eyes, like Scarlett O'Hara's abode, if Tara had gotten shrunk in the wash). Becky picked up her bag and walked briskly across the park to her restaurant, Mas.

It was three o'clock in the afternoon, and the little kitchen was already steamy and warm with the scent of braised pork shoulder in a cinnamon-spiked sauce, cilantro and garlic salsa, and roasting peppers for the savory flan. Becky took a deep, happy breath and stretched her arms over her head.

"Thought you were off today," said Sarah Trujillo, her partner and best friend.

"I'm just stopping by," Becky said, as her cell phone trilled again.

"Let me guess," Sarah said.

Becky sighed, looked at the number, then smiled, and flipped the phone open. "Hi, honey," she said. They'd been married for two years, and they'd dated for three years before that, but the sound of Andrew's voice still gave her butterflies.

"Hi. Are you all right?"

She looked down at herself. Bag, boobs, belly, feet, all present and accounted for. "Yeah, I'm fine. Why?"

"Well, my mother just paged me and said she's been trying to reach you, but you weren't picking up your phone."

Shit, Becky thought again.

"Look, I know she can be demanding. I had to live with her, remember?"

"Yes," Becky said. *And how you turned out normal is one of the mysteries of the ages,* she refrained from adding.

"Just humor her a little bit. Ask her how things are going with the move."

"I can humor her," Becky replied, "but I don't have time to run her errands."

"I know," her husband answered. Becky could hear hospital sounds in the background, some doctor being paged. "You don't have to. I don't expect you to. Mimi doesn't, either."

Then why does she keep asking? Becky wondered.

"Just talk to her," Andrew said. "She's lonely."

She's crazy, Becky thought. "Okay," she said. "Next time she calls, I'll talk to her. But I have to turn my phone off soon. Yoga."

Sarah raised her eyebrows. *Yoga?* she mouthed.

"Yoga," Becky repeated and hung up the phone. "Don't laugh."

"Why would I laugh?" Sarah said, smiling sweetly. Sarah had eyes the color of bittersweet chocolate, glossy black hair, and a dancer's body, although she hadn't laced up her pointe shoes since she'd blown out both knees at seventeen. She was the reason that Mas's six-seat bar was packed three deep every week night and four deep on Fridays; the reason that of all the restaurants on Rittenhouse Square, Mas could keep each one of its thirty-six seats full all night long, in spite of the two-hour wait. When Sarah would put on red lipstick and snake-hip through the throng, a plate of complimentary empanadas in her hands and high-heeled sandals on her feet, the grumbles would evaporate and the watch-glancing would cease. "What's the soup again?" Sarah asked.

"Garlic and white-bean puree with truffle oil," Becky said, as she picked up her bag and surveyed the still-empty dining room, each of the twelve tables set with fresh linen and wineglasses and a little blue glass dish of spiced almonds in the center.

"And why do you think I'd be laughing about yoga?"

"Well," said Becky, picking up her canvas bag. "Just because I haven't exercised in . . ." Becky paused, counting the months. The years. ". . . in a while." Her last experience with organized fitness had been in college, where she had to pass a semester of phys. ed. before she graduated. She'd let Sarah talk her into Interpretive Dance, where she spent four months waving a scarf around, pretending to be, alternately, a tree in the wind, a child of alcoholics, and resignation. She'd been half hoping that her obstetrician would put the kibosh on exercise and tell her to just stay home with her feet up for the last twelve weeks of her pregnancy, but Dr. Mendlow had been almost indecently enthusiastic when Becky had called for permission to enroll.

"You probably think yoga's for wimps."

"No, no!" said Sarah. "Yoga's very demanding. I'm impressed that you're doing this for yourself and, of course, for your darling little wee one."

Becky stared at her friend and narrowed her eyes. "You want something, right?"

"Can you switch Saturdays with me?"

"Fine, fine," Becky grumbled. She didn't really mind working Saturday night. Andrew was going to be on call, which, more than likely, meant she'd be abandoned in front of the television set at least once so that her husband could go tend to someone's inflamed appendix or obstructed bowel. Or, most likely, she would have to field more phone calls from Mimi.

Sarah scraped the jicama she'd been julienning into a bowl, wiped her cutting board, and tossed the towel into a basket in the corner. Becky retrieved it and threw it back to her. "Two towels a night, remember? The laundry bill last month was killer."

"A thousand pardons," Sarah said, as she started scraping kernels of corn off the cob for the roasted-corn salad.

Becky headed up the back staircase to a tiny room at the top—a converted closet in the old row house that was Mas. She closed the blinds and took another appreciative sniff of dinner coming together—the mole simmering, the spice-rubbed brisket slow-roasting, the undertone of garlic, and the bright notes of cilantro and lime. She could hear the sounds of the dinner crew arriving—waitresses laughing in the kitchen, the dishwashers turning the radio from WXPN to the salsa station. She set her bag onto the desk, on top of the stacks of invoices and ordering forms, and reached into the locker where she'd put her yoga outfit. "Loose-fitting, comfortable clothing," the yoga flyer had said. Which, luckily, was pretty much all she ever wore.

Becky pulled off her elastic-waisted black pants, exchanging them for a pair of elastic-waisted blue ones and added an exercise bra that had taken her forty-five minutes on the Internet to find at a site called, God help her, Bigmamas.com. She pulled on a long T-shirt, slipped her feet into her sneakers, and pulled her curls into a bun that she skewered into place with one of the chopsticks Sarah had left on the desk. "Gentle, rhythmic stretching," the flyer had said. "Creative visualization and meditation for the mother-to-be." She figured she could handle that. And if not, she'd just say something about heartburn and head for the door.

As she stuffed her clothes into the bag, her fingertips brushed against something cold and unfamiliar. She dug around and pulled out a silver baby rattle. She felt around in her bag some more, but she couldn't find a card or wrapping paper or a ribbon. Just one little rattle.

She turned it over, gave it a shake, then headed down the stairs to the kitchen, where Sarah had been joined by the dishwasher, the sous chef, and the pastry chef. "Is this from you?" she asked Sarah.

"No, but it's nice," she said.

"I don't know where it came from."

"The stork?" Sarah offered.

Becky rolled her eyes, then stood sideways in front of the mirror beside the dining-room door for another round of what was becoming her favorite game: *Pregnant or Just Fat?*

It was so unfair, she thought, as she twisted and turned and sucked in her cheekbones. She'd dreamed of pregnancy as the great equalizer, the thing she'd been waiting for her entire life, the moment when all the women got big so nobody talked or worried about their weight for nine blissful months. Well, fat chance. Pun intended. The skinny girls stayed skinny, except they developed adorable little tight-as-a-drum basketball bellies, whereas women Becky's size just looked as though they'd had too much for lunch.

And plus-size maternity clothes? Forget about it. Normal-size women get to wear little Lycra-blend sporty numbers that proclaim to the viewing public *Hey! I'm pregnant!* Meanwhile, any pregnant woman bigger than a breadbox gets to choose from the offerings from exactly one—yes, one—maternity-wear manufacturer, whose stirrup pants and oversized tunics scream *Hey! I'm a time traveler from 1987! And I'm even fatter than normal!*

She looked at herself in profile, straightening her shoulders, willing her belly to stick out farther than her breasts did. Then she turned to Sarah. "Do I look . . ."

Sarah shook her head as she sailed toward the deep fryer with a tray of corn fritters that Becky had prepared that morning. "Can't hear you, can't hear you," she sang, as the fritters started to sizzle. Becky sighed, did a quarter turn, and looked over at Juan the dishwasher, who'd suddenly become very involved in the plates he was stacking. She shot a glance toward the grill and found two waitresses with their eyes averted, busily mixing, chopping, and even, in Suzie's case, reading over the week's schedule as if there'd be a quiz on it later.

Becky sighed again, picked up her bag along with a copy of the schedule for the week and the specials for the weekend, and headed out the door to cross the park, walk eighteen blocks east toward the river, and keep her date with New Age destiny.

"Ladies, welcome." The instructor, Theresa, wore loose black pants that rode just below her hipbones and a strappy brown tank top that showed off exquisitely defined deltoids and biceps. Her voice was low and lulling. Hypnotic, really. Becky stifled a yawn and looked around the studio on the fourth floor of Theresa's Society Hill town house. The room felt warm and cozy without being stuffy. The lights were dim, but votive candles burned on the sills of high windows that looked west over the city's twinkling skyline. A fountain burbled in one corner, a boom box in another played the sound of wind chimes, and the air smelled good, too, like oranges and cloves. In her pocket, her cell phone vibrated. Becky hit Reject without looking, felt instantly guilty, and promised herself that she'd call Mimi back as soon as class let out.

She replaced the phone and looked around at the seven other students, who all looked to be somewhere in their third trimesters. On Becky's right was a tiny girl with a ponytail of cornsilk-fine blond hair and a perky little belly. She wore one of those maternity workout ensembles that came in sizes Small and Smaller—white-striped track pants, black tank top with contrasting trim hugging her bump. She'd given Becky a friendly "Hello" before spritzing her mat with a bottle of Purell. "Germs," she'd whispered.

On Becky's left was the most beautiful woman Becky had ever seen outside of a movie. She was tall and caramel-skinned, with cheekbones that could have cut butter, eyes that looked topaz in the candlelight, and a drum-taut tummy pushing at a light-brown cashmere hoodie. She had perfectly manicured fingernails and, Becky could see once she'd pulled off her socks, perfectly pedicured toenails and a diamond on her left hand the size of a sugar cube. *I know her,* Becky thought. She couldn't come up with a name immediately, but she knew her occupation. This woman—her name was something exotic, Becky thought—was married to the man who the Sixers had just traded a center and a point guard to get, a superstar from Texas with some ridiculously high points-per-game average who also, Andrew had explained during the one game Becky had watched with him, led the league in rebounds.

Theresa sank to the floor without using her hands. *As if,* Becky thought. "Let's begin," Theresa said in a slow, lulling voice that made Becky feel like curling up and taking a good, long nap. "Why don't we go around the circle. Everyone can share their names, how far along they are, how the pregnancy's been, and a little bit about themselves."

Yoga Barbie's name turned out to be Kelly! An event planner! This was her first pregnancy! She was twenty-six years old, and she was twenty-seven weeks along! And she felt great, even though things had been hard in the beginning because she'd been spotting! And on bed rest! *Yay, team,* thought Becky, stifling another yawn. Then it was her turn.

"I'm Rebecca Rothstein Rabinowitz," she said, "and I'm twenty-nine and a half weeks. I'm having a girl. She's my first baby, and I'm feeling pretty good, except . . ." She glanced ruefully at her belly. "I feel like I'm not really showing yet, which is kind of a bummer." Theresa gave a sympathetic nod. "What else? Oh, I'm a chef and manager at a restaurant called Mas in Rittenhouse Square."

"Mas?" gasped Kelly. "Oh my God, I've been there!"

"Great," Becky said. Whoa. Her own mother hadn't been that enthusiastic about eating at Mas. But the restaurant had just been written up in *Philadelphia Magazine* as one of its "Seven Spots Worth Leaving the Suburbs For," and there'd been a very nice picture of Becky and Sarah. Well, of Sarah mostly, but you could see the side of Becky's face at the edge of the frame. Some of her hair, too, if you looked carefully.

"I'm Ayinde," the beautiful woman on Becky's other side began. "Thirty-six weeks. This is my first pregnancy as well, and I've been feeling fine." She laced her long fingers over her belly and said, half defiantly, half apologetically, "I'm not working right now."

"What were you doing before the pregnancy?" Theresa asked. Becky bet herself the answer would be *swimsuit model.* She was surprised when Ayinde told them she'd been a news reporter. "But that was back in Texas. My husband and I have only been here a month."

Kelly's eyes got wide. "Oh my God," she said, "you're . . ."

Ayinde raised one perfectly arched eyebrow. Kelly closed her mouth with a snap, and her pale cheeks blushed pink. Theresa nodded at the next woman, and the circle continued—there was a social worker and an investment banker, an art gallery manager and a public radio producer, and one woman with her hair in a ponytail who had a two-year-old already and said she was a stay-at-home mom.

"Let's begin," said Theresa. They sat cross-legged, palms upraised on their knees, eight pregnant women sitting on a wood floor that creaked beneath them as the candles flickered. The women swayed back and forth. "Let the breath flow up from the base of your spine. Let it warm your heart," she said. Becky rocked left to right. *So far so good,* she thought, as Theresa led them through a series of neck rolls and mindful inhalations. It wasn't any harder than Interpretive Dance had been.

"And now we're going to shift our weight to our hands, lift our tails in the air, and slowwwly ascend into Downward Dog," Theresa intoned. Becky eased herself onto her hands and feet, feeling the sticky yoga mat against her palms, and sent her tailbone sailing up. She heard Yoga Barbie beside her sigh as she got herself into position and the beautiful woman—AyeINday—groan softly.

Becky tried to lock her elbows so that her arms wouldn't shake. She hazarded a glance sideways. Ayinde was wincing, and her lips were pressed tightly together. "Are you okay?" Becky whispered.

"My back," Ayinde whispered back.

"Feeeeel yourself rooooted in the earrrrth," said Theresa. *I'm going to feel myself* landing *on the earth in about a minute,* Becky thought. Her arms wobbled . . . but it was Ayinde who dropped first and rocked backward on her hands and knees.

Theresa was kneeling beside her in an instant, one hand on Ayinde's back. "Was that posture too challenging?" she asked.

Ayinde shook her head. "No, the posture was fine; I've done yoga before. I'm just . . ." She gave a small shrug. "I'm not feeling right today."

"Why don't you just sit quietly for a moment?" Theresa said. "Focus on your breath."

Ayinde nodded and rolled onto her side. Ten minutes later, after Proud Warrior and Triangle Pose and an awkward kneeling posture that Becky decided she'd call Dying Pigeon, which was probably a lot easier if you didn't have breasts, the rest of the class joined her. "Shivasana," Theresa said, turning up the sound of the wind chimes. "Let's hold our bellies gently, breathing deeply, filling our lungs with rich oxygen, and send our babies a message of peace."

Becky's stomach growled. *Peace,* she thought, knowing that it wasn't going to work. She'd felt exhausted for her first trimester, queasy on and off for her second, and now she was just hungry all the time. She tried to send her baby a message of peace but instead wound up with a message of what she was going to have for dinner. *Short ribs with blood-orange gremolata,* she thought and sighed happily, as Ayinde sucked in her breath again.

Becky pushed herself up on one elbow. Ayinde was rubbing at her back with her eyes squeezed shut.

"Just a cramp or something," she whispered before Becky could ask.

After Theresa had clasped her hands over her enviably firm chest and wished them all *namaste,* the women made their way down the twisting staircase and walked out into the twilight. Kelly followed Becky. "I just love your restaurant," she gushed, as they walked south on Third Street toward Pine.

"Thanks," Becky said. "Do you remember what you ordered?"

"Chicken in mole sauce," Kelly said proudly, pronouncing the Spanish word with a flourish. "It was delicious and . . . oh my God!" Kelly said for the third time that night. Becky looked to where she was pointing and saw Ayinde leaning with both hands against the passenger's side window of a tank-size SUV with something white fluttering on its windshield.

"Wow," said Becky, "either she's taking that parking ticket awfully hard or . . ."

"Oh my God!" Kelly repeated and race-waddled away.

Ayinde looked at them helplessly as they approached. "I think my water broke," she said, pointing at the sopping hem of her pants. "But it's too early. I'm only thirty-six weeks. My husband's in California . . ."

"How long have you been having contractions?" Becky asked. She put her hand between the other woman's shoulder blades.

"I haven't had any," Ayinde said. "My back's been hurting, but that's it."

"You might be having back labor," Becky said. Ayinde looked at her blankly. "Do you know about back labor?"

"We were going to take a class at the hospital in Texas," Ayinde said, pressing her lips together, "but then Richard got traded, and we moved, and everything just . . ." She sucked in a breath, hissing, with her forehead pressed against the car window. "I can't believe this is happening. What if he doesn't get here in time?"

"Don't panic," said Becky. "First labors usually take a while. And just because your water broke doesn't mean you'll be having the baby soon . . ."

"Oh," said Ayinde. She gasped and reached for her back.

"Okay," said Becky. "I think we should go to the hospital."

Ayinde looked up, grimacing. "Can you hail a cab for me?"

"Don't be silly," said Becky. *Poor thing,* she thought. Being in labor all by herself—no husband around, no friend to hold her hand—was about the worst thing she could imagine. Well, that and having her midriff appear on one of those "Obesity: A National Epidemic" news reports. "We're not just putting you in a cab and abandoning you!"

"My car's right here," said Kelly. She raised her keychain, hit a button, and a Lexus SUV across the street started beeping. Becky helped Ayinde up into the passenger's seat and buckled herself into the back. "Can we call someone for you?"

"I see Dr. Mendlow," Ayinde said.

"Oh, good, me, too," said Becky. "So his number's in my cell phone. Anyone else? Your mom or a friend or someone?"

Ayinde shook her head. "We just moved here," she said, as Kelly started the car. Ayinde turned around and grabbed Becky's hand. "Please," she said. "Listen. My husband . . ." Her forehead furrowed. "Do you think there's a back door to the hospital or something like that? I don't want anyone to see me like this."

Becky raised her eyebrows. "Well, it's a hospital," she said. "They're used to seeing people come in with gunshots and stuff. Wet pants won't faze them."

"Please," Ayinde said, squeezing her hand even tighter. "Please."

"Okay." Becky pulled her big black sweater out of her bag, along with a baseball cap. "When we get out, you can wrap this around your waist, and if you think you can manage the stairs, we can get to triage that way, so you won't have to wait for the elevator."

"Thank you," Ayinde said. She pulled the baseball cap over her eyes, then looked up. "I'm sorry. I don't remember your names."

"Becky," said Becky.

"Kelly," said Kelly. Ayinde closed her eyes as Kelly started to drive.

AYINDE

"Well, your water's definitely broken." The young resident pulled off her rubber gloves with a snap and took her umpteenth peek toward the door, as if she expected the great and exalted Richard Towne to come walking through it at any moment. *Not an unreasonable thing to wish for,* Ayinde thought, smoothing the flimsy blue gown over her bare legs. In the past forty-five minutes, she had left dozens of messages at a dizzying array of numbers. She'd called Richard's cell and his pager; she'd left messages with his agent and his coach, the team's front office, the maid at their new house in Gladwyne. So far, nothing. No surprise there, she thought bleakly—it was the first round of the playoffs, and everyone had their game faces on and their phones turned off. Just her luck.

"But you're just one centimeter dilated. When this happens, we generally want to see a baby within twenty-four hours, or the risk of infection goes up. So you've got a few choices," the resident said.

Ayinde nodded. Kelly and Becky nodded, too. The resident— DR. SANCHEZ, her name tag said—peeked toward the door again. Ayinde looked away and wished she could put her hands over her ears to block out the chatter coming from the bed next to her own.

"Richard Towne! From the Sixers!" There was a curtain between Ayinde's bed and the next one. Evidently, Ayinde's neighbor had de- cided that a curtain was as good as a wall, and she was stage- whispering at the top of her lungs in spite of the PLEASE DO NOT USE

CELL PHONES sign. "Yes. Yes! Right next to me!" She dropped her voice incrementally. Becky and Kelly and Ayinde could still hear every word. "I don't know if she is or not. Mulatto, maybe?" The woman giggled. "Are we allowed to say that anymore?"

Ayinde closed her eyes. Becky put her hand on her shoulder. "Are you okay?"

"Fine," Ayinde murmured.

Kelly poured her a glass of water. Ayinde took a sip and set it aside.

"No, no, not here," yakked the woman in the next bed. "I haven't seen him yet, but he's got to be around here somewhere, right?"

You'd think so, Ayinde thought. She swung her legs over the side of the bed and yanked off her blood-pressure monitor. The ripping sound of the Velcro made her neighbor shut up. The resident managed to turn her eyes away from the door.

"Can I go to labor and delivery?" Ayinde asked.

"Ayinde, are you sure?" Becky said. "You could go home, walk around, try to take a nap and get some rest in your own bed. You know, studies show that the longer a woman labors at home, the less time she spends in the hospital, the less risk there is of an emergency C-section or the use of forceps or vacuum during delivery."

"Huh?" asked Kelly.

"I'm taking natural-childbirth classes," Becky said, sounding slightly defensive.

"I don't want to go home. I live out in Gladwyne," said Ayinde. "It's too much trouble to go out there and come back again." And, she thought, there'd be no way she could—how had Becky put it?— "labor at home" in full view of the cook and the maid and the driver who'd be there.

"Do you have someone to stay with you?" Becky asked. "We could come and drive you back to town when you're ready . . . or you could just come to my house for a while."

"That's very nice of you, but I'll be all right here." She handed her cell phone to Becky. "Would you mind stepping into the hall and calling my house?" she asked. "Ask to speak to Clara. Tell her that I need my suitcase—it has a yellow ribbon tied around the handle and it's right inside my dressing room—and then have her ask Joe to drive it to the hospital."

"Are you positive?" Becky asked. "There's no reason for you to be in the hospital unless you have to. And this could take hours."

The resident nodded. "First labors are often on the slow side."

"Just come," said Becky. "I'm a fifteen-minute walk from here, or we can drive you back in no time."

"I couldn't . . ." Ayinde said.

"I'll come, too," said Kelly. "It's better than spending another night sitting home reading *What to Expect When You're Expecting*."

"You'll be perfectly safe. My husband's a doctor," Becky said.

"Are you sure?" Ayinde asked.

"You shouldn't be here all by yourself," Becky said. "Even if it's just for a few hours. We'll call your husband, and you can try to relax."

"That would be my advice," said the resident. "If you want my opinion, go with your friends."

Ayinde didn't bother to correct her. "Thank you," she murmured to Becky. Then she took her clothes and disappeared into the bathroom, closing the door quietly behind her.

Friends, Ayinde thought as she pulled on her pants and smoothed her hair with shaking hands. She hadn't had a real friend since something like second grade. Her whole life she'd felt out of place; half black, half white, not quite one thing or the other, never fitting in.

Be brave, her parents used to tell her. She remembered them bending over her bed when she was little, their faces serious in the darkness, her mother's the color of milk chocolate and her father's the color of snow. *You are a pioneer*, they'd explain, their eyes shining with earnest good intentions. *You are the future. And not everyone's going to understand it, not everyone's going to love you the way we do, so you have to be brave.*

It was easy to believe them in the nighttime, in the safety of her canopied bed at the center of her bedroom, which was on the second floor of their eight-room Upper East Side duplex. The days were harder. The white girls she went to prep school and boarding school with had been perfectly nice, with a few notable exceptions, but their friendship had always had a kind of cloying undertone, as if Ayinde were a lost dog they'd rescued from the rain. The black girls—the handful of them she'd known at Dalton, the scholarship winners at Miss Porter's—hadn't wanted much to do with her, once they got past the exotic name and found out that her pedigree made her more like the rich white girls than like them.

She opened the door. Becky and Kelly were waiting. "All set?" Becky asked. Ayinde nodded and followed her outside.

She'd known there were risks to marrying a man like Richard, and if she'd had any doubts, her mother, the former Lolo Mbezi, 1970s supermodel, was all too eager to fill her in. "You'll have no private life at all," Lolo proclaimed. "Public property. That's what athletes are. Their wives, too. I hope you're ready for it."

"I love him," Ayinde told her mother. Lolo had tilted her face, the better to display the perfection of her profile. "I hope that's enough," she'd said.

Up until now, she thought, as Kelly started the car, *it had been.* Richard had been more than enough; his love had more than made up for everything she'd missed during her childhood.

She'd met Richard at work, when she'd been a reporter for the CBS affiliate in Fort Worth, sent off to interview one of Richard Towne's teammates, an eighteen-year-old third-round draft pick named Antoine Vaughn. She'd gone striding right into the locker room as if Gloria Steinem herself had been holding the door. She almost kept walking, right into an open locker, when the first player ambled by, still wet from the shower with nothing but a towel wrapped around his waist.

"Just keep your eyes above the equator," Eric the cameraman whispered. She swallowed hard and cleared her throat.

"Excuse me, gentlemen. I'm Ayinde Walker from KTVT, and I'm here to see Antoine Vaughn."

She heard silence. Sniggers. Whispers she couldn't quite make out. "They finally got some hot reporters, huh?" called a man who was, blessedly, still wearing his warm-up suit.

"You replacin' old Sam Roberts's tired ass?"

"Hey, baby, never mind the kid. Come over here. I'll give you an interview!"

"Keep it down, fellas," called the obligatory team minder from the corner, a middle-aged guy in a rumpled suit who didn't look as if he had much interest in keeping the peace, or moving at all.

She swallowed again and squinted through the shifting field of half-clad male bodies. "Does anyone know where Antoine Vaughn is?"

"You can call me Antoine!" offered the guy who asked if she'd be replacing Sam Roberts, the station's sports reporter. "You can call me anything you want, lovely!"

She shot the guy in the corner a desperate glance, which he pretended not to see.

"I'm right here."

She turned . . . and there was Antoine Vaughn, lounging on his back on one of the benches. She recognized him from the picture the team had sent over. Of course, that picture had been just head and shoulders. And he'd been wearing clothes.

"See, it's true," he said, gesturing south and starting to laugh— clearly, he'd had this line prepared—"everything is bigger in Texas!"

Ayinde lifted one eyebrow and locked her knees so that none of them would see how they were shaking. The whole thing brought back bad memories. At her very exclusive private school in New York, a few of the other girls (*whitegirls,* she'd thought of them then, just one word) had shoved her into the boys' bathroom. Nothing had happened—and, really, the boys had been more upset than she was— but she'd never forgotten her initial terror when the door had swung shut behind her. Now, in the locker room, she drew a deep breath, the way she'd learned, so that her words would come from her diaphragm and would carry.

"If that's so," she said, "then you must be from out of town."

"Oh, dip!" called one of the other players.

"Yo, Antoine, man, she told you!"

Antoine Vaughn glared at Ayinde through slitted eyes and pulled a towel around his waist.

"Wasn't that funny," he muttered, sitting up and hunching forward.

"Hey."

Ayinde turned around and looked up . . . and up. "Take it easy on the kid," said Richard Towne. His uniform left his arms and legs bare. His chestnut skin gleamed with sweat, and his teeth glistened when he smiled. But she wasn't going to back down yet . . . not even if Richard Towne—who was one of the most famous athletes in America at that moment, who never gave interviews to anyone, and who was, in person, even more attractive than his pictures—told her that she should.

"Tell him to cover up and I might."

"Go get dressed, man," Richard said to Antoine Vaughn, who jumped off the bench so fast it was as if God Himself had told him to put on his jockstrap. Then Richard turned back to Ayinde. "Are you all right?" he asked, pitching his voice so softly that nobody could hear it but Ayinde.

"I'm fine," she said, even though her knees were now shaking so hard she was surprised they weren't knocking together. Richard put one world-famous hand on her shoulders and steered her out of the locker room and into one of the courtside seats in the echoing stadium.

"They were just teasing you," he said.

"It wasn't funny." She blinked furiously at the tears that had appeared out of nowhere. "I'm just trying to do my job."

"I know. I know. Here," he said, handing her a cup of water. She sipped it, fanning at her lashes, knowing that if just one tear fell, it would ruin her mascara and she'd look like hell on camera.

She took a deep breath. "You think he'll talk to me?"

Richard Towne considered. "If I tell him to, he will."

"Will you tell him to?"

He smiled again, and that smile was like stepping onto a beach after three months of hard winter and feeling tropical sunshine on your skin. "If you have dinner with me, I will."

Ayinde said nothing. She wasn't quite able to believe it. Richard Towne, asking her for a date.

"I've seen you do the news," he said. "You're good."

"Except around naked teenagers."

"Oh, you were winning that battle," he said. "I was just speeding things along. So will you have dinner with me?"

Ayinde heard her mother's voice in her head, her mother speaking in the quasi-British accent she'd affected after spending ten days in London when Ayinde was twelve or so. *Make them work for it,* Lolo lectured. "I don't think so," she said automatically. She would have said it even if Lolo hadn't chosen that moment to rise up from her subconscious and whisper in her ear. Richard Towne had a reputation.

He laughed. "So it's like that, huh? You got a man already?"

"Don't you have a basketball game to play?" Her voice was cool, and she turned away slightly, but she couldn't keep herself from smiling.

"You're playing hard to get," he told her, as he let one finger trail over the back of her hand.

"I'm not playing at all," she told him. "I'm working." She looked him full in the face, a move that took all the courage she had. "And honestly, I can't see having a relationship with a man who wears shorts to work."

There was a moment when he just stared at her, and Ayinde felt her heart sink, thinking that she'd pushed it too far, that probably nobody ever teased him, nobody would even dare . . . and that she shouldn't have said "relationship" when he'd only asked her to dinner. Then, finally, Richard Towne threw back his head and laughed. "What if I promised to wear pants?"

"To work?"

"To dinner."

She looked at him from under her eyelashes. "A shirt, too?" She wanted to hear him laugh again.

"Even a jacket and tie."

"Then . . ." She let her voice trail off, making him work for it, making him wait. "Then I suppose I'd consider it."

She called to the cameraman, who'd gone off to shoot B-roll of the dance squad, twelve women shaking their hips and hair, and looking like they were in the grip of some communal form of epilepsy. "Eric, you ready to take another shot at Antoine?"

Eric tore his attention away from the dancers and went all googly-eyed at the sight of Richard Towne. "Hey, man, nice game against the Lakers!"

"Thank you, sir," Richard said and returned his attention to Ayinde. "Friday night?"

A *basketball player,* she thought to herself. What was it the young girls called them? *Ballers.* Her social life had never included one. There had been doctors and lawyers and businessmen, and once, much to the delight of her program director, a fling with the anchor at the NBC station, which got both of their names in the papers for the three months it had lasted. "Look," she said. "I want to be clear about something. I'm grateful for your help, but if you're looking for some damsel in distress, I'm not her."

Richard Towne shook his head. Ayinde found herself intoxicated with the sight of his body, the bulge of biceps, the sinewy forearms, those enormous hands.

"Don't worry," he said. "I don't have any kind of savior thing going on. I'm a simple man," he said, spreading his hands. "I just want to play a little basketball, maybe win another ring. Enjoy life, you know? You're a serious lady. I appreciate that. But even working girls have to eat."

"True," she said, allowing herself a smile.

"I'll call you at the station." And with that he gave a courtly little half bow and trotted onto the hardwood. By the time she was back at the station, there was an enormous bouquet of lilacs and lilies on her desk. *This is what they call the full-court press,* the card read. Ayinde had laughed out loud before picking up the phone to call Richard Towne and tell him that Friday night was fine.

Ayinde closed her eyes and tried to make her way through the contraction. "Okay," said Becky. "Breathe . . . breathe . . . you're doing just fine, keep breathing . . ."

"Ohhh," Ayinde sighed, as the contraction finally loosened its grasp. Becky had her balanced on a giant blue ball set in the middle of her tiny living room on one of the narrow little streets near Rittenhouse Square. Ayinde had been rocking back and forth, trying not to scream.

"Sixty seconds," said Kelly from the corner of the couch where she'd bundled herself in a blanket with a notebook and her watch.

"Shouldn't you girls go to the hospital now?" asked a voice from the staircase.

"Ma, you're hovering," Becky said without turning her head.

"I'm not hovering," said Edith Rothstein, who had, indeed, been hovering on the staircase, visible only from the waist up, never setting a foot into the living room and practically wringing her hands since the three women had walked through the door five hours earlier. "I'm just concerned."

"Hovering!" Becky said. Her mother, a trim woman with a carefully styled cap of reddish-blond hair and a string of pearls she'd been twisting nonstop, pursed her lips. Edith had ostensibly come north for a cousin's wedding in Mamaroneck but, Becky confided, her real business involved staring at Becky's belly and conversing nonstop with her as-yet-unborn granddaughter. "I wouldn't mind it so much," Becky said, "except she hardly ever talks to me anymore. It's like her field of vision stops at my neck."

Ayinde wiped her forehead and looked around. Becky's living room was about the size of her own dressing room, and she was sure that no decorator had helped with the selection of the overstuffed bookshelves and the afghans that lay over the couch and the chairs, but the room was charming anyhow and it felt warm and safer than the hospital had.

But not warm and safe enough for Becky's mother. "Andrew," she whispered loudly enough so that the three women could hear her, "are you sure this is all right?"

"It's fine, Edith," Andrew said from the kitchen in the basement. "The ladies sound like they've got it under control."

"What are they doing down there?" Ayinde asked, thinking how lucky Becky was to have such a sweet husband—a husband who, most important, was here and not three thousand miles away. Andrew reminded her a little bit of her own father . . . or, rather, she admitted, the parts her father would play on Broadway or occasionally on the big screen. He'd carved out quite a niche for himself by playing caring, warmhearted fathers and, lately, even grandfathers.

"Andrew's online, and Edith's probably alphabetizing my canned goods," Becky whispered back. "We're fine, Mom," she called. "Really." Edith shook her head again and vanished, like a rabbit disappearing down into its burrow. Ayinde reached for her cell phone for what felt like the hundredth time since her water had broken, hit the button for Richard's cell, then sucked in her breath as the phone rang and rang and another contraction started grinding through her.

"Another one," she said, curling her body around her belly.

Kelly's face went pale as Ayinde tried to breathe through the pain. "What's it feel like?" she asked when the contraction was over.

Ayinde shook her head. It was a horrible pain, worse than anything she'd ever felt, worse than the ankle she'd broken while riding horseback when she was fourteen. It felt as if her midriff was surrounded by iron bands, and they were squeezing her tighter and tighter as the contraction unspooled. It was like being adrift, drowning in a vast ocean with no shore and no rescue in sight. "Bad," she gasped, pressing her fists against her back. "Bad."

Becky put her hands on Ayinde's shoulders and looked into her eyes. "Breathe with me," she said. Her eyes were as calm as her voice, and her hands were strong and steady. "Look at me. You're going to be all right. Let's give your baby some air. Come on, Ayinde, breathe . . ."

"Oh, God!" she groaned. "I can't do this anymore . . . I want my mother." The contraction finally loosened its grip. Ayinde started crying, miserable, defeated tears.

Just then—at last—her cell phone rang.

"Baby?" Richard sounded harried and distracted. She could hear the noise of the crowd in the background.

"Where are you?"

"On my way to the airport. On my way home. I'm sorry, Ayinde—I turned my phone off when practice started . . ."

"And nobody told you?"

She could hear a car door slamming. "Not 'til just now."

Not until the game was over, Ayinde thought bitterly. Not until they didn't need him anymore. "Hurry," she said, gripping the phone so tightly she thought it would break into pieces in her hand.

"I'll be there as soon as I can. You're in the hospital, right?"

"Not now," she said, feeling another contraction beginning, knowing she wouldn't have the time or the breath to explain where she was and how she'd gotten there. "But I'll meet you there. Hurry," she said again, and broke the connection, and bent over double, one hand clutching the phone, the other one clawing at her back, which felt like it was on fire.

"Sixty seconds," Kelly said, clicking the stopwatch.

"Okay," said Becky, in a voice so calm and lulling that she could have filled in for the yoga instructor. "I think it's time to go." She helped Ayinde back onto the couch. "Do you want me to call your mom?"

A chuckle worked its way through Ayinde's lips. "Mom," she repeated. "I never even called her that. She wouldn't let me. She wanted me to call her Lolo. People we'd meet who didn't know us would think that we were sisters. She never would correct them, either." She made an abrupt, strangled sound. It took Kelly and Becky a minute to realize she was laughing. "You know what she said when I told her I was pregnant?"

Kelly and Becky shook their heads.

"She said, 'I'm too young to be a grandmother.' Not *Congratulations.* Not *I'm so happy for you. I'm too young to be a grandmother."* Ayinde shook her head, then grabbed at her back and bent over again. "Don't . . . call . . . her," she panted. "She wouldn't even come."

Becky's hand moved in small circles in the center of Ayinde's back. "Okay," she said. "Let's get to the hospital," she called softly. Edith popped into the room like a jack-in-the-box, so fast that Ayinde figured she had to have been sitting on the stairs, waiting for them to need her. *Not fair,* she thought. Becky had her mother; Becky had her husband. Ayinde was starting to feel as though she had nothing at all.

"Can you grab some extra clothes—T-shirts and stuff, in case we're there awhile? And some bottles of water?" Edith scurried away. Ayinde bit back a groan as Kelly bent and slipped on her shoes and led her, in mincing baby steps, out the door, where Andrew Rabinowitz was waiting with the car. "Kelly, you get in the front seat," Becky instructed, helping Ayinde into the back. A homeless guy stood across the street and watched them, rocking back on his heels as he cackled, "Yo! You ladies need a SHOE-horn!"

"Very helpful," Andrew muttered, holding the door for his wife. Ayinde squeezed her eyes shut, one hand working at the seat belt, the other clutching her cell phone. The pain was moving through her body like a predator, leaping from her legs to her back to her belly, shaking her between its jaws like a lion shakes a half-dead gazelle. She felt as if she would fly apart if she opened her eyes. Becky smoothed her hair away from her temple.

"Hang on. We'll be there in no time," Becky said.

Ayinde nodded, breathing, counting backward from one hundred, hitting zero and starting the count again, thinking that she only had to survive this long enough to get to the hospital and then they'd give her something, something to take away the pain and the humiliation that bit at her more sharply than contractions. *Knocked up, no husband.* That's what anyone who saw her would think, ring or no ring, because where was her man?

Andrew pulled up to the emergency room entrance at Pennsylvania Hospital, and the women worked their way out of the car—Ayinde in the T-shirt and pajama bottoms Becky had lent her, Becky in leggings and a sweater, with her curls swept into a bun. Kelly had refused Becky's offer of clothing and was still in her chic maternity workout wear, its jaunty stripes and clingy Lycra an uneasy contrast to the scared look on her pale face.

"Triage," Becky said, leading Ayinde and Kelly into an elevator. Then they were on the third floor, and Ayinde was grasping the edge of the admission desk, trying to spell her name.

"A-Y-I-N . . ."

"Amy?" guessed the nurse.

"It's Ayinde!" Ayinde gasped. "Ayinde Towne! Richard Towne's wife!" She was past caring who knew who she was. Past remembering whether the publicist had told her to sign in with her maiden name or not, past everything except getting the pain to stop.

"Well, why dintcha say so, hon?" the nurse asked complacently, pointing toward a cubicle and handing Ayinde a gown. "Everything off from the waist down, lie on the bed, the resident will be along soon." She looked over Ayinde's head, toward the door. "Is your husband parking?"

Ayinde grabbed the gown and lurched toward the bathroom without a word.

"Well," sniffed the nurse, "nice addy-tood!" She turned to Becky and Kelly. "Is he coming?"

Kelly shrugged. "We think so," Becky said. The nurse's tired face lit up.

They left the nurse dialing her phone and found Ayinde on her knees in the bathroom, her pajama bottoms crumpled on the floor, the gown draped over her shoulders.

"Drugs," Ayinde said. She wiped her mouth, fumbled for the handle, and managed to flush the toilet and push herself onto her feet. "Please help me find a doctor. I want drugs."

"Okay," Kelly said. "Come on, let's get you into bed." She opened the bathroom door. Instantly, a group of three people in scrubs—a man and two women—backed away. "That's her?" Ayinde heard one of them whisper. She closed her eyes and let Becky guide her onto the bed. Seconds later, a beaming doctor appeared.

"Hello, Mrs. Towne!" he said, as if he'd known her all his life. "I'm Dr. Cole."

"I'd like my epidural," said Ayinde, as she thrust her legs into the stirrups, not caring if she kicked the doctor in his chest in the process, not caring who saw what.

"Well, now, let's just have a look," the doctor said briskly, inserting his fingers as Ayinde bit back a scream and tried to hold still. "You're six centimeters, maybe seven. We'll page Dr. Mendlow, and we'll send the anesthesiologist right up."

The pasty-faced nurse helped Ayinde into a wheelchair and took her to her room. "Time to say good-bye," she said. "Only immediate family's allowed in labor and delivery unless you cleared it ahead of time."

"We're her sisters," Kelly said.

The nurse stared at them with her mouth falling open: three women, two white, one black, all three of them pregnant.

"It's been a very big year for our family," Kelly said cheerfully. From her bed, Ayinde managed to smile.

"Well, I suppose we can make an exception," said the nurse. "No cell phones, no pagers, no food," she said.

Ayinde sipped from the cup of water Kelly handed her. She could hear the woman in the next room who sounded like she had to be nearing the end. "Come on, honey, push, push, PUSH!" her husband cheered. She wondered if the father was a Little League coach on the weekends, the kind of guy who'd stand behind half a dozen six-year-olds and show them how to wrap their hands around the bat.

"Are you okay?" Kelly whispered. Ayinde nodded, then gripped the edges of the sheet, twisting her body, trying to get away from the pain of the strongest contraction yet. "He . . . better . . . hurry," she managed to say. Becky squatted beside the bed, holding her hands. Kelly rubbed her back and watched the door.

"Good news," she said. "Your epidural has arrived."

Ayinde opened her eyes and saw a compact, red-headed man who introduced himself as Dr. Jacoby, said he was delighted to meet her, and managed to get off the topic of the absent Richard Towne in less than thirty seconds. As Ayinde rested her weight on a nurse's shoulders, Dr. Jacoby swabbed her back with Betadine, then reached for a needle so long it made even stalwart Becky blanch and leave the room, saying something about getting some water.

"Hey," said the nurse Ayinde was leaning on, "when things calm down a little, could your husband give me an autograph?"

"I'm sure that won't be a problem," Ayinde said, straining to be polite because she wanted the drugs to work. She started to nod, and the doctor and nurse both said, "Oh, no, don't move!" So she held herself nodless, perfectly still, while the warmth and then the blessed numbness spread down from her hips.

She let her eyes slip shut, and when she opened them, it had somehow become five in the morning and the door was swinging open, admitting a wedge of harsh light.

"Look who's here!" said Becky.

Ayinde saw Dr. Mendlow at the foot of the bed, his lanky frame and disarming grin, his curly brown hair tucked into a surgical cap, lifting the hem of her gown. And behind him was Richard, unshaven and weary, all six feet nine and a half inches, still wearing his warm-up suit and beaming at her, with a quartet of nurses in his wake.

He reached for her hands. "Hey, baby." His eyes crinkled at the corners. His smile looked the same way it did on TV, where it sold cereal and soft drinks and his own line of sneakers. Ayinde closed her eyes, leaning her face against the warm leather of his jacket, breathing his comforting smell of soap and aftershave and the faint whiff of sweat, no matter how long it had been between games and workout sessions . . .

Ayinde jerked her head back.

Dr. Mendlow looked up from between her legs. "Did I hurt you? I'm sorry."

"Shh, it's okay. Daddy's here," said Richard, bending close, smiling at his own joke. Ayinde breathed deeply, and yes, there it was, a whiff of something different mixed into her husband's comforting scent. *Perfume.* Her mind turned the possibility over, then dismissed it fast. He'd been at the game, then probably a press conference, then the plane back home. Reporters . . . stewardesses . . . fans outside the arena and the hotel, craning their necks as he passed, pressing moist scraps of paper into his hands . . . there could have even been a nurse who'd waylaid him in the hall. Or maybe she was just so exhausted that she'd hallucinated the whole thing and conjured up a little Chloe or Obsession out of nothing more than her own pain and fear.

"Nine centimeters. Almost ten. Just a little lip left," said Dr. Mendlow. He looked from Ayinde's face to Richard's. "You guys ready to have a baby?"

The nurses charged into the room, breaking down the bed, folding away its bottom third, and propping Ayinde's feet up. Richard held one hand. Becky gripped the other. "Do you want us to go?" she whispered, as Richard was being helped into gloves and a gown. Ayinde squeezed Becky's hand hard and shook her head.

"Stay. Please," she said. "You, too," she said to Kelly, who was watching from the armchair. Kelly looked so tired. Ayinde imagined that she looked even worse. The night felt like it had stretched out forever, and the hardest part was still to come.

"Okay, going into a contraction," called Dr. Mendlow. "You ready to start pushing?" Ayinde nodded, and the room filled with noise and people—the anesthesiologist, nurses, the nurse who was, unbelievably, clutching a notebook and a pen, the machines were beeping and pinging, and someone by Ayinde's head was saying that it was time to *"PUSH! PUSH! Tuck your head down, take a deep breath, and give me everything, little more, little more, little more, come on, come on now, Anna . . . Anya . . ."*

"Ay-IN-day!" she gasped and dropped her head back onto the pillow, where someone slipped an oxygen mask over her cheeks. "Like it's spelled!"

"That's my baby," Richard said. The pride in his voice was unmistakable. Becky squeezed her hand. Ayinde opened her eyes and peered into her husband's eyes.

"Good job," he said, bending his head over hers. "Now, come on, baby. Let's bring it on home."

"PUSH!" called the nurses. Ayinde locked her eyes with her husband and bore down with all her strength.

"Here comes the head!" said Dr. Mendlow.

And there were nurses holding her legs, Richard holding her hand, the nurse talking into her ear again, *"Come on, bear down, do it now, come on, give me more, PUSH, PUSH, PUSH."*

"Reach down!" said Becky. Ayinde did, reaching blindly, oxygen mask askew, eyes squeezed shut, and oh, there it was, the warm silky sleek wedge of his head, right there against her fingertips, more alive than anything she'd ever touched or dreamed of. She groped for Richard's hand.

"Richard," she said. "Look. Look what we did."

He bent down, pressing his lips against her ear. "Love you, baby," he whispered.

She bore down again, until she was almost sitting upright in the bed, until the world began to flicker. "Oh, God, I can't do it anymore!" she screamed.

"You can, you can, you are," said one of the voices in her ear. "Just one more, Ayinde, one more, you're almost there, come on and PUSH!"

Perfume, Ayinde's mind whispered in a voice that sounded suspiciously like the voice of the formidable Lolo Mbezi (born Lolly Morgan, but her mother had left that name behind). *He came back to you smelling of some other woman's perfume.* And then she shut her eyes and gritted her teeth and held her breath and pushed so hard it felt as if she were turning herself inside out, hard enough to silence the voice that whispered in her mind, to forget that smell forever. She pushed until she could neither see nor hear, and then she fell back on her pillow, exhausted and spent and breathless . . . and certain. *Perfume.*

A babble of voices rose up around her. *"Okay, honey, ease off now . . . slow, slow, gentle . . . here come the shoulders."*

She felt a sensation of slipping, of a great, twisting release, a sudden, shocking emptiness that reminded her, somehow, of her first orgasm, how it had taken her entirely by surprise and stolen her breath away.

"Ayinde, look!" Dr. Mendlow called, beaming underneath his blue surgical cap.

She looked up. And there was her baby, sheathed in a coat of grayish white, a head full of black hair slicked along his skull, full lips parted, tongue quivering, fists trembling in outrage.

"Julian," she said. *Perfume,* her mind whispered. *Be quiet,* she told it, and she stretched out her arms and reached for her son.

May

KELLY

"Okay, so there's Mary, Barry, then me, Kelly, then Charlie, Maureen and Doreen—they're twins—Michael, and Terry. She's the baby," Kelly said. "Maureen's in San Diego and Terry's in college in Vermont. Everyone else is still in New Jersey. Everyone except me." She and Becky had been in Ayinde's house for half an hour, lavishing compliments on ten-day-old, six-pound-ten-ounce baby Julian, and accepting Ayinde's thank-yous and the Kate Spade diaper bags she'd given them both as gifts ("Oh, really, this is way too much," Kelly had said, while inwardly she was thrilled and only wished that the bag had said Kate Spade in larger, more visible letters). Then they'd toured the house's ground-floor living room, dining room, granite-countered kitchen with a Sub-Zero refrigerator and a Viking range, butler's pantry, solarium. Finally the talk had turned to Kelly's unfashionably large family, whose members Kelly could recite in a single breath—*MaryBarrymeCharlieMaureenandDoreenthey'retwinsMichael andTerryshe'sthebaby*—and Kelly was eager to return to a topic that would put her on more equal footing with her new friends.

"My husband's a big Sixers fan," she said. "He grew up in New York, and he used to be a Knicks man, but ever since he went to Wharton, it's all about Allen Iverson. And Richard, of course." She sat back, satisfied that she'd found an unobtrusive way to work Wharton into the conversation.

"How long have you guys been married?" Becky asked.

"Almost four years," said Kelly.

"Lord, you must have been a child bride," Becky said.

"I was twenty-two," Kelly said. "I guess that's young. But I knew what I wanted." The women were sitting in Ayinde's movie-theater-sized living room. Ayinde was nursing baby Julian, a tiny, sleepy-eyed pouty-lipped bundle in blue footie pajamas with a matching blue cap pulled over his curls. Kelly and Becky were side by side on the couch, sipping the tea and nibbling the cookies that a maid in a black-and-white uniform had carried in. Kelly couldn't get over the room. Everything in it, from the richly patterned rugs to the tassled pillows on the couches and the gold-framed mirror that hung over the marble fireplace, was absolutely right. Kelly wanted to stay in this room forever or, better yet, have a room just like it herself someday.

"Do you guys want a big family, too?" Becky asked.

"Oh, God, no," said Kelly, with a shudder she couldn't quite suppress. "I mean, it wasn't so bad. We had a big van that the church gave us a good deal on—we're Catholic, I know, big surprise—and we had a really big dining-room table, and . . ." She shrugged. "That was about it."

"It must have been nice," said Ayinde, sounding wistful as she stroked her baby's hair with her free hand. "You must have always had someone to talk to."

Kelly nodded, even though it wasn't precisely true. Maureen was the only one she could really talk to. The rest of her brothers and sisters thought she was bossy, a tattletale, and too big for her britches when she tried to tell them what to eat or what to wear or how to behave. God, if she'd had a nickel for every time she'd heard *You're not my mother!* from one of them. Like their actual mother was such great shakes. Kelly remembered how Paula O'Hara had discovered the scrapbook she'd kept when she was eight years old. The scrapbook was an old photo album that was meant to be the twins' baby book, but her mother had gotten bored with it, so there were only a few snapshots of

Maureen and Doreen when they'd come home from the hospital. The rest of it Kelly filled with her own pictures, ones cut out of copies of *Ladies' Home Journal* and *Newsweek* and *Time* that she'd take from the dentist's office at the end of the block after the receptionist left the magazines bundled up on the curb. Kelly wasn't interested in pictures of people, just pictures of things. She'd cut out shots of big Colonial houses where the paint on the shutters wasn't flaking off in long, curling strips; pictures of shining new minivans where you couldn't still make out the words MARY MOTHER OF PEACE painted over on the side; pictures of blue vases full of daffodils and patent-leather tap shoes and a pink Huffy bike with a glitter banana seat. Pictures of dresses, pictures of shoes, a picture of the coat with real rabbit fur on the collar and cuffs that Missy Henry had worn to school last winter. Her mother had escorted Kelly into the living room, where none of the children were normally allowed, told her daughter to have a seat on the plastic slipcovered gold-and-green couch, and brandished the book in her face, shaking it so hard that a picture of some duchess's hunting lodge came loose and fluttered to the floor. "What's this?"

There was no sense in trying to lie. "It's just pictures of things I like."

Her mother's eyes narrowed. Kelly surreptitiously sniffed her breath, but no, it was just coffee. So far. "Covetousness is a sin."

Kelly dropped her eyes, and even though she knew she should just be quiet, she couldn't keep herself from asking, "Why is it bad to want nice things?"

"You should be concerned with the state of your soul, not the state of your bank account," said Paula. Her brown curls were cut short in a wash-and-go style that she hardly ever even bothered to comb, and she was wearing one of her husband's old plaid shirts over her jeans. "Easier for a camel to fit through the eye of a needle than a rich man to enter Heaven."

"But why? Why is it bad to be rich? Why is it bad to have nice things?"

"Because God doesn't care about nice things," her mother had said. Paula had been trying to sound pleasant—instructive, too, like a Sunday-school teacher—but Kelly could hear that she was losing patience. "God cares about good deeds."

"But why doesn't God want good people to have nice things?" Kelly asked. "What if you have nice things and you do good deeds, too? What if . . ."

"Enough," her mother had said, tucking the book under her arm. "I'll be keeping this, Kelly Marie. I want you to go to your room, and I want you to tell Father Frank about this on Sunday."

Kelly never told anyone about her book. That Sunday, she just confessed to her usual complement of little transgressions—*Bless me, Father, for I have sinned. It's been one week since my last confession. I took the Lord's name in vain and I fought with my little sister.* What was she supposed to say? Why was what she'd done so wrong? *Bless me, Father, for I have sinned. I cut a picture of a movie star's black-and-white kitchen out of a three-month-old issue of* Life? Her mother had done a poor job of hiding her scrapbook. She'd just shoved it in her closet, underneath the white leatherette book with the words OUR WEDDING tooled in gold leaf on the cover. The book contained a few dozen snapshots of the wedding at St. Veronica's and the reception at the Knights of Columbus hall after. Her father's tuxedo had had disco-era wide lapels; her mother's Empire-waisted gown had failed to hide the bulge that would be baby Mary five months later. Kelly rescued her scrapbook the next night, and she'd kept it until she went off to college.

Kelly sat back in Ayinde's leather couch and set her teacup carefully into its saucer and smoothed her hair. She knew that, objectively, she looked okay, or at least as okay as a seven-and-a-half-month pregnant woman could look. At least her hair was right. Dr. Mendlow had probably thought she was crazy because the first question she'd asked during her first office visit wasn't about diet or exercise or the birth itself but, "Can I get my hair highlighted?" Then again, Kelly thought, Dr. Mendlow didn't know that her hair was the exact shade of dirty dishwater if she didn't keep up with her color.

She took another sip of tea. She'd kill to have hair like Becky's.

She'd just bet those were natural curls. Hair like Becky's and a house like Ayinde's, and she'd be all set.

"So tell us about event planning," Becky said. "Do you do weddings?"

"Only a few and only the very high-end ones. Brides are crazy," Kelly said, wrinkling her nose. "I mean, they have a right to be, of course, it's their big day and all, but it's much easier dealing with corporations. It's not as personal for them."

Becky rolled her eyes. "Someday I'll tell you about my wedding."

"Why? What happened?"

Becky shook her head. "It's a long and tragic story. Some other time."

Kelly hoped there would be another time and that the three of them would turn into those women she'd seen in the park or on the sidewalks, chatting easily as they wheeled their babies along. Maureen had always been her best friend, but Maureen had married an investment banker and moved out west, and none of her college friends were having babies yet. Only a few of them even had husbands.

"Do you guys have brothers and sisters?" she asked. She ran one finger quickly over the gold rim on her saucer and wondered if it would be tacky to flip it over and see who'd made it. She decided, regretfully, that the answer was yes. She and Steve had gotten Wedgwood for their wedding, the same pattern that one of her favorite actresses had registered for, according to *In Style* magazine. But Ayinde's china was more beautiful than anything she'd seen in any of the stores. Antique, probably.

Ayinde shook her head. "I'm an only child." She pressed her lips together, and shifted the baby in her arms. "I think my mother didn't want to risk her figure with any more than me."

"Seriously?" asked Kelly.

"Oh, yes, indeed," said Ayinde. "Lolo takes her figure very seriously. She was a model in the seventies. She was the second woman of color ever on the cover of *Vogue.* Which she'd tell you herself, about ten minutes after she met you."

"And where are you both from?" Kelly asked. Oops. Bad move. Kelly the Cruise Director, her brother Barry used to call her. At family dinners, after grace, her mother would slump in her chair, staring listlessly at her plate, and her father would glare from face to face to face, looking alternately furious and bewildered, as if he couldn't figure out how all those kids had gotten there. Her brothers and sisters would just shove food into their mouths, and Kelly was the one trying to keep the leaden ball of the conversation aloft, with an effort that made her teeth ache. *How was school today, everyone?* she'd ask. *Doreen, how was field hockey?* Her sister would say, *Shut up, Pollyanna. You're not my mother.* And Paula would be glaring at Kelly from her chair. *No, you're not their mother,* she'd mumble sometimes, in a voice both angry and somehow confused, as if she was saying it out loud to convince herself that it was true. But somebody had to be their mother, Kelly thought; someone at least had to try, and after four in the afternoon, there was no way that Paula was up to the task. So she'd try. *Michael, how was your science test? Terry, did you remember to get Mom to sign your permission slip?* One by one, her siblings would carry their plates into the family room to eat in front of the television set, leaving Kelly and her parents alone at the table, in a room gone so quiet that you could hear their knives and forks moving over their plates.

Becky told them she'd grown up in Florida and had come to Philadelphia for her husband's residency. Ayinde was born in New York City, but had gone to Miss Porter's in Connecticut for high school, then Yale for college, and she'd spent her summers abroad. *Abroad.* Kelly didn't think that she herself could ever get away with using that word in a sentence, even though technically she could because she'd gone to Paris for her honeymoon. You had to be beautiful to use a word like that. It also helped if you didn't come from New Jersey.

Ayinde settled Julian over her shoulder to burp him, and Becky shifted on the couch, giving her belly small pats, as if it were a dog that had settled in her lap, and Kelly felt the silence stretching uncomfortably. There were a million questions she wanted to ask

Ayinde—*What was labor really like?* foremost among them. Her mother had had so many babies, Kelly thought she'd have some idea, but she didn't. Paula would leave either in the middle of the night or the middle of the day, and she'd come home a few days later, looking even more exhausted than normal, with a new little bundle in her arms for Kelly to wash and diaper and coo over. She'd tried to ask her sister Mary, the only one with children, some of her questions, but Mary had brushed her off. "Your labor will be fine, and your baby will be perfect," Mary said, as her own three kids screamed in the background during the sisters' first-of-the-month conference call. "And if it's not, you'll just return it for store credit."

"Ha, ha, very funny," Kelly had said.

"I have to give him a bath," Ayinde said. "His little stump fell off last night . . ."

"Oh, we should get going," Becky said, struggling out of the plush couch. Kelly got to her feet.

"Thank you so much for the bag," she said. "You really didn't need to."

"Actually," Ayinde said, smoothing the baby's blanket, "I was wondering if you'd stay and supervise. The nurses showed me how to do it in the hospital . . . they made it look so easy."

"Of course we'll stay!" Becky said.

"I can help," said Kelly. She blushed, hoping she hadn't sounded too eager. "I gave my brothers and sisters a million baths." She could remember standing over the chipped kitchen sink, the lullabies she'd sing as she squeezed a washcloth over their tiny heads to rinse away the shampoo.

"I'm glad one of us knows what she's doing," Ayinde said. She led them upstairs to the bathroom, which was stocked with hooded towels, washcloths, and, Kelly was pleased to see, the same blue plastic tub that Kelly herself had purchased four weeks before. Becky filled the tub. Ayinde undressed the baby, then looked at him, naked in her arms, and took a deep breath. "Do you want to get him started?" she asked.

"Sure," Kelly said. She took Julian and eased him, feet first, into the water. "Here you go, mister, your first bath. Isn't this fun? You just go slowly," she told Ayinde, "so it's not a big shock . . . there!" She settled the baby into the tub. Julian made a little *eh, eh, eh* noise, then began splashing his hands into the water with a shriek.

"Hey, cutie," Kelly said, trickling water over Julian's belly. "I think he likes it." After a few minutes in the water and some work with the washcloth, she spread a towel across her chest, lifted the baby out of the water, and bundled him like a burrito before handing him back to his mother. "Thanks," Ayinde said. "Both of you, thank you so much."

Kelly made it back to her apartment just as her own phone started ringing for the monthly all-girl conference call. "Hey, sis," said Doreen. "How goes the pregnancy?"

"Just great!" said Kelly. She set down her grocery bags in the empty hallway and carried the box from Pottery Barn Kids through the empty living room and dining room and into the nursery, which, other than their bedroom, was the only room in the apartment that had furniture. Kelly didn't want to buy cheap stuff they'd just have to replace, so she decided to wait until they could afford exactly the things she wanted: the perfectly curved celadon-green upholstered couch, the window treatments of Robert Allen farmhouse-print toile, the mahogany console tables and credenzas, the Mitchell Gold loveseat in mushroom-colored suede, all of them bookmarked and catalogued in the Favorites file on Kelly's computer. *Still cutting out pictures?* her mother had asked the last time Kelly saw her (her mother had been in the hospital then, the exact yellow of a ripe banana). *I don't have to anymore,* Kelly said. She remembered the first time she'd seen this apartment—and, more to the point, its rent. *Steve, we shouldn't,* she told her husband, and he'd taken her hand and said, *We deserve it. You deserve it,* and signed the lease on the spot.

"So what can we get you?" asked Mary. "What do you need?"

"Nothing, nothing," Kelly said hastily, not even wanting to think about what constituted an appropriate baby gift in her sister's mind. "The nursery's actually been done for a while."

Her sisters laughed. "That's our Kelly," Maureen said.

Kelly frowned as she sat down on the rocker with its custom-ordered red-and-white slipcovered seat cushion. Lemon, the golden retriever they'd bought from a breeder last year, curled happily at her feet. "I just didn't want to take any chances. Even if you register, people get things wrong. Like, for example, say you register for the red-checked gingham crib sheet on page thirty-two of the Pottery Barn Kids catalog . . ."

"For instance," said Mary. Her rumbling laugh turned into a coughing fit. She'd been trying to quit smoking again, but from the sound of things, she hadn't succeeded.

"You register for that," Kelly continued doggedly, "but someone could decide to get you a red gingham sheet from somewhere else or even just a red sheet that they bought on clearance . . ."

"Oh, God forbid," said Doreen.

"Well, then you can't return it!" Kelly said. "And then you're stuck!"

"The horror," said Mary, rumbling her laugh again. Kelly closed her eyes, cursing herself for telling her sisters anything. Mary and her husband and their three kids lived in the old house in Ocean City, where everything was dingy and falling apart and smelled like cigarettes. Mary wouldn't care what color a sheet was, as long as it was clean. And maybe she wouldn't even care about that.

"Never mind," said Maureen. "If the nursery's done, what do you need? Some toys or a diaper bag or something?"

"I've got hand-me-downs," Mary offered. Kelly made a face and changed the subject to Doreen's boyfriend, Anthony the police officer, and what Doreen should bring when she went to meet his parents. "Flowers are always nice," Kelly said.

"Not wine?"

"Well, you don't know if they drink, and you don't want them to think that you do."

"But I do drink!"

"Yes," Kelly said patiently, "but they don't need to know that right away. Get a nice bouquet. Don't spend more than twenty-five bucks, or it'll look like you're trying too hard, and no carnations."

Once the phone call was over, Kelly turned on the light and looked proudly at the baby's room. The rocker was white-painted wood with red-and-white-striped cushions. The dresser was already filled with washed and folded outfits—socks and overalls and little hats and scarves that she'd been buying and squirreling away long before she got pregnant, before she'd even met Steve. Not in a crazy Miss Havisham way, but just an adorable sunhat here, a pair of perfect denim Oshkosh overalls there. So she'd be ready. So it would all be right.

Kelly kicked off her shoes and ran her toes over the Peter Rabbit rug, sighing in satisfaction as Lemon licked her hand.

New friends. Kelly shut her eyes, Ayinde's living room still hanging like a vision behind her lids, and rocked. She'd had friends in high school and in college, but ever since Steve, she'd fallen out of touch with her girlfriends. They were still doing the single-in-the-city thing—happy hours and blind-date horror stories, blowing their paychecks on makeup and shoes. Kelly was just in a different place now. A better place. No more worrying about whether a guy would call or if she'd sit home alone on a Saturday night. She rocked back and forth, sighing in contentment, thinking about Steve and whether he'd ever get to meet Richard Towne and whether he'd make a fool of himself if he did. Steve had occasionally been known to go off the deep end, to hang on to a handshake past the point where the other person was clearly uncomfortable, to talk too long or too loudly about gay marriage or the flat tax or any one of the dozens of topics on which he held a strong opinion.

She didn't like to think about it, but the truth was that she'd met her husband on the rebound, after the guy she'd dated her sophomore and junior years had broken up with her. His name was Scott Schiff. She'd been desperately in love with him, and she thought he'd been in love with her, too. Then one night she'd gone to his apartment and tried to sit down on his bed, and he'd jumped up as soon as her bottom had hit the quilt. *Oh, dear,* she thought, as her heart sank. *Not good.*

He paced across the room, rubbing his hands together like they were cold, and she'd known what he was saying without really hearing a word of it. "Fine!" she had said, cutting off his speech about how he cared for her a great deal but didn't think they'd have a long-term future together. He made their relationship sound like she was a bond he didn't want to risk his capital on. "It's fine!"

She knew why he was ending it. She'd seen the look on his face when they pulled up outside the O'Hara family house for her mother's funeral. She caught the way his nostrils had flared at the sight of the ancient van in the driveway, the frayed carpet on the stairs, the single bathroom on the second floor that all eight kids had shared. His parents' walls were hung with original watercolors; the walls at Casa O'Hara were decorated with framed eight-by-tens of each child's high school graduation portrait and—oh, how she'd kicked herself for not getting Maureen to take it down—a huge crucifix with a buff Savior in a skimpy loincloth with gaudy drops of blood painted onto His hands. Scott was a major catch, four years older than Kelly, getting his MBA at Wharton. She hadn't lied, not exactly, when she'd told him she'd grown up on the shore. It was technically true, but, clearly, he imagined something more along the lines of the six-bedroom summer cottage his parents owned in Newport instead of this shabby house in a crummy working-class town on the Jersey shore. She guessed she should have been grateful that he stayed with her for even a minute once her mother was in the ground.

"Are you okay?" Scott asked, as she bounded off his bed.

"I'm fine. You know, it's actually kind of a relief," she said. "I've been thinking the same thing. I didn't see a strong long-term picture here, either." She forced herself to look at him, blinking rapidly so the tears in her eyes wouldn't spill onto her cheeks. "I hope you weren't thinking of . . . you know . . . a future together. Because I wasn't." She crossed the room to where he was standing, feet shoulder-width apart, hands clasped, the very portrait of the modern CEO-to-be, and took his hands. "I'm sorry if I misled you." Her little speech left him flummoxed and silent, the way she'd hoped it would. She made a fast sweep of his place, gathering up her things—a hairbrush, a pair of running shoes, her copy of *Smart Women Finish First*—because she knew that having to see him again with a box of her stuff in his arms would send her right over the edge.

"Hey," he said, his voice so gentle that she knew she couldn't look at him or she'd start to cry and beg him to let her stay. "You don't have to do that now." He looked miserable as he cleared his throat. "I know this has been a hard year for you. Your mother . . ."

"Oh, that was a long time coming. We'd made our peace. Really. It's okay!" she said. Toothbrush. Dental floss. Perfume from the Gap that she'd poured into the Boucheron bottle her roommate had tossed. She went to his kitchen for a plastic bag. "I'll see you around. Take care now!"

She made it to the elevator in his high-rise building before she had to lean against the wall. *Breathe,* she told herself, the way she had when the phone had rung four months ago and it had been Mary, twenty-six but sounding six years old, crying and calling her by her little-girl nickname. "Kay-Kay, Mommy's gone."

Kelly forced herself off the wall in case Scott thought to stick his head out the door to look for her. She tucked the plastic bag under her arm, took the elevator down to the ground floor, crossed the campus, and found a bar, which was loud and hot and crowded. She pushed her way through the crowd and ordered a double vodka, straight up, and gulped it down like a kid swallowing cough syrup. She didn't make a habit of this. She'd only done it once since high school, the night before her mother's funeral, at a bar in Ocean City with her sisters beside her, and it hadn't been vodka then but Maker's Mark, their mother's beverage of choice. Paula O'Hara had poured it into her Tab and plopped in front of the television set, the pink can in her hands, the blue glow painting her cheeks, watching *Dynasty* and *Dallas* and tapes of *Days of Our Lives* while the eight of them came and went.

The bartender held the bottle in the air.

"Do it again," Kelly said. *Stupid.* God, she'd been so stupid, thinking that Scott Schiff was The One, turning down the other guys who'd asked her out, putting all her eggs in one biscuit, or basket, or whatever it was you weren't supposed to put all of your eggs into. She gulped her second shot, ordered her third, and was reaching for her purse, trying to remember how much money she had, when suddenly there was a hand on top of her own.

"Let me get that."

Kelly looked up and saw a guy in a navy-blue suit. *Nice looking enough,* she thought—a little pale and pinched, his eyes a little too intense—but who in the entire University of Pennsylvania, professors excepted, wore a suit on a Saturday night? A suit with—she looked down, feeling herself wobble on the barstool—wingtips?

She peered through the cigarette smoke at the guy, who had pale-blue eyes, thin red lips, carefully combed brown hair that was already thinning a bit, and a prominent Adam's apple above his blue-and-gold tie.

"What's with the suit?" she said, yelling to make herself heard over the babble of voices and Hootie and the Blowfish issuing from the jukebox.

"I like suits," the guy yelled back. "I'm Steven Day."

"Congratulations," she said and emptied her glass.

"Whoa, slow down," he said. She squinted at him. Her head was already feeling fuzzy.

"Don't tell me what to do. You're not my father." *Because if you were,* she thought, *you'd have three days' worth of stubble and you'd be trapped with a family you hated, and you'd deliver the mail for a living, and your only suit would be twenty years old.*

Steven Day did not look the least bit abashed. "Come outside, Kelly," he said, as he took a firm grip on her elbow. "Let's get some fresh air."

She made a face but allowed him to maneuver her off of her seat and out of the bar. "How do you know my name?"

"I've been watching you."

She stared, trying to place him. "You have? Why?" She realized that she was talking too loudly—it had been noisy in the bar, but outside, the fall air was crisp and her voice was carrying. "Why?" she asked again, more quietly.

"Because I think you're beautiful," he said, steering her down the sidewalk. She could feel his breath against her cheek as he formed each word. "We were in economics seminar together."

She remembered meeting a guy in the graduate-level economics seminar she'd talked her advisor into letting her take, but it had been Scott Schiff. Although something was tugging at her memory—a guy in a suit who sat in the back of the room and could turn any question into a passionate defense of the free market, a guy who wore suits while everyone else came to class dressed in jeans and sweatshirts and sneakers.

Alex Keaton wanna-be, she thought, as she wobbled sideways, almost crashing into a bus shelter. Steven Day steadied her. "Are you all right?"

Half a dozen of her typical responses bubbled to her lips. *Sure! Fine! Great!* Instead Kelly sagged against him and let her eyes slip shut. "No, I'm not. Not really."

"Are you worried about finals?"

She shook her head. "Finals are about the least of my problems right now."

"So what's wrong?"

"Well, for one thing, you didn't let me get another drink." She shoved her bangs out of her eyes. All through high school in Ocean City, she'd permed her hair. Her first day at Penn she noticed that nobody else had permed hair. She couldn't afford to have hers straightened, so after the second day of classes, she found a West Philadelphia barbershop a few blocks off campus. She parked herself in the black leather chair in front of the astonished barber and said, *Cut it all off.* She had a pixie cut for the rest of college. It was her signature look, and at twelve bucks per trim, it was one she could afford.

She peered up at him. His face in the darkness hung above her like the moon. "Do you really think I'm beautiful?"

He nodded at her, very seriously. "Come on. Let's go to my place."

She drew herself upright, mustering what was left of her dignity and her sobriety. "I am not going back to your place. I just met you." She licked her lips and ran her hands through the mess of her hairdo and peered at him through her vodka haze. "You have to buy me dinner first."

"Sit here," Steven Day instructed, and he parked Kelly on the bench inside the bus shelter. "Don't move."

She closed her eyes and held perfectly still. Five minutes later, Steven Day, wingtips and all, was standing in front of her with a fragrant, grease-spotted bag from McDonald's in his hand. "Here," he said, pulling her to her feet. "Dinner."

For two blocks, Kelly wobbled past clusters of chattering undergrads and sorority girls all in a row, popping french fries into her mouth and telling Steven the short but tragic story of Scott Schiff.

"He wasn't such a good guy, anyhow," she said through a mouthful of fried potato. At that moment, after the vodka, she felt as though she could tell Steven Day anything, as if nobody had ever understood her the way Steven Day did. "You wanna know what I think?"

Steven Day panted and pulled Kelly away from the pile of recently raked leaves she was attempting to lie down on top of. "Sure."

"I think he wanted a rich girl. Someone with a fancy last name and a big dowry."

"I don't think women really have dowries anymore."

"Oh, you know what I mean. I'm from New Jersey, you know? It's not fancy. My dad's a postman. My mom . . ." She stopped herself.

She was drunk but not drunk enough to start talking about her mother. "It's not that impressive."

"I think," he said, "that America's more of a meritocracy these days."

She blinked until her muddled brain coughed up a definition of meritocracy. "Yeah, well, the meritocracy hasn't made its way to Scott Schiff's bedroom yet." She swallowed her french fry and started to cry. And she never cried. Not even when Mary had called her, not at the funeral, not after, when her father, freshly shaven and wedged into a suit that Kelly remembered from her baby sister's first communion, told her that her mother left a will. Doreen got Paula's pearl earrings, Terry the diamond solitaire necklace their father bought her for their tenth anniversary, and Maureen the gold bracelet she'd gotten from her own mother. She left Mary her wedding rings. Her mother had left Kelly her rosary beads and her Bible. When her father handed over the Bible, a St. Joseph prayer card fell into Kelly's lap. The card had marked the page from Ecclesiastes, yellow highlighter marking the verses Paula O'Hara wanted her daughter to have instead of diamonds and pearls: *I made me great works; I builded me houses. . . . And behold, all was vanity and vexation of spirit, and there was no profit under the sun.*

"I'm such an idiot," Kelly wept, as he unlocked the door of his apartment. She knew that her nose was running all over the lapel of Steven Day's suit, but she couldn't stop herself. "I thought he loved me."

"Shh," Steven said, smoothing her hair off her face. He pulled off Kelly's shoes and sweater and slipped one of his T-shirts over her head. "Let me," he whispered, and she'd blinked at him. His breath smelled of mint toothpaste, and it was cool against her cheek. At that moment, she was so weary, so sad, so completely empty—no Scott, no mother, no nothing—that she would have let him do anything at all, as long as she didn't have to be alone.

She sat up in Steve's cluttered bedroom with his blue plaid sheets bunched in her hands. "Let you what?" she whispered back.

He eased her head down onto the pillow and kissed her, first on the forehead, then, lightly, on the lips. "Let me take care of you."

Later that night, she'd woken up alone in the unfamiliar bed and looked across the room at the man who'd brought her there. He was still fully dressed, right down to his wingtips, with a blanket pulled up to his chin. His eyelids glimmered in the dark. It was five o'clock in the morning. *You,* she thought. She knew that she sounded like a housewife selecting a melon at the supermarket. She knew that she was still drunk, still chagrined and furious at the thought of Scott Schiff—and, for that matter, at the thought of her mother and that mocking bit of Scripture. None of it mattered. Her mind was made up. And when Kelly decided on something, that was what she got. She'd been that way since she was six years old. *You,* she thought, and that was that.

By the next night, they had kissed, and that weekend, they slept together, and six months later, right before graduation, they were engaged, and six months after that, just after Kelly's twenty-second birthday, they were husband and wife, living in this three-bedroom apartment on the eighteenth floor of a brand-new building on Market Street where the whole city was spread out, sparkling at her feet. The rent was technically more than they should have been spending—according to the formulas she'd seen, you were supposed to spend something like a third of your income on your residence and they were spending more like half—but she hadn't been able to resist the place. There were two full bathrooms, and they each had Jacuzzi tubs and marble floors. The wall-to-wall carpeting was brand new and so were the kitchen appliances, and the walls didn't smell of decades of someone else's meals—just of fresh paint. True, the lack of furniture was a problem—her sisters had practically busted a gut laughing when they'd seen the empty living room and complained about having to eat on the floor—but it was a minor inconvenience, and one that Kelly was certain wouldn't last long. If Steve kept earning as much money as he did, in a year or two she'd be able to buy exactly what she wanted. And Oliver would have the best of everything—no hand-me-downs, no winter coats that smelled like cigarette smoke, no toys that some older sibling had broken. If he wanted something, all he would have to do is ask.

She heard Steve's key in the door, and she got to her feet. *Oliver James,* she whispered. She kissed her fingertips and tapped them on top of the crib's mattress. Perfect. It was all going to be perfect.

LIA

On my first flight to Los Angeles, when I was eighteen, I had the middle seat. The man sitting by the window was maybe thirty, with curly blond hair and a wedding ring and a briefcase full of candy—his daughter, he said, had loaded him up before he left. The entire five-hour flight I talked to him, flipping my freshly dyed blond hair over my shoulders, telling him about the parts I'd played in my high school's musicals, the acting classes I was going to take, and the agent's name I'd gotten. For five hours, the man had fed me Hershey's Kisses and fruit-flavored chews, laughing and nodding, being—what? Bemused, I guessed. With my bad dye job and my delusions of what Los Angeles would be like, I must have been a bemusing sight. When we started our descent, he'd even changed places with me, giving me the window seat so that I could see California—"the promised land," he'd called it—before he did.

My flight back to Philadelphia eleven years later was different. I staggered through the airport like a zombie, paying for two seats so there'd be no chance of flying with a baby beside me. The week before, I'd been walking through the Beverly Center, just to have something to do, and a baby had started to cry and my breasts had started leaking and I'd wanted to die right there, just die on the spot. I paid cash for the rental car in Philadelphia, laying bills on the counter as the clerk at the Budget desk stared and asked me again and again whether I wouldn't prefer to just put it on a credit card. But a credit

57

card would have made it easy for Sam to find me, and I wasn't ready to be found. Not yet.

I was worried that I wouldn't remember the way home, but I did. It felt like the red Kia I'd rented was driving itself—out I-95, past the Franklin Mills Mall, its parking lot packed as usual, past the sprawl of chain restaurants and cheap apartment complexes with RENT ME NOW banners flapping limply above the trash-littered ditches. Left onto Byberry, across the Boulevard, left and right and left again, the rented car's wheels turning over streets that felt smaller and dimmer than they had when I'd lived here. The aluminum siding on the small ranch houses and even the asphalt on my street had faded, and the houses themselves seemed to have shrunk in the shadows of the trees, which had gotten taller. But some things hadn't changed. My old key, the one I'd kept on my keychain for all that time, still turned in the lock. I set my bag at the foot of the stairs and sat in the living room without turning the lights on, watching the minutes tick past on the VCR clock.

My mother came home at 4:15, which was exactly half an hour after the last bell rang at her school. She always came home at exactly that time. In the summertime, she'd simply shift her routine a little, and instead of going to Shawcross Elementary at 7:15, she'd go to a diner for breakfast, go to the Y for a swim, and then go to the library, where she'd arrive as soon as the doors opened at nine and leave precisely at four o'clock, with a break at around noon to sit on the front steps and eat the sandwich (which alternated between tuna on rye and cream cheese and olives on white) that she'd packed in her purse. "What do you do there all day?" I'd asked once, when I was fourteen or so and we were still talking. She'd shrugged. "I read," she'd said. Maybe she hadn't meant it as a criticism, or for me to imagine the inevitable *And it wouldn't kill you to pick up a book every once in a while instead of lying in the backyard in your bikini, combing lemon juice through your hair,* but that was what I heard.

She walked into the living room with her black nylon book bag in one hand, her purse in the other. She blinked at me twice. Other than that, her face didn't change. It was like I stopped over every week to sit in her living room with the shades pulled and the lights off.

"So," she said. "I can defrost another chicken breast for dinner. Do you still eat chicken?" Her first words to me. Her first words in eleven years. I almost laughed. Everything I'd been through, the distance I'd come, just to wind up back where I'd started, sitting on the same old blue couch, with my mother asking me if I still ate chicken.

"Yes," I said. "I do."

"I'm asking," she said, "because I thought maybe you'd become a vegetarian."

"Why would you think that? Just because I moved to California?"

"I thought I read it somewhere," she muttered. I wondered what else she'd read about me, how much of the story she knew. Not much, I decided. She'd never been much for the movies or the movie magazines. "Trash," she'd said. "Brain rot." My father was the one who'd taken me to the movies, who'd buy me buttered popcorn and rattling boxes of Good & Plenty and wipe my face carefully before we drove back home.

She brushed by me on her way up the stairs, pulled off her shoes, and walked through the kitchen in her panty-hosed feet. She was wearing black pants—"slacks," she'd call them—a white blouse with a bow at the neck that I thought I'd remembered from before I'd left home.

I followed her up the stairs and watched as she put the chicken in the microwave, then reached for the box of bread crumbs, an egg from the refrigerator, the cracked white bowl. She'd dipped the chicken pieces into that bowl before putting them on a cookie sheet to bake since time immemorial. She'd shrunk in my absence, just like the rest of the neighborhood. Her sandy-blond hair looked faded, her shoulders were slumping underneath her cotton-polyester-blend blouse, and there were brown patches on the backs of her hands. She was getting old, I saw, and it startled me. Time passing in the abstract was one thing, but seeing her was something else. I opened my mouth, thinking that I had to start somewhere, with someone; that I had to start figuring out how I would tell my story. *I went to California and I fell in love . . .* My throat felt like it was swelling shut. I imagined Sam standing in the movie theater lobby, maybe holding a tub of popcorn, wondering where I'd gone. I blinked rapidly, licked my lips, found a head of iceberg lettuce in the refrigerator, and started tearing it into chunks. My mother looked at my Vera Bradley monstrosity crouching at the base of the stairs. "Nice bag," she said, handing me a bottle of low-fat ranch dressing.

"So," she continued, once the chicken was in the oven and a pair of potatoes were rotating in the microwave, "what brings you back to town?"

Her tone was carefully neutral. Her eyes were on her feet. The answer was right on the tip of my tongue, but I couldn't make myself say the words. And I might have been wrong, but it seemed as if she was having the same trouble: She'd open her mouth, then close it. Once she said my name, but when I turned my head, she only shrugged and cleared her throat and stared at the floor some more.

She pulled two plastic place mats out of the drawer where the plastic place mats had always resided. "Your grandmother died," she said. "While you were gone. I would have called you, but . . ." She shrugged. She didn't have my number, and she didn't know my new name.

"Did they pound a stake through her heart to make sure?"

She pursed her lips. "I see California hasn't changed that smart mouth of yours."

I didn't say anything. My father's mother had lived in Harrisburg, around the corner from her other daughter and my three cousins. She'd never had much time for me. I would see her once a year, the day after Thanksgiving. She always wore a sweatshirt with three painted handprints—one for each of my cousins. When I was eight, I asked why my handprint wasn't there. She thought about it, pointed to the smallest of the handprints, and told me I was welcome to pretend that that one was mine. Gee, thanks.

"Mom," I began, before realizing I had no idea how to start this story, no idea what to say. I looked down at my plate and poked at my chicken.

"You're welcome to stay if you like," she said quietly, her eyes not meeting mine.

"Mom," I said again. *I met a man and we got married, and something terrible happened . . .*

"You're my daughter," she continued, "and you'll always have a place here." I waited for her to touch me, knowing that she wouldn't. She had never touched me when I'd lived with her. My father gave the hugs. "You remember where your bedroom is," she told me, pushing herself away from the table, scraping her mostly untouched plate into the trash can that was, I swear, the exact same trash can she'd had since we'd moved to this place twenty years before. "There are clean sheets on the bed." And with that, she was gone.

My bedroom was just the way I'd left it—pink shag carpet, Tom Cruise posters on the wall, a tiny single bed that creaked and listed to the left when I lay down on it. The bed was draped in a Strawberry Shortcake comforter, the one I'd coveted and nagged my parents for when I was eight years old. My mother had told me I already had a perfectly good comforter and that I'd be bored with Strawberry in a year. *No*, I begged. *Please! I really, really want it, and I'll never ask for anything again.* In the end, it was my father who caved in and bought me the comforter for my birthday. Once he was gone, my mother made me keep that comforter on my bed all through high school. "Comforters don't grow on trees," she said. But she had enough money to spend on her own clothes, and mine, and, I noticed, a new comforter for herself—beige on beige, filled with some kind of starchy polyester filling, which made a scratching sound every time you touched it. It wasn't about the money. The comforter was my punishment, a reminder of what girls got when they whined and nagged—a father who'd bolted, a ratty quilt stained with spilled Kool-Aid, bearing the face of a cartoon character nobody could even remember. By the end of ninth grade, I quit asking for a new comforter, and I quit bringing friends up to my bedroom. We hung out in the family room instead while my mother was at work, watching MTV and pilfering swallows of Baileys Irish Cream from the dusty bottles in the liquor cabinet.

I stretched back on the bed and put my hands over my eyes. It was seven o'clock at night, four o'clock in California. I thought about my husband in our apartment, which had miniature rosebushes growing in pots on the narrow balcony and sheer golden curtains in the bedroom and nothing at all that was beige. *We can get a house,* Sam had told me, once he'd signed the contract for the sitcom. *Maybe up in the hills. Nothing too big, but something nice.* We made plans to start looking—we called agents, visited a few open houses, drove up the twisting roads with the seat belt stretched tight over my belly. I remembered Sam's smile underneath his baseball cap, the way he made me laugh by trying to pronounce the abbreviations exactly the way they were spelled in the classified ads. Three bdrms! Hdwd Fl! Bldrs Spcl! Canyon Vu!

I imagined him sitting alone at our dining-room table with the paper or with the frozen pizzas he'd eat when I wasn't around, or out by the pool, an old cowboy hat cocked back on his head, fishing each leaf and dead insect out of the water with the long-handled mesh skimmer. The apartment complex had a guy who came every other day, but Sam had taken over skimming duties. "It's how I meditate," he told me. "And it's cheaper than yoga, right?"

He wouldn't be able to find me here, any more than my mother would have been able to find me on the West Coast. Like thousands of women before me, I'd used the move to Los Angeles to reinvent myself. I'd chosen a new name to go along with my slimmed-down body, the lips I plumped up, the nose I pared down, and the hair whose color I changed at least three times a year. *Lia Frederick,* I called myself on my credit cards and driver's license. Frederick was my father's first name, and Lia was my own name, minus an S. I gave friends and boyfriends—Sam included—the biography of the girl I'd roomed with during two weeks of Girl Scout camp in the Poconos. As far as my husband knew, I was from Pittsburgh, where my father had been a bank manager and my mother taught fifth grade. I had one little brother, and my parents had been happily married. *Had been* was the operative phrase. Once I realized that Sam would, quite naturally, be interested in meeting and spending time with the close-knit, loving clan I'd described, I killed them all in a car accident when I was away on spring break my senior year of high school. *Poor baby,* Sam had said.

But I did give him a little piece of the truth. My mother was a fifth-grade schoolteacher, who'd been in charge of the same classroom at the same rambling red-brick elementary school I'd attended myself. Through budget cuts and layoffs and six different principals, my mother, Helen, had stayed the course, teaching social studies and English and spelling to ever-enlarging classes of ten- and eleven-year-olds. She kept framed copies of all of her class pictures hung along the stairs, a laminated march through time. With each step up, my mother got older and the classes went from eighteen white kids to twenty-eight kids of all races. In each of the pictures, my mother wore a version of the same lipstick, the same outfit, and the same smile. My class picture was there, too, framed and hung at the top of the stairs. I hadn't been a pretty girl. That would come later. In fifth grade, I still had buck teeth and braces and brown hair that hung to my waist. I was in my mom's homeroom, but I took pains to position myself as far away from her as I could. In the picture, I'm wearing a red-and-green kilt and a white blouse and tights, and she's wearing black slacks and a white blouse. She's giving her typical cool smile as she holds the sign reading MRS. URICK GRADE FIVE, and I'm looking sideways, not smiling at all, clearly desperate to be somewhere else, away from this, away from her.

In bed, I laced my hands over the skin of my belly, which felt loose and pleated. Downstairs, the television set clicked on. First *Wheel of Fortune,* then *Jeopardy!* My mother called out the answers as she walked through the den in her blouse and her slacks and her pantyhose. I could imagine the stack of papers set on the coffee table, the mug reading WORLD'S GREATEST TEACHER filled with decaf on the arm of the couch, listening to everything ABC had to offer until after the eleven o'clock news. In this house, the channel never changed. I'd broken the remote control years ago (in an accident that probably had something to do with those purloined swallows of Baileys), and she'd never bothered to replace it.

I rolled over so that my cheek was pressed against the pillowcase. It still smelled the same here, like fabric softener and fried eggs. The same scuff marks on the wall from when I'd tried to move my bed, the same bashed-in corner of the closet door that I'd kicked in a fit of fury when I was eighteen. "You don't listen to me!" I cried. "You don't ever listen to me!"

She stood watching me from the doorway, her arms crossed over her chest. "Quite a performance," she said, when I'd paused to draw a breath. "Are you done, or is there an encore?"

"Screw you!" I yelled. She stared at me impassively. "*Fuck* you!" I said. She gave a tiny pained wince, as if she'd stubbed her toe. "I HATE you!" Nothing. "And you know what? You hate me!" That, finally, made something real happen on her face. She looked, for one brief instant, shocked and desperately sad. Then her features smoothed out into a look of bland expectation, like a theatergoer awaiting the final curtain so she can find her coat and go home. "I'm going to live with Dad!"

"Fine," she said. "If you think he wants you." That was when I kicked the closet door in. Three weeks later, I'd gone down to a pawnshop on South Street and sold the diamond-and-gold engagement ring that my great-grandmother had left me when she'd died. Two days after that, I was on my way to California, taking candy from a stranger and talking nonstop, hurtling toward my new face and new name and the future that would lead me, inexorably, to Sam. And, eventually, back here. Back home.

Downstairs, my mother called questions at the television set. *Who is Tab Hunter? What is mercury? Who is Madame Bovary? What is Sydney, Australia?* I closed my eyes. *By and by, by and by, the moon's a slice of lemon pie* . . . the bed tilted sharply sideways, and I woke up with a start.

My mother sat on the corner farthest from my body, perched on the tiniest amount of pink quilt and sheet she could manage without sliding to the floor. In the light from the hallway, I could see that her hair had gotten thinner. "Lisa," she said. "Can you tell me what's wrong?"

I closed my eyes and kept my breathing even, and when she reached out her hand—to touch my hair, my cheek, I didn't know— I rolled away. When I opened my eyes again, it was morning, and the sun was shining on Strawberry Shortcake and on me. I got out of bed, pulled on my L.A. clothes, slid behind the wheel of the rental car with no destination in mind, taking the turns as they came. Two hours later, I was back in the park where I'd sat with my father, shivering in the late-winter chill with an untouched sandwich in my lap. I closed my eyes and tilted my face into the thin sunshine. *Why,* I thought. *Why, why, why?* I waited, but no answers came. Just the woman I'd been watching, one hand on her belly, her curls bouncing as she walked.

BECKY

"There's this woman in the park who's always staring at me," said Becky.

"Whah?" asked Andrew, who'd fallen asleep with one arm flung over his face. Without opening his eyes, he reached over to the bedside table, picked up the tube of Rolaids, and handed them to his wife.

"I don't have heartburn," Becky said. It was two in the morning, the thirty-second week of her pregnancy, and she'd been awake for the last three hours. Andrew sighed and replaced the antacids. "No, actually, you know what? I do." Andrew sighed again and tossed the Rolaids across the bed. "I can't sleep. I'm worried," said Becky. She chewed, rolling from her left side to her right.

"What are you worried about?" Andrew asked, sounding marginally more awake. "The woman in the park?"

"No, no, not her. I'm worried . . ." In the darkness, Becky bit her lip. "Do you think things are going to be okay with Mimi? I mean, do you think she'll calm down a little once she's settled?"

"What do you mean?" Andrew asked. Now he sounded entirely awake and not, Becky noted, entirely happy.

"Well, you know. The phone calls. The e-mails. She seems very lonely." Becky said carefully, thinking that *needy* would have been a better word. That, and *insane*.

"It's hard to leave a house and move halfway across the country."

"Yes, but it's not like Mimi hasn't done it before." *Five times.* Her mother-in-law had been married to more men than Becky had ever seriously dated. In the wake of her failed fifth marriage to a real estate magnate in Dallas, she'd packed up her things, collected her alimony, and purchased what she invariably referred to as her "li'l patch of Paradise" in Merion. "You're the one man who'll never let me down," she'd said, flinging her arms dramatically around Andrew's neck after she'd told them about the move. *But he's my man,* Becky had thought, as Andrew patted his mother's back. *Not yours.*

"She's just high strung," Andrew said. "She'll settle down. We just need to be patient with her."

"Promise?"

He rolled over and kissed her cheek and wrapped his arm around her belly. "Promise," he said. He rolled over again and was instantly asleep, leaving Becky wide awake and uncomfortable.

The baby kicked. "Oh, don't you start, too," Becky whispered and rolled over again. She rested her hand on Andrew's shoulder and nudged him until he held it.

She'd met Andrew eight years ago. She was twenty-five and living in Hartwick, New Hampshire, where she'd gone to college. A bad choice but a lucky one, she'd think, looking back. She chose Hartwick after being dazzled by the gorgeous pictures of New England fall that came with its admissions packet, thinking that a change from Florida's endless summer might suit her. Hartwick, whose unofficial motto was Not the Ivy League, but At Least We're Nearby, hadn't been the perfect fit. The oh-so-pretty campus turned out to be peopled with oh-so-pretty blond girls, many of them equipped with the BMWs Daddy had bought them for graduation. Becky had always felt a little out of place. *Oh, Florida!,* the whippet-thin girls would say as Becky, dressed in slenderizing black, tried not to feel enormous or inadequate. *We go on vacation there every year!* Plus, she wasn't a big drinker, and that was pretty much the only thing that Hartwick students did on the weekends . . . and the weekends started on Thursday and didn't end until the wee hours of Monday morning.

She'd walked past Poire, the only nice restaurant in town, at least a dozen times before she'd worked up the courage to go in and ask about the HELP WANTED sign in the window. From the day she'd been hired as a busgirl on probation, the restaurant's polished hardwood floors and starched white tablecloths and its cramped kitchen and gleaming fumed-oak bar had felt more like home to her than any place on campus ever did. And Sarah, who was a part-time grad student and Poire's bartender, became her first New Hampshire friend.

Becky went from bussing to hostessing and waitressing. When she graduated, Darren the manager had hired her full-time. She'd been learning to cook for a year when she met Andrew. It had been the spring of the diet pills, which marked Becky's first, last, and only attempt at organized dieting. "They're a miracle!" Edith Rothstein had claimed, showing off her own sixteen-pound loss when Becky went home for Chanukah. "Now, I made you an appointment with Dr. Janklow . . ."

Becky rolled her eyes. Her mother rolled her eyes right back.

"If you don't want it, you'll cancel. It's not a big deal."

Becky dragged her feet, but in the end she allowed her mother to drive her to Dr. Janklow's office the next morning, and Dr. Janklow had written her a prescription and wished her good luck. A year later, Dr. Janklow had taken a hasty early retirement in the wake of a rumored malpractice suit brought by the family of a woman who'd wanted to drop a quick twenty pounds before her wedding and wound up dropping dead in the middle of her rehearsal dinner instead. "Before dessert or after?" Becky wondered, and her mother had glared at her, hissing, "Who asks these things?"

The pills made her heart race. They made the inside of her mouth feel as though she was sucking on a wad of cotton. They quintupled her energy level, making her feel twitchy and jittery. She lost twenty pounds in twelve weeks. For the first time since junior high, she could buy clothes at the Gap. True, she could barely squeeze herself into the largest size they carried, but still! She bought a denim miniskirt that she'd wear to work at Poire, and after work she'd leave it inside-out on the floor of her apartment just for the pleasure of walking by and seeing the label.

On the nights she wasn't cooking, she'd top the miniskirt with a low-cut blouse of wine-red velvet, dangling silver earrings, and high-heeled black boots. She wore pink lipstick and lots of mascara and let her curls tumble free. Guys made passes at her. Not just drunk ones, either. But from the first time she saw him, she only had eyes for Andrew.

He came into Poire on a busy Thursday, the obligatory skinny girl on his arm, on a night when two servers had called in sick—because, Sarah would later decree, you couldn't call in *hooked up, hung over, and deeply ashamed.* The servers were overwhelmed, and Becky, who was hostessing that night, had been happy to take over Table Seven.

"Hello, and welcome to Poire," Becky said, handing the couple their menus. "May I tell you about our specials?"

"Sure," said the guy. *Oh,* she thought, looking at him. *Oh, yum.* He was handsome, with his close-cropped curls and wide-set eyes and broad shoulders, but it was more than that. There was something about him, the way he ducked his head, smiling, as she described the osso bucco over polenta, or the way he watched her as she spoke, that made Becky wonder what his hands would feel like, how that voice would sound first thing in the morning. Or maybe it was just that she was so damn hungry all the time, and thinking about the sex she most likely wouldn't be having had become a substitute for dwelling on the food she was trying not to eat.

"Oh, God," moaned the girl. "Osso bucco. Five million calories!"

"Six million, actually," Becky said. "But it's worth it."

"I'll give it a try," he said. "What do you recommend to start with?"

Me, Becky thought.

All through the meal, she felt him watching her as she served and cleared, uncorking the wine, offering fresh silverware, more bread, more butter, a new napkin when he dropped his. By the time they'd gotten around to dessert (espresso for the date, a quivering square of chocolate-walnut bread pudding floating in crème anglaise for the love of Becky's life, who'd taken a spoonful, sighed, and said there was nothing even close in the hospital cafeteria), she had married him, chosen their china pattern, and named their babies Ava and Jake. When their meal was over, she did something she'd never done before—she wrote her name and phone number on the check before setting it in the center of the table and walking away with her heart pounding harder than usual, praying that Miss Espresso-for-dessert wouldn't try to pay.

Luckily, Andrew picked up the check. He looked it over, smiled, tucked his credit card inside . . . and by the time he'd left, Becky had a note with "I'll call you . . . Andrew Rabinowitz" written on it and a thirty-percent tip, too.

Andrew Rabinowitz! Andrew. Andy. Drew. Mr. and Mrs.—no, Dr. and Mrs.!—Andrew Rabinowitz. "Rebecca Rothstein-Rabinowitz," she said, trying it out. Sarah raised an eyebrow and said, "But how will anyone know you're Jewish?" Becky gave her a loopy smile and floated into the parking lot, heading to her little apartment, where, sure enough, there was a message from Andrew on her answering machine.

They dated for six weeks—cups of coffee; lunches and dinners; movies where they'd hold hands, then kiss, then grope; the obligatory long walks by the river that would quickly turn into long make-out sessions on the picnic blanket Becky had brought, along with the herb-roasted chicken and crusty French bread. But they'd never been to bed until the night of Sarah's twenty-fifth birthday.

The party had started after Poire shut down. There were shots of vodka with Budweiser chasers. Shots of tequila with more tequila chasing that. Finally, when there were only six people left, Darren, Poire's owner, broke out a bottle of twenty-five-year-old, single-malt Scotch, and they toasted Sarah. Becky and Andrew staggered out onto the street and ended up at Hartwick's only diner. It was an unseasonably balmy April night. All of the diner's windows were wide open, along with the front door. Becky could feel the spring breeze against her flushed cheeks. "I like you," she told him and took a big, dreamy bite of griddle-crisped sticky bun. "I really, really like you."

Andrew had reached across the table and twined one of her curls around his finger. "I like you, too," he said.

"I know," she said, beaming at him. "So. Your place or mine?"

Neither of them had any business driving, but after another half hour and three cups of black coffee, they made it to Andrew's car. Becky imagined that she could feel the road wavering underneath them as he drove, undulating like a warm, slow-moving river. She wandered through his apartment, taking in the hideous brown-and-orange shag carpeting, the walls that looked bruised from furniture being hauled in and out, the obligatory plywood and cinder-block bookcases freighted with medical textbooks and magazines, and a state-of-the-art computer on a desk in the corner.

And the futon, his only piece of furniture. She circled it slowly, as if it were a dog that might bite. "I don't like futons," she said. "They can't commit. I'm a bed! I'm a couch! I'm a bed! I'm a couch!"

"I'm a starving med student," Andrew said, handing her a bottle of chilled white wine and his keychain, which had a bottle opener attached. Eight ninety-nine, the price tag on the wine announced. *Hey, big spender,* Becky thought, uncorking the bottle, pouring them each a glass, and swallowing half of hers in one gulp.

He took her hand and led her to the futon, which was still in its couch position, and they leaned into each other until her velvet-clad shoulder was pressing against the Oxford cloth of his shirt. Up close, the skin of his neck looked scraped, like he'd been shaving with a blunt razor, and she could see that his front teeth overlapped ever so slightly. These flaws only made her feel more tender toward him.

She breathed in his ear and felt him shudder. Emboldened, she kissed him there. Then licked. Then sucked at the lobe, gently, then harder. He sighed.

"Oh, God . . ."

She hummed in his ear and thought of things she hadn't eaten since the diet-pill diet had begun. Chocolate pudding, chocolate mousse, coconut ice cream served with dollops of real whipped cream. Mandarin oranges.

"Mandarin oranges," she whispered. "I'd like to feed you mandarin oranges and let you suck the juice off my fingers."

"Oh, wow," he breathed. She smiled at him sweetly, grabbed his right hand, and licked the palm as delicately as a cat skimming cream.

"Becky," he said, pressing her shoulders against the futon. *Now,* she thought, making sure to arch her back so that her breasts were displayed at their best advantage. She could feel the length of him rubbing against her thigh, dispelling her fears that she was revolting him instead of arousing him. "Becky," he said again, sounding more like a schoolteacher than a man who'd just had his palm licked. He sighed. It wasn't a passionate exhalation. It sounded more like the noise her father had made when he discovered Becky's brother finger-painting on the hood of his sports car.

"Becky," Andrew said, "I don't think we should do this."

She sat up, her breasts dangerously close to tumbling out of her top. "Why not?"

"Well," he said, clearing his throat and sitting back, his hands pressed tightly together. "Um. It's just that . . ." Another pause. "I've never really had a girlfriend."

"Oh," she said. *Huh?* she thought. He was twenty-eight. Who hadn't had a girlfriend at that age? "Are you saving yourself for marriage?"

He closed his eyes. "Not really. It's just that . . ."

She was beginning to have a sinking feeling in her somewhat-diminished stomach. In her experience, sentences that started with *It's just that* rarely led anywhere good. Particularly if they were being uttered by a man whose palm you'd just licked.

I don't want to hear this, she thought. But she couldn't stop herself from asking. "Just that what?"

Andrew sighed and stared at his lap. His face was drawn and unhappy. "I want a girlfriend. But. Um." He bit his lip. "I guess it's that you're not exactly what I had in mind."

"Because I'm fat," she said.

He didn't say yes. But he didn't say no, either.

"Well," she managed, straightening her top, "good luck with Cindy Crawford." Her legs felt wobbly as she found her purse, but somehow Becky made it to the door and managed to give it a very satisfactory slam before remembering that she had no way of making it five miles back to her apartment. Then she remembered that she still had his car keys in her pocket. She could take his car, but then how would he get to campus? She decided, slipping behind the wheel of his car, that she didn't much care.

She left his car keys in his office mailbox that Monday morning with a can of Slim-Fast on top, in case he missed the point, and proceeded to spend the next two weeks feeling like a popcorn box that had been run over by a moving van: flattened, empty, and altogether miserable.

"Screw him," said Sarah, sliding an Irish coffee across the bar. "It's not like he's Cary Grant, first of all. And you're beautiful."

"Yeah, yeah," Becky said.

"Oh, no moping," said Sarah with a shudder. "I hate moping. What you have to do is go find another guy. Immediately, if not sooner."

Becky took her friend's advice and moved on. Waiting in line for the movies one night, she met another guy, an engineering graduate student who was tall and thin and mostly bald—not quite handsome, not anywhere near Andrew quality, but he was sweet. He was the tiniest bit boring, too, but she didn't mind because in the wake of Dr. Andrew cheap-wine-drinking, futon-sleeping, tacky-apartment-dwelling, you're-not-quite-what-I-had-in-mind Rabinowitz, boring wasn't looking so bad.

The trouble was, her cooking fell off. She scorched a panful of stuffed Cornish game hens on a busy Friday night and sent out a Dover sole that was slimy and half raw and forgot to add sugar to the chocolate-hazelnut mousse. Her chicken with preserved lemons, which should have been a happy marriage of sweet and sour, tasted as bitter as Becky's thoughts had become, and her soufflés deflated with a sigh the instant she pulled them out of the oven.

"A woman with a broken heart's got no business cooking," said Eduardo the sauté chef, scraping the skin off one of Becky's blackened game hens. He pointed his knife at Becky. "You got to figure this out."

Becky tried. She concentrated on her new boyfriend. And just when she'd started to believe that she wasn't the size of Pluto, or at least one of its moons, Andrew came back to Poire.

It was June, two weeks before Becky's birthday. The air was soft and lilac-scented, and the campus and the town had a riotous, swoony feeling, an end-of-the-school-year anticipation, as if at any moment everyone would throw down their books and tear off their clothes and roll around on the freshly mown grass.

It was raining that night, a gentle gray drizzle. Sarah came back to the kitchen and said that Andrew was sitting at the bar, alone. "Do you want me to spit in his glass?"

"That's a generous offer, but no." *I don't need him,* she told herself. But she couldn't stop herself from looking. Andrew wore a brown suede jacket and a hangdog look, and there were purplish circles under his eyes. *I have a boyfriend,* Becky thought. And she was going home to fix him a late supper, after which they would have satisfactory, if slightly vanilla, sex, so screw you, Andrew Rabinowitz. But after she'd wiped down her station, wrapped up her knives, and walked out the back door, there was Andrew, waiting for her, his arms wrapped around himself in the drizzle, standing next to her car.

"Well, well," she said, "look who's here."

"Becky," he said. "I wanted to talk to you."

"I'm busy."

"Please." He sounded desperate. It was all she could do to shore herself up, remembering how he'd hurt her, what he'd said.

"I have to get going." She paused to give her next statement its full impact. "My boyfriend's waiting for me."

"It'll just take a minute." His voice was so quiet she could barely hear it. "The thing is . . ." He mumbled something she couldn't make out.

"Pardon me?"

He raised his head. "I said, I think I'm in love with you."

"Oh, blah blah, whatever." She managed to sound nonchalant, even though her heart was pounding so hard she was sure he'd be able to hear it. "You know what?" She lifted her wrapped satchel. "You should know better than to fuck with someone who's carrying knives."

"I am. Becky, you're funny and smart . . ."

" . . . and fat," she finished. She leaned down, unlocked her car, tossed the knives in the backseat, and sat down behind the wheel. Andrew walked around the car and put his hand on the passenger's side door.

"Oh, no," she told him. "Step away from the vehicle."

"I didn't exactly say that," he said. "And it's not what I think. I think you're beautiful, but I was pushing you away because . . ."

She stared at him through the mist.

"I have to tell you something," he said and cleared his throat. "A private thing."

"Go ahead," she said, looking around the empty parking lot. "I don't think anyone's listening."

"Could I just—" he said, reaching for the door handle.

"No."

"Fine." Andrew took a deep breath and rested his hands on the roof of her car. "First of all, I'm sorry I hurt your feelings."

"Apology accepted. No big deal. I've been called worse by better."

"Becky," he pleaded. "Please. Look. Please just let me finish this."

She paused, curious, unable to help herself.

"See. Um." He shuffled his feet. "The thing is, I'm . . . shy."

She laughed incredulously. "That's your big secret? That's the best you can do? Oh, please." She slammed her door.

"No. Wait! That's not it. The thing is . . ." His voice was muffled by the rolled-up window.

"What?"

Andrew said something Becky couldn't hear. She leaned over and rolled the passenger's side window down. "What?"

"It's a sex thing!" he hissed, then looked around as if expecting to see an audience hanging on his every word.

"Oh." A sex thing. *Oh, God.* He's a cross-dresser. He's impotent. He's an impotent cross-dresser, and he wears a smaller size than I do.

Andrew leaned into the car and didn't lift his head to look at her as he spoke. "You know when you get used to doing something a certain way and then that's the only way you can do it? Like, you drive to work a certain way every day and after a while it's like there's no other way you can do it?"

No, she thought. "Yes," she said.

"Well, I'm like that. It's like that for me. It's like that with . . ." He gestured toward his crotch.

"Sex?"

He nodded miserably.

"So you can only do it, like, in missionary position?"

He sighed. "I wish. I've actually never . . ."

It took her a minute to realize what he was saying. "Never?"

"I can only do it by myself. I have this very specific method, and . . ."

"What?" she demanded, shifting her weight so that her thighs were rubbing together. She was intrigued. And very turned on. "Tell me! Unless it involves, you know, your mother's girdle or something. In which case you should feel free to lie."

There was a thunk as he banged his forehead against the roof of the car. "I can't."

Becky poked his chest through the opened window. "Can't tell me or can't do it?"

"It's idiotic," he said. "It's so dumb, and I've never talked about this with anyone."

"What?" Her mind was ticking off possibilities, each more horrific than the last. Leather. Whips. Plastic wrap. Oh, my.

He winced. "I can't believe this," he said, as if he was talking to himself. "I can't talk about this anymore."

"Yes, you can," she said, reckless in the warm June rain, willing herself to forget, for the moment, her earnest engineering-student boyfriend, who was probably waiting for her in his bed, on his beige percale sheets. "Take me home and tell me." She unlocked the passenger's side door. "I promise I won't laugh."

Half an hour later, Andrew and Becky were back on his futon. The room was lit by two candles burning on top of the television set. Andrew had a juice glass full of Scotch in his hand, and his eyes were squeezed shut, as if he couldn't stand to even look at her. "My mother . . ." he began.

Oh, Lord, Becky thought. Please don't let this involve something inappropriate with his mother.

"She's very. Um. Intrusive. When I was a kid, she didn't let me have a lock on my bedroom door. The only place I could get any privacy was the bathroom. So I learned to . . ."

"Get off," Becky supplied.

He smiled a little, his eyes still closed. "Right. Um. Lying on my stomach on the bath mat. Kind of, um, rubbing back and forth."

She exhaled the breath she hadn't realized she was holding. Given the possibilities—nurse's outfits, enema bags, stuffed-animal costumes, and worse—she was pretty sure that she could deal with a bath mat. "That's not so bad." She glanced toward the closed bathroom door, trying to remember whether she'd ever even seen his bath mat and whether jealousy was appropriate.

"It's not so bad until you try to do it any other way." His voice got softer. "Like with a girl."

"So you never . . ."

He swallowed a mouthful of Scotch and shook his head, his brow furrowed, eyebrows knitted. "No. Never. Not even once."

God. She felt so sorry for him . . . sorry, and aroused. A virgin. She'd never been with a virgin. She could barely remember being a virgin herself.

"Tell you what," she said. "I think we should do an experiment."

"It won't work," he said. "I've tried before."

Her mind tingled with possibilities and with questions. She wondered what had happened during his experiments. Would he get to a certain point with a girlfriend, then dash off to the loo and belly-flop on top of the bath mat for the finale? Or fake orgasm? Could men do that?

"What's the worst thing that could happen?" she asked

He gave her another ghost of a smile. "I don't know. Dying a virgin?"

Becky winced. "Okay, that actually is the worst thing that could happen. But I bet we can figure this out."

He opened his eyes. "I appreciate that. Really, I do. No matter what happens, I'll never forget that you were so . . ." His voice cracked. ". . . Nice about this."

"You're welcome," she said. A plan was forming in her mind. "So what do you think? Should we try?"

He got up off the futon, reaching for his belt buckle.

"Whoa, cowboy! Slow down!"

He dropped his hands, looking puzzled. "I thought we were going to . . ."

"Oh, we are. But not tonight. Tonight," she said, "we're just going to make out."

He grinned, looking honestly happy for the first time since he'd arrived at Poire. "That," he said, "I can handle."

Three hours later, Becky's lips were swollen, her cheeks and chin rubbed raw from his stubble. "Please," Andrew groaned, pressing his whole length against her. "Please, Becky, I know it'll work, please . . ."

With a force of will she hadn't known she'd possessed, Becky wrenched herself away. She knew that if they kept kissing, if he kept touching her, if his fingertips grazed the crotch of her panties one more time, she wouldn't be able to wait.

"Friday," she gasped. "After work." She'd have to make some excuse to her boyfriend. "Can you pick me up?"

He could, he said. She kissed him, kissed him, kissed him, planning the menu in her head.

In spite of Becky's career at Poire—and in spite of what people might have inferred from her figure—good cooking did not run in the Rothstein family. When Becky was a teenager, most of her mother's meals had come in the form of a powdered shake mix that she'd blend with ice cubes and, if she was feeling really sporting, bananas. Ronald Rothstein had eaten whatever was set in front of him, without ever seeming to taste it or even really looking. "Delicious," he'd say, whether it had been or not.

Grandma Malkie was the cook in the family. With her shelf of a bosom and wide, quivering hips, she was also Edith Rothstein's worst nightmare. "Ess, ess," she'd croon to little Becky, slipping bits of rugelach and hand-rolled hamantaschen into her mouth when her mother wasn't looking. Becky loved spending nights at her grandmother's house, where she could stay up late, sprawled on her grandmother's peach satin comforter, playing Crazy Eights and eating salted cashews. Grandma Malkie was the one Becky had come to in tears after Ross Farber had chanted "Fatty, fatty two-by-four" at her on the bus back from the Hebrew-school field trip. "Never mind him," Grandma Malkie had said, handing Becky a clean handkerchief. "You look just the way you're supposed to. Just the way your mother should, if she'd let herself eat a meal once in a while."

"Boys won't like me," Becky said, sniffling and wiping her eyes.

"You're too young to worry about boys," Grandma Malkie decreed. "But I'll tell you a secret. You know what boys like? A woman who's happy with herself. Who's not making herself miserable with the Jane Fonda videotapes and complaining all the time about whether this part or that one's too big. And you know what else they like?" She leaned close, whispering into her granddaughter's ear. "Good food."

Becky had started cooking when she was fourteen, out of self-defense, she'd later joke, but really, it was to honor her grandmother. With the help of Julia Child and a copy of *The Joy of Cooking* her mother had gotten as a wedding gift and never even opened, she discovered heavy cream and chives and shallots, lamb chops seared on the gas grill she'd bought herself with her bat mitzvah money, quiches and soufflés, napoleons and éclairs, stews and daubes and ragouts, and fresh Florida fish baked in parchment with nothing but lemon juice and olive oil.

She'd cooked for men before. She had a boyfriend her sophomore year who was heavily into salmon, after he'd read that it could help prevent prostate cancer, but he could only afford the canned stuff, which he'd bring her in bulk from the grocery store. "Prostate patties," Becky would announce . . . or, once, feeling ambitious and wanting to get rid of a half can of bread crumbs and three eggs, "Prostate loaf."

But this would have to be her very best effort—food fit for a king. Or at least food fit for a man who'd spent the last decade or so making love to the bathroom carpeting.

Figs, she thought. Figs for starters. But were whole figs too obvious? She remembered a fig-jam pizza she'd had once at a restaurant in Boston, on crispy flatbread with prosciutto and asiago cheese. She could pull that off. And some kind of meat for the main course, seared crisp on the outside, juicy and pink-tender in the center. Mashed potatoes with heavy cream. Asparagus, because it was supposed to be an aphrodisiac, and then something completely decadent for dessert.

Maybe a cheese course with organic lavender honey. Baklava! Chocolate truffles! Fresh raspberries with cream!

Her mind was racing. Her mouth was watering. Her bank account wouldn't be able to withstand the assault she had planned—the wines alone would cost in the triple digits. Becky happily busted out her For Emergencies Only credit card without even bothering to worry about what she'd do when she got the bill.

Andrew was waiting for her at the bar again on Friday night, looking considerably less hangdog than he had the time before.

"Are you two friends again?" Sarah asked.

"Something like that," Becky said, but her tone must have given her away because Eduardo and Dave immediately began chorusing in a combination of English and Spanish about how Becky, even with her diminished *culo,* was back in love and would, God willing, stop ruining paying customers' dinners as a result. She pulled her bags of groceries out of the walk-in where she'd stashed them, added a loaf of bread and two bottles of wine, and hurried out to meet Andrew at the bar.

"What's all this?" he asked, eyeing the bags.

"Food."

"You're going to cook?" he asked. Clearly, whatever he'd been imagining, dinner hadn't been included.

"I'm going to cook," she said. *I'm going to knock your socks off,* she thought. *I'm going to make you forget every other girl you ever kissed. I'm going to make you love me for the rest of your life.*

Back at his apartment, Andrew lit candles while Becky spread fig jam on the flatbread, added drifts of cheese and thin slices of prosciutto, and popped it under the broiler.

"What are you making?" he asked, watching her every move as she worked in his closet-sized kitchen. She hoped he liked what he was seeing. She was wearing Old Faithful, her Gap denim miniskirt, and what she hoped wasn't too much perfume.

"Appetizers," she told him. He wrapped his arms around her waist and leaned her back against the kitchen counter, nuzzling her neck. "You smell nice."

Okay, then, not too much perfume.

"I bought us something," he said, reaching over her head into a cabinet. She smiled when he handed her a can of mandarin oranges. He'd remembered. That was good.

She pulled the pizza out of the oven, set water to boil for the asparagus, and dredged the pounded-thin slices of veal in flour while he took his first bite of the flatbread. "Wow," he said, "this is amazing."

"Isn't it?" This wasn't a night, she'd decided, for false modesty. And the pizza was fantastic, the pungent cheese blending perfectly with the sweet fig jam.

"Come here," he said. She wrapped an apron around her waist, set the veal to sauté in olive oil and butter, and complied. "You feel so good," he whispered. "And everything smells delicious."

"Patience," she said, smiling against his neck. "We're just getting started."

She poured the wine, trimmed the asparagus, crumbled blue cheese over the veal slices, and set them in the preheated oven. The potatoes were bubbling away; the cheeses were warming on the counter. She handed him the plates, the glasses, the wine, two linen napkins, and the forks she'd already decided they wouldn't be using for long, and led him into the living room.

"Relax," she told him. With his shoulders tensed and the corner of his mouth twitching, Andrew looked more like a man with a dentist appointment than someone gearing up for a night of gustatory and sexual ecstasy. "I promise, whatever happens, this won't hurt a bit."

Twenty minutes later, dinner was served. Andrew spread a sheet out over the floor, and he sat there, cross-legged, one knee jouncing up and down.

"Oh," he said. "Oh, wow."

They ate in silence for a few minutes, looking at each other shyly, tasting everything.

"It's so good," he said, pushing his plate away. "I'm just not that hungry." He tried to smile. "I'm nervous, I guess."

"Close your eyes," Becky said. He looked worried—perhaps imagining that she'd be breaking out restraints, or a video camera—but complied.

She lifted the glass of wine to his lips. "Take a little sip," she told him. "And keep your eyes shut."

He drank. His lips curved up in a smile. "Open," she said and fed him a morsel of veal. He chewed slowly. "Mmm."

"Want to try?"

He gave her a spear of asparagus, easing it slowly into her mouth. She heard him breathing harder as she brushed his fingertips with her lips. Then he took a pinch of rice. She licked the grains off his fingers, then sucked, hearing him sigh. "Can I . . . ," he whispered. She opened her eyes a slit. He'd dipped his fingers in the wineglass and was holding them out for her to suck.

He groaned out loud as she drew his index finger between her lips. Becky took a mouthful of wine, held it in her mouth, leaned forward, and kissed him, letting it trickle over his tongue. They kissed and kissed, pushing the plates away, and then Andrew was on top of her, grinding against her in the flickering candlelight, and her head was full of every good smell—wine and cheese and fresh-baked bread and the smell of his skin. "Becky," he breathed.

She pushed herself up onto the futon. Andrew ground himself against her.

"Does this mean," she gasped, "that we're skipping the cheese course?"

"Now," he panted. "I can't wait anymore."

"Just one more thing." She hurried into the kitchen, past the cheeses, the honey, and the champagne she'd brought, finding his little can of mandarin oranges, popping the top, spilling the fruit and syrup into a bowl. Back in the living room, Andrew was lying on the futon, his shirt off, staring at her so intently she felt dizzy.

"Dessert," she said, as she took one of the segments of orange between her fingers, sliding it slowly into his mouth.

He sighed. "Becky," he murmured.

"Just wait," she whispered. She sent up a quick prayer that he wouldn't burst out laughing at what she had planned next and then figured, really, would a man who'd shared his most intimate moments with a piece of rubber-backed rope-spun cotton laugh at anything? *Fuck it,* she thought, *here goes.* She pulled off her shirt, leaving only the lacy black underwire bra, and tilted the bowl, spilling a trickle of syrup down her neck, over the tops of her breasts.

"Come here," she said, drawing him toward her. His tongue worked hard at her neck. She eased another slippery segment down between her breasts, and he dove for it. She thought of pigs digging for truffles, pioneers sending buckets down wells, hoping for sweet, clear water. The candles flickered, sending shadows dancing across his face. She felt him, hard against her thigh, as she took a slippery segment between her teeth and kissed him, using her tongue to ease the orange between his lips. With that, she reached for his zipper, eased his pants down over his hips, and . . . *Oh, my God.* "Is this a joke?" she asked, staring down at him.

"No joke," he said, in a strangled-sounding voice as he tried to yank his pants off over his shoes.

"It's real?"

"Real," he confirmed.

"Jesus Christ," she said. "Have you ever been in pornos?"

"Just medical school," he said, grabbing her hand.

"How big is it?"

"I don't know."

"Oh, come on, of course you do."

"I never measured."

"Yowza," she said, trying not to stare. She let him wrap her fingers as far as they would go. She thought about French baguettes, still warm in their paper wrappers. She thought about plums, rice paper–wrapped spring rolls, crepes filled with apricot jam, beggar's purses stuffed with caviar and sour cream, every delicious thing she'd ever tasted. She wanted it to be the best blow job he'd ever had, but it quickly became apparent that it was more than likely the only blow job he'd ever had. He laced his fingers in her hair and pumped his hips so vigorously that she felt herself gagging.

"Easy," she said.

"I'm sorry," he said, sitting up.

"Not to worry," she told him. "Hang on. I have an idea."

She padded into his kitchen, opening the cupboards and the refrigerator until she found what she was looking for—the olive oil she'd been using to cook. He'd put it in the refrigerator, which was twenty-seven kinds of wrong, but she figured it would warm up quickly enough and she could lecture him later. Back in the living room, she arranged herself on the futon. "Come here," she whispered. As he stood over her, still wearing his shirt and his shoes, she unhooked her bra, picked up the olive oil, and poured some into his hands.

He swung himself over her, straddling her side with his thighs, rubbing himself with his oiled hands, cupping her breasts and rubbing himself between them.

"Ah," he said, sliding back and forth, getting the idea quickly.

"Okay?" she whispered, as he worked himself back and forth.

"I think . . . ," he panted. "I need . . ."

She poured more oil in her hand and tucked her hand underneath him, her palm rubbing against the swollen flesh as it moved back and forth over her, breathless underneath his weight.

"Ah," he groaned and shoved himself up on his hands. A moment later, he collapsed against her, groaning her name into her hair.

Ten minutes later, they were spooning on the futon. "Wow," he said. The ruins of dinner were scattered across the floor—plates still crusted with melted Gorgonzola and potatoes on the floor, half-filled, fingerprint-smeared wineglasses balanced next to his digital clock.

"I know."

"Can I do anything for you?" he whispered. She shook her head. There was a worm of guilt twisting in her belly as she thought about her boyfriend, probably waiting up for her with two fillets of swordfish, white and inoffensive, in the fridge. She thought that if they didn't actually have intercourse, it was somehow less like cheating, more like a humanitarian mission, the kind of thing ex-presidents won the Nobel Peace Prize for.

"Becky," Andrew whispered. "My hero."

"Go to sleep," she whispered back. A minute later, still smiling, he did.

They dated for two years while Andrew did the fourth and fifth years of his residency, then when he landed a fellowship at Pennsylvania Hospital, they moved to Philadelphia. Becky convinced Sarah to dump the Marxist grad student she was dating and move with her. They pooled their savings, plus the money Becky's father had left her, and rented the space that would become Mas. Life was wonderful. And Becky was sure she knew what was coming the night Andrew led her to the couch and sat down, holding both of her hands and looking into her eyes.

"There's something I want to ask you," he began.

"Okay," Becky said, hoping that she'd guessed right as to what would be coming next.

Andrew smiled and pulled her close. She closed her eyes. *Here it comes,* she thought and wondered if he'd bought a ring already or if they'd be shopping for one together.

He brought his mouth close to her ear. "I'd like you to . . ."

Be my wife, Becky's mind filled in.

" . . . meet my mother," said Andrew.

Becky's eyes flew open. "What?"

"Well, I think you should meet her before we get married."

She narrowed her eyes. "Andrew Rabinowitz, that was lame."

Her husband-to-be looked chastened. "Really?"

"I insist that you do it again."

Andrew shrugged and dropped to his knee in front of her. "Rebecca Mara Rothstein, I will love you forever, and I want to be with you every day for the rest of my life."

"That's better," she murmured, as he pulled a black velvet box out of his pocket.

"So that's a yes?"

She looked at the ring and squealed with delight. "That's a yes," she said. She slipped the ring on her finger and tried not to think about how even as he was proposing to her, his mother had come first.

"Are you awake?" Andrew asked, nuzzling her curls.

"Mmmmph," Becky said and groaned, peering over her husband's shoulder and hazarding a glance at the clock. Seven o'clock already? "Need more sleep," she said, pulling the pillow over her head.

"Do you want me to call Sarah and tell her you're sick? You can stay in bed all day."

Becky shook her head, sighed again, and pushed herself up and out of bed. Her intention was to work right until she went into labor. Sarah, who'd agreed to serve as Becky's doula and assist her during the birth, had raised her eyebrows. "You know best," she said. But lately, she'd started following Becky around the tiny kitchen with the PISO MOJADO sign and insisting that the chefs keep a large pot of water boiling on the back burner "just in case."

Becky gulped down her prenatal vitamins and held out her arms. "Quickly," she said. "While it's just the two of us." Andrew tilted up her chin, and they kissed. Becky's eyes slipped shut.

The telephone started ringing. Andrew gave a guilty start. "Let me just get that," he said.

Becky sighed and shook her head. She knew who was on the line without even looking at the caller ID. E-mail was Mimi's first line of communication, and if she didn't get a response within an hour, she'd start calling, no matter how early in the morning it was, or how late at night. And if Andrew didn't call her right back, she'd have him paged. "What happens if you don't return the page?" Becky had once asked. Andrew's brow furrowed. "I guess she'd start calling hospitals. And morgues."

Becky curled on the couch. "Hi, Mom," Andrew said, giving his wife an unhappy shrug. Andrew knew she didn't like his mother much, but she didn't think he had any sense of the way that during nights when she couldn't sleep she'd entertain long, vivid fantasies of her mother-in-law dying of some rare disease that would render her conveniently mute before whisking her off to the land from which you couldn't page, e-mail, phone, or fax your son every fifteen minutes. She tried not to complain about Mimi because when she did Andrew would look serious and give her a speech that inevitably began with the words *Becky, she is my mother, and she does this out of love.*

It would have helped if she and Mimi had something other than Andrew in common. They didn't. For starters, Mimi had little use for food. She was a champion noneater, a world-class under-orderer. If you asked for two poached eggs and whole-wheat toast, she'd have one poached egg and sliced tomatoes. If you were only having coffee, she'd just have water, and if you just wanted water, she'd have a glass without ice.

And Mimi hated the little rowhouse Becky and Andrew had bought the year before. "Your kitchen's in the basement!" Mimi had shrieked in dismay when she'd flown in from Texas for a visit. Becky bit her lip at the spectacle of Mimi, who only ever made reservations, getting in a tizzy over the location of the kitchen. Instead, Becky pointed out the hand-glazed tile floor and the built-in bookcases were big enough for all of her cookbooks. Andrew, wearing an old pair of scrubs, painted each floor of their house a different color—rich wine-red for the kitchen, goldenrod-yellow for the ground-floor living room, robin's-egg blue for the third floor, where he'd put up walls, turning what had been one big bedroom into one medium-sized bedroom, a short hallway, a closet, and a sunny little nook where their baby would sleep. He'd come to bed that night with paint in his hair, and she'd told him that it was just what she'd wanted. *And it was,* Becky thought, as Andrew said his final good-bye to Mimi and pulled her off the couch for a hug.

"You sure you don't want a day off?" he asked.

She shook her head. "Can you feel that?" she asked, pressing his hand against her belly.

Andrew nodded. Becky closed her eyes and leaned against her husband's shoulder as the baby swam inside of her.

June

June

LIA

"So," my mother asked me during my ninth week under her same-as-it-ever-was roof, "are you here to stay?" She bared her teeth in the first-floor bathroom mirror, checking for lipstick. Another day, another white blouse/black slacks combo, here in the House Where Time Stood Still.

I sat on the couch with my head bent over the basket of laundry I was folding, feeling even more off-balance than normal. I'd woken up thinking not of the baby but of Sam. In Los Angeles, there'd been a homeless woman who hung around at the corner by the gate to our apartment building in Hancock Park. Morning after morning, wearing three dirty coats in the seventy-degree weather, she'd be there, jabbing her finger in the air and talking to herself. After we'd come home from Korean barbecue one night and she'd been gesticulating wildly at our car as we drove by, Sam had made it his project to win her over. It was for my own good, he told me. "I understand that there are crazy people everywhere," he explained, "but if there's going to be one around the baby, I'd rather she was a benevolent crazy person." One morning, he headed out early, in a T-shirt and jeans and a baseball cap, all cleft chin and bright blue eyes, with an apple in his hand. Ten minutes later, he came back, sans apple, with a welt on his forehead.

"She threw it at me," he reported, sounding both indignant and amused, and I teased him, saying she was the first woman in a long time who hadn't been won over by his good looks and Texan charm. I'd thought that would be the end of his homeless outreach project, but every morning for two weeks he'd carry something out the door—a yogurt, a bagel, a packaged Zone meal (we'd had a huge fight about that, with me arguing that homeless, hungry people should not be given low-cal commodities and Sam saying that it wasn't fair to treat our lady any differently than the other dieting denizens of L.A.). I don't think she ever spoke to Sam, but I do know that she never threw anything at him again . . . and that once the baby came, when I pushed my stroller past her, she stepped back respectfully, looking at us with a hungry avidity, as if she were watching a parade.

My mother was staring at me, looking at my gray high school–era sweatpants and washed-out Pat Benatar T-shirt with her nose scrunched. "Do you have any plans?"

I folded a washcloth and set it in the basket. "I'm not sure."

"What have you been doing all day long?" I examined her voice for criticism, for her typical thinly veiled anger, but didn't find it. Her eyes were focused on the scarf she was tying around her neck, and she just sounded curious.

"Sleeping, mostly," I said. It was partially true. I did sleep as often as I could, long, fuzzy hours on the Strawberry Shortcake comforter with the dusty blinds pulled down. I'd wake up from the naps with my heart thudding, a sour taste in my mouth, and my body covered in sweat, feeling less rested than I had when I'd laid down, and then I'd get into the rental car and head to the city, to the park, and to the woman I'd been . . . what? *Stalking* was the shameful word that surfaced in my mind. The week before I'd left a pacifier in the window box of the restaurant where she worked, but that wasn't hurting anyone, was it?

So what else was I doing all day long? In between four-hour naps and trips to the park, I'd been trying to compose a letter to my husband. I wasn't sure what it should say. All I knew for sure was that

Hallmark didn't make a card for it. *Dear Sam,* I'd begun. *I'm sorry.* That was as far as I'd gotten.

"Why don't you tell me what's going on?" my mother asked.

I shook my head. "Something happened," I told her as the world started to spin. I gripped the laundry basket and shut my eyes.

"Well, Lisa, I managed to figure out that much," she told me. I waited for her voice to rise into the taunting singsong she'd used to such devastating effect when I was a teenager. It didn't. "You might feel better if you talked about it," she said. I blinked at her to make sure it was still the same old Mom—sensible shoes and neat hair, the same long, sharp nose that I had, and lipstick that would undoubtedly wind up on her teeth at some point during the day.

"I can't," I said. "Not yet."

"Fine, then," she said. "Whenever you're ready."

"I don't know why you're asking," I said, gathering the laundry. "It isn't like you care."

"Oh, Lisa, don't start that adolescent nonsense. I'm your mother. Of course I care."

I thought about what I could tell her and what it would do. I could imagine her face crumpling, the way she'd hold out her arms to me—*Oh, Lisa! Oh, honey!* Or maybe not. Maybe she'd just wipe her teeth with her finger and look at me as if I was kidding or inventing things ("Young lady, I want the truth, not one of your inventions!"). She'd looked at me a lot that way before I left. She'd looked at my father that way, before he'd left, too.

I got to my feet, holding the laundry to my chest.

"Lisa," she said. "I do care." If she'd touched me—if she'd put her hand on my arm, even if she'd just looked at me, just looked—I might have told her the whole thing. But she didn't. She glanced at her watch and picked up her car keys from the table by the door. "Here," she said. She reached into the closet, rummaging past my junior-high-era denim jacket and one of my father's discarded raincoats, and handed me something—a down coat, calf-length and bulky, electric blue, with snaps running up the front. "It's cold today."

I looked at myself in the mirror once she was gone, seeing the circles under my eyes, the hollows in my cheeks, my greasy two-toned hair. I looked about ready to join the apple-chucking bag lady. I pulled on the coat, lay down on my tilting bed, and pulled out my cell phone. *You have twenty-seven new messages,* said the voice mail. *Lia, it's me. Lia, where are you? Lia, could you please . . .* And then just *Please.* I hit "delete" twenty-seven times, and then lay there in the semidarkness, thinking about my husband. It still felt strange to think of Sam that way. We'd been dating for less than a year when we got married, and we'd only been married for ten months when I left.

Sam and I had met at a club where we'd both been working. Sam was tending bar. My job was to open the doors of cars as they pulled up to the curb, lean down low enough to let the passengers get a good view of my cleavage, and say, "Welcome to Dane!" with a smile that suggested the possibility, if not the likelihood, of hot anonymous sex in the ladies' room.

"Not Dane's!" the owner had screamed at the six model/actresses he'd hired, as five o'clock approached. "It's not Dane's; it's just Dane! Welcome to Dane! Let me hear you say it!"

"Welcome to Dane," we'd chanted.

"We're like the world's best-looking Hare Krishnas," I said an hour later, leaning surreptitiously against the bar with one high heel slipped off so I could massage a blister in progress.

Sam had laughed when I'd said that . . . and, later, he'd handed me a vodka gimlet and hadn't charged me. "Welcome to Sam," he said. There was a hint of Texas in his voice, even after six years of struggling-actordom in Los Angeles. He was handsome, but so were most of the men in that town. Sam was better than handsome. He was kind.

"Are you sure?" I'd asked him when he'd slipped a coiled paper-straw wrapper band around my ring finger, the day after the three take-home pregnancy tests had come back positive, positive, and, you guessed it, positive. I'd twisted the bit of paper around and around, feeling happy and excited and scared.

"I'm sure," he'd said. He'd reached into his pocket and pulled out a travel agent's envelope with two tickets to Las Vegas. "I'm sure about you."

Las Vegas was perfect. It eliminated the potential unpleasantness of a big wedding, with his family present and my family absent—absent and dead, as far as Sam was concerned, in that long-ago car-crash tragedy. "Go get a massage," Sam told me after we'd checked in. "They do prenatal ones. I checked." When I got back to the room, there was a green garment bag lying on the bed. "I know you don't have a family to do this for you," he'd said. I'd shaken the gown out onto the bed. It was a creamy color somewhere between ivory and gold, full-skirted, made of silk that was as soft as petals. "Let me be your family now," he'd said.

There were birds in the hotel lobby, I remembered, parrots and macaws and lorakeets with brilliant yellow and emerald-green feathers. Their eyes seemed to follow me from their bamboo cages as I walked by with my husband, holding my frothy skirt, hearing my heels click on the marble floor. If I could rewrite the story in the manner of the Brothers Grimm, I would have the birds call out warnings: *Turn back, turn back, thou pretty bride!* Then I would erase what I'd written, going back and back and back to the night we'd met. If he hadn't smiled at my joke; if he hadn't given me the drink; if I hadn't liked the look of his face and his hands when he passed his jacket across the bar, telling me that I looked cold in my hot pants.

I pulled my mother's coat around me and got to my feet. The diaper bag was at the foot of the stairs where I'd left it. I slung it over my shoulder, worked my engagement ring off my finger, and slipped it into my pocket. I'd locked the door behind me before I remembered that the letter for Sam was still on top of my old bed. I decided to leave it there. Let her try to figure it out. Let her try to make sense of who Sam was and what I'd done to be sorry for.

Forty-five minutes later, I was back in the pawnshop I'd first visited eleven years ago, with a different diamond ring in my hand. The guy behind the counter spent what felt like an eternity peering through the loupe, from the diamonds to my face, back to the diamonds again.

"It's from Tiffany's," I'd said to fill the silence.

"Seven thousand," the guy had said—his first words. "And if it's stolen, I don't want to know."

I wanted to argue, to bargain, to tell him that the ring was worth more than that, and found I didn't have the energy. I just held out my hand for the money, and he'd handed it over, a thick wad of hundred-dollar bills that I folded and refolded and finally crammed into one of the bag's many pockets, a zippered plastic one intended for dirty clothes or wipes.

Then I walked to a coffee shop on South Street, picked up a copy of one of the free weeklies, and began circling ads for apartments. I kept my head down and tried to ignore Sam's voice in my head, the way he would have had me laughing by trying to pronounce STDIO SBLT and RD BRCK GDN and asking why the advertisers couldn't just pay extra and spring for the vowels.

"SUBLET, RITTENHOUSE SQUARE," I circled. "ONE BEDROOM, HARDWOOD FLOORS, PARK VIEWS, AVAILABLE IMMEDIATELY." It sounded perfect, and the rent wouldn't put an unsustainable dent into my cash wad. I dialed the number and was surprised to find myself talking to an actual person instead of an answering machine. I made an appointment and headed west, first up Pine Street, then up Walnut, where my feet slowed down of their own volition in front of an Internet café.

My fingers felt clumsy on the keyboard. My login was the one I'd given myself years ago—LALia. The password was our baby's name. I had a hundred and ninety-three new messages, including one from Sam for every day I'd been gone. PLEASE, read the memo line of the most recent ones. NOT PLEASE READ THIS. Just PLEASE. I held my breath and clicked one open.

Dear Lia. I'm honoring your wishes and not trying to find you, but I'd give anything just to know that you're all right.

I think about you all the time. I wonder where you are. I wish I could be there with you. I wish there was some way to make you believe that none of this was your fault, it was just a terrible thing that happened. I wish I could tell you that in person. I wish I could help.

Can I?

He hadn't signed his name.

I hit reply before I could lose my nerve. *I'm home,* I wrote to my husband. *I'm safe. I'll write more when I can.*

I paused, my fingers quivering over the keyboard. *I think about you, too,* I wrote. But I couldn't. Not yet. I hit Delete, shoved a five-dollar bill in the tip cup at the counter and pushed through the heavy glass door.

Forty-five minutes later I was knocking on a door on the sixteenth floor of the Dorchester.

"It's a six-month sublet," said the super, a middle-aged man in khakis and a tie that he kept tugging. He opened the door on an empty one-bedroom unit with parquet floors, two big closets, a galley kitchen, and a view of the park. "Dishwasher, garbage disposal, coin-op laundry in the basement."

I walked through the apartment, hearing Sam's voice in my head. Dshwshr! Gbg dspsl! Pk Vu! The super was watching me closely. I pulled my mother's coat tightly around me and looked down, noticing that my little pink slides, so perfect for traversing the three feet of sidewalk between valet parking and any given Los Angeles destination, were looking a little worse for the wear after weeks in Philly.

"And here's your view," he said, pulling open the blinds with a theatrical flick of his wrist.

I touched the glass with my fingertips and looked down into the park where I'd spent the last weeks sitting, watching, and waiting.

Sixteen floors below me, a man and a little boy were crossing the park hand in hand. The man had on jeans and a blue shirt, and the boy, who was maybe six years old, was pushing a silver scooter.

"Oh, God," I whispered, and placed both palms flat on the glass.

"Are you okay?" asked the super.

"Dizzy," I managed.

He hurried up behind me, close enough to grab me if I fell, and then paused like he was frozen, unsure of whether or not to touch me. "You need to sit down?" *You needa siddown* was what I heard. Philly accents. I'd forgotten about them.

"I'm fine. Really. I was just a little dizzy. Too much coffee. Or maybe not enough." I was trying to remember how people talked to each other. I'd gotten out of practice since I'd been back. "A goose walked over my grave," I blurted, then bit my lip. That was one of my mother's favorite sayings, and it had just popped out of my mouth like a dove flying out of a magician's hat.

"You sure you're okay?"

"Sure," I said. "Yes. I'm fine." I tightened my grip on the diaper bag and tried to think of what I should say next; how normal-people conversations went. It felt like forever since I'd had one.

"So what do you think?" the super asked, giving his tie another tug.

Okay, Lia, you can do this, I thought. "It's nice. Very nice."

"So what brings you to town?"

A goose, I thought. *It walked over my grave, and it flew me back home. Like the stork, only in reverse.* "Homesick, I guess. I'm from here. Well, not *here* here, but Somerton. Near. Near here." *God, Lia, shut up,* I told myself.

"Are you going to be working in Center City?"

I looked down at my dirty shoes and prayed for a response to deliver itself directly to my mouth. "I will be," I said. "Eventually. Soon. I mean, I'm okay for money," I hastened to add, because I didn't want him to think that I was a deadbeat waiting to happen. I wanted this apartment. It had good vibes, or feng shui, or whatever. It felt safe. "I'd like to take the apartment."

"Good," he said, as if I was a first grader who'd completed some bit of addition. "Good for you." I filled out an application, noticing the way the super's thick eyebrows rose when he glimpsed the wad of cash in the bag when I handed over my deposit.

"You don't have a check? Well, lemme just write you a receipt for this," he said, fingering the bills a little uneasily.

"Don't worry, I'm not a drug dealer or anything," I said, and then mentally kicked myself, knowing how guilty that made me sound. "I'm not," I said in a smaller voice. "The number I gave you is my mom's number. You can call her if you need, you know, a character reference . . ." And I kicked myself again, wondering what my mother would actually say about me if he were to call. "I'm sorry," I said helplessly.

"Don't worry," he said kindly, taking down my cell phone number. "I'll be in touch by tomorrow morning. You can stay as long as you like. The door'll lock behind you."

I wandered into the bedroom, then into the closet, where I breathed in the scent of Murphy's oil soap and the ghosts of outfits past. There were a dozen empty hangers, a few dust bunnies, empty metal racks where shoes had once been.

Tired. Oh, I was so tired. I hadn't been asleep in hours. I checked the door to make sure it had locked. Then I spread the down coat on the floor of the bedroom, pulled down the blinds and curled up in the center of the room, holding perfectly still until the world stopped spinning and I was asleep.

I dreamed the dream I'd been having since the night I arrived. It always started the same way—I'd find myself standing in the doorway of Caleb's room. I saw the cream-colored carpet, the walls Sam and I had painted pale yellow, the bookshelf full of board books, the poster of Babar doing yoga on the wall.

The crib was where it was supposed to be, waiting in the center of the room. I walked toward it, looking down at my stained pink shoes, the ones that had carried me from Los Angeles back home, holding my breath, knowing what I'd find even as I leaned over the crib, because the dream always ended the same way. I'd reach down and pull back the blanket, only to find a pile of leaves where the baby should have been. When I brushed my fingertips against them, they all blew away.

AYINDE

"I wish you wouldn't go," Ayinde said, staring at Richard's shoulders silhouetted in the lights from the walk-in closet, as she cradled Julian in her arms. The baby was four weeks old and he'd finally topped eight pounds, but he still felt light as a bag full of feathers in her arms, and every bit as fragile.

"I wish I didn't have to," he replied, selecting a suitcase from the row of suitcases just inside the closet door. "But I promised the sneaker company I'd do this more than a year ago, and I shouldn't back out." He opened the suitcase and took a look inside, knowing before he'd even finished with the zipper what he'd find—a suit, still in dry-cleaner's plastic, a sports jacket and two pairs of pants, three button-down shirts, the appropriate complement of pajamas, socks, and underwear. He had half a dozen bags like this, each one packed for stays ranging from an overnight visit to a week out of town. Actually, Ayinde thought, there were two week-away bags—one stocked with bathing suits and beach shoes, the other containing a ski parka, cashmere scarves and sweaters, and a pair of size fifteen fur-lined boots. When Richard came home, he'd just leave the suitcase by the door, and someone—the maid, the butler, someone—would unpack it, wash the underwear, dry-clean the suits, probably even change the blade in his razor, repack the whole thing, and replace it in the closet, where it would be ready to go for the next trip.

He walked out of the closet, looking cheerful. She knew that, in his head, he was already traveling, shaking hands and smiling his game-day smile. Maybe he was thinking about the airplane, that big seat in first class, with a drink on the armrest and headphones shutting out the noise. No babies crying, no exhausted, bedraggled-looking wife who flinched every time he touched her. He crossed the room with a spring in his step, retrieving a pair of cufflinks from the dresser drawer, and a pair of loafers from one of the specially built cubbyholes that held everything from dress pumps to golf cleats. Then he looked at his wife and baby, both of them sitting in an upholstered armchair that the decorator had sent over that morning. "Do you really want me to stay?"

Yes, she thought. "No," she said. "No, you go on ahead. I know this is important to you."

"Important to both of us," he said, adding the latest issues of *Sports Illustrated* and *ESPN: The Magazine* to his leather carry-on duffel bag.

She nodded reluctantly. She understood that Richard's willingness to do anything his corporate sponsors required—to show up at their events, dine and golf with their executives, autograph endless basketballs for their kids—was part of what made him so valuable. It was funny, she mused, shifting in the chair, still feeling tender between her legs, even though Dr. Mendlow had assured her that her stitches had healed beautifully. They thought they were giving Richard a vacation—a week on the golf course in Paradise Island; a long weekend on the slopes at Vail—but Richard treated the trips like work, and he took them seriously, researching the names and histories of the men he'd be meeting days ahead of time so that he could watch their eyes widen each time he'd work a name or place into a conversation. *How are Nancy and the boys? They've got to be getting big now, right? Eight and ten? Or, I was sorry to hear about your mother passing. How are you holding up?* The men's delighted faces would say, *Can you believe it? Richard Towne knows my wife's name! He knows how old my boys are!*

When it had been just the two of them in Texas, Ayinde hadn't minded the travel. Sometimes she'd stay in their big, modern mansion, picking up weekend shifts at the station to make up for the game weekends she'd be gone. Or if Richard was heading east, she'd fly with him and visit her parents in New York. She'd go to the theater with her father, and her mother would drag her to Bergdorf Goodman or Barneys after dumping Ayinde's suitcase on the bed, pinching a skirt or a jacket between her fingertips, and saying, "Is this what passes for high fashion out in the sticks?"

She watched her husband pack, wondering when all the trips, the weekends away, the ceaseless courting of businessmen who sold soft drinks and sneakers and cereal would end, when Richard could finally let himself relax into a well-deserved retirement. Chasing after endorsements was a full-time job in itself, and one that Richard didn't really need. But it was more than the money, she thought. It was about the security that Richard had never had growing up, the rock-solid certainty that there would always be enough money for food, for clothes, even for college.

"You know I don't like leaving you two all by yourselves," he said. Ayinde nodded, thinking how strange it was, because in her life, *all by yourselves* meant all by yourself except for the maid, the cook, the driver, the gardener, the Pilates instructor who came Friday mornings, and the decorator, who had her own key and wasn't afraid to use it—Ayinde had already bumped into Cora Schuyler, of Main Line Interiors, twice before eight o'clock in the morning, once when she'd let herself in to deliver a plate she wanted hung in the kitchen and again when she'd been dropping off handcrafted soaps for the powder room.

There was a business manager, who toiled in the twelve hundred feet of office space above the six-car garage; the part-time publicist, who worked in the office next to his; and the bodyguard, who earned what Ayinde felt was an exorbitant sum for the job of driving up and down their street in a menacing-looking Hummer, taking down the license plates of anyone who turned into their cul-de-sac. There'd also been a baby nurse Richard had hired to stay for three weeks. Ayinde had sent her away after five days. The nurse, who was a perfectly nice lady in her fifties named Mrs. Ziff, had let it slip that her next client was a working woman with a two-and-a-half-year-old who only had twelve weeks of maternity leave. Ayinde felt guilty since Julian was her only baby, her only responsibility, and she had no business hogging this woman's time, even though she—well, Richard—had paid for it already.

"Call your yoga friends," he said, zipping up his bags and setting them outside the door. During the night, the driver would fetch them and place them in the trunk of the town car that would take Richard to the airport first thing in the morning. "Have a hen party."

"Friends," she repeated. Richard looked at her.

"They are your friends, right?"

She nodded, still feeling a little surprised by it.

"So go to a spa or something," Richard said. "Relax."

"Please stay," she said, surprising them both, struggling out of the armchair with Julian in her arms, hurrying across the perfect room, their bed with the pillows that Clara plumped at least twice a day, the marble fireplace and mahogany mantelpiece with newly framed photographs of the baby on top.

"Aw, baby," Richard said. Ayinde burrowed her face against his upper arm, feeling the warmth of his skin through his cashmere sweater.

"Stay," she repeated in a small voice. "Please stay."

Richard reached down to hold her, and Ayinde caught the look of confusion in his eyes. She wasn't like this. She wasn't needy, or clingy, or whiny, or any of the things that most of the women in Richard Towne's orbit—the ones who didn't work for him, at least—usually were. *I'm not a damsel in distress,* she'd told him . . . and it had been true at the time.

"I'm sorry," she said, making an effort to look normal—*Chin up, shoulders back, have some pride, girl!* she heard Lolo whisper. She smoothed her hair with her free hand and wished that she wasn't still wearing the bathrobe and pajamas she'd spent the whole day—actually, the better part of the week—in. "I'll be fine." And it was true. She'd always done just fine on her own. She remembered Christmas when she was eight years old. Her parents had left the night before for one Greek island or another, but Ayinde handn't wanted to miss her school play, in which she had two lines as one of the Three Wise Men. She made arrangements to sleep at a friend's house, and her parents had hired a car to pick her up there and take her to the airport. Unfortunately, they'd accidentally taken her passport with them.

"We'll be back as soon as we can," her mother had said, her voice faint but angry over the crackling overseas connection, as if the whole thing had been Ayinde's fault, not hers. "Monday at the latest."

Ayinde had a house key that she wore on a ribbon around her neck. "Back so soon?" the doorman had asked as she wished him a merry Christmas and headed for the elevator. She knew if she told him the truth, he'd be worried about her and maybe even miss his own Christmas. She knew he had kids—he kept a picture of them at his desk. So Ayinde said she was fine, waved at him as the elevator doors slid shut, and spent a very happy two days in the empty apartment, wrapped in her down comforter, eating butter cookies from a tin the housekeeper had left as a Christmas gift, making hot chocolate and noodle soup with water from the kitchen taps because she wasn't allowed to use the stove, and reading Nancy Drew books until her parents (Lolo chagrined, Stuart apologetic, the both of them bearing enough gifts for a dozen eight-year-old girls) had come back home.

More than twenty-five years after that Christmas, Ayinde lowered her eyes. She had known the deal she'd made when they married, and it was too late to change its terms. She had been the very model of the modern woman—strong, smart, self-sufficient, barely bothered by even a locker room full of hostile, naked men. And once Richard promised to do something, he'd do it, no matter what. She'd known that, too. "Don't worry about us," she said, wondering whether it would have even occurred to him to worry about her in the first place.

"Have fun," he said, and smiled and kissed her, then bent carefully, knees creaking, to address the baby. "Little man, you take care of your momma."

Take care of me, Ayinde thought, and looked down at the top of her husband's head and was shocked to see what looked like the beginning of a bald spot. *Take care of me,* she thought again, and cradled Julian close to her heart.

BECKY

"Sorry I'm late," Becky whispered to Kelly, thumping into a seat in the hospital auditorium five minutes into the Breast-Feeding 101 lecture. "Restaurant crisis. Our supplier sent us pine nuts instead of avocados. Total disaster." On stage was the instructor, an off-duty nurse in a pair of dark-blue scrubs over a long-sleeved T-shirt. In her right hand she had a laser pointer; in her left, a larger-than-life-sized model of a breast, complete with retractable nipple.

"Good evening, ladies," the nurse said. "Gentlemen," she added, waving the breast at the pair of fathers-to-be who'd braved the auditorium. "And congratulations on being here. You've taken a very important step in making sure that your baby gets off to the best possible start. How many of you were breast-fed?" Becky was shocked when Kelly raised her hand.

"Really?" she whispered.

"Don't be impressed," Kelly whispered back. "My mother wasn't progressive or anything like that. I just think they couldn't afford eight kids' worth of formula."

"We have some props tonight," the nurse said, walking backstage and returning with a cardboard box filled with infant-sized plastic dolls. "Take one doll and pass the rest along." Becky got an Asian-looking baby in a disposable diaper and a Pennsylvania Hospital T-shirt. Kelly reached into the box. "Oh, look, I got a black one!" she said. People two rows in front of her turned around to stare.

"Won't Steve be pleased," Becky whispered. Kelly's fair skin flushed.

"Now," said the instructor, once each woman had a baby, "have any of you had breast surgery? Breast implants?" A few hands went up. Kelly craned her neck.

"Don't stare," Becky said, whacking Kelly's shoulder with her Frequently Asked Breast-Feeding Questions handout.

"Breast reductions?" A few more hands went into the air. Kelly looked studiously down at the notebook she'd brought. "How many of your doctors have asked if you'll be breast-feeding?"

Everyone raised their hands.

"How many of your doctors have looked at your nipples?"

Nobody raised their hands except one woman in the front row.

"Okay, how many of you know what an inverted nipple looks like?" the nurse asked. There was absolute silence. The nurse shook her head, frowning. She raised the stuffed breast into the air, then jammed the nipple down. "Ouch," Becky whispered.

"That's a flat nipple," said the instructor, "and that"—she gave the nipple another shove—"is an inverted nipple. Both can make breast-feeding a challenge, but there are things we can do to help."

"We can rebuild you," Becky murmured. "We can make you better."

"There will be nurses in the bathroom during the break if anyone wants her breasts inspected," said the instructor.

"Are you going to go?" Kelly asked.

Becky shook her head. "My breasts are okay," she said. "And honestly, I'm sick of being looked at." She pressed her lips together, remembering the misery of her five-month ultrasound, lying on the table while some sadist in scrubs squirted her belly with warm goop and proceeded to press and shove the receiver against Becky's stomach so hard she gasped.

"Can you please be a little more gentle?" she asked.

The nurse shrugged and said without looking away from the screen, "Because you're obese, it's harder for me to visualize the baby."

Obese. Becky could have died. She squeezed her eyes shut, feeling pride and excitement draining from her heart and being quickly replaced with shame. She was only glad that Andrew had been tied up in surgery and wasn't there to hear it as she sat up on the table, gathered the sheet over her midsection, and told the technician that she wanted to see her supervisor.

Up on stage, the instructor was using her doll and the giant breast to demonstrate different positions—the cross-cradle, the football hold, "which works best for large-breasted mothers."

"And here are some handouts you might find helpful," she said. Becky pulled one off the stack and made a face.

"Pacifiers: The Devil's Teats," she read.

"Really?" said Kelly.

"I'm giving you the condensed version," Becky said. She looked at her watch and got to her feet. "Come on. Let's go."

Ten minutes later, they met Ayinde in a coffee shop on South Street, where they ordered noncaffeinated beverages, cooed over baby Julian, and told the stories of how they'd gotten pregnant.

"It was like a bad joke," Kelly said, scowling at the mint tea she'd ordered instead of the espresso she told them she really wanted. "My mother got pregnant every time she so much as looked at my dad, my sister Mary's completely fertile, and it took us six months of trying, and Clomid."

"Six months is average," Becky said. The bells on the doorknob jingled briefly as the door opened and closed, and a woman in a bright blue coat walked tentatively up to the counter.

"Yeah, well, it felt like forever. And it turns out that I wasn't ovulating regularly, so I took the Clomid, and that worked. But it really threw my schedule off."

"Your schedule?" asked Becky.

"Well, I'd planned on getting pregnant when I was twenty-five instead of twenty-six. That way, I'd have my first when I was twenty-six and my second when I was twenty-eight . . ."

"Wait. Hold up. Your second baby?" Ayinde asked.

"Right. Steve and I want two."

"I'm just trying to survive this one," Ayinde said, gazing down fondly at Julian. "I can't believe you're already planning number two."

Kelly dumped the packets of sugar and sweetener onto the table and started arranging them by color. "I like to have a plan," she said. "If you want to know the truth, my ideal situation would have been twins."

"You're crazy," Becky said. "Do you have any idea how much work that would be? Ayinde, tell her!"

"It's hard," Ayinde said, smiling wearily. "You two shouldn't even be here. You should just go home and sleep while you can."

"Well, I know it would be really hard for the first few months, but then you'd have two kids and you wouldn't have to try to get pregnant again, and you wouldn't have to be pregnant again . . . and you can breast-feed two babies, remember?" Kelly said.

"Just because the instructor can do it with two dolls doesn't mean it's going to work in real life," Becky said.

"So how about you?" Kelly asked. "Did you and Andrew get pregnant right away?"

"Oh, Ayinde can go next," Becky said. "My story's kind of short."

"I guess we were average," said Ayinde. "It took us about six months. Maybe a little longer." She slipped off Julian's hat and tucked it into her purse. "Although I think Richard thought he'd hit the jackpot on his first try . . ." She shrugged. "He's used to getting what he wants." She sipped her glass of milk. "I know I'm lucky," she said. "So many of the players have kids everywhere, they're hit with paternity suits left and right . . ."

"Oh, yeah, same with doctors," Becky said. "The groupies are unbelievable." She turned one curl around her finger. "Andrew actually wasn't in a hurry, either. He'd say that we were having such a good time by ourselves and that a baby would complicate things. Which it will, of course. But in a good way. At least that's what I hope."

"Did you get pregnant right away?" Kelly asked.

"It was kind of a joke," said Becky. "We wanted to wait until Andrew had finished his fellowship so he'd be home a little more, but we got pregnant the first month I went off the Pill. We weren't even officially trying yet, but I'd already convinced myself that I was never going to get pregnant."

"Why not?" Kelly asked.

"Well, I was doing all of this reading on the Internet about, um, heavier women and pregnancy. I had really long menstrual cycles . . ." Becky took a sip of her water and took a minute to ponder the strangeness of discussing her menstrual cycles with her still-new friends before deciding she just didn't care. "Anyhow, I thought I had polycystic ovarian syndrome, where you get your period but you don't actually ovulate, so you can't get pregnant. Lots of, um, larger women have it. I even called an infertility specialist before I went off the Pill, just to get a checkup. They didn't have any openings for six weeks, and by the time I got there . . ." She shrugged, unable to keep from smiling, remembering how thrilled she'd been and how the doctor had shaken her hand and told her to go home and stay healthy. It had been the first time since she was twelve that she'd felt anything other than shame in a doctor's office, where visits started on the scale and always included a variation on the *What are we going to do about your weight?* lecture. "And that was thirty-seven wonderful weeks ago."

"Wonderful?" asked Kelly, wrinkling her nose.

"Well, adequate. I was tired all the time at the beginning and queasy in the middle. Oh, and there was a week when I didn't eat anything except English muffins. But other than that, it's been a normal, boring pregnancy." She smiled again, remembering how she'd felt her daughter give her first little flutter at week nineteen. *Gas,* Andrew had said. *Gas,* her mother-in-law Mimi had pronounced with a magisterial nod, as if she'd birthed dozens of children instead of just Andrew. But Becky had known that no matter what they said, it wasn't gas. It was her baby.

Kelly took another sip of tea and grimaced. "My pregnancy's been awful. I've had so many things go wrong that I'd turn my uterus in for a refund if I could. I was spotting for the entire first trimester, so I had to go on bed rest for a while, and then my quad screen came back questionable, so I had to have an amniocentesis and go back on bed rest again after that. And I'm just so uncomfortable!" She looked down at herself, resting her hands on the mound of her belly. "I've never been this big in my entire life!"

"You're still smaller than I was before I got pregnant," said Becky. "Take heart."

"I threw up every morning until my sixth month," Kelly continued, "and I've got killer heartburn . . ."

"Oh, heartburn. Me, too," said Becky. She'd forgotten about the heartburn. Maybe pregnancy wasn't as blissful as she'd been telling herself.

"I had to get prescription medication," said Kelly. "The over-the-counter stuff wasn't helping." She looked at Ayinde. "How about you?"

"It was fine," Ayinde said, resting one hand on the edge of the car seat, smoothing Julian's blanket as her enormous diamond flashed. "Up until the surprise ending."

"Oh, come on," Kelly wheedled. "You can tell us."

Ayinde said nothing.

"Did you have killer heartburn?" Kelly asked. "Morning sickness? Did you pee when you laughed?"

A tiny flicker of a smile moved across Ayinde's face. "My feet," she said, with an I-give-up shrug. "My feet have gotten bigger. My calves, too. I have these boots that zip up . . ."

"Ugh, zippers," said Kelly. "Don't get me started."

"My hands were swollen, too," Ayinde said, looking down at them regretfully. "Still are, actually. I ought to take my rings off."

"Soap and warm water works," said Becky.

"Oh, I think I could squeeze them off," Ayinde said. "But I won't."

"Why not?" asked Becky.

" 'Cause then I'm just another baby mama without a man,"
Ayinde drawled in a flawless around-the-way accent. "And I don't
want people looking at me that way."

Her confession knocked Kelly and Becky into silence. "You really
think that people . . . ," Kelly began.

"Oh, yes," Ayinde said with a large, insincere grin. "Oh, yes, indeed. Black girl, no ring, it's an obvious conclusion."

"Even though you're . . ." Kelly's voice trailed off.

Ayinde raised her eyebrows. "Biracial? Light skinned?"

"Rich, I was going to say." Kelly's cheeks were so pink that they
practically glowed. "I didn't know you were biracial."

Ayinde put her hand on Kelly's forearm. "I apologize," she said.
"I shouldn't have assumed. My father's white, and my mother's black.
Well, African-American and one-quarter Cherokee, to hear her tell it.
But that's not what most people see when they look at me."

"You guys?" Becky's voice was quiet as she looked over Kelly's
shoulder. "Don't stare, but that woman in the corner keeps looking
at us."

Kelly's head swiveled so abruptly that Becky heard her neck
creak. "Don't stare!" Becky whispered sharply, thinking that the
woman looked so off-balance that one wrong look would cause her to
bolt. Ayinde cut her eyes discreetly to the right, where a woman in a
blue down parka with lank blond hair hanging past her shoulders sat
with her hands wrapped around a mug and a newspaper spread on her
table.

"Do you know her?" Ayinde whispered.

"I keep seeing her," Becky whispered back. "I don't know who she
is, but I see her everywhere."

"Is she pregnant?" asked Kelly.

"I don't think so. Why?" said Becky.

"Well, ever since I've been pregnant, I've been seeing pregnant
women everywhere. Have you guys noticed that?"

Becky nodded. "But I don't think she's pregnant. She's just everywhere. I know I've seen her in the park . . . and on the street . . ."

Kelly turned her ahead again. "Don't stare!" Becky said. "Or I'll hit you with the breast folder again!"

"She looks . . ." Kelly wrinkled her nose. "Lost."

"Like I-can't-find-Independence-Hall lost, or . . ."

"No," Kelly said. She tried to come up with something better, but the first word was the only one that seemed to fit. "Lost lost."

The woman raised her head and looked at them. *Lost,* thought Becky. Kelly had it right. The woman looked lost, and sad, and haunted. When she spoke, her voice sounded rusty and underused. "Little boy?"

The three women exchanged a fast, worried glance.

"I'm sorry," said the woman. The hesitancy with which she talked made Becky wonder whether English was her first language, or if she was translating from her native tongue into theirs in her head. "Is your baby a little boy?"

"Yes," said Ayinde cautiously. "Yes, he is."

The woman nodded. She seemed about to say something else or to stand up and approach them, but when she got to her feet, she changed her mind, gave them one last despairing look, and bolted out the door.

KELLY

Kelly Day sat at the desk in her high-rise apartment, looking through the floor-to-ceiling windows at the leafy tree tops that lined her street. There was a telephone headset clamped to her ears, the desktop computer's screen was glowing in front of her, her Palm Pilot and notebook were at the ready, and Lemon was curled contentedly in a corner, languidly licking his privates. She'd never felt more efficient, more together, more happy than she did at that moment, with one hand resting lightly on her belly and Dana Evans, head of Special Programs for the Philadelphia Zoo, rattling off requests into her ear.

"All right," Kelly said, starting to review. "So that's no onions, no garlic, no curries, no yellow foods . . ."

"No yellow vegetables," Dana Evans said. "I think that saffron rice would be acceptable but not yellow peppers."

"No yellow vegetables," Kelly said, making a note and thinking that Prince Andres-Philipe, head of some small, wealthy European nation known for the excellence of its chocolate and the liberality of its divorce laws, sounded like a major head case. "No coffee, no chocolate, no alcohol, no alcoholic flavoring in the dessert . . ."

"It's a shame, too," said Dana. "That Grand Marnier mousse you guys served last time was out of this world."

"I'm so glad you enjoyed it," Kelly said, making a notation of the compliment in her Dana Evans file for the next person handling a zoo event. "Now, in terms of the order of events, the students from Creative and Performing Arts will sing our national anthem, then his national anthem . . ."

"And the brass band?"

"Trumpets when he enters," Kelly said. "A string quartet will be playing during the meal. Butlered hors d'oeuvres starting at six o'clock, lasting forty-five minutes as the guests arrive, open bars on both sides of the tent. At 6:35, the prince arrives through the back. I'll have security hold a parking place right by the door and escort him into the tent. We'll start asking people to take their seats at 6:40. At 7:00, the head of Special Gifts will introduce the prince. He'll make brief remarks—I've got four minutes blocked off—thanking the attendees for their generosity to the zoo. Dinner service will start at 7:10—French service, as we discussed—and the desserts will be buffet style, with petits fours accompanying the coffee service. Dancing will start at 8:15, and I've got the prince scheduled to leave at 8:30."

"One more thing," said Dana. "The prince prefers male waiters."

Kelly shook her head and made another note. "Does he have any strong feelings about direct eye contact?"

"None that he's mentioned," Dana said. "And the hotel knows he'll need his tuxedo cleaned and pressed?"

"He can either drop it at the front desk as soon as he checks in or ring the front desk to pick it up once he's in his room," said Kelly.

"You're an angel," Dana said. "So will I see you at the event?"

"Not me," Kelly said, grinning. "My maternity leave starts tonight. A whole year!"

"Then I won't keep you. Good luck!"

"Thanks," said Kelly. She hung up the phone and rested her bare feet on Lemon's warm side as she finished typing a memo to her boss containing the final details of the prince's visit. Then she flipped her laptop closed and her Palm Pilot open. The man from the fabric store was coming to measure their windows tomorrow at ten. They still couldn't afford the leather couch with nailhead detail she'd had her eye on—not to mention the plasma television set she'd lusted after ever since she'd first seen it advertised—but curtains were at least a start, and . . .

"Hi," said a hollow voice. She gasped, jumping up out of her seat, spilling a cup of coffee (decaf and, lucky for her, lukewarm) over her desk (from IKEA and destined for replacement—there was an antique secretary in a lovely shade of gold-green with cabriole legs that she'd seen in a shop on Pine Street) and her dog. Lemon yelped and scurried out of the office with his tail between his legs.

"Steve! You scared me!" She lifted her laptop and started mopping up coffee with her sleeve. "What are you doing home?"

Her husband stood motionless in the middle of their empty living room. The suit that had fit him fine when he'd left for work in the morning seemed bigger now. The jacket hung around his arm in loose folds, the pants drooped at his waist, and the cuffs puddled over his shoes. He looked at the beige carpet and mumbled something Kelly couldn't hear.

"What?" she asked. She could hear the echo of her mother's voice in her own, her mother berating her children or giving her husband the third degree—*Where were you? Who broke this? What were you doing last night until two in the morning?*—and it set her teeth on edge. She lowered her voice. "I'm sorry, Steve. I didn't hear you."

Steve's hair was curling limply over his collar. *Haircut,* Kelly thought, reaching automatically for her Palm Pilot before she forced herself to look at Steve again.

"What is it?" she asked again, feeling fear creep up her spine, wrapping around her belly. Steve never looked this way. He'd always been . . . not cocky, exactly, not like Scott Schiff, who'd probably looked like a successful investment banker from birth, but quietly confident, sure that his intelligence and drive would lead, inevitably, to his success. Only now, with his head hanging down and his hands dangling at his sides, Steven Day didn't look like the head of e-business for one of the country's largest pharmaceutical companies. He looked like a scared little boy.

"Laid off," Steve repeated, his Adam's apple jerking with each

word. "I fucked something up, and they . . ." He paused. "They decided to cut back on their e-business initiatives."

She stared at him, taking a minute to figure out what he meant.
"You got fired?" she blurted.

"Laid off."

The words felt like a shot to her heart. "Are you kidding me?"

"No, I'm not," said Steve, hunching his shoulders. "Me, Philip,
half of the programmers, three of the receptionists . . ."

Kelly pressed her hands down hard on the lid of her laptop and
found that she wasn't interested in the plight of the programmers or
the receptionists or Steve's friend Philip. Instead, she felt a rage so
black and absolute that it scared her. *Those assholes,* she thought,
drawing in a shaky breath. *I'm going to have a baby! How could they have
done this to us?*

"Do they know that I'm pregnant?" she asked, hating the shrill
sound of her voice.

"Yeah," said Steve. "That's why they're giving me three months'
severance instead of two."

Three months. Kelly's mind started clicking. Three months' pay,
minus their rent, minus credit-card payments, car payments, utili-
ties, health insurance . . .

"Do we still have our health insurance?" she asked, hearing her
voice waver.

"I can pay for it," Steve said. "We'll have COBRA. We'll be okay,
Kelly. Don't worry about that."

She drew a deep breath. "What happened?" Almost without
thinking, she touched her cell phone, her Palm, the neat stack of bills
that she was going to use Quicken to pay that night. *What now?* she
thought, feeling her head spinning. "Why would they do this to
you?"

"I just screwed up, okay?" he yelled. "It wasn't like I meant to do
it. It just happened." He raked his hands through his hair. "I feel like
an idiot," he muttered. Kelly went to the living room and started rearranging things—the tape measure she'd left on the floor, copies of

Forbes and *Money* and *Power* magazines and *What to Expect When You're Expecting* that were stacked in the space where a coffee table would go. There was a picture she'd torn out of *Traditional Homes* magazine of the window treatments she wanted. She folded it into a tiny square and shoved it into the pocket of her maternity jeans.

"What are we going to do?" she asked, thinking of the deal they'd made—she'd take a year off to stay home with the baby; he'd work and support them.

Steve pushed himself away from the table and walked past her without meeting her eyes. "I'm going for a run," he said.

"You're going for a run," she repeated, thinking that this was his bizarre idea of a joke, waiting for him to tell her that he was kidding about all of it. Running. And losing his job.

She went to the kitchen with one hand on her belly, which felt heavier than it ever had, and started pulling things out of the refrigerator—chicken breasts, broccoli, chicken broth for rice. Five minutes later, Steve stalked out of the bedroom, dressed in shorts and a T-shirt and his running shoes. "I'll be back soon." And then he was gone.

Kelly stood in the quiet of the kitchen for a minute, waiting for Steve to come back and tell her he was kidding, that everything would be all right, that he'd keep the promise he'd made that first night, that he would take care of her. When he didn't reappear, she put the chicken in the oven and put water on to boil for broccoli. Then she shuffled into the bedroom, where her husband's suit and shoes and tie lay in a pile on the bed and curled up on top of them, resting her forehead on a sleeve that was still damp and smelling of coffee. He'd screwed up, and what could she do about it? She'd already arranged their whole glorious future in her mind—the big wedding, the beautiful apartment, the babies, all of it predicated on the career her husband would have, the salary that would make it all possible. *Wrong again, dumbo,* a voice whispered in her mind. And what would happen now? There wasn't a lemon law for husbands. She couldn't bring him in for a tune-up or call his boss and try to fix the mistake that had cost him his job.

When she heard the door open an hour later, Kelly pulled off her clothes, wrapped herself in a bathrobe, and walked into the living room. Steve was lying on the floor, where a couch should have been. He'd kicked his sneakers off. His T-shirt clung to his chest as it rose and fell.

Kelly looked down at him, struggling to find the proper—the wifely—tone of voice. Sympathetic. Empathetic. Something-thetic. "Look," she finally managed. "These things happen. Mistakes get made . . ."

"Nice use of the passive voice there," Steve said.

"Well, what do you want me to say?" Kelly asked. Steve flinched as if she'd slapped him. It didn't slow her down. "Do you want me to say that this is all fine? That I'm going to have a baby and my husband doesn't have a job, but it's okay?"

Steve finally raised his head. "Something's burning." The smoke alarms went off with a whoop. Lemon started barking furiously.

"Shit," Kelly said. She went into the kitchen and saw that the water had boiled away and the bottom of the pot was burned. She turned off the burner, dumped the pot into the sink, and ran cold water into it. A hissing cloud of steam rose around her head. The fire alarm seemed to shriek even louder.

Kelly ran into the bathroom, pulled half a dozen scented candles from underneath the sink—cinnamon, vanilla, Spring Rain, Sugar Cookie. She carried them back to the kitchen and lit each one. She could hear Steve on the phone with the building's super, telling him everything was fine. "Just a little cooking accident." *And a little unemployment,* Kelly thought. She set the candles on top of the stove, ran to the front bathroom for a can of air freshener, and started spraying. Lemon whined and cringed away from the can.

Steve grabbed her wrist. "What are you doing?"

She opened her mouth to try to explain the way her mother's kitchen back in Ocean City had been—dishes eternally piled in the sink, the dishwasher perpetually half-emptied, and its smell, most of all, the smell, as if the walls had absorbed the residue of every meal that had ever been cooked there, every pan of bacon and pot of Brussels sprouts, every cigarette that had ever been smoked, every beer that had ever been opened (and every can of bourbon and Tab). "I just don't want it to smell like smoke in here," was all she said. She reached for the air freshener and saw that her hand was shaking. Steve took the can out of her hand and put it down.

"I'm going to sleep," she said. It was seven o'clock at night, and she hadn't eaten dinner, but Steve simply nodded and said, "Okay." Kelly balled her hands into fists and resisted the urge to reach for the air freshener again. "Look," she said. "I'm sorry about what happened. Things will be all right." The words hung in the kitchen alongside the smoke. Steve didn't look at her.

"Well, good night," she said and marched past him, through the empty living room, down the hall, past the office and the baby's room, into their bedroom. She remembered the first time she'd seen this apartment, how it had been everything she'd ever wanted. High ceilings and floor-to-ceiling windows, en suite bathroom with Jacuzzi tub and separate shower, marble countertops and hand-painted porcelain fixtures. A bathtub that nobody else had ever used, two full bathrooms for the two of them. *We deserve it. You deserve it,* Steve would say, making dinner reservations at the priciest place in town, surprising her with a gold bracelet, an iPod, a trip to Jamaica. *Why not?* she'd think. She was making good money, and Steve's salary, after bonuses, was so big it surprised them both. Things were only getting better, so why not?

"Why not?" she whispered, burying her face in her hands.

July

July

AYINDE

The book that would change her baby's life arrived the first week of July, when Julian was eleven weeks old. Its title page was half covered in Lolo's oversized scrawl. THOUGHT YOU MIGHT FIND THIS HELP-FUL, her mother had written. "Helpful" had two *l*'s at the end. Ah, well. Spelling had never been her mother's strong suit. Ayinde would have showed it to Richard, and they would have both laughed at it, but Richard was gone again. Golfing, then lunch downtown with executives from the video-game company, who were currently in the midst of developing a game based on Richard's moves. "I'm sorry," he'd said, standing at the foot of their bed, a butterscotch suede jacket draped over his broad shoulders and his golf spikes in his hand. "I'll be back in time for dinner."

Ayinde lowered her eyes. Every time he left, she thought about the perfume she'd smelled when he'd come so late to the hospital, and every time she'd started to ask him about it, something kept her from getting the words out. Her mother, maybe. She didn't want to be pathetic, chasing after the man who'd already married her, checking his collars for lipstick and going through his wallet for receipts. So she merely lifted Julian's pudgy forearm in her hand. "Wave bye-bye to Daddy," she said. Richard had kissed them both and Ayinde had snuggled back into bed with Julian curled against her. When she opened her eyes, her husband was gone and so, inexplicably, were two hours of her morning.

Priscilla Prewitt's Baby Success! read the cover of the book Lolo had sent. Underneath the title was a picture of a woman with warm brown eyes and silver hair in a no-nonsense bob and a beaming baby in her arms. GIVE YOUR BABY THE BEST BEGINNING read the back cover. PRISCILLA PREWITT SHOWS NEW MOTHERS THE WAY!

Julian pumped his arms in the air. Ayinde gave him her index finger to grasp and turned the pages with her free hand. *Priscilla Prewitt,* she read, *has been a childcare professional for more than thirty years, both in her native Alabama and in Los Angeles, where she developed her easy-to-follow, five-point plan for* Baby Success! *In her patented "down-home" prose backed up by the latest scientific studies, Priscilla Prewitt teaches every mother how to get her baby off to a successful start, ensuring success in preschool and beyond, and peace and harmony for the whole family!*

Five-point plan, Ayinde mused, flipping to the table of contents and chapters entitled "Sleep, Baby, Sleep!" and "Starting a Schedule" and "Keep On Keepin' On." It was eleven o'clock in the morning and she hadn't even managed to get herself out of bed yet. The day before, she hadn't gotten dressed until three and hadn't eaten until dinner. The cook had prepared her a beautiful niçoise salad for lunch that had sat on the kitchen counter, the tuna turning brown and curling up at the edges, because Ayinde had stayed in bed for the duration of Julian's nap, marveling at his long-fingered hands and his lips, moving through the bedroom in a kind of milky underwater haze that was caused, she figured, from having been awakened the previous night at one, four, and five-thirty in the morning because Julian was hungry or Julian was wet or Julian was just being a newborn and needed her around. Had she even brushed her teeth? She ran her tongue over her incisors and decided that the answer was no. Scheduling didn't sound bad at all.

Julian batted at the braids she had put in the week before, figuring they were as low maintenance as she could handle and she wouldn't have to worry about offending conservative Philadelphia television viewers anytime soon. She hummed to him, some wordless lullabye that her nanny had sung to her, opened up a page at random, and started reading. *A baby on a schedule—a baby in a familiar daily routine—is a happy baby. Think about your own life, darlin'. How would you feel if you got up in the morning not knowing whether it's six o'clock or ten o'clock? Not knowing whether your next meal would come in fifteen minutes or two hours? Not knowing what your day would hold? You'd be a big ol' grouch, and rightly so! Babies crave routine and regularity. They want to know what's coming next, whether it's a nap or a nursing or a bath or bedtime . . . and the sooner you get them started on a pleasant, predictable, easy-to-manage routine, the happier you and Dumpling will be.*

"Dumpling," Ayinde said experimentally. Julian tugged at her braid and gave a squeak. She flipped through the book, thinking that the *Baby Success!* plan, with its required logs and charts and timers, sounded fairly time-consuming . . . but what did she have besides time? She had no job. She couldn't travel with Richard to away games or business trips even if she'd wanted to. She was rattling around the gigantic house she'd insisted upon with nothing to do but mind the baby.

Ayinde stared into Priscilla Prewitt's warm brown eyes, wondering what her own mother would make of *Baby Success!* So far, Lolo was shaping up to be as effective and engaged a grandmother as she'd been a mother. She and Stuart had hired a driver to bring them in from New York once. Her parents had spent a total of three hours with Julian since his birth, and the baby had been asleep for two of them. They'd sat stiffly, side by side on the couch, beautifully overdressed, as if they'd come to audition for the roles of doting, and extremely wealthy, grandparents. Her father had bounced the baby on his knee (a little too vigorously for Ayinde's taste, but she'd kept quiet). Then he'd sung "Danny Boy" in his ringing baritone. That, evidently, constituted the entirety of his baby-entertaining skills. He'd vanished into the guest house where she'd found him an hour later, playing pool with the publicist.

Lolo wasn't much better. She held the baby once, tentatively, and pretended not to mind when he'd drooled on her Jil Sander suit, but Ayinde had caught her dabbing furtively at the stain on the cream-colored sleeve. They'd dropped off a teddy bear that was easily five times as big as the baby and a complete layette of Petit Bateau outfits they'd purchased duty-free during their last trip to St. Barth's. That, so far, had been the extent of the Mbezi/Walker's involvement with little Julian.

"All Through the Night" read chapter six. Julian opened his eyes and started to cry. Ayinde sighed, thinking she'd settle for her baby's sleeping All Through Three Hours. She carried Julian to the glider and began nursing him, supporting his body with her right hand while she turned pages with her left.

By the next morning, Ayinde had all of her tools in place—an electronic timer, so she could see exactly how long Julian was nursing, and the brands of slings and strollers and baby bathtubs and baby soap and baby shampoo that Priscilla Prewitt recommended. (*Now I want y'all to know that I'm not getting one red cent from these manufacturers. These are simply the products that I've liked the best over the years.*)

Ten minutes into her *Baby Success!* program, she had her first problem. *Brand-new babies should be nursing a maximum of thirty minutes per feeding,* Priscilla Prewitt wrote. *Longer than that, and they're just usin' you as a pacifier.* But after thirty minutes, Julian was still going strong. Ayinde squinted at the book, looking for further instructions. *If Dumpling is reluctant to let go of the booby, tell him nicely but firmly that mealtime's over, and there will be more to come later. Then ease him off the breast, and offer him a pacifier—or, if you're going all-natural, your finger to suck on.*

"Julian!" Ayinde said, in her best estimation of a tone that was nice but firm. "Mealtime is over!" He ignored her, eyes squeezed shut, jaw working. Ayinde let him nurse another minute, which slid into another two, which was almost five when she was accosted with a vision of her son running home from kindergarten and opening her blouse himself.

"Okay!" she said in her firm-but-cheerful tone. She tried to pull him off gently. The baby's head slid backward. Unfortunately, her nipple came with it.

"Ow!" she hissed. Julian opened his eyes, startled, and began wailing. Just then, the telephone rang. *Kelly,* she thought, groping for the Talk button without so much as glancing at the caller ID. Maybe it was Kelly, or Becky, and she could tell her what to do . . .

Alas, it was Lolo. "I hear that sweet boy!" she announced. Ayinde could imagine her mother standing in the white-on-white kitchen in which nothing other than tea was ever prepared, misting her orchids, dressed, as always, in couture—a pencil skirt or a wrap dress, high heels, and one of the dramatic hats that had become her signature look.

"Hello, Mother."

"Hello, my love. How are you doing?"

"Just fine," Ayinde said, as Julian blatted.

Lolo's tone was dubious. "That doesn't sound like a happy baby."

"He's just a little cranky," Ayinde said, as Julian wailed even more loudly. She set him down in his Priscilla Prewitt–approved bouncy seat, tucked the receiver under her chin, and tried to refasten her bra. "It's his cranky time."

"Are you using that book I sent? It came very highly recommended. My masseuse swears by it!"

"High praise," Ayinde murmured.

Lolo raised her voice until she was shouting over the baby's cries. "Well, Ayinde, the point of the book is that once you get your baby into a routine, he won't have a cranky time!"

"I understand that," Ayinde said, fumbling her breast pad back into place. "We're working on it."

"You know," Lolo said, "you never cried like that by the time you were Julian's age."

"Are you sure?"

She gave a brittle laugh. "I think I can remember what my own daughter was like."

With all the drugs it was rumored Lolo had taken in the 1970s, Ayinde wasn't so sure. "I should go."

"Of course, love. Take good care of that darling baby!"

Ayinde hung up the phone, rehooked her bra, and picked up Julian, whose wails had given way to little whimpers. "Hey, sweetheart," she whispered. His eyes were beginning to close. Oh, dear. She picked up the book. **DO NOT ALLOW DUMPLING TO SLEEP AFTER A FEEDING!** Priscilla Prewitt admonished. *Do you want to take a big ol' nap after eating a heavy meal?* "Yes," Ayinde said. *No!* Priscilla Prewitt wrote. *The ideal order for Baby's development is meal, then activity, and then a little visit to Dreamland.*

"Julian. Dumpling." She kissed his cheek and wiggled his toes. He opened his mouth and started to cry again. "Playtime!" She dangled the fuzzy butterfly in front of the baby's face. Richard hated the fuzzy butterfly, along with the blue teddy bear and the crinkly-winged insects. "It's sissy stuff," he'd said.

"How very evolved of you," she'd replied and explained that there were very few options available for newborns in the dump-truck-and-bulldozer category, even if she'd wanted to seek them out, which she didn't. "What did you play with when you were a baby?" she asked.

His face closed. Ayinde regretted the question immediately. Richard had grown up in Atlanta in half a dozen houses—his grandmother's, an aunt here, a play-cousin there, places Ayinde had only seen on TV and in the profile *Sports Illustrated* had run a few years ago. No toys there. Worse, no mother. It was part of what drew them together. Even though Ayinde had been abandoned in a posh apartment and enrolled in boarding school as soon as she hit fourteen, and Richard had been dumped in apartments in the projects, it all came down to the same thing—parents who had better things to do. But Ayinde, at least, had had a consistent adult in her nanny, Serena, who'd cared for her from the time she was six weeks old until her eighth birthday. She'd had toys and clothes and grand birthday parties, a roof over her head, and the guarantee of three meals. Richard's life hadn't been like that.

"You want to know what I played with?" he asked shortly. Then he'd smiled to soften the blow of his words. "Basketballs, baby." Julian had basketballs, of course—a regulation-sized sphere that bore the autographs of all of the Sixers and a miniature one that Richard kept tucked in Julian's crib.

"Let's shake a leg," she told her son, who peered at her through slitted eyes as she wiped his face with a burp cloth, replaced his dirty T-shirt with a clean one, fastened a blue-and-white bib around his neck, and carried him into the sticky air outside.

"Just be patient," Becky was saying from her perch on a bench in Rittenhouse Square Park, where she and Kelly and their respective bellies were sitting side by side in short-sleeved shirts and sneakers, squabbling about the right way to give birth. *Like it was going to be up to them,* Ayinde thought with a smile.

"I am being patient," Kelly replied. She lurched to her feet and stretched her arms over her head, then grabbed her left elbow with her right hand and pulled. "I've been patient. But it's thirty-eight weeks, which is full term, so why can't they just induce me already?" She blew out a frustrated breath and switched elbows, then moved on to hamstring stretches.

Ayinde wheeled Julian over to the bench, thinking that Kelly, with her wisp of a blond ponytail and translucent skin, was looking considerably less chipper than she had in that first yoga class. Her lips were chapped, her blue eyes were sunken, and her body, in her black-and-white maternity workout ensemble, seemed to be all belly. Her arms and legs had moved past skinny toward scrawny, and she had dark circles under her eyes.

"Babies know when they want to be born," Becky said. "What's the rush?" Becky's appearance had also changed in the past weeks. She had the same full cheeks and tumble of curls, the same uniform of sneakers, leggings, and oversize T-shirts. The difference was, she'd finally started to show. Which was good news, Becky said, insofar as she finally looked pregnant, but bad news because people kept asking her whether she was having twins. Or triplets. And whether she'd taken fertility drugs to get them.

"You need to relax," Becky said, unscrewing the top of her water bottle and taking a gulp. Kelly made a noncommittal noise and started doing torso twists. The two of them were polar opposites when it came to their birth plans. Becky wanted an all-natural birth: no drugs, no medical interventions, laboring at home for as long as she could manage with her husband and her friend Sarah there to help. She'd taken classes in something called the Bradley Method and was fond of parroting expressions from her instructor such as "Babies know when they're ready to be born" and "Women were having babies just fine long before doctors got involved" and "You have to let your labor unfold in its own time."

Kelly, on the other hand, had long ago announced her intention to get her epidural right away—in the hospital parking lot, if possible—and none of Becky's facts and figures and offer to loan her a videotape of women in Belize giving birth without any medication while they squatted in rope hammocks they'd woven themselves had changed her mind. Kelly's own mother, Kelly explained, had simply disappeared in the middle of the night five times and come back a day or two later with a deflated belly and a brand-new little bundle of joy. No muss, no fuss, no pain that Kelly had seen, and that was just what she wanted for herself.

"Let's get this over with," Becky said, getting slowly to her feet. They started their laps around the park. Kelly pumped her arms vigorously and lifted her knees high. Becky tended to amble and to stop every few minutes to readjust her ponytail. Ayinde kept her eyes on Julian, sleeping in his stroller, and had almost fallen twice because of it.

"I can't stand this anymore," Kelly groaned. "Do you know I'm so miserable I actually thought about having sex, just to see if it would get things going?"

"Oh, no," said Becky. "Not sex!"

Kelly looked at her. "Are you having sex?"

"Well, sometimes," Becky said. "You know. When there's nothing good on cable."

"I just don't see why they can't induce me. Or give me a C-section. That would be ideal," said Kelly, pumping her arms even harder as they rounded the corner on Nineteenth Street, passing a trio of art students carrying portfolios. She waved away the cigarette smoke. "I hate waiting."

"You know, statistically, the average first pregnancy lasts anywhere from seven to ten days past the medical establishment's arbitrary forty-week deadline," Becky said. "I'm forty-one weeks tomorrow, but you don't see me complaining. And a C-section's major surgery. There are risks, you know." She nodded, looking satisfied at having worked another natural-childbirth nugget into the conversation, and glared at a pair of joggers who'd brushed a little too close to her shoulder as they completed another lap. "Are we done yet?"

Kelly shook her head. "Once more around the park," she said. "How are things going with Julian?"

"Wonderful," Ayinde said reflexively. She rolled her shoulders, readjusting her grip on the stroller's padded handlebar, and thought that "Wonderful" was the only answer anyone really wanted to hear from a new mother. The truth was, caring for a newborn was infinitely more demanding than she'd imagined. The baby needed her all the time, and whenever she started to do something—check her e-mail, take a shower, look at a magazine, take a nap—his cries would call her back, and he'd need his diaper changed or he'd need to nurse, which he did at a rate of what felt like once every thirty minutes.

Richard had watched it all with increasing skepticism. "You don't need to work so hard," he told her the night before, when she'd left the table after three bites of dinner to nurse the baby on the living-room couch. "We can get that baby nurse to come back."

Ayinde had told him no. In her view, the only women who were entitled to pay someone else to care for their children were working women. She had no job except for the baby, and she'd been good at every job she ever had. It pained her to think of admitting that she couldn't handle Julian by herself. "We're fine," she'd told Richard. "We're fine," she told her friends, as they completed another lap. She reached down to reattach Julian's teddy bear wrist rattle. "Have either of you ever heard of a book called *Baby Success?*"

"Oh, absolutely!" Kelly said.

"That's the one that says you're supposed to have your baby on a schedule, right?" Becky asked. She winced and stopped to twist from side to side. "Cramp," she explained, as Kelly high-stepped in place.

"That's the one. My mother sent it," Ayinde said.

"I looked at it in the bookstore. It sounded kind of rigid," Becky said. "I mean, I agree with the scheduling idea in principle, but I like the idea of a morning nap and an afternoon nap instead of a nap every day at 9:15 and 3:32. And, did you get to the chapter on working mothers?"

Ayinde had. "Back to Work?" the chapter was entitled, with the question mark built right in. Priscilla Prewitt, unsurprisingly, was not a fan. *Before you head back to the salt mines, think carefully of the consequences of your choice,* she wrote. *Babies are meant to love their mothers and to be cared for by their mothers—it's basic biology, darlings, and neither feminism nor daddy's good intentions can fight it. Work if you must, but don't kid yourself. Remember that the woman you bring into your house to love your dumpling is going to get some of the hugs, some of the smiles, some of the sweet little giggles—in short, some of the love—that any baby would rather give to Mom.*

"She makes it sound like you're a horrible person if you leave your baby with a sitter for the afternoon, and you're about two steps away from a psycho killer if you hire a nanny. But some women have to work," Becky said, as they started walking again. "Like me."

"Do you really have to?" asked Kelly.

"Well, I don't think we'd starve if I didn't. But I love what I do. I don't know how I'll feel after the baby comes, but for now, working three days a week sounds like it'll give me a nice balance."

"What will you do with the baby?" Kelly asked.

"Day care," said Becky. "Andrew's hospital has on-site day care that a bunch of the doctors use. I'll be with her in the morning, drop her off at noon, and Andrew will take her home if he's done before I am—ha, ha, like that ever happens. What'll probably happen is I'll pick her up when I'm done working. But he'll be nearby. I feel good about that." She looked at Ayinde and Kelly. "You guys are staying home, right?"

Ayinde nodded. Kelly didn't. "I was going to," she said.

"What do you mean?"

"Well." She looked down at her sneakers, the bows perfectly tied, as they rounded the corner again. "Steve's decided to make a career transition. He'll take paternity leave once the baby comes, and probably I'll go back to work until he finds something. But I'm sure it won't take long," Kelly said. She flipped her ponytail and wiped a trickle of sweat off her cheek.

"Are you okay?" Becky asked.

"Oh, sure! I'm fine!" Kelly said.

Ayinde took a deep breath. She didn't want to discourage them or tell them what it was really like at home with a new baby, but she couldn't keep from remembering something Lolo had told her about her own infancy, an anecdote her mother liked to break out at cocktail parties. "That baby cried and cried so much her first week home, I swear, if someone had shown up at my front door—some normal-looking person, mind you—and promised me they'd give her a good home, I would have handed her over in a minute!" The guests would laugh, as if Lolo was kidding. Ayinde wasn't so sure. After almost three months with Julian, her lovely little boy who seemed constitutionally incapable of sleeping for more than two hours or not crying for longer than one, she was starting to understand what her mother had meant and why Lolo had been able to hand her daughter over to Serena at six weeks. Serena was the one who'd sung Ayinde lullabyes, who'd cut the crusts off her sandwich, given her baths, and comforted her the day the mean girls had pushed her into the boys' room. That was the kind of mother she wanted to be (except for the part about taking the train back to Queens every night, to be with her own children, the way Serena had). "You're both going to be wonderful mothers."

"I hope so," Kelly muttered, rubbing her hands on her belly. "Come out, come out, wherever you are!" She looked at her watch again, then over at Becky, who wiped her forehead and said that it was time for gelato.

BECKY

Becky peered over her belly at Dr. Mendlow as he examined her the next morning. "Anything doing?" She was forty-one weeks and four days pregnant, and even though she'd been telling everyone that her baby would come when she was ready and that patience was a virtue, the truth was she was getting a little desperate. *There had to be something doing by now,* she thought. *People didn't just stay pregnant forever.*

Dr. Mendlow pulled off his gloves and shook his head. "I'm sorry, Becky, but the head's still up; you're still not dilated or effaced at all."

She squeezed her eyes shut, willing herself not to start crying before she'd taken her feet out of the stirrups.

"That's the bad news," the doctor said. "The good news is, you had a nonstress test this morning, and the heart rate's still perfect, and the amniotic fluid looks fine."

"So can't I just wait?"

He pulled up a wheeled stool and sat down on it as she sat up, holding the gown closed over her chest. "I'm sure from all the reading you've done you know that the risks of having something go wrong with the birth, or the baby, increase after forty-two weeks."

She nodded. Even her holistic, all-natural, have-your-baby-at-home-or-in-a-nearby-field books had acknowledged that that much was true. She hadn't paid much attention at the time, though. She'd just assumed that she wouldn't have that problem, that as a result of her good intentions and strenuous preparation, her baby would be born not only on time but in a manner that was just what she'd planned for and dreamed of. "So what do we do now?"

Dr. Mendlow flipped a few pages in her chart. "Given that we're this far along, and given what the last ultrasound told us about the size of the baby's head, my recommendation would be a C-section."

Becky buried her face in her hands. Dr. Mendlow touched her shoulder gently.

"I know this isn't what you wanted," he said. He'd been listening to Becky talk about natural childbirth almost from the day she'd first come to see him, and he was completely supportive. "But pregnancy's a balance between the wishes of the parents—the mother, really— and what's going to be safest for the baby." He wheeled the stool over to the wall and consulted a small calendar taped to it. "How does tomorrow sound for a birthday?"

"Can I think about it?"

"Sure. Think," Dr. Mendlow said, getting to his feet. "Just don't think too long. I'm going to go ahead and pencil you in. Let me know by five."

"Okay," Becky said, wiping tears off her cheeks. "Okay."

She called Andrew on his cell phone and met him in the cafeteria for lunch. "I know you must be disappointed," he said, passing her handfuls of flimsy paper napkins so she could wipe her eyes. "But Dr. Mendlow knows how strongly you feel, and he wouldn't be advising this if he didn't have very good reasons."

"I just feel like such a failure," Becky wept.

"You shouldn't," Andrew told her. "It's just a case of knowledge outstripping evolution. We know more about good nutrition and not smoking and drinking than any other generation. So the babies are getting bigger, and the moms aren't."

"Fine," Becky sniffled. She knew he understood how she'd dreamed about the birth; how she'd read a book that talked about how women needed to be brave and strong, to be warriors for their babies; how she wanted to be a warrior for her daughter, laboring in water, on her hands and knees, squatting, stretching, doing whatever it took, working in harmony with her baby until her daughter had made her way into the world. And now here she was, facing exactly the kind of birth she didn't want—a cold, sterile operating room, bright lights and surgical scrubs, nothing gentle or peaceful or meaningful about it.

She walked home slowly along the heat-sticky pavement. She called her mother, who told her that she was leaving for the airport immediately and she'd be there late the next morning. She called Kelly, who tried and only partially succeeded in not sounding envious, and Ayinde, who dropped the phone twice in the course of a five-minute conversation because she didn't want to put Julian down even for an instant. "In Guatemala, the women carry their babies constantly," Ayinde said. "And there's lots of benefits to it. Bonding and all."

"Whatever you say," Becky said, and Ayinde had laughed.

"No, it's not whatever I say, it's whatever *Baby Success!* says. Call us as soon as you can."

Becky said that she would. Then she called Sarah to tell her that her doula services wouldn't be required, and made a reservation for an early dinner at her favorite sushi place. She hadn't eaten sushi during her entire pregnancy, but now, what did it matter? The baby was practically in nursery school, and a few slices of raw tuna weren't going to hurt.

Ow. She rolled over, grimacing, and looked at the clock. It was three in the morning, and her stomach was killing her. She closed her eyes. Her mother would be there in nine hours; she'd be having her C-section . . . no, she thought, reframing the statement the way her books had taught her, she'd be having her baby in less than twelve hours. She tried to breath deeply, listening to Andrew's raspy exhales, concentrating on her baby. *Ow!*

Okay, she thought, bunching a pillow underneath her head. It was 3:10 and, clearly, the sushi had been a mistake. "Andrew?" she whispered.

Without opening his eyes or even seeming to wake up at all, her husband reached over to the bedside table, groped unerringly for the antacids with one long-fingered hand, and tossed them across the quilt. Becky chomped two and closed her eyes again. At the ultrasound the day before, they'd said her baby looked to be in the nine-and-a-half-pound to ten-pound range, which meant that the size Newborn clothes she'd bought and stashed at Sarah's house probably weren't going to do her any good. She wondered if she could return them. Kelly would know. Maybe she'd even want to take them back herself. It would be something to keep her busy while she waited and . . . *Ow!*

She looked at the clock again—3:20. "Andrew?" she whispered again. Her husband's hand spidered out from underneath the sheets and started groping on the bedside table again. "No, no, wake up," she said. "I think I'm in labor!"

He blinked at her, then pulled on his glasses. "Seriously?"

"I just had three contractions in a row, ten minutes apart."

"Huh," he said and yawned.

"Huh? Is that all you've got to say?" She maneuvered herself upright, reached across him, and called Dr. Mendlow's service. *Press one for an appointment, two for a referral or a prescription refill, three if you are a patient in labor* . . . "I'm finally getting to press three!" she announced.

"What?"

She shook her head, giving the answering service her name and her number. Then she eased herself out of the bed and lifted her suitcase onto the mattress. "Nightgowns, pajamas, book," she said out loud.

"I'm not sure you're going to get a lot of reading done," said Andrew.

The telephone rang. Andrew handed it over. "Dr. Mendlow?" Becky said. But it wasn't Dr. Mendlow; it was Dr. Fisher, his older, grumpier colleague. Becky had seen Dr. Fisher once, at her three-month visit, when Dr. Mendlow had been called away for a delivery.

Dr. Fisher had completely ruined her day by looking revolted as he'd palpated her belly. "Ever tried Weight Watchers?" he asked when her feet were in the stirrups. And he hadn't so much as cracked a smile when Becky had blinked at him and asked, breathlessly, "What's that?"

"I'm having regular contractions," Becky said.

"Dr. Mendlow's notes said we'd decided on a C-section," Dr. Fisher said.

"Well, that had been my decision," Becky said, hitting the *had* and *my* with equal emphasis. "But now that I'm in labor, I'd like to go back to my birth plan and give natural childbirth a shot."

"If you want to try it, that's fine," he said in an *It's your funeral* tone. "Come on in when your contractions are four minutes apart . . ."

" . . . one minute long, for over an hour."

"You got it," he said and hung up the phone.

Becky's mother, dressed in a light-blue velour warm-up suit and pristine white sneakers, stared as she saw her daughter and her son-in-law beside the baggage carousel. "What are you doing here?" she asked Becky, letting go of her suitcase and grabbing for Becky's hands. "Why aren't you in the hospital?"

"I'm in labor," Becky said.

Her mother's eyes darted around, taking in the crowds of travelers dragging suitcases and the uniformed limousine drivers holding placards with names written on them. "You're in labor here?" She looked at Andrew. "Is that safe?"

"It's early labor. It's fine," Becky said, leading her mother to the car, where she'd already packed her aromatherapy oils, relaxation tapes, a dog-eared copy of *Birthing from Within* and Naomi Wolf's *Misconceptions* for inspiration. "There's no reason for me to be in the hospital yet."

"But . . . but . . ." Her mother looked past Becky at Andrew. "What about the C-section?"

"We're going to give vaginal delivery a shot," Andrew said. Edith Rothstein flinched—whether from the idea of her daughter in labor, walking around in public, or her son-in-law saying *vaginal*, Becky wasn't sure.

"It's okay," Becky told her, as Andrew started driving. "Really. I heard the baby's heartbeat on the monitor yesterday, and it's fine. Ooh, ooh, contraction." She closed her eyes and swayed slowly back and forth, breathing, picturing the warm sand of a beach, hearing the waves roll in, trying not to hear her mother muttering what sounded like *This is crazy* underneath her breath.

"So you're just going to stay here?" Edith asked incredulously once they were back in the house and Becky had installed herself on top of her inflatable birth ball. Edith's pale-blue eyes widened. "You're not going to have the baby here, are you?"

"No, Mom," Becky said patiently. "But I'm not going to the hospital yet."

Her mother shook her head and headed for the stairs and the kitchen, where she'd probably start in on rearranging Becky's spice rack.

Andrew put Edith's suitcase in the closet. Then he knelt down and rubbed Becky's shoulders. "I'm so proud that you want to do it this way," he said. "Are you feeling all right?"

"I'm feeling great," Becky said, leaning her head against his chest. "But I know it's still early." She squeezed his hand. "Stay with me, okay?"

"I wouldn't leave for anything," he said.

Two long baths, one CD's worth of whale songs, and twelve hours' worth of on-and-off contractions later, Dr. Mendlow finally called. "Why don't you stop on in, let us have a look?" he said, so casually that he could have been suggesting joining him for a cup of coffee.

Fifteen minutes later, just before ten o'clock at night, they were in triage.

"Hmm," said the nurse, looking from Becky to the narrow bed in triage and back to Becky again.

"You all need some BIG GIRL beds!" Becky announced and hoisted herself aboard. Today of all days she was not going to let anyone make her feel ashamed about her size.

The nurse scratched her chin and wandered away. Becky closed her eyes and blew out a great frustrated breath.

"You're doing fine," Andrew said.

"I'm tired," said Becky, as the nurse reappeared and tried to wrestle a too-small blood pressure cuff around Becky's upper arm.

A resident came in to examine her. "Three centimeters," she announced.

Becky turned to Andrew. "Three? THREE?!? That can't be right," she said, looking past the mound of her belly to the bored resident. "Can you check again, please? I've been in labor since three o'clock this morning."

The resident pursed her lips and put her hand back. "Three," she said.

Shit, thought Becky. After all that time, she'd harbored the secret dream that she'd be more along the lines of eight or nine centimeters dilated and ready to push.

"Do you want to go back home?" asked Andrew.

Becky shook her head. "Can't do it," she said. "My mother's about to have a nervous breakdown. Let's just get a room already."

"Should I get Sarah to come?"

"Only if she's coming on a bus full of morphine," Becky said and tried to smile. "Sure. Go call her." She raised her voice and called to the nurse. "Hey, me and my crappy three-centimeters-dilated cervix would like to be admitted."

"I'll alert the media," the nurse called back.

An hour later, which was forty-five minutes longer than it had taken with Ayinde, Becky and Andrew were in their room.

"Did you ever think about playing professional basketball? Because I've noticed that it really improves the service around here,"

Becky said, plopping down on the rocking chair, trying not to notice the way it pinched at her hips, and rocking back and forth in preparation for the next contraction.

Andrew shook his head. "Want me to call your mom?"

"Tell her we've been admitted, but tell her not to come yet," Becky said. "I don't want her sitting in a waiting room all night. She really would have a nervous breakdown. At least at our house there's stuff for her to organize."

He nodded, then cleared his throat. "Can I call my mom?"

"She knows I'm in labor, right?"

Andrew nodded. From his silence, she could guess exactly what Mimi's opinion of Becky opting for labor rather than the scheduled C-section had been. "Let's just call her once the baby's here, okay?"

Andrew frowned at her.

"Oh, don't make the pouty face," Becky said. "That was the plan, right?"

"It's just that it's a happy occasion," Andrew said. "I feel bad that we're not letting my mother be a part of it."

"If she was capable of acting like a normal human being," Becky began, before a contraction interrupted her. A good thing, too. Andrew looked miserable every time Becky complained about his mother, which, she had to admit, happened more than she would have liked every time the subject of Mimi came up. "Look," she said, once the contraction had eased off. "She's a little anxious, as you know, and I just think it would be better for me—better for the labor, better for the baby—if I didn't have to worry about her being here. As soon as the baby comes, call away, but for now, I want this to be just the two of us. Well, the two of us, and Sarah. And the baby." She stared down bleakly at her belly. "Soon, I hope."

Andrew nodded and stepped into the hall to call Edith. When he came back, he was rubbing his eyes.

"Lie down," Becky said, half hoping that he wouldn't take her up on her offer. No such luck. Andrew made a beeline for the bed. "I'm just gonna close my eyes for a minute," he said. Approximately ten seconds later, he was sound asleep, leaving Becky lonely in the dark. "Dammit," she whispered. She'd forgotten that Andrew's seven years of fourteen-hour days in hospitals had given him the uncanny ability to fall asleep at the drop of a hat in anything that even resembled a bed.

Another contraction started. "You know," she gasped, "this hurts a lot more than Naomi Wolf would have had me believe." Andrew snorted in his sleep. Becky clutched her belly, groaning, trying to breathe through it the way she'd practiced, feeling ashamed of herself. When she'd been in a room down the hall with Ayinde, a small secret part of her had believed that she'd be stronger than her friend, that no matter how bad the pain she wouldn't scream or writhe or call on Jesus. Well, the joke was on her. Here she sat, screaming and writhing like a pro, and the only reason she hadn't called on Jesus yet was on account of being Jewish. And Becky was sure that in another hour or so, given the intensity of her contractions, all bets would be off, and she'd be taking whatever divine intervention she could get.

A nurse poked her head into the room and picked up the clipboard next to the bed, where Becky's birth plan was prominently displayed. "Okay, so we're going to do this natural," she said with a smile.

No, Becky wanted to shout. *No, no! I was high when I wrote that! I didn't know what I was talking about! Bring on the drugs!* But she kept her mouth shut and tried to hold still while the nurse found the baby's heartbeat with a handheld Doppler device.

"Ow, ow, ow," Becky moaned, shifting her weight from foot to foot as the contraction tore through her. Andrew's cell phone started ringing.

"Oh, you have got to be kidding me," Becky groaned, knowing instantly who their mystery caller was. "You're not even supposed to use cell phones in here!"

"I'll just be a minute," he said, angling his body away from her, pressing the phone to his ear. Becky could hear every one of Mimi's words.

"An-DREW? What's going on? I haven't heard from you in hours! I called your house, but someone—" Becky grimaced. For reasons she'd never understood, Mimi had taken an instant disliking to Becky's mother, and refused to so much as utter her name. "—said you weren't there. Where are you?"

"Andrew," Becky whispered, "it's the middle of the night and I'm in labor. Where does she think we are? Key West?"

"Well, Mom, we're actually a little busy right now."

No, Becky mouthed frantically. *No!*

"Shh," Andrew whispered and turned toward the window, leaving Becky to pound fruitlessly on his plaid-shirted shoulder.

"Oh mah GAWD!" Mimi shrieked. "Is the baby comin'? Is this it? Oh, ANDREW! I'm gonna be a GRAND-ma!" There was a click, then silence. Andrew closed his eyes and banged his forehead against the wall.

"Just keep her in the waiting room," Becky said. "Please. Seriously. If you love me at all, keep her in the waiting room."

He bent down and squeezed her hands. "I promise," he said.

"You'd better," she said. "Because I've had about all I can take here."

There was a knock on the door, and there was Sarah, in a sweatshirt and jeans, her hair pulled back in a ponytail, grinning at them with a brimming tote bag over her shoulder. "Hey, you two," she said. Becky felt better just looking at her. She let Sarah lead her back to the rocking chair and told Andrew to go back to sleep. "Take a nap," Sarah urged him. "We'll need you later."

Ten minutes later, Andrew was snoring again, arms outstretched, glasses askew on his face, and Becky was squatting on the birth ball, with Sarah crouching behind her, digging her knuckles into the small of Becky's back. "Does that feel any better?"

"Yes. No. It's still awful," Becky said. She felt as limp as a wet washcloth, more tired than she'd been in her entire life. "It hurts, it hurts, it hurrrts," she moaned, shaking her head back and forth, her sweaty hair sticking to her cheeks. "Make it stop, make it stop, make it stop."

Sarah wrapped her arms around her shoulders and rocked with her. "You're doing fine," she said. Becky wasn't so sure. Maybe this was the great equalizer she'd been hoping for—not pregnancy itself, but birth that put all women, large and small, black and white, rich and poor and in between, on the same playing field, battered by fear, begging for drugs, wanting nothing except for the pain to stop and the baby to arrive.

"Shh," Sarah soothed, as the contractions rose and fell, rose and fell. She flipped open to the page Becky had bookmarked in *Birthing from Within.* "Visualize your cervix. See it opening like a flower." Sarah set the book down. "I can't believe I just said that out loud."

"FUCK my cervix," Becky wept, leaning against Sarah's shoulder. "How do women do this?"

"Fucked if I know," said her friend. "Want me to call a nurse?"

Becky shook her head, feeling sweaty tendrils sticking to her cheeks as Sarah helped her to stand up and lean against the wall. "This cannot get any worse."

The door to her room opened, and a triangular wedge of light spilled into the darkness, followed by a familiar voice. "Hahyahhh." Which was Mimi's approximation of "Hi."

"Oh, shit," Becky whispered into Sarah's shoulder. "Wrong again."

Mimi narrowed her eyes and squinted past Sarah, toward the nurse who'd just walked through the door. "What is SHE doing here?" she demanded. Her voice was its standard two or three decibels too loud for the room. "I was told nobody was allowed!"

Becky bit her lip. Maybe lying had been a mistake.

The nurse glanced at the chart, then at Sarah. "She's Becky's doula," she said.

"Well, that's my son, who is a surgeon in this hospital, and that," she said, gesturing toward Becky's abdomen, "is my grandchild."

And what am I? Becky thought. *Tupperware?*

Mimi extended her trembling finger toward Sarah. "If SHE gets to stay, then I do, too!"

Andrew sat up in the bed. "Mom?"

"Mimi," Becky whispered, "Andrew and I really wanted our privacy for this."

"Oh, don't worry! You won't even notice I'm here!" She kicked the birth ball into the corner, sat down on the rocking chair, and pulled a video recorder out of her purse. *Unbelievable,* Becky thought. "Smile pretty," Mimi said, flicking on the overhead lights and pointing the lens at her daughter-in-law. "Oh, dear. You could use a little lipstick."

"Mimi, I do not want lipstick! Please turn the light off, and . . . oh, God," Becky groaned as another contraction started up.

"Well, there's no need to be dramatic," Mimi announced and moved closer with the camera, speaking into its recorder. "Hah there, this is me, Mimi, your grandmother, and we're in the hospital on Saturday morning . . ."

"MiMIIIIIII!"

"Okay, Mom," Andrew said. He grabbed his mother's elbow with one hand, her handbag with the other, and began propelling her toward the door. "Let's go sit in the waiting room."

"What?" Mimi shrieked. "Why? I have every right to be here, Andrew. This is MY grandbaby, and I don't understand why you'd want some . . . some doo-doo or whatever she is in there with you while your own mother gets left in the cold . . ."

The door blessedly swung closed behind them. Sarah raised her eyebrows. "Don't even ask," Becky panted. The contractions went on and on, unspooling over the hours. Andrew and Sarah took turns walking with her, rubbing her feet and her back until the sun came up, and then they started spacing out, dwindling to one every five minutes . . . then one every seven . . . then one every ten.

Dr. Mendlow's normally cheerful face was grave, his high forehead wrinkled as he finished his exam.

"Still three centimeters," he said. Andrew held one of her hands, and Sarah held the other. Becky started to cry.

"That's the bad news," the doctor continued. "The good news is, the heartbeat still sounds strong. But for whatever reason—and it might be the size of the baby, which, as you know, we've been keeping an eye on—the baby's head is just not descending enough to get the cervix to really dilate." He sat down on the edge of Becky's bed. "We could try some Pitocin to see if that'll start the contractions again."

"Or?" Becky asked.

"Or we could have a C-section. Which, given that we're right up against forty-two weeks, and given what we suspect about the size of this baby's head, is what I'd recommend."

"Let's do it," Becky said instantly. Andrew looked shocked.

"Becky, are you sure?"

"I don't want Pitocin," she said. She gathered her damp curls off her cheeks. "Because then the contractions will kill me, and I'll need an epidural anyhow, and I could still wind up needing a C-section after all that, so I might as well get one now. Let's do it."

"Why don't you take some time to talk about it," said Dr. Mendlow.

"We don't need any time," said Becky. "I just want a C-section. Let's go, let's go, let's go!"

It wound up taking two hours. Because Becky refused an IV earlier that night, they hooked one up to get her hydrated. The anesthesiologist's arrival didn't improve things. He introduced himself as Dr. Bergeron, and he looked like a dissolute French poet, skinny and pale, with long hair and a goatee, the kind of guy who made his own absinthe on weekends and might have a body or two stashed in his basement. There was a splatter of blood on the cuff of his scrubs. "Do you think he's on heroin?" Becky whispered to Andrew, who took a long look at the doctor before shaking his head.

Then she was in the operating room, with a half dozen new faces introducing themselves—Dr. Marcus, one of the residents . . . Carrie, the nurse-anesthesiologist . . . I'm Janet, and I'll be assisting Dr. Mendlow. *Why did the doctors get last names and the nurses just first ones?* Becky wondered. One of the nurses helped her to sit up and drape herself over Carrie's shoulders while the goth-looking anesthesiologist swabbed her back with something icy. "You'll feel a little pinch, then some burning," he said. She could smell rubbing alcohol, and the room suddenly seemed too bright, too cold, and her entire body was shivering.

"I've never had surgery before," she tried to tell Carrie. "Not even a broken bone!" Carrie eased her back down onto the table.

"Hi, Becky." Finally, Andrew was there, gowned and be-hatted, with a surgical mask on inside out. It made Becky laugh as they lifted a sheet at her waist level. He must be so nervous, she thought, to get that wrong.

"Hey, hon," said Dr. Mendlow. Becky couldn't see his face, but his eyes were warm and reassuring over his mask.

"You okay?" Andrew whispered, and she nodded, feeling tears sliding down her cheeks and pooling in her ears.

"Just a little scared," she whispered. "Hey, if I can feel them cutting, you'll make them stop, right?"

"Time of incision, 10:48."

Incision? "They started already?" Becky asked.

Andrew nodded. She could see the action reflected in his glasses. There was a lot of red. She closed her eyes. "Is the baby out yet?"

Laughter. "Not yet," said Dr. Mendlow. "You're going to feel a lot of pressure."

She squeezed her eyes shut. *Baby,* she thought, *hang in there, baby.* "Suction," called Dr. Mendlow. "Ooh, she's wedged in there tight."

And then she heard someone say, "Oh, there she is!" and there was a scream—not a little, puny baby scream, either, but a gusting, furious *What are you DOING to me?* kind of scream.

"Look up," said Dr. Mendlow. "There's your baby!"

And there she was, her skin the pink of the inside of a seashell, in a coat of blood and white vernix, eyes squinched shut, head perfectly bald, tongue vibrating as she wailed.

"What's her name, Mom?" one the nurses asked.

Mom, Becky thought wonderingly. "Ava," she said. "Ava Rae."

"Dad, you want to come over here?"

Andrew slipped away from her side. She watched as he went over to the scales and to the table where they wiped Ava's flailing arms and legs, weighed her, wrapped her in a blanket, and pulled a striped cap over her head. "She's perfect, Becky," he said, and he was crying, too. "She's perfect."

The next few hours were a blur. Becky remembered Dr. Mendlow asking Andrew if he wanted to look at her uterus and ovaries—"See, right here, very healthy!"—and thinking that he sounded like a used-car salesman trying to talk a customer into making a purchase. She remembered Andrew telling her that their mothers were outside and that a nurse had wheeled Ava by to show them. She remembered being pushed into Recovery, which was nothing more than a curtained-off section of the labor and delivery floor. She remembered lying on the too-narrow gurney, shivering from her head to her feet. Every so often she'd run her hands over her belly, reaching for the hard rise of her stomach, feeling instead something that felt like a warm, deflated inner tube. And her toes . . . she could see them for the first time in weeks. "Hi, guys!" she said and tried to wiggle them. It didn't work. Becky wondered whether that was something to worry about.

Another nurse bustled into her curtained cubicle, bearing a bundle wrapped in a blue-and-pink-striped blanket. "Baby's here!" she announced. And there was Ava, with a perfectly round pink face and one of her ears sticking out at a funny angle from underneath her cap.

"Hi," Becky said, running one finger along her cheek. "Hi, baby!"

They let her hold the baby for a minute. Becky pressed her against her chest. "I'm so glad you're here," she said. She offered the baby her breast, but Ava wasn't interested . . . she just blinked and looked around, looking somewhere between thoughtful and disgruntled, like someone who's fallen asleep reading a really great book and is still trying to figure out which world they're in, the real one or the one they imagined while they read. "Sweetheart," Becky whispered, before the nurse whisked the baby away.

Andrew sat down on a wheeled stool and scooted himself up by Becky's head. "You are amazing," he said and kissed her forehead.

"I know!" Becky said. "But I can't stop shivering!"

"It's the anesthesia. It'll stop. Do you want me to get you a blanket?"

"No. No. Stay with me." Becky closed her eyes, imagining that somewhere not too far away she could hear Mimi elbowing her way past Becky's mother and screaming. *Give her to me! Let me hold her! She's my grandbaby! Mine! MINE!* She sighed, thinking that her father would have put a stop to Mimi's nonsense, if he'd been around. He would have been so happy . . .

She wiped her eyes. "You okay?" Andrew asked.

Becky nodded. "You should stay with the baby," she said.

"Are you sure? Our moms are both out there and Sarah's sleeping in the waiting room."

"Then you should definitely go," said Becky, unable to shake the image of Mimi snatching up the little blanket-wrapped bundle and making a break for it.

Andrew kissed her again and left the cubicle, and Becky was alone, without even a machine's beep to keep her company. "I'm a mother," she whispered. Somehow it didn't feel quite real. She waited for the feeling she'd imagined, that rush of pure bliss and unmitigated, unconditional love for everyone in all the world to wash over her. It didn't seem to have kicked in yet. Why had Ava screamed so much when they'd pulled her out? Why hadn't she been interested in nursing? Why did she only weigh eight pounds four ounces when the doctors thought she'd be closer to ten pounds? Was there something wrong with Ava? Something they weren't telling her?

A nurse came in wheeling a clear bag attached to a pole. "Your morphine pump!" she announced.

"Woo hoo!" said Becky. Not that anything hurt yet, but she wasn't interested in exploring the possibility that at some point after the surgery, something would. The nurse handed Becky a button and explained that she could press it once every ten minutes for an extra dose. "Do you have a stopwatch?" Becky asked. The nurse laughed, gave her some ice chips, and pulled her curtain shut.

"I'm a mother," she whispered again. She waited to feel changed, transformed, turned inside-out, and rendered completely different. So far she didn't. She conjured up a picture of her mean Aunt Joan, who'd showed up at her tenth birthday party and pulled her aside before the cake and presents to hiss that she didn't need such a big slice of cake and wouldn't she like an apple instead, and waited for the magic of maternity to wash her mental slate clean. Nope. Nothing doing. She found that she still hated Aunt Joan . . . which meant that motherhood would leave her unchanged. She'd be herself, basically, only with less sleep and a new scar. Oh, dear. Becky hit the morphine button hopefully, figuring that if she couldn't have emotional tranquillity, she could at least have narcotics.

As if the sigh had summoned her, the nurse reappeared.

"Your room should be ready soon," she said. "Do you want a little more morphine? Dr. Mendlow left orders saying you could have more."

"Sure," she said, figuring, why not? It couldn't hurt. She hit her button again as the nurse injected something into her IV bag. She wasn't shivering anymore. She felt pleasantly warm all over, like she was lying on a beach. And she could finally wiggle her toes! "Check me out," she told the nurse and pointed toward her toes. "I'm a mother!"

"Yes, you are," the nurse said, patting her shoulder. Becky closed her eyes, and when she opened them again, she was floating through the halls, giggling, and Andrew was hovering above her, looking concerned.

"How much morphine did they give you?" he asked.

"Press my button, press my button!" Becky said.

Instead of pressing her button, he looked over her head at the nurse. "How much morphine has she had?"

Becky started to laugh even harder, even though she could feel a vague but disturbing pulling sensation at the base of her belly. Where they'd taken the baby. "Hey, I had a baby!"

"That's right," said Andrew, with a big, worried-looking smile.

"Ava," Becky told the nurse, as they wheeled her into her room and eased her, still giggling, onto the bed. "Her name is Ava. Isn't that a beautiful name?"

"Here she is!" said the nurse, as she came through the door pushing a wheeled table with a plastic rectangle on top. And inside of the rectangle, wrapped in fresh blankets, in a little striped blue-and-pink cap and an electronic bracelet around one tiny ankle, was Ava. She wasn't screaming anymore but blinking and peering around.

Becky held out her arm, still dangling with the IV tube. "Baby," she instructed. Andrew scooped the baby up from her little nest and handed her to Becky. "Baby," Becky whispered to Ava.

"Baby," Andrew whispered to his wife.

"Press my button," Becky whispered back.

"I think you've had enough morphine."

"I'm trying to stay on top of the pain," Becky explained. "Press it, press it, press it!"

"Okay, already," he said, as Edith walked into the room, eyes brimming.

"Oh . . . oh, Becky!" Edith said, bursting into tears as she took in the sight of Becky with the baby in her arms. "Oh, Becky . . . she's so beautiful . . . I just wish your father . . ."

"I know," Becky said, feeling her own eyes well up. "I miss him, too."

Edith blew her nose as Ava opened her mouth and started to cry. Andrew and Becky looked at each other.

"Oh, shit," Becky said. "Take the baby, take the baby!"

"You've got her," he said, in a manner that she supposed was meant to be encouraging.

"I'm *high!*" Becky protested. "I can't have the baby! You take her! Oh, God, she's crying. Call a nurse!"

"It's okay," he said, laughing a little. "It's okay." He tucked the baby back against her chest. "Shhh, shhh," he said. Ava stopped crying and looked up at them, her eyes no color and every color at once.

"Hello, gorgeous," Becky whispered. Ava batted her wispy eyelashes and yawned. Becky stared at her until, finally, they both fell asleep.

"Hahyahhhh."

Becky cracked one eyelid open. The hospital room was a blur— the morphine, she supposed—and was silent except for Andrew's snoring and that horrible noise of her mother-in-law.

"Hahyahhhh."

There was her mother-in-law, Mimi Breslow Levy Rabinowitz Anderson Klein, flanked by two of her friends, teeny-tiny women in cashmere sweater sets and low-rise jeans exposing their sixtysomething hip bones. *Mutton dressed as lamb,* Becky thought, eyeing the wrinkled cup of her mother-in-law's navel. The three of them were lined up over Ava's bassinet. Mimi's head was dangling inches from the baby's, so close that their noses were practically touching.

"Hah, Anna Banana," Mimi said, inching her face forward.

Oh, Becky thought. *Oh, no.* Anna had been Mimi's mother's name.

Becky knew that Andrew had told his mother that they were planning on naming their baby after her. But Andrew certainly must have told his mother that they'd named the baby Ava, not Anna. And even if he hadn't, Ava's name was written plain as day on the pink three-by-five notecard taped to her bassinet.

"Sweet little Anna," Mimi crooned to her friends. "And just look what I bought her!" She reached into her purse with her free hand and pulled out a miniature pink tank top with the word HOTTIE spelled out in sequins on the front. "Isn't it adorable?" she asked, as her friends cooed their approval. Becky wondered if the outfit came with a matching G-string. And the purchase-separately pimp. "Let's see how it looks!" one of Mimi's friends said.

Mimi lifted the baby out of her bassinet, appearing not to notice as her head flopped forward, and began pulling on the tank top. "Hey," Becky tried to say, but her throat was so dry that the words came out as a whisper. She stared at Andrew, willing him to wake up and put a stop to this, as Mimi inched her hand underneath the bassinet and stealthily removed one of the bottles of formula the night nurse had left there. Becky waited until Mimi had almost maneuvered the nipple into her baby's mouth. Then she pushed herself up until she was upright, gritting her teeth at the pain, not even noticing as the sheet one of the nurses had laid on top of her slipped off her chest.

"What are you doing?" she asked. Mimi jumped at the sound of her daughter-in-law's raspy voice. The bottle flew out of her hand.

One of Mimi's lady friends stared at Becky. "Oh, dear, she hasn't got a stitch on underneath that gown," she said.

"What are you doing?" Becky asked again, pointing at the bassinet with the hand that didn't have the IV needle.

"I . . . she . . ."

Andrew rolled over on his cot.

"Excuse me! She was hungry!" Mimi said shrilly. "I was just going to . . ."

"I'm breast-feeding," Becky said, pointing at the notecard that announced to all the world that AVA ROTHSTEIN-RABINOWITZ IS A BREAST-FED GIRL! "If she's hungry, just give her to me."

Mimi grabbed the baby under the armpits with less care than she would have shown to a ten-pound sack of flour and handed her over.

"And her name is Ava," Becky said.

Mimi's eyebrows drew down, and her freshly lipsticked mouth folded in on itself. She turned toward her son, who was still lying on his cot. "What? WHY? She was supposed to be named after my mother! This was supposed to be my honor!"

"She is named after your mother," Andrew said mildly. "She's named Ava."

"My mother's name was not AVA! My mother's name . . ."

"Started with the letter A. And so does Ava's," Becky said and looked at Mimi, practically daring her to start a fight, knowing what she'd say if her mother-in-law took the bait—*you got to name your son whatever you wanted; we have the same right.*

Mimi's mouth opened and closed, opened and closed. Becky pulled her gown open. Mimi flinched.

"We can talk about this later," she said, backing out of the room so fast that she almost tripped on her high heels. Her friends scurried out after her. Becky settled Ava against her and looked over at Andrew, who was staring at the baby in her HOTTIE tank top.

He rubbed his eyes again. "Is that what the hospital's giving the baby girls now?"

"No, that would be what your mother's giving little girls now. And why was she trying to feed the baby without asking us first?"

"I'm not sure," he muttered, gathering the bottles of formula and hiding them in his suitcase, "but it won't happen again. I'll talk to her."

For all the good it'll do us, Becky thought. "And HOTTIE?" she asked, pointing to the offending shirt. "I know we haven't discussed this, but I think we should wait a while before we let the baby wear things that say HOTTIE. Six months, at least." Then she giggled. "Did you see how fast Mimi got out of here? My nipples are her Kryptonite!"

Andrew bit his lip. Becky could tell he was struggling not to smile. "Becky, she is my mother," he said, but he delivered the sentence quickly and without conviction. Ava stopped sucking and opened her eyes. "Don't worry," Becky whispered to her daughter. "We won't let her bother you a bit."

KELLY

"Okay," Kelly called, as she walked into her apartment with baby Oliver in her arms and her husband, her dog, and three sisters in her wake. "Terry, there's a lasagna in the freezer. Preheat the oven to 350 degrees and bake it for an hour. Mary, would you mind bringing my laptop into the bedroom? I want to send out an announcement . . . oh, and can you bring me the digital camera so I can download the pictures? Steve, if you go to the My Documents folder on the desktop, there's a spreadsheet labeled 'Oliver Week One.' Can you please enter one wet diaper at 10:45? And Doreen, can you take Lemon for a walk?"

Her sisters and her husband dispersed, leaving Kelly alone with her baby, who was sleeping, eyes tightly shut and mouth open, in her arms. He had her husband's ears and his chin, but his eyes and mouth were shaped exactly like hers. "Hello, Oliver," she whispered. "Welcome home." She set him gently into his crib and knelt by the bookshelf. Her stitches hurt, but she managed to pull her copy of *What to Expect When You're Expecting* off the shelf and replace it with *What to Expect the First Year.* When she looked up, Steve was standing in the doorway, shuffling his feet.

"The wet diaper has been entered, and the pacifier is clean."

"Could you take your shoes off?" Kelly asked. She wanted to ask him to take a shower and change his clothes because she was sure he was still crawling with hospital germs, but she wasn't sure how he would take it.

He set his sneakers by the door. "Hey, I'm sorry about the pictures," he said.

Kelly stood up and walked slowly back to the rocker, listening to what sounded like her sisters going through her closet. "Is this a good color for me?" she heard Terry ask.

"Terry, no touching!" she called toward the bedroom. "It's okay," she said to Steve, easing herself down into the rocker. "The nurses took some nice shots. You know, once they revived you."

"I don't know what happened," Steve said. "It was just . . ." He swallowed hard. "There was an awful lot of blood."

It wasn't as if it was your blood, Kelly thought. Her delivery had been awful. She'd torn before her episiotomy and lost so much blood that she'd needed a transfusion, and Oliver had been running a fever, so he'd spent the first two nights of his life in the NICU, and Steve, instead of being helpful and loving and supportive, had passed out during the delivery and split his forehead open on the edge of the table. They'd both come back from the hospital with stitches.

Terry and Doreen stood in the nursery doorway. Terry was holding a pale-blue silk blouse; Doreen had a gold chain in her hands. "Can I borrow this just for tonight?" Terry asked, turning the question into one long word. "And this?" Doreen asked, holding the necklace. "Anthony and I are going out to dinner."

"Fine, fine," Kelly said wearily, knowing it was unlikely she'd ever see the shirt and the necklace again, or that if she saw them, they'd be stained or ripped or broken. In the crib, Oliver gave a tiny, catlike yawn. "It's all right," Kelly said. "Now, Steve, why don't you download the pictures, choose the best one, go to the website that I've bookmarked, and we can order the birth announcements."

"Hey, you're online here?" asked Mary, wandering in just as Terry and Doreen left with the blouse and the necklace. "Can I check my e-mail real quick?"

"Sure," said Kelly. Mary left. Steve sighed and leaned against the wall. The bandage on his forehead was starting to look dingy around the edges. Kelly wondered if she could change it. "I'm whipped," he said.

Kelly tried to be sympathetic. She was whipped, too. She'd suffered through the hospital noise and the nurses, too, who'd woken her and the baby up every four hours to check their vital signs. "How about some coffee?" she asked, and stuck her head out the door. "Hey, Terry, can you make some coffee?"

"You shouldn't drink coffee," Terry said, loping back into the nursery. Kelly's youngest sister wore tight, faded jeans, a blue-and-purple shirt whose cuffs drooped past her wrists, hand-sewn moccasins, and feathered earrings. "It does terrible things to your insides. I had a series of high colonics in Vermont, and you would not believe the stuff that came out of me."

"Terry, nobody wants to hear about the stuff that came out of you," said Doreen. Doreen also wore jeans, but hers were stiff and new looking, and she'd paired them with a pink sweatshirt and sensible sneakers . . . and, Kelly saw, her gold necklace.

"Seriously," said Mary. Mary wore a Wing Bowl T-shirt and khaki shorts with bulging pockets. Kelly wondered what was in them. Makeup, maybe. Mary's last visit had coincided a little too neatly with the disappearance of Kelly's favorite eyeliner.

"You guys!" Kelly said. Her sisters turned to face her. "Mary, go get Steve his coffee. Doreen, can you bring my suitcase to the bedroom? The dirty clothes are in the plastic bag, and anything that's folded you can just leave on the bed. Terry . . ." Her voice trailed off. Her baby sister, the prettiest and, alas, most vacuous member of the family, stared at her, strawberry lips parted. "What are you doing with the sterilizer?"

"Oh, is that what it is?" Terry asked, pulling her thumb out of the device. "Guess I won't have to wash my hands for a while." The three of them drifted out the door.

A minute later, Oliver started to cry. Kelly looked at her watch. It was four o'clock, an hour after she'd been discharged from the hospital, and Oliver had last eaten . . . She pulled out her Palm Pilot. Wet diaper at 9:00, nursed for fifteen minutes at 10:00, then again at 11:20, poop diaper at noon, forty-five-minute nap . . . "I think he's hungry," she said. She went to lift Oliver out of the crib. Steve beat her there.

"Hey, baby boy," he said, hefting the baby into the air. Oliver's neck wobbled. Kelly bit back a scream.

"Steve, be careful!"

"What?" Steve asked. He was wearing one of his old Penn T-shirts, jeans, and three days' worth of stubble. Since his job had ended, he'd given up regular shaving, and Kelly had been trying, with some success, not to nag him about that or about the clothes and shoes and magazines he left on the floor.

"His neck! Be careful!"

Steve looked at her as if she was crazy, then shrugged and handed the baby over. Kelly settled Oliver into the crook of her arm and sat in the rocker, where she pulled her shirt up and struggled to unhook her bra cup.

"Need some help?" Steve asked.

She shook her head and guided Oliver's face to her breast. Where nothing happened.

"Come on," Kelly whispered, jiggling Oliver on her knee, "come on, come on, come on!" She was trying to remember everything she'd learned in breast-feeding class and practiced in the hospital. Support the head. Pinch the nipple and get it lined up with the baby's mouth. Wait until the baby's mouth is wide open, then push his face toward your breast. She lined up. She waited. She pushed. Nothing. Oliver turned his face sideways and started to scream.

"Are you okay in there?" Steve asked.

"Fine!" Kelly called back, hoping he'd go for a run soon. She wanted him out of the house, out of her hair, and away from her sisters, who were starting to ask a few too many questions about how work was going. Even Terry, who was a world-class ditz, would be able to figure out that Steve wasn't saying much about his job because

Steve didn't have one anymore. And what about her friends? Becky's husband was a doctor, Ayinde's husband was Richard Towne. How long could she keep up the fiction of "paternity leave" and "job search" before it become obvious that what her husband was really doing was nothing?

"Come on, honey!" she whispered to Oliver, who turned his face away, wailing. He'd been nursing like a champ in the hospital, but in the hospital there were nurses and lactation consultants just a phone call away. At home she only had Steve, who'd been napping while Kelly did the feedings, and Doreen and Terry, who didn't have kids. Kelly couldn't remember what Mary had fed her babies. Kelly had been in high school when they were born, just a baby herself. Either way, she couldn't ask them for help. She was the one who helped them, who lent them clothes and money when she could, who advised them on haircuts and boyfriends, car purchases and job interviews. If she told them she needed something, they'd probably look at her as if she'd started talking backwards. She'd have to figure this out on her own.

"Come on," she whispered again. Breast-feeding had been easy enough in theory—insert Tab A into Slot B, wait for nature and hunger to take over—but what were you supposed to do when Slot B was wriggling and screaming, and you needed at least one hand free to get Tab A into place?

"The wheels on the bus go round and round, round and round, round and round, the wheels on the bus go round and round . . ." The baby kept screaming. "The wipers on the bus go round and round . . ." No. Wait. The wipers didn't go round and round, they did something else. But what?

Steve stuck his head into the room again. "Swish, swish, swish." *Thank you, Mr. Rogers,* Kelly thought. "Do you want me to take him for a while? They gave us some bottles at the hospital."

"No, we cannot give him a bottle," Kelly said. She flicked her bangs out of her eyes and took a deep breath. "We just have to figure this out."

"Do you want me to get one of your sisters?"

Kelly closed her eyes, wishing for Maureen, her favorite sister, all the way in California. Wishing, God help her, for her mother. Even though she'd spent many of her final years muttering to herself or half-passed out in front of her soap operas, Paula O'Hara had at least known how to nurse a baby. She could hear her sisters in the living room. From the sound of it, they were trying to get Lemon to walk on Kelly's treadmill. "She's got a sterilizer in there!" Terry reported breathlessly.

"That's our girl," Mary said, laughing her death-rattle laugh as she walked to the kitchen. The oven door opened and closed.

"Lasagna," Doreen grumbled. "Just perfect when it's ninety degrees outside."

Kelly wriggled in the rocker, hating the way her jiggly stomach pushed against the elastic waistband of the maternity jeans she'd worn home and the way her breasts felt like two footballs some doctor with a mean sense of humor had Krazy-Glued onto her chest. "Tell them to go get some coffee or something. And bring me my purse, okay?" She pulled out her wallet and the business card with the lactation center's number. "Could you call and leave a message?"

Steve pinched the card between his first two fingers. "What should I say?"

"That I can't get him latched on!"

Steve fled for the telephone. Kelly kept trying as she heard her sisters file out the door. Oliver kept trying and shaking his head back and forth as if he was deliberately trying to avoid her nipple.

"What can I do?" Steve asked, staring over her shoulder at the red-faced, writhing baby as if he were a grenade.

"Call Becky," she said. "Her number's on the notepad on the right-hand side of the refrigerator."

Two minutes later, Steve was back. "She wasn't home, but I left a message."

Kelly rested Oliver over her shoulder, against the burp cloth she'd placed there in the hope that there'd be some need of it in the near future, and rocked him, nuzzling his fuzzy, blue-veined head, praying he'd stop crying. "Can you call Ayinde?"

His eyes lit up. "You've got Richard Towne's home phone number?"

"Please just call, okay? And don't bother Richard if he answers!"

Steve nodded and came back a minute later carrying the phone. "Ayinde," he whispered.

"Ayinde? It's Kelly. Um, can you . . ." Her voice broke. Twenty minutes into at-home motherhood, and she already needed to be bailed out. She clenched her fists. "I can't get Oliver to latch on, and he hasn't had anything to eat in hours." Kelly nodded. "Oh, no, you don't have to . . . are you sure? Uh-huh. Uh-huh. Thank you. Thank you so much." She recited her address, hung up the phone, and handed it to Steve. "She's on her way."

The phone trilled again. Steve handed it over. "It's Becky."

"Becky? Listen. Oliver won't nurse. I can't get him latched on, and I've been trying forever, and . . ." She shot a frenzied look at her watch. "He hasn't had anything to eat in hours."

"Okay, okay, shh, shh, he's not going to starve in one afternoon," Becky said.

"Are you making baby noises at me?" Kelly demanded.

"Yeah. Sorry," said Becky. "It just happens. You'll see. Andrew tried to hug me the other night, and I wrapped my arms around him and started burping him. Ava just woke up. We'll leave as soon as I change her."

"Thank you," said Kelly. She wiped her nose on the burp cloth and looked down at Oliver, who'd fallen asleep with his fists clenched.

Half an hour later, Becky and Ayinde had arrived with their babies. Julian was tucked into his car seat, swaddled so tightly that just the top of his fuzzy curls and his big brown eyes peeked out, and Ava, ten days old, was nestled in a sling against Becky's chest. "She's beautiful," Kelly said.

"She's bald," Becky corrected. "Wow. Monogrammed burp cloths!" Becky marveled, taking in Oliver's Peter Rabbit rug, the bunny-shaped night-light and rabbit-print crib bumpers, his educational black-and-white mobile, the stacks of *Baby Einstein* DVDs on the bookshelf. "Your nursery has a theme. Do you know what the theme of Ava's nursery is? Laundry." She set Ava, who was gray-eyed, pink-cheeked, and bald, into Oliver's crib. "Okay. Show us what's going on."

Kelly picked up the baby, holding her breath, hoping against hope that in front of an audience he'd start nursing like he'd been doing it all his life. No dice. Align face, open mouth, insert nipple, miss, try again, and then brace herself for Oliver's screams.

Becky looked at Ayinde, then back at Kelly. "Hmm. It looks like he's missing your nipple." She pulled her curls on top of her head and rolled up her sleeves. "I'm just going to go wash my hands. Is it okay if I touch you?"

"Sure! Touch! Take pictures! Post them on the Internet! Just please get him to eat something!"

"No worries. We're going to figure this out. Kelly, you hold his head." Kelly tucked Oliver's sweaty scalp into her palm, looking into his scrunched-up face. Becky put one hand underneath Kelly's breast and pinched the nipple at a different angle than what Kelly had been trying. "Wait . . . wait . . ."

When Oliver opened his mouth, she pushed him forward, but he missed again.

"He's almost got it," said Ayinde.

"Yeah, well, almost won't get him fed," Kelly said, wiping her eyes on her shoulder.

"Do you have any formula?" Becky asked.

"I don't want to give him formula!"

"No, not to feed him, just to give him the taste. I was thinking we could squirt a few drops on your nipple, just so he knows that there's food there."

Steve, who'd been waiting just outside the door, handed Ayinde a bottle.

"Okay, Ayinde, squirt."

Kelly looked down and had to laugh at the way her torso looked like some weird three-handed Rube Goldberg feeding machine.

"Okay, now!"

Becky pinched. Ayinde squirted. Kelly brought the baby to her breast. She closed her eyes and prayed, even though, strictly speaking, she hadn't believed in God since her mother had found her scrapbook and taken it away, along with Kelly's allowance for the month, just when she'd almost gotten enough money for a pair of Calvin Klein jeans. And, then, wonder of wonders, she felt the sharp pulling sensation of Oliver starting to suck.

"He's doing it," she said, as Steve applauded quietly from the doorway. "Oh, thank God."

They spent the next hour practicing—getting Oliver latched on, taking him off, getting him latched on again, first with Becky and Ayinde's help ("it takes a village to feed my child," Kelly joked), then with just Kelly and Becky, and finally, with Kelly all by herself. Oliver had nursed himself to sleep by the time her sisters, smelling of Mary's cigarette smoke, filed back into the nursery.

"Terry wants to sterilize her hand again," Doreen said, giggling.

"Go ahead," Kelly said. She was afraid to look at them. She was so worried they'd be staring at Ayinde like she was a gazelle that had wandered into the house or, worse, they'd ask for her husband's autograph.

After her sisters had gone back to New Jersey and Steve had headed to the bedroom for a nap, Kelly and Ayinde and Becky and their babies sat down on the living-room floor.

"If I ask you something," Becky blurted, "do you promise not to laugh?"

Kelly and Ayinde promised. Becky lifted her daughter, unsnapped her overalls, and pulled them up, along with Ava's onesie.

"Okay," she said. She took a deep breath and pointed to a spot just underneath the crease of Ava's armpit. "Is that a third nipple?"

Ayinde raised her eyebrows. Kelly stared down at the baby. "Are you serious?"

"You said you wouldn't laugh!"

Ayinde reached for Ava and looked at her closely. "I think it's just a freckle or a birthmark. Did the doctor say anything when she went for her checkup?"

Becky shook her head dolefully. "No. But really, what are they going to tell you? 'We're sorry, ma'am, your daughter's a freak?' " She sighed. "Maybe they just hoped I wouldn't notice the third nipple."

"It is not a third nipple!" said Kelly.

"Poor Ava," Becky said, refastening Ava's clothes. "Maybe we'll travel all over the country and exhibit her. See the Girl with Three Nipples."

"I don't think people will pay to see just one act," said Ayinde.

"The Girl with Three Nipples and the Incredible Screaming Mother-in-Law," said Becky. "And me, too. I used to be able to juggle a little bit. You want to see something else weird?"

"Is it a second head?" asked Ayinde.

Becky shook her head, reached into her diaper bag, and pulled out a blue-and-white toile-print bib. "I found this in my diaper bag a few days ago."

"Pretty," said Kelly, fingering the bib's silk trim, then flipping it over to inspect the label. "Ooh, Neiman-Marcus. Very nice."

"Yeah," Becky said, "except I don't know where it came from. And this morning, someone put a silver spoon through my mail slot."

"Well," Ayinde said, "you did just have a baby." Julian, who'd been dozing in his receiving blanket, opened his eyes and yawned with his little hands curled into fists.

"I know, but it wasn't wrapped, and there wasn't a card." Becky shrugged. "It could've been from one of the fellows at the hospital. There are six of them who Andrew works with, and I swear, there's one working set of social skills between them. And the one I get stuck talking to at parties is never the one who's got it." She got to her feet and slipped Ava back into her sling. "Are you guys up for a walk in the morning?"

They agreed that, barring naps or breast-feeding emergencies, they'd meet at ten o'clock by the goat statue in Rittenhouse Square Park. When they were gone, Kelly set a dozing Oliver back into his crib, then stretched out on the nursery floor, with her hands by her side so she wouldn't run the risk of encountering her belly flab. She closed her eyes and started imagining how it would be; the things she'd buy and where she'd put them; the couch and the lacquered rattan armoire, the inlaid coffee table, the plasma TV. Everything clean, everything new, everything perfect, the way her baby boy deserved. She didn't open her eyes when she heard Steve walk into the room.

"Hi," said her husband. "Listen, if you want to rest for a while, I'll take care of the baby." Kelly kept her eyes closed, focusing on the vision of her living room that seemed so close she could almost touch it—the Vladimir Kagan high-backed barrel chairs, the Turkish rug she'd seen at Material Culture, the antique maple sideboard, framed and matted professionally shot photographs of their son on the wall . . .

"Kelly?"

She made a sleepy noise and turned onto her side. After a minute, Steve tiptoed out of the nursery, and she and her son were left alone to dream.

AYINDE

"Baby?"

Ayinde opened her left eye. She was lying on her side, with her body curled around Julian's, and Richard's body curled around hers. Julian was fourteen weeks old and, so far, he hadn't spent a single minute in his beautifully appointed crib. During the daytime, when he napped, he was in his stroller or, more likely than not, in his mother's arms. And at night, he slept beside her, nestled next to her breast while she lay beside him, breathing in his scent, tracing his face, the curve of his cheek, or his ear with her fingernail.

"Ayinde?" Richard whispered, a little more loudly.

"Shh," she whispered back. It was two fifteen in the morning. Julian had been sleeping for less than an hour. She shook Richard's hand off her hip. "What?" she whispered.

"Could you just . . ." His voice was apologetic. ". . . Maybe move over a little bit?"

Ayinde shook her head, then realized her husband wouldn't be able to see the gesture in the dark. "There's no room," she whispered. "I don't want the baby to roll off the bed."

She heard Richard stifle a sigh. "Tell me again why he can't sleep in his crib."

Ayinde felt guilt surging through her. There was no earthly reason for the baby not to be in his crib, except for the fact that she didn't think she could stand to have him so far away. "He's happy here," she whispered.

"Yes," Richard said reasonably, "but I'm unhappy here. I'm about to fall out of my own bed."

"Well, can't you just stick it out?" Ayinde asked. "He's just a baby!" She leaned down to look at her darling boy, so sweet in his blue footie pajamas, to touch his lips with her finger and plant a feather-light kiss on his cheek. "He's brand new."

"How long are you planning on keeping him in here with us?" Richard asked.

"I don't know," Ayinde said. *Forever,* she thought dreamily, as she gathered Julian into her arms, nuzzling her baby behind his ear, drinking in the whistle of his exhalations. Lucky for her, Priscilla Prewitt was on the same page as she was concerning sleep. *For thousands of years, the family bed was the order of the day,* she wrote. *And when you think about it, it's still what makes the most sense. Where is Baby going to feel the safest and most secure? What's most convenient for the breast-feeding mom?* (In Priscilla Prewitt's world, Ayinde quickly learned, every mom was a breast-feeding mom. Formula was acceptable "only in the event of a true emergency, and by true emergency I don't mean you're bored or you're busy or you just want a break; I mean you're in the hospital or somebody's dyin'.")

Richard sighed.

"Maybe we could get a bigger bed," Ayinde offered.

"I had this one custom made," Richard said. And she wasn't imagining it. He sounded impatient. "Look, Ayinde, babies sleep in cribs. It's what they do! You and I both slept in cribs, and we turned out fine."

"Yes, we slept in cribs," she whispered back. "And my mother drank and took diet pills and snorted God knows what when she was pregnant with me, and your mother . . ." Ayinde shut her mouth, knowing that she'd wandered into the briar patch. Richard hardly ever talked about his mother, who'd been sixteen when she'd had him, with no husband or even a steady boyfriend in sight, and God only knew what she'd indulged in when she was expecting. Family legend was that Doris Towne hadn't even known she was pregnant, that she'd mistaken labor pains for indigestion brought on by bad fried clams, and wound up giving birth to Richard in the hospital parking lot in the backseat of one of her girlfriend's cars. Ayinde cleared her throat and reached for her husband's hand. "We know better now. That's all. And there are lots of studies about the benefits of shared sleep."

"Shared sleep?" Richard scoffed. "Nobody's sharing any sleep with me. I'm afraid to roll over because I'll roll on the baby; I'm afraid to clear my throat because I'll wake him up . . ."

"I'm sorry," Ayinde said. Richard reached for her, pulling her bottom against his crotch.

"Come here," he said. His fingertips grazed her breasts.

"Ouch!"

"Sorry," he said, jerking his hands and his body away.

"Oh, Richard, that hurts!" Tears sprang to her eyes. Ayinde was committed to breast-feeding, even though some of the other players' wives had taken her aside to whisper that it would ruin her figure. She didn't care about her figure, but she wished someone had told her how painful it would be; how her breasts alternated between feeling as floopy as half-filled water balloons and as swollen and painful as if they were made of hot glass. Her nipples felt as if some ill-tempered animal had been chewing at them while she slept. And Julian didn't have teeth. How would she survive once he got them? She'd have to figure it out. The American Academy of Pediatrics recommended breast-feeding for the first year, and Priscilla Prewitt, big surprise, said there was no reason to stop then and that it was "better for Dumpling and better for Mom" to keep nursing "right up 'til nursery school if you can!"

"I'm sorry," he said again, sounding both apologetic and indignant. After a moment's silence, he rolled over and sighed. "Is it supposed to be this hard?"

"What? Breast-feeding?"

"No," he said sadly. "Everything." There was a rustle of the sheets, cool air against her legs, and then Richard was unfolding himself from the bed. "I'm gonna go sleep down the hall," he said. He bent down and kissed his wife's forehead; the dry, chaste kiss that a grown-up uncle gives a sixteen-year-old niece. "Good night." He bent down toward Julian.

"Don't wake him up!" Ayinde whispered, more sharply than she'd meant to. *Please,* she thought, curving her body even more closely against her son's. *Please just leave and let us sleep.*

"Don't worry." He brushed one thick fingertip against the baby's cheek, then shut the door with barely a click. Ayinde pulled the covers up to her chin, resting her own cheek against Julian's curls.

August

BECKY

"Okay," Becky said, yelling into the telephone to make herself heard over Ava's wails. "What kind of cry would you say this is?"

"What kind of cry?" Andrew repeated. Becky tilted the phone so that he'd be able to hear every nuance of Ava's screams. It was five in the morning; her baby was four weeks old, and her husband was in the hospital, called away at midnight to tend to the various internal injuries of six teenagers who'd decided it would be fun to get lit up on apricot brandy and drive into a tollbooth. "I don't know. What's it sound like to you?"

She tucked the baby under her arm, anchored the telephone under her chin, and thumbed through the T. Berry Brazelton guide to newborns that had become their less-than-reliable road map to figuring out Ava. "Is it a shrill, rising cry or a low, rhythmic cry?"

"Let me listen for a minute."

Becky rolled her eyes and rocked the baby in her arms. For the past two days, in an attempt to improve Ava's mood and sleeping habits, she'd been giving her an all-natural colic remedy called gripe water. It was made with caraway and dill, and while it hadn't helped much with the crying, it had given Ava a scent pleasantly reminiscent of a fresh loaf of rye bread.

"I give up," Andrew said.

"So what should I do now?"

"Is she wet?"

Becky sniffed Ava's diaper, a move she would have never believed herself capable of a few short weeks ago. The baby was looking less than lovely. Her elastic-bottomed sleep sack, pink and printed with bees and flowers, was rucked up underneath her armpits, and her face flared with the whiteheads and juicy pustules of a case of baby acne so bad that Becky had to sit on her hands to keep herself from slapping a pore strip on Ava's nose. After four weeks, the baby was still completely bald, and although Becky would never have admitted it to anyone, she thought that much of the time Ava looked like the world's smallest angry old man. Especially when she was crying. "No. Not wet."

"Is she hungry?"

"I nursed her half an hour ago."

"Oh, yeah," Andrew said. *Oh, yeah, indeed,* thought Becky. Nursing Ava had turned out to be a million times more complicated than she'd thought it would be. She had overactive letdown, which meant that the instant the baby got near her breasts, it was like a spigot going off. Which meant that she had to wear nipple shields—little bits of silicone that looked like tiny see-through sombreros and had a nasty habit of falling to the floor just as she was getting Ava into nursing position—so that her daughter wouldn't choke to death on her dinner.

"Try the bouncy seat," said Andrew.

"Tried it," Becky said. "Nothing doing."

"Maybe you could sing to her?"

Becky took a deep breath and looked down at her daughter. "Love," she sang. "Exciting and new. Come aboard. We're expecting you . . ."

Ava wailed even louder.

"Facts of Life?" Becky offered. The baby drew in a breath and paused, silent, with her mouth wide open. Becky knew what was coming next—Ava Rae's Nuclear Scream of Death. Patent Pending.

"I'm sorry, honey," Andrew said in her ear, as Ava unfurled her shriek. "I'm sorry I can't be there to help."

Becky struggled with the screaming baby and the telephone. "Why does God hate me?" she said to no one in particular. She hugged Ava against her and rocked her back and forth. Ava had been crying for the past thirty minutes, with no sign of stopping. *Can't you help me?* she seemed to be asking with each wail. *Can't anyone help me, please?* Becky was starting to feel desperate. She wished her mother was still there. Edith Rothstein had somehow managed to survive not one baby but two. Maybe she had some kind of secret formula, a magic lullabye she'd invented when she wasn't occupied picking specks of invisible lint off the couches. But Edith had to get back to Florida and to her job. She had packed up and departed after a week during which she'd rocked the baby, changed the baby, washed and folded every piece of clothing the baby owned, and wiped down every single item in Becky's kitchen, up to and including the four ramekins buried in the back of her cabinet. It was too early to call her; too early to call her friends on the chance that their babies, unlike Ava, were asleep.

"Maybe I'll take her outside," she said.

"At five in the morning?"

"Just on the front step," Becky said. "I don't know, maybe a change of scenery will work."

"Take the phone," said Andrew.

"Got it," said Becky. They said good-bye. She wrapped Ava, who was still screaming, in a receiving blanket, pulled Andrew's bathrobe around her shoulders, shoved her feet into the nearest shoes she could find (from the way the left one pinched and the right one gaped, she deduced she'd gotten one of her prepregnancy shoes and one of her husband's sneakers), twisted her hair into a bun, and clomped down the stairs.

"Taking the night air, taking the night air," she sang as she opened the front door. A woman—the same one she'd seen in the park and in the coffee shop, with the streaky blond hair and the long blue coat—was sitting on the front step across the street, underneath a streetlamp, staring at Becky's front door.

"Oh, hi!" said Becky, somewhat startled.

The woman jumped to her feet and started walking rapidly east, toward the park, her hair swinging against the back of the coat, a giant pink bag bouncing against her shoulders.

"Hey!" Becky called. She crossed the sidewalk, turning sideways to squeeze between two SUVs, and then she was out on the street, with her curiosity overriding her fear. The woman didn't feel dangerous. Although, Becky thought, maybe extreme sleep deprivation meant that her instincts weren't what they should be.

"Hey, wait!" Becky yelled. The woman in the blue coat kept moving toward Eighteenth Street, head down, feet moving faster. Becky picked up the pace, closing the distance between them. "Please slow down!" she called. "Please" was, as her mother had always told her, the magic word. The woman stopped in her tracks, hunching her shoulders with her back to Becky, as if she were afraid she was going to get hit.

"What are you doing here?" Becky called from behind her, squinting through the darkness and holding her daughter tight against her chest. With her free hand, she reached for the bathrobe pocket, feeling the comforting weight of the telephone.

The woman turned to face her. Becky saw that she was beautiful . . . and that she was crying. She had on the long blue down coat Becky had seen before, dirty pink shoes, blue jeans peeking out from underneath the jacket, long hair that was blond at the ends and dark at the crown. She looked to be about Becky's age—early thirties, give or take. *Hollywood tragedy,* Becky thought, and then she stepped forward without trying to figure out why those words had popped into her head.

"I'm sorry," the woman said, looking desperately unhappy. "I'm sorry."

Becky settled Ava—who, miraculously, had stopped crying and now appeared to be watching the proceedings with a degree of interest—against her shoulder.

"What were you doing in front of my house?" Becky asked. She wondered if maybe the woman was homeless. That would make a certain kind of sense. Homeless people were a fact of life in Philadelphia. There was a woman who'd pretty much adopted the Dumpster behind Mas. Becky and Sarah would leave lunch on the back step for her every afternoon. She tried to think of what she had in her kitchen.

Apples, leftover bread, and tomato salad . . . "Are you hungry?" Becky asked.

"Am I hungry?" the woman repeated. She appeared to be considering the question as she looked down at her shoes. "No, thank you," she said politely. "I'm all right."

"Well, how about some tea, then?" Becky asked. *This is so bizarre,* she thought. *Maybe I am dreaming. Maybe the baby finally stopped crying and I fell asleep* . . . The woman, meanwhile, was edging toward her, stepping sideways, balanced lightly on the balls of her feet, ready to run if Becky pulled her phone out of the bathrobe pocket and called the cops. Becky looked at the big pink bag over her shoulders and finally figured out what it was. A diaper bag.

The woman looked up at Becky. "I heard your baby crying," she said.

Becky looked at the woman. She had wide-set eyes, a full, pink mouth, high cheekbones, a heart-shaped face with a pointy chin that should have been too sharp for her face, but on screen . . .

"Hey," she said. "Hey, I know you! You were in that movie about the cheerleaders."

The woman shook her head. "Nope. Sorry. That was Kirsten Dunst."

"But you were in something."

The woman reached out with one fingertip and almost touched Ava's bare foot. "She's so beautiful," she said. "You must be so happy."

"Happy. Yeah, well, when she sleeps . . ." Becky's voice trailed off. Lia Frederick. That was her name. Lia Frederick. And her married name was Lia Lane. Which Becky had no reason to know except that she was a devotee of *Entertainment Weekly* and *People* and the nightly tabloid TV shows on which Lia Frederick was a regular. Lia Frederick had played half a dozen small roles in big-budget shoot-'em-ups, and she'd played a nuclear scientist with a rare blood disease and a stalker ex-husband in a movie on Lifetime that Becky had seen twice in the past four weeks when she'd been stuck inside with her brand-new squalling baby.

Lia reached into the diaper bag and pulled out a burp cloth, a fancy one in a blue-and-white print that matched the bib Becky had found. "Here," she said and tried to put it in Becky's hand. "This is for you."

So this was where the little baby gifts had been coming from, Becky thought. This was who'd slipped the spoon through her mail slot and who'd put the rattle in her bag and left a pacifier at Mas.

"Here," said Lia, trying to put it in the pocket of Becky's bathrobe. "Please, take it. I don't need it anymore."

Becky searched her memory. *Hollywood tragedy,* she thought again, and then she had it. Some normally bubbly anchorbabe, face arranged into an unfamiliar somber expression. *Our condolences go out to Sam and Lia Lane, whose ten-week-old son Caleb died last week.* "Oh my God."

"Please," said Lia, looking desperate and sad as she pushed the little bib at Becky. "I'm sorry. I'm sorry I scared you. I'm sorry I was in front of your house; I couldn't sleep so I went for a walk, and I was just resting for a minute when I heard the baby start to cry. Please. Please just take it. Please."

Becky put the cloth in her bathrobe pocket, and she took Lia by the hand. "Come with me," she said.

Ten minutes later, Lia was sitting at her table, still looking as if she might bolt, and Becky was sitting in the rocking chair she'd installed in the corner of the kitchen. Ava, it turned out, had been hungry after all, and she was nursing contentedly while whapping at the side of Becky's breast with one tiny fist and looking like an angry old man who was now trying to get his change back from a broken vending machine. *Twix bar! Twix bar! Goddamnit, I wanted a Twix bar!* Becky smiled, burped the baby, and set her into her Moses basket on the kitchen table. "Scrambled eggs. I'm going to make scrambled eggs," she said, before Lia could answer.

Becky cracked four eggs one-handed into a bowl and reached for her sea salt, her pepper mill, and her whisk. "Whenever my brother and I got sick, my mother used to make us scrambled eggs. I have no idea why, but, well . . ."

"I'm not sick, though," Lia said with a tiny smile. She took a long breath and let it out slowly. "I used to live here, you know. I mean, not here, here—not downtown—but in Philadelphia. In the Great Northeast."

Becky put a chunk of butter in the pan and flicked on the heat. "Tea?" she asked. When Lia nodded, she put the kettle on to boil. "So you came back home, after . . ." Her voice trailed off.

"After," Lia said. She looked ruefully at her diaper bag. "I got on the plane with this bag. I wasn't even thinking. I had all this stuff, this baby stuff, and then I saw you in April."

"Did I look pregnant?" Becky blurted, then shook her head at herself. Here she was, with incontrovertible evidence of her condition, and she was still playing Pregnant or Just Fat?

"Yeah," Lia said. "And I just thought . . . oh, I don't know. I don't know what I was thinking. I guess I kind of lost my mind."

"I can understand that," Becky said. She poured the eggs into the pan and turned down the heat. "I mean, I can imagine . . . well, I can't imagine, really. It's the worst thing I can think of." She tilted the pan, stirred the eggs, and popped two crumpets into the toaster.

"I watched you for a while," Lia said. "You and your two friends. But I don't know their names." She smiled. "I didn't even know Ava's name. You never call her Ava, you know? She's the baby of a thousand names. Tiny Toes, Grumbelina, Princess Plumberbutt . . ."

"I think we were having diaper issues that day," Becky said. "Anyhow, the blond woman is Kelly and her baby's Oliver. She keeps flow charts, and her big recreational activity is returning things. She's basically the Meg Ryan of Babies R Us, but she's really nice. The black woman's Ayinde and her baby's Julian. Her husband's on the Sixers, and she lives in this mansion in Gladwyne. I'm not sure I would have gotten to know either one of them, before." She shrugged. "Babies make strange bedfellows."

Ava stirred in her basket, raising one clenched fist above her head. "The baby power salute," Becky said.

"Caleb used to do that," Lia said. "That was my baby's name. Caleb." She seemed about to say more, then she closed her mouth and stared down at Ava.

"Where's your husband?" Becky asked, struggling to come up with his name. "Sam, right?"

Lia shook her head. "Back in Los Angeles. I kind of just left. I wanted to tell him . . . it wasn't his fault, but . . ." She shook her head again. "I just couldn't stay," she said softly.

Becky turned off the flame and reached for plates and napkins. Ava started flailing her arms. "Can you hold her?" Becky asked.

"Oh," Lia said. "I, I don't think . . ."

"She doesn't bite," Becky said from the stove. "And even if she did, it would probably be okay, as she is still in the situation of having no teeth."

Lia smiled. She shrugged off her coat, bent down, and lifted Ava into her arms. She settled the baby against her a little awkwardly and rocked her back and forth as she rocked across the kitchen, singing in a voice that was high and sweet and silvery.

> "Bye and bye, bye and bye,
> the moon is half a lemon pie.
> The mice who stole the other half
> have scattered star-crumbs in the sky.
> Bye and bye,
> bye and bye,
> my darling baby, don't you cry.
> The moon is still above the hill.
> The soft clouds gather in the sky."

Becky held her breath. Ava reached up with one wandering hand and tangled her fingers in Lia's hair.

KELLY

"How was your doctor's appointment?" Steve asked, with his right hand on her knee.

Kelly took a deep breath and tried to wake up. She had known this question would be coming, and she knew that in spite of how it sounded it had nothing to do with Steve's concern for her health. *How was your doctor's appointment,* loosely translated, meant *Can we have sex?*

"It was fine," she said slowly, knowing what would come next. Knowing and not wanting it one bit.

The truth was, she was cleared for takeoff. "You're fine," Dr. Mendlow had said, still buried practically wrist-deep in what she amusingly used to think of as her private parts. That was before she gave birth in a teaching hospital and wound up pushing in full view of a parade of residents, interns, medical students, and, she could have sworn, a junior high school field trip, although Steve insisted that she'd hallucinated that part. "Whenever you're ready, you can start having intercourse." Kelly would have laughed longer than thirty seconds, but she knew the doctor was busy, and she had to get back home as fast as she could because Oliver would need to nurse again. That, and she couldn't think of a polite way to say that she'd never wanted to have sex less in her entire life and that the spectacle of her shorts-clad, couch-bound husband, who kept telling her that he was taking a much-needed mental health break before starting his job search in earnest, wasn't doing much for her libido.

There was also the matter of the couch. She'd come back from walking Lemon and Oliver one afternoon to find a giant orange-and-brown-plaid three-seater squatting in the middle of her formerly vacant living room. She'd closed her eyes, certain that when she opened them again the ugliest couch in the history of furniture would have vanished. But no. The couch was still there.

"Steve?"

Her husband, still wearing the boxer shorts he'd slept in, wandered into the room.

"What is this?"

"Oh," he said, looking at the couch as if he, too, was seeing it for the first time. "The Conovans were throwing it out, and I told them we'd take it."

"But . . ." She struggled to find the right words. "But it's hideous!"

"It's a couch," he said. "It's something to sit on." He flopped down defiantly. Kelly winced at the sour smell of mildew and eau de old people that wafted out of the cushions. The thing smelled as if someone had died on top of it. And then stayed awhile. And it looked . . . God, she thought and swallowed hard. It looked close enough to the couch she'd had in her house growing up to be its evil twin.

"Steve. Please. It's awful."

"I like it," he said. And that was that. The couch had stayed.

Dr. Mendlow looked at Kelly as she wiped her eyes with the hem of the pink paper-towel gown. "Why don't you step into my office?" he said. He looked as boyish as ever in his customary blue scrubs and white coat, but she saw a tie peeking out from underneath his collar. She wondered where he was going and whether he'd be bringing his wife.

"No," she said, still snorting a little, "no, really, I'm fine. Just a little exhausted." Which was such an understatement that it set her off on another gale of laughter. She'd fed Oliver at 11:00 at night, at 1:30 in the morning, at 3 A.M., at 5 A.M., and literally had been forced to drag her nipple out of his mouth so that she could make her 8:30 appointment.

"My office," he said, washing his hands. Kelly wiped herself off, pulled on her panties, her sweatpants, and her T-shirt (stained with spit-up on both shoulders, she noticed, but what could she do?), and arranged herself in one of Dr. Mendlow's leather chairs.

"Listen," he said, sitting behind his desk five minutes later, jolting Kelly out of the light doze she'd fallen into, "whatever you want to tell your husband, I'll back you up."

Her jaw must have dropped. "You want to tell him I said nothing but holding hands until six months, you go right ahead."

"I . . . really?"

"You're breast-feeding?"

Kelly nodded.

"Then you're not sleeping much. And you're adjusting to what's probably the biggest change in your life. Sex probably isn't very high on your list right now."

"My husband," Kelly said and then stopped. The truth was that the six weeks after Oliver was born felt like a vacation. "Nothing in the vagina," Dr. Mendlow had said. "No intercourse, no tampons, no douching," he told them. "You can have oral sex," he said. Kelly thought Steve was going to vault over her hospital bed and hug him, until he continued, "That means you can sit around and talk about all the sex you aren't having." Steve's face fell. "Come see me in six weeks, and we'll see where you are." Then the doctor had whacked Steve lightly on the forearm with Oliver's medical chart and headed out the door.

But now her reprieve was over, and Steve's hand was inching up her thigh. "Can we?" he asked. Kelly ran through her options. There weren't many. She could tell him no and just postpone the inevitable, or she could tell him yes, bite the bullet, and hope for a fast conclusion.

"Is the baby sleeping?" she whispered. Steve peered down to the foot of the bed, where Oliver reposed, snug in his Pack-n-Play (after his first night at home, Kelly had quickly figured out that the gorgeous, perfect little nursery was going to remain unused as long as the baby was waking up three or four times a night). Steve nodded, smacked his lips, and dove.

He started by kissing her neck, gentle nibbles up and down. Umm. She closed her eyes and tried not to yawn as he pressed against her. He was kissing her collarbones . . . pushing up her nightgown . . . shaking her shoulders.

"Wha? Huh?" She blinked.

"Did you fall asleep?"

"No!" she said. Had she? Probably. Kelly pinched herself hard on the thigh and vowed that the least she could do would be to stay awake for the entirety of this encounter. She owed her husband that much.

"Where were we?" she asked. She kissed his earlobe and nibbled at his chest. He moaned, and circled her breasts with his hand, rubbing at the nipples with his thumbs.

"Whoa!"

"What?" She couldn't have fallen asleep again, she thought. It wasn't possible.

He raised his hands in front of her face, shaking them, with a look of such disgust that she expected to see blood dripping from his fingertips. Instead she saw a few innocuous white drops. Milk.

"Honey, it's no big deal."

He shook his head, still looking pale and disconcerted, and resumed his efforts. Off went the nightgown. Off went the granny panties, stained the color of faded ketchup at the crotch (she hoped he wouldn't notice in the flickering blue light of the baby monitor). In went the KY jelly he'd subtly placed on the nightstand after they'd finished dinner. On went the condom. Ribbed for her pleasure, said the box. Hah.

"Ow!"

"Sorry," he panted. *Ouch.* What on earth was going on down

there? Had the twelve-year-old resident who'd sewn up her epi-siotomy accidentally revirginized her? Kelly shut her eyes and tried to relax.

"Oh, God," he breathed in her ear. "Oh, God, Kelly, you feel so good."

"Mmm," she moaned back, thinking that she didn't feel good at all. Her belly was still loose and flabby; she felt as if there was a half-deflated inner tube around her midsection, and its skin looked as if someone had dipped a rake in red paint and stroked it up and down. She knew the stretch marks would fade, but for the time being, she couldn't stand to look at them. Steve, however, didn't seem to mind.

"What do you want?" he gasped and grabbed her ankle, pulling her right leg up toward his shoulder. Kelly bit back a yelp and tossed her head in pain that she hoped he would mistake for passion. "What do you want me to do?"

And instead of some ribald response, some variant of *Do it to me harder,* which would be her typical prepregnancy answer, his question set off an echo in her head, courtesy of one of the books she'd been reading to Oliver before he'd fallen asleep. *Mister Brown can moo, can you?*

"Kelly?"

Oh, the wonderful sounds Mr. Brown can do. Mr. Brown can moo like a cow . . .

"Moo!" she said.

Steve stopped moving long enough to stare at her. "What?"

"I mean, mmmm," she moaned. Louder this time. *Goddamn Dr. Seuss is ruining my sex life.*

"Kelly?"

Boom, boom, boom, Mr. Brown is a wonder . . .

"Kell?"

Boom, boom, boom, Mr. Brown makes thunder! "Oh, God!" she said. Generic, but acceptable. At least it didn't rhyme.

She clutched Steve's shoulders as his breathing sped up. *Thank you, God,* she thought, as he gasped, and Oliver started to cry.

"Argh!" sighed her husband.

"Wah!" cried her baby.

Cow goes moo, sheep goes baa, went her head, which had evidently abandoned Dr. Seuss and moved on to the board books of Sandra Boynton. *I am never going to sleep again, ever,* Kelly thought, rolling out from beneath her husband and lifting her baby into her arms.

AYINDE

Ayinde smoothed her jacket over the mushy area where her waist had once been and tried not to fidget as the news director looked at her tape. "Good stuff, good stuff," he murmured, as a televised Ayinde talked onscreen about house fires and car crashes, bond issues and benefits rodeos, and the real-time Ayinde realized with a sinking feeling that she'd forgotten to stick breast pads in her bra before she'd left the house. Then again, Paul Davis, the WCAU news director, hadn't given her much notice. Her agent had sent her tapes to the station— to this one and to every other shop in town, up to and including the second public station, which was located in the middle of a neighborhood in Roxborough she knew Richard would never let her drive to alone—months earlier, when Richard had been traded. But that had been months ago, and she hadn't gotten so much as a nibble until the night before when Davis himself had called to ask whether she had a minute to stop by the station that morning. It was going to be a crazy day, Ayinde realized—once she was done she'd have to turn around, go home, pick up the baby, and drive all the way to New York to meet her mother—but if she got a job offer, it would have been worth it.

Paul Davis—fiftyish, white, handsome in a tweedy, goateed way—clicked the set into silence and looked down at the résumé on his desk.

"Yale, huh? And a master's from Columbia."

"Don't hold it against me," said Ayinde, and they both laughed.

"West Virginia for ten months . . ."

"Which was about eight months too long," said Ayinde. More laughter. She let herself relax a bit as she pulled her jacket tightly across her chest.

"Six years in Fort Worth."

"I started out doing general assignment work and features, and, as you'll see, I was promoted to weekend editor, then to anchor of the five o'clock news, which had a twelve percent rise in ratings the first year I was there."

"Very nice, very nice," he said, scribbling something on the résumé. "Look, Ayinde. I'm going to be honest with you."

She smiled at him. He'd said her name right on the first try, which had to count for something.

"You've clearly got the skills to succeed in this market. You've got the look—well, I don't need to tell you that."

She nodded again, her heart rising. "In Texas they had to test-market my hair a few times to get it right . . ."

"Your hair's not the issue," Paul Davis said. "Your husband is."

"My husband," Ayinde repeated.

"You're intelligent. You're warm. You're smart but not conde-scending." Paul Davis looked at the screen again, where Ayinde's face was frozen, lips parted, eyes half-shut. "You're sexy but not in an ob-vious way. I'm just afraid that you're not going to work as an anchor in this market. Nobody's going to tune in to see you read the news."

"They're not?"

Davis shook his head. "They're going to tune in to see what kind of woman Richard Towne married. They'll tune in to see what you're wearing, and what your ring looks like, and how you're doing your hair. I'm just not sure they'd buy you as the person telling them about the school strikes and the car crashes."

Ayinde straightened her back. "I think my skills as a reporter speak for themselves. You can ask any of my colleagues in Fort Worth. Getting married to Richard Towne didn't knock fifty points off of my IQ. I'm professional, I'm committed, I work hard, I'm a team player, and I don't ask for special treatment."

Paul Davis nodded. The look on his face was not unsympathetic. "I'm sure all of that's true," he said. "And I'm sorry for the position your marriage has placed you in. But I don't think there's a news director or GM in town who'd tell you any different. Your status—your celebrity—would be a distraction to the viewer."

"But I'm not a celebrity! Richard's the celebrity!"

Paul Davis hit Eject and handed Ayinde's tape back to her. "Let me tell you what we're thinking," he said.

Fifteen minutes later, Ayinde wandered back into the parking lot, feeling as if she'd walked through a tornado. *Special correspondent,* she thought, unlocking her car and tossing her tape into the passenger's seat, where it bounced off the caramel-colored leather and landed on the floor. Yale and Columbia and ten months in West Virginia lugging her own camera around; four years as a reporter and two years anchoring in a top-twenty-five market and they wanted her to be a quote-unquote special correspondent? To go to Sixers games and—how had that loathsome Paul Davis put it—"use your access to give viewers a behind-the-scenes look at the team"? Profiles of the players. Profiles of the coaches. Profiles of the dancers, for heaven's sake!

She yanked the seat belt in place. "Bullshit," she whispered, putting the car in gear, heading home to pick up Julian, who was napping in his bassinet with the maid standing guard at his nursery door. "Richard called," Clara told her. Ayinde sighed, loaded the baby and all of his gear into the car, and called his cell phone. Richard had watched her get dressed that morning, advising her on the plum-colored suit versus the gray one. He'd kissed her and told her she was going to knock them dead.

"How'd it go?" he asked eagerly.

"Not very well," she said. She pulled out onto the Schuylkill Expressway. It was probably for the best, she thought, as Richard made indignant noises and asked whether Ayinde wanted to switch agents and if there was anything he could do to help. Maybe this was nothing short of God's way of telling her that she was supposed to be a stay-at-home mom, that her time was best spent with her baby.

"Where is my darling boy?" Lolo trilled two hours later—more for the benefit of the assembled photographers, makeup artists, hair stylists, and assistants than for Julian, Ayinde was sure.

"Right here," Ayinde sang back, setting down the car seat and overstuffed diaper bag on a table lined with platters of bagels and pastries, and turning sideways so that her mother could see Julian in his *Baby Success!*–mandated front carrier. The photo shoot was being held in a Chelsea studio, a long, rectangular room with a concrete floor and rolls of black paper hanging from the ceiling to serve as backdrops. There was a screened-off area for makeup and wardrobe, and techno music blasted from the speakers suspended from the ceiling. "This is my daughter," Lolo said grandly. "She's an anchorwoman."

"Not anymore," said Ayinde, thinking of how she'd spent her morning. "I'm just a mom now." She looked down at Julian, thinking that the words didn't sound any better out loud than they had in her head on her way out of the WCAU parking lot. She'd have to work on that. *Darlin', you are now the proud owner of the best job title there is!* was what *Baby Success!* said.

Her mother looked at Ayinde. "Back down to fighting weight?" she asked.

"More or less," Ayinde said, determined not to let Lolo bait her. She'd agreed to this photo shoot for *More* magazine—"Generations of Beauty," they were calling it, or something equally ridiculous—as a favor to Lolo and over her husband's objections. "I don't want our baby in a magazine," Richard said, and Ayinde had agreed. Normally, she hated the way the media turned wives and children of athletes into disposable accessories, whose only job was to look good cheering in the stands. But Lolo had insisted. More than that, really. Lolo had begged. "You know how hard it is to find work at my age," she said. "And if this goes well, Estée Lauder might consider me for their Face Over Fifty." By Ayinde's calculations, Lolo was actually eligible to be a Face Over Sixty, but the less said about that, the better. There was a part of her, a part she usually managed to keep hidden and quiet, that was still desperate for Lolo's approval, or even Lolo's acknowledgment, and it was that part that had agreed to bring Julian into Manhattan for a family portrait, while the more rational part of her mind was insisting, *No way.*

"What a sweetie!" Three girls dressed all in black, with low-waisted pants and cruelly pointed shoes, were clustered around Julian. Ayinde hugged her son, taking a deep, restorative sniff of his hair and warm skin.

Lolo's voice rose above the girls' coos. She'd already been to makeup. Her coppery skin and green-gold eyes looked as lovely as ever, her lips ripe and her cheekbones high and fine and her eyelashes thick and black as a bird's wings. "They're ready for you, darling." She looked at the baby, as if he'd turned into a large tumor attached to her daughter's chest. "Where's the nanny?"

Ayinde took another deep breath of Julian's scent and nuzzled his curls before answering. "Mother, I don't have a nanny."

"Well, the sitter, then."

"No sitter."

Lolo lifted an immaculately groomed eyebrow. "Au pair?" she asked, without much hope in her voice.

Ayinde forced herself to smile. "Just me." She let one of the pointy-toed girls lead her to a chair. Julian sat in her lap while a man named Corey applied blush and bronzer and coppery eyeshadow to her face and arranged her braids in a twist at the nape of her neck. "Breast-feeding," she said ruefully, after the third couture gown failed to fit over her chest. She could hear her mother sucking her teeth from ten yards away. A champion tooth-sucker was Lolo Mbezi. It made up for the fact that she never frowned. "Wrinkles, darling," she'd say, whenever she caught her daughter doing it.

"Hmm," said the wardrobe man, helping her slip into a Vera Wang dress, a shimmering column of pale-gray silk. It didn't zip, but he told her not to worry. "A few pins, a little tape, and we'll be just fine." He looked over Ayinde's head. "Oh, my," he breathed. Ayinde turned and saw her mother, resplendent in ruched and pleated chiffon in a dozen shades of pink ranging from blush to magenta. A strapless bodice showed off her shoulders and collarbone, her flawless mocha skin, and the length of her slim neck. The skirt was a bell-shaped explosion of layers, puffing out gracefully as Lolo glided across the room, hands holding up the skirt, elbows bent just so. Ayinde suddenly felt as drab as a pigeon. "And here's the star of the show!"

A pointy-toed girl handed Julian to his mother. The baby was completely naked. "You know, I'm not sure this is a good idea . . ." Ayinde said.

"Oh, don't be such a worrier!" said Lolo, beaming at her daughter and grandson. "Darling, you look lovely. Very chic. Spin round." Ayinde did. "Marvelous. Bobby, you're a miracle worker . . . with the pinning, you can hardly tell about the zip."

Ayinde closed her eyes and prayed for patience as the photographer arranged them—Lolo standing on an eighteen-inch platform, Ayinde sitting below her, trying to suck in her stomach, the naked baby in her lap.

"Wonderful, Lolo, that's amazing with the eyes," called the photographer. Ayinde tried not to yawn as Julian squirmed. "Chin up, Ayinde . . . no, not quite so high . . . tilt your head a little, nope, nope, other way . . ."

Ayinde was starting to sweat underneath the lights, and the muscles in her legs and back were trembling with the effort of sitting perfectly erect. Julian wriggled harder, batting at the dangling silver earrings they'd given her.

"I think we need to take a break," she managed to say before her son successfully snagged one of the earrings and yanked at it hard. "I need to feed him . . ."

"One of the girls can give him his bottle," said Lolo, shaking out the pleats of her gown.

"He doesn't get bottles, Mother. I'm breast-feeding . . ." *Just like that book you sent told me to,* Ayinde thought.

"It's okay, we're almost done. Eyes this way, please. Perfect. Ayinde, let's try the baby held on your other side."

Ayinde shifted Julian from her right arm to her left. The baby responded by peeing down the front of her gown. Lolo sucked in a horrified breath. Ayinde closed her eyes to a faint patter of giggles from the pointy-toed girls.

"And thank you, ladies, that'll be all," said the photographer.

"I don't understand why you don't have a nanny," Lolo said. It was an hour later, and they were eating a late lunch of chicken paillard in a back booth at La Goulue. Ayinde had changed into leggings and one of Richard's jerseys. Lolo was impeccable as ever in a Donna Karan pantsuit. And she was eating, while Ayinde's plate sat untouched in front of her because Julian was nursing and both of her hands were occupied, much to her mother's unstated but evident irritation.

"I want to raise him myself," Ayinde said.

"Well, of course, that's wonderful, but don't you want to have a life of your own?"

"This is my life right now."

"All that expensive education . . . ," her mother murmured.

"What do you want from me?" Ayinde snapped. Lolo blinked at her coolly.

"I want what every mother wants for her children, darling. I want you to be happy."

"No, really," said Ayinde. "I know you want something, and I can't figure out what. You send me this book . . ." Julian started whimpering. She switched him from her right breast to her left as discreetly as she could manage it, smoothed his hair, and continued. "You send me this book that says that the purest bond in the world is the bond between a mother and a child, that says that I should breast-feed until he's three and let him sleep in my bed, and that leaving him with a nanny is tantamount to child abuse . . ."

Lolo looked puzzled. "The book says that?"

Ayinde bit back hysterical laughter. Trust Lolo to not even have skimmed the back cover of *Baby Success!*, which had become Ayinde's scripture. "Look. Raising Julian is my job right now. This is my work. And it's important work."

"Well, of course it is," said Lolo, sounding nonplussed. "But it doesn't mean you should never have any time for yourself."

"Like when it's convenient for you," Ayinde said.

Lolo tilted her head. "Oh, darling, let's not fight." She speared a piece of chicken on her fork and held it out. "Here. Open up."

"Mother . . ."

"You must be hungry. Here." She waved the forkful of chicken near Ayinde's lips, and Ayinde reluctantly opened her mouth. "There you are!" her mother said. She gave a pleased smile and sat back, her face glowing underneath her makeup. (Ayinde had washed hers off the instant she could, knowing that makeup in combination with Julian's wandering hands would spell ruin for her clothes.) "All I'm saying," Lolo continued, "is that there's nothing wrong with having some help. You have to give yourself a rest every once in a while, even if you're the best mother in the world."

"Well, maybe I should just enroll him in boarding school," Ayinde said, trying to keep her tone light, remembering the way Lolo had flitted in and out of her childhood. She'd breeze into Ayinde's room a half hour past bedtime, getting ready to leave the apartment for dinner and dancing, to bestow a kiss on her daughter's forehead, usually waking her up in the process. "Sleep well!" she'd trill, her heels tap-tapping on the marble foyer. Then there'd be the sound of her father's heavier tread and the door clicking quietly shut behind them. At breakfast time, her parents' bedroom door would be shut, the living-room blinds drawn. Serena would pour out milk and cereal, and Ayinde would eat quietly, set her dishes in the sink, and creep out the door.

"Well, I think you're doing a wonderful job," Lolo said. "But you shouldn't take it all so seriously! It's diapers and strollers, not rocket science!"

Ayinde looked down at Julian cradled in her arms, his cheeks working as he nursed, her perfect, beautiful boy, his mouth the exact shape of Richard's, his long fingers just like her own, and her mother's. "I just want to do it right."

"You do the best you can. That's what every mother does. Here," said Lolo, waving another forkful of chicken at her daughter. Ayinde sighed helplessly before she opened her mouth and let her mother feed her lunch.

September

BECKY

"Hahyahhh."

Becky winced, holding the phone away from her ear. It was seven o'clock in the morning, and she'd finally gotten Ava back to sleep after a six A.M. feeding and ensuing fret-fest. It seemed that seven A.M. was a perfectly acceptable time for a phone call in the Mimi-verse. "Hi, Mimi," she said, not making any effort to sound more awake than she was.

"Did I wake you?"

"A little bit," said Becky, with an ostentatious yawn, hoping Mimi would take the hint.

Fat chance. "Oh, then, I'll be quick. Let me speak to my son."

Becky rolled over and poked Andrew with the phone. "Your mother," she whispered.

Andrew took the phone and turned onto his side. "Hi, Mom." There was silence. A disturbing amount of silence. "All right," said Andrew. "Okay. For how long?" More silence. "No, no, of course not! Calm down, Mom. It's fine. No. No! Well, if I did, I apologize. Right. No. Of course you do! Okay. We'll see you later, then. Love you, too. Good-bye."

He clicked the End button, rolled onto his back, and closed his eyes.

"What?" asked Becky.

Andrew said nothing.

"You better tell me, or I'm just going to assume the worst," said Becky.

More silence.

"She got married again?" Becky guessed.

Andrew pulled the pillow over his face so that his words were muffled, but Becky could still make them out. "There's something wrong with the air-conditioning in her house."

Becky swallowed hard. "It isn't even that hot out anymore."

"It'll just be for a few days," said Andrew.

Becky said nothing. Andrew reached for her.

"Becky, she is . . ."

"Your mother. I know. It's been pointed out to me. But we don't even have a guest room! Wouldn't she be more comfortable in a hotel?"

"She doesn't want to spend the money." He burrowed his face deeper into the pillow. "She's still complaining about what our wedding cost her."

"Oh, please," muttered Becky, as she got out of bed. "Remember, I wasn't the one who wanted three hundred guests. Nor was I the one who commissioned ice sculptures of the bride and groom. How long will Madame be staying?"

He got to his feet without meeting her eyes. "She wasn't exactly sure."

"And where's she going to sleep?"

Andrew said nothing.

"Oh, come on!" said Becky. "Andrew, she can't expect us to give up our bedroom! Ava sleeps up here, and I have to be near Ava . . ." She stuck her head into Ava's nook to make sure the baby was still asleep, then made her way down the stairs. Andrew pulled on his bathrobe and followed her. "This is bullshit," Becky said, measuring out the coffee.

Andrew pressed his lips together. Whether he was getting angry or just trying not to smile, Becky wasn't sure. She set a mug in front of him. "Let me ask you something. And I want you to tell me the truth. Have you ever said no to her? Ever? Just flat-out, 'No, Mom, I'm sorry. That isn't going to happen'?"

Her husband stared into his cup. Becky felt her heart sink. She'd long suspected that this was the case—that Mimi ordered, Mimi demanded, Mimi threw fits until she got what she wanted, and Andrew, patient, kindhearted Andrew, was powerless in the face of her tantrums.

"It won't be for too long," he said. "And it means a lot to me."

"Fine, fine," Becky said with sigh. An hour later, when Andrew had left for the hospital and Ava had been fed and changed and dressed, the doorbell rang, and there was Mimi on the top step, dressed in skintight jeans, a denim jacket, and a halter top, with four pieces of matching Vuitton luggage, trunk included, lined up on the sidewalk behind her.

"Hahhh, darlin'!" she said, sweeping into the house and snatching twelve pounds of startled bald baby out of her mother's arms, leaving Becky to drag her luggage up the stairs. "Ooh, is that coffee I smell?" She trit-trotted down to the kitchen, where Becky poured her a cup. Mimi sipped. "Decaf?" she demanded.

Becky considered lying. "No," she said. "I could make some . . ."

"Oh, honey, would you mind?" Mimi's eyes never stopped moving, bouncing from the kitchen walls to the floor to the sink to the stove to the shelves of cookbooks. Looking for what, Becky wasn't sure. Possibly evidence that the kitchen was doubling as a meth lab, which would prove that Becky was every bit the low-life trailer-park queen that Mimi seemed to think she was. "I don't suppose you'd have something for me to nibble on?" Mimi asked innocently. She rejected white bread ("I'm staying away from processed flour"), whole-wheat bread ("doesn't agree with me"), and cantaloupe ("just never liked it"). "How about I keep an ear out for my granddaughter, and you could run to the market?"

Sure, Becky thought. *How about I chop my hand off and feed it to the Rottweiler across the street?* And would it kill Mimi to call Ava by her name? Possibly. Ever since the morning in the hospital, Mimi hadn't called the baby anything except "my granddaughter" and "my grand-baby." Never once had the name *Ava* crossed her lips. Maybe she was still clinging to the hope that they'd decide to call her Anna after all.

Throw her a bone, Becky told herself. "Okay. I'll just jump in the shower first . . ."

Mimi waved her away. "We'll be fine! Just leave me with a bottle!"

And so it begins. "We're breast-feeding, remember?"

Mimi's eyes widened. "Still?"

"Still," Becky said.

"And the doctors think that's okay?"

"It's the best thing for her," Becky said. "The breast milk helps her immune system develop, and—"

"Oh, that's what they say now," Mimi interrupted. "In my day, formula was best. And it certainly seems to have worked with Andrew!" She cut her eyes at Becky. "And I read that breast-fed babies can have problems." She dropped her voice to a whisper. "With obesity." A merry little giggle. "Of course, my Andrew's never had a problem there, either!"

I'm going to kill her, Becky thought with a kind of distant wonder. *I really am.* "I'll be down in ten minutes," she said, hurrying up the stairs, where she stood under the shower with her eyes closed, singing "I Will Survive" until the hot water ran out.

Down in the kitchen, Mimi was at the table with the baby in her arms and a half-eaten blueberry muffin in front of her. "She had almost the whole muffin top!" she said.

"What?" Becky said.

"She's a good eater," Mimi announced. "Just like her daddy was."

"Mimi! She can't have food yet!"

"What's that?"

Becky's hands balled into fists. "She can't have food until she's four months old at the very earliest, and then just rice cereal!"

Mimi waved her hands. "Oh, I'm sure this is all right. I was feeding Andrew when he was just six weeks old, and he turned out just fine! It's just a fad," she prattled. "Feeding babies, not feeding babies, breast milk, formula . . . although maybe you'd know more than I do. Being in food services and all."

Becky pressed her lips together, picked up the telephone, locked herself in the bathroom, and called her pediatrician's office, where the very nice nurse practitioner on call told her that while a blueberry muffin might upset Ava's tummy, it probably wouldn't do any lasting damage. Then she walked back down the stairs.

"Hi, sweetie," she said to Ava. Ava looked at her from Mimi's lap, then tilted her head back. The skin underneath her chin unfolded like the pleats of an accordion. Mimi stared down in disgust.

"Oh, MAH!"

Becky peered over her mother-in-law's shoulder at the rings of grayish-brownish schmutz in her daughter's neck.

"Aren't you giving her baths?" Mimi demanded.

"Of course we are, I just . . ." Becky shook her head. She had tried to wash underneath Ava's chin, but the baby didn't make it easy. Half the time, she wasn't sure that Ava even had a neck. Her head seemed to fit squarely between her shoulders, and who knew what was collecting in there? Well, she did now. She grabbed a wipe from her diaper bag and handed it to Mimi.

"I honestly don't know where that stuff came from."

Mimi made a huffing noise.

"I'll go to the store now," Becky said. "Please don't feed her anything while I'm gone."

Another huffing noise. Becky grabbed her keys and headed out the door. When she returned, carrying two bags of Mimi-mandated groceries, her mother-in-law and baby were settled on the living-room couch. "Who's my princess? Who is? Who is?" Ava blinked and gave a gummy grin. Becky stifled a sigh and went down to the kitchen. Five minutes later, Mimi's voice pulled her back up the stairs.

"And now we'll do our crunches! One! Two! One! Two! Got to look good! So all the boys will call!"

Excuse me? Becky hurried into the living room. "Mimi. Listen. I'm sure you don't mean any harm, but Andrew and I don't want Ava to grow up worrying about her body."

Mimi stared at her as if Becky had just gotten out of her spaceship for her first visit to Planet Earth. "What are you talking about?"

"Crunches. Boys. We don't want Ava to have to worry about any of that." Becky attempted a smile. "At least not until her first birthday."

Mimi's lips curled into a scowl. "And Andrew agrees with this . . . this . . ." Becky could almost hear her saying *nonsense.* "Philosophy?" she concluded.

"One hundred percent," Becky said and headed for the door before she succumbed to the temptation to tear Ava out of her grandmother's arms and boot Mimi and her designer luggage back onto the street.

The backyard was Becky's favorite part of the house. It was barely the size of a pool table, but she'd filled every inch with planters and pots in which she grew impatiens, petunias, and gerbera daisies, and the herbs and vegetables she used in the kitchen—tomatoes and cucumbers, mint and basil, sage and two kinds of parsley, even a watermelon vine. She hummed to herself as she tended to the plants, pinching off dead leaves, pulling up weeds.

Five minutes later, Mimi, with Ava in her arms, invaded her sanctuary. "Let's see what Mommy's doing!" she caroled, swooping Ava into the air and then down toward the ground in a manner practically guaranteed to induce spit-up within five minutes. *At least that'll get rid of the muffin,* Becky thought.

"We're watering plants!" she said, squirting water in the air, watching as Ava tried to grab for it and frowned as the spray slipped through her fingers. Then she raised her dripping hand and tried to stick her thumb in her mouth. Mimi slapped it away.

"No, no thumb-sucking! Bad girl!"

Becky turned off the hose and began to pray. *God grant me the serenity to accept the things I cannot change, courage to change the things I can, and the patience not to strangle my mother-in-law, chop her into little pieces, and dump them down a sewer.* "Actually, Mimi, thumb-sucking's okay."

"Excuse me? That can't be right. She'll ruin her teeth!"

"That's an old wives' tale," Becky said, feeling guilty for enjoying the way Mimi flinched at the word *old*.

Mimi's lips pursed. "If you're sure," she finally said.

"Yes, I'm positive," Becky said, holding out her arms. "Let me change her."

Becky carried Ava upstairs. Her diaper was dry, but she figured that one more minute of Mimi would cause her to do something she didn't want her daughter to see.

She refastened Ava's onesie, sank onto the rocker, and pulled up her shirt. Ava latched on eagerly. It had been less than an hour since she'd last eaten, but she seemed ravenous. Or maybe she just wanted some soothing. Mimi could put anyone on edge; why would a newborn be exempt?

Becky closed her eyes, rocking slowly, drifting into a doze as her baby nursed in her arms.

"Are you nursing?"

Becky lurched forward, jerked out of her nap. Ava's eyes opened wide. She pulled away from the breast and started to cry.

"We were," Becky said pointedly, pulling her shirt down, patting Ava's back until she belched.

"Oh, excuse YOU!" Mimi said.

Becky wiped the baby's pursed pink lips with the corner of a receiving blanket and snuggled Ava against her. *It's the best feeling in the world,* her own mother had said the first time she'd held Ava. Becky hadn't believed her then—she'd been so scared of hurting the baby, who seemed like such a fragile, floppy thing that she'd start sweating before every diaper change. But now that Ava was holding her head up better, looking around and noticing things, now that she'd gotten over her baby acne, Becky loved to hold her. Ava's skin was soft and sweet-smelling, her long-lashed gray-blue eyes and full pink lips the most beautiful things she'd ever seen. She could spend hours kissing the back of Ava's neck or nuzzling her head, still completely bald, the skin so pale that she could trace the veins that ran beneath it.

"We're going to take a little nap," Becky told Mimi. Without waiting for a response, she settled the baby into her crib and went to the bedroom, where she slipped off her shoes, pulled down the shades, and gazed at the skylight she and Andrew had installed during the halcyon days before Mimi had moved to town. She called Andrew's office, then his cell phone, and when he didn't answer either one, she did the thing she'd long resisted, the thing she despised Mimi for doing with such regularity. She paged him. *Yes, please, could you ask him to call home? No, no, not an emergency. It's just his wife.* Thirty seconds later, the phone was ringing. Becky lunged for it. She was fast, but Mimi was faster.

"Andrew! What a nice surprise!"

"Hi, Mom. Is Becky there?"

"I imagine," Mimi purred. "But don't you have a minute to talk to your old mom?"

Becky hung up the phone and balled her hands into fists. *God grant me the serenity to accept the things I cannot change . . .* Ten minutes later, Mimi was screaming up the stairs. "BeckEEEE! My son wants to talk to you!"

The baby started crying. "Tell him I'll call him back," Becky called, and went into Ava's room, where she spent ten minutes easing the baby back into sleep. When she called Andrew's cell phone again, he picked it up.

"How are things?"

"Not good," Becky said.

"Is she being impossible?"

"Well, let's see. So far she's fed our daughter a blueberry muffin, woken her up from her nap, slapped her thumb out of her mouth . . ."

"What?" Andrew sounded properly incredulous. Becky relaxed into the pillows. *He's on our side,* she reminded herself. *On my side. Not on hers.*

"She gave stomach crunch instructions so that the boys will call . . ."

"She said this to the baby?"

"Well, she didn't say it to me, now, did she?"

Andrew sighed. "Do you want me to come home? I've got . . ." Becky could hear him reaching for his schedule. "A hip replacement I'm scrubbing in on at three, but I could have Mira cover for me."

"No, no, you go replace your hip. I just needed to vent."

"I'm sorry, Becky," Andrew said. "Hang in there."

"I'll try," she said and hung up the phone. Back in the nursery, Ava was on her side, and Mimi was leaning over the crib in a replay of the first morning in the hospital, black hair dangling, nose roughly six inches from Ava's. Becky couldn't see her expression, but Mimi's pose made her think about cats who'd suck the breath out of sleeping babies. Her hands formed fists; her short nails dug into the flesh of her palms. *Get away,* she wanted to scream. *Get away from my baby, you crazy lady!*

"She's so perfect," Mimi whispered.

Becky's hands unclenched. Horrible as she was, Mimi at least had it right about Ava. "She is, isn't she?" she whispered back.

"I always wanted a little girl," Mimi said. "But I had two miscarriages after Andrew, and the doctors said no more for me."

Becky felt her heart melt. Ava's eyelids fluttered as she slept. "Her eyelashes are so pale," Mimi whispered. "I wonder how she'd look with a little mascara?"

Becky felt her heart reconstitute itself. "We should let her sleep," she said. She held the door pointedly open until Mimi gave up and followed her back down the stairs.

Back in the living room, Becky deployed her secret weapon. "Would you like some wine?"

Mimi did. Two glasses of Chablis and a remote-control handoff later, Becky was free. "We're just going for a little walk!" she called, knowing as she carried the stroller down the stairs that Mimi wouldn't join them. Her four-inch heels tended to preclude recreational strolling. Becky decided to see if Lia was home. Lia would help her keep things in perspective. Not even Screaming Mimi was so bad when you considered what Lia had lost.

It had been a week since she'd met Lia, and they'd had coffee once, in the park, conducting the kind of getting-to-know-you conversation that felt a little like a bad blind date until Becky had got Lia going on her secret addiction—Hollywood gossip. After only an hour with Lia, Becky knew more about who was gay in Hollywood and who was merely a Scientologist than she'd learned after decades of *Access: Hollywood.* She'd asked about movie stars; Lia had asked about her friends and their babies. A fair trade, Becky thought.

She pushed Ava around the perimeter of the park, into the lobby of Lia's building, and had the doorman call up to her apartment. "Want to go for a walk?" she asked. Lia walked out of the elevator wearing a pair of Gloria Vanderbilt jeans that had to date back to her high school days. Her two-toned hair was tucked tidily underneath a Phillies baseball cap, but she looked uncomfortable as she darted a glance at the stroller, then looked quickly away. Becky reached for her cell phone. "Let's see if Kelly and Ayinde are around." She paused, feeling uncomfortable. "That is . . . I mean . . ." She looked at Lia, biting her lip. "Do you not want to be around other babies?"

"No, it's okay," Lia said. She shoved her hands in her pockets and gave a small shrug. "The world is full of babies. It doesn't bother me much. Not if the babies belong to people I know. It's just that sometimes . . ." She touched Ava's cheek. "Sometimes it's hard," she said softly. "When it feels like everyone except you has a baby that isn't going to die."

Becky swallowed hard. "We can just walk around the park," she said. "We can get some coffee."

"No, no." Lia shook her head. "I want to meet your friends."

•   •   •

Half an hour later, Ava was napping in her stroller, and Becky, Ayinde, and Lia were sitting on a horrific orange-and-brown-plaid couch in Kelly's formerly vacant living room. Oliver, who appeared to have doubled in size since his birth, was lying underneath his Gymini, chewing on one drooly fist. And Kelly, dressed in what looked like her old maternity workout wear, was talking on her telephone's headset, keeping one eye on her baby and one on her computer screen.

"Paul, let me make sure I understand," she said. She smiled at Becky and Ayinde, beamed at the babies, and nodded at Lia, who'd whispered her name. "There was a typhoon? And that's why the candles are still in Thailand? Well, what's our contingency plan?" She listened, frowning, tapping a pen against her desk. "So we have no contingency plan. And there's no candle in the entire tristate region that would be acceptable. Right. Yes. Yes, I'll wait." She put her hand over the mouthpiece and made a face. "This is why I don't do weddings," she whispered, as someone—Paul, presumably—started screaming on the other end of the phone. "Paul. Paul. PAUL! Listen to me! We are talking about centerpieces, not the AIDS vaccine. I really don't think a call to the consulate is going to get us anywhere. What I suggest you do is start calling suppliers in New York. I can fax you a list, and I'll put stars next to the best bets. Pick out half a dozen candles in the same color palette. I'll stop over in the morning, and we'll speak to the bride together. Right. Yes. Ten o'clock. Right. Okay, I'll see you then." She hung up the phone and sank onto the floor where she sat cross-legged beside her baby and her sleeping dog.

"Oh my God!" she said, staring up at Lia. "You're famous!"

"Well, not exactly," Lia said with a smile. She pointed to the phone. "That sounded interesting."

"Are you working?" Becky asked.

"Agh. Not exactly," Kelly said. "My former boss had an emergency, and I told her I'd help out. The bride fell in love with these candles from Thailand. Unfortunately, three hundred of them are stuck in a boat in a harbor because of a typhoon. They won't be here in time for her wedding."

"So what happens now?" Becky asked.

"Bad things," said Kelly. She lifted Oliver into her arms, rolled onto her back, and started pressing the baby over her head. Oliver's pudgy legs dangled, and his hands opened and closed as his mother pumped him up and down. "The noble duke of York," Kelly chanted. "He had ten thousand men! He marched them up to the top of the hill and he marched them down again!"

Ayinde looked at her watch. "Can I borrow your crib?" she asked.

"Go . . . right . . . ahead," Kelly said between presses.

"He doesn't even look sleepy!" Becky said.

Ayinde shrugged apologetically, scooped Julian into her arms, and carried him to the nursery.

"Don't mind her; she's joined the cult," Becky whispered to Lia. "Priscilla Prewitt. Ever heard of her? She's Ayinde's guru. Ayinde's got Julian's entire life scheduled in five-minute increments, and . . ." She looked at Kelly. "Are you exercising?" she demanded, as Kelly continued to loft Oliver into the air.

"Triceps," Kelly grunted and rested the baby on her chest.

"Well, you're a better woman than I am," Becky said. Lemon snuffled at Oliver's head. Ayinde tiptoed back into the room.

"If I don't lose ten pounds, I won't be able to fit into any of my clothes," Kelly said. "And I can't afford a new wardrobe."

Steve, in shorts and a T-shirt and bare feet, walked into the living room. "Can I get any of you ladies some lunch?"

Kelly was so lucky, Becky thought. She'd kill to have Andrew home for a day. He could bring her lunch, and take the baby for a walk, and help her get through the five baskets of laundry that seemed to have accumulated overnight. While Steve took salad orders, Kelly set Oliver back underneath his Gymini and started walking on the treadmill with five-pound weights in each hand.

"Boy, you're lucky to have Steve here," Becky said. "How's his job search going?"

Something moved across Kelly's face at the word *lucky,* but the expression was gone before Becky had a chance to figure out what it might have meant. "Just fine!" she said, hitting the acceleration key until she was jogging. "Lots . . . of . . . exciting . . . opportunities!"

Becky set Ava on her back on the floor and stretched luxuriously. "Can I just stay here for the rest of my life?" she asked.

"Is your mother-in-law . . . really . . . that . . . bad?" Kelly asked, as she picked up her pace.

"Heh. Really that bad doesn't even begin to cover it," Becky said.

"So what did she do?" asked Lia.

"You wouldn't believe me if I told you."

"Try us," Ayinde said.

"Okay," said Becky. She cleared her throat. "She wore a wedding dress to my wedding, and she sang 'The Greatest Love of All' during the reception."

Lia and Ayinde looked at each other. "Is she a singer?" Lia asked carefully.

Becky rolled over and nuzzled Ava's belly. "No, she is not!"

"So she was singing it to both of you?"

"Nope. Just to Andrew."

"And the wedding dress . . ." Lia's voice trailed off.

"Actual wedding dress," Becky confirmed. "Versace, I believe. Tight. White. Low cut. Slit high. Lots of sixty-four-year-old cleavage, which, let me assure you, was not what I wanted to see as I was coming down the aisle. I think she recycled it from one of her previous engagements."

"I . . . know . . . you're . . . kidding . . . ," Kelly panted. Her ponytail bobbed with each stride.

Becky sat up, rummaged in her diaper bag, and pulled out her wallet. "Here," she said, showing her friends a photograph. "In case you were wondering, I keep this for evidence, not sentimental attachment."

Kelly slowed down and then hopped off the treadmill, and she and Lia and Ayinde bent their heads over the picture. "Oh," said Lia. "Oh, my. Are those hoopskirts?"

"They are indeed," Becky said. "Although Mimi was in couture, my entire bridal party, such as it was, wore hoopskirts as a tribute to her Southern heritage. With matching mint-green parasols." She giggled. "We looked like a lost tribe of Mummers."

"I can't believe you're laughing about this!" Kelly said, lifting her shirt to wipe her forehead.

Becky shrugged. "Believe you me, I didn't think it was funny at the time," she said. "But it was four years ago. And you have to admit that it is slightly hysterical."

Ayinde stared at the picture. "I think that is the worst wedding story I've ever heard." Ava rolled onto her side and passed gas noisily.

"Good one!" Becky said, patting her daughter's bottom. "Do you know, I was so shocked the first time she farted in the hospital that I called the nurse to make sure that was, you know, a done thing?" She shook her head. "Just one more little fact the baby books don't tell you about."

Kelly smiled brightly. "In my house, we call them tushie bubbles!"

Becky rolled her eyes. "In my house, we call them baby farts!" She leaned back against the brown-and-orange couch. "I just want to know how someone turns out the way Mimi did? I mean, the husbands! And the drama!"

Lia shrugged and fiddled with her baseball cap. Becky wondered whether it had been a mistake to bring her, whether three little babies, two of them boys, might have been more than Lia wanted to see. "Don't ask me. I can't figure out my own mother, let alone someone else's," Lia said, "but I think . . ."

"Tell me," Becky said. "Please. Help me out."

"People like Mimi," Lia said. "I think they're like that because they've been hurt."

"I'd like to hurt her," Becky muttered.

Lia shook her head. "Come on," she said. "Violence is never the solution. And Becky . . ."

" . . . She is his mother," Kelly and Ayinde recited. Lia laughed, as Becky's cell phone rang.

"Honey?" Andrew said. "You're not home."

"And they say men aren't perceptive. We went for a walk," Becky said.

"You left my mom by herself?"

Becky's heart sank. "Well, you know Mimi. She's not much of a walker. And the baby needed some fresh air."

"Two hours' worth?"

Had it been that long? "Look, Andrew, your mother's a grown woman . . ."

"She wants to spend time with her granddaughter," Andrew said. "And Becky . . ."

"Yeah, yeah, right, I know," she said. "Don't even say it. I'm leaving right now." She hung up the phone and picked up her baby. "Hey, were you supposed to fax something to the candle man?" she asked.

Kelly clapped her hand over her mouth. "Oh my God," she muttered and hurried to her computer.

"No rest for the wicked," Becky said, wheeling her daughter out of the door.

LIA

"Get job" had been on my list, right after "get money" and "find place to live." But when Becky offered me a job at Mas on our way home from Kelly's, I turned her down.

"I'm not a good cook," I said, as we walked side by side, pushing Ava down Walnut Street. "I used to get Zone meals delivered. I never even turned on the stove in my old apartment."

"Not to worry. It isn't rocket science." Becky pushed the stroller into a coffee shop and bent down to readjust Ava's pink sunhat, which coordinated nicely with her pink overalls and pink-and-white-striped shirt. "Do you know somebody stopped me on the street yesterday and said, 'What a cute little boy'?"

"Weren't you supposed to go home?" I asked.

"And I am!" Becky said cheerfully. "Just as soon as I have some coffee. And nurse the baby. For half an hour or so. Anyhow," she continued, settling herself at a table in the back. "The job I'm talking about is about as entry level as you can get. Washing spinach, peeling shrimp . . ." She shot me a sideways glance. "You're not, like, a vegan or something? No philosophical objections to cooking living things?"

I shook my head, remembering how my mother had asked a version of the same thing.

"It's not much money," Becky said. "And it's not glamorous. And you're going to be on your feet a lot . . ."

"I'm used to that," I said. "Acting's a lot of standing around."

"Ah, but it's standing around Brad Pitt, as opposed to Dash the dishwasher," Becky said. She looked over her left shoulder, then her right, like a spy in a movie. "Cover me," she muttered out of the corner of her mouth. She draped a pashmina the size of a picnic blanket over her shoulder, picked up the baby, and lifted her blouse. "Okay, can you see anything?"

I looked down. I could see Becky, and the blanket, and a vaguely Ava-shaped lump underneath. "You're fine."

"Good," said Becky. "Watch her, though. She's a sneak. Yesterday she pulled the blanket off, and I wound up with my boob hanging out at the Cosi on Lombard Street. Not good. So, you gonna take the job?"

"If you're serious. And if you don't mind that I've never done this before."

She shook her head. "Believe me, everyone will be delighted to have you. Especially Dash the dishwasher."

"Thank you," I said.

"De nada," she answered. She burped the baby, wiped her mouth, spent ten minutes in the bathroom changing Ava's diaper, and finally, regretfully, and very slowly, I noticed, headed toward her house.

I started work the next afternoon, standing in front of the sink in Mas's steamy kitchen, and peeling carrots until my fingers were numb. "Are you doing okay?" Becky asked, over and over. "Are you doing all right? Do you want to take a break? Do you need anything to drink?"

"I'm fine," I told her. I straightened my back and flexed my fingers. It was hard work physically, boring and repetitive, but everyone in the kitchen was nice (especially, as Becky had predicted, Dash the dishwasher, who I guessed was about nineteen and was also, if I had to bet, a fan of some of my early direct-to-video work). It was the first time since I'd left Los Angeles that my mind was truly quiet. And

Sarah was going to show me how to make vinaigrette. Things were okay.

The following Monday, my first day off, I unfolded the list I'd made for myself. Every single thing had been checked off except for the last item. "Get help." I couldn't put it off forever, I thought, bundling my hair underneath my baseball cap again and walking into the twilight.

I'd come across the listing for Parents Together in the same newspaper that had led me to my apartment, but three minutes into the meeting, I didn't think the group would turn out as well as my sublet had.

What I wanted—what I needed—was to know when I'd stop waking every morning in pain, when I'd stop in the trench of a sorrow so deep and wide that I didn't think I'd even make my way out of it. How long would this hurt? When will Caleb not be the first thing I think of in the morning, the last thing I think of at night? When will I stop seeing his face every time I close my eyes? I didn't think I'd find my answers in Pennsylvania Hospital, in the fifth-floor conference room with its faint smell of illness and institutional cleanser. The walls were beige, the carpet was gray, and the long table was surrounded by people sipping from Styrofoam cups of coffee and tea.

The woman who spoke first was named Merrill. She had frizzy shoulder-length brown hair, horn-rimmed glasses too big for her face, a gold wedding band too big for her finger. Merrill was forty. Her son's name was Daniel. He'd had leukemia. He'd been eleven when he died. That had been four years ago, but Merrill still sounded as bewildered and brokenhearted as if she'd gotten the news that morning. *It's still happening,* I thought, gripping the table as the ground seemed to lurch underneath me.

"And those Wish Foundation people just keep jerking us around," Merrill said. There was a blossom of shredded tissue in her hand, and every few minutes she'd raise it to her cheek, but she looked too angry to cry. "It's make a wish, right, not make a politically correct wish, not make a wish some do-gooder who's never had a sick kid thinks is okay, and if Danny's last wish was to meet Jessa Blake, who are they to say they don't work with porn stars?"

The man sitting beside her—her husband, I guessed—laid a tentative hand on her shoulder. Merrill shrugged it off. "He only knew her from the music videos. It wasn't like we let him watch porn," she said. "And then they wanted to send him Adam Sandler, and I know for a fact it was only because Adam Sandler was already coming to Philadelphia to see some girl in renal failure . . ."

I tried to disguise my snort of laughter as a cough gone wrong. The leader looked at me. "Would you like to go next?"

"Oh, no," I said, shaking my head.

"Well, why don't you tell us your name?"

"I'm Lisa." It popped out just like that, even though I'd been Lia for years. A few months back in Philadelphia and, hey, presto, I was Lisa again. "But really, I don't want to talk. I'm not even sure I belong here."

"Jessa was his favorite," Merrill said again. She lifted the tissue blossom to her cheek. "His favorite."

"Okay, Merrill. Okay," the leader said gently, as Merrill's husband drew her head onto his shoulder, and she started to cry. Suddenly, I hated Merrill. Her son had been eleven. She'd had eleven years' worth of birthday parties and Christmas presents, skinned knees and soccer games. She'd gotten to watch him crawl and walk and run and ride a bike. Maybe she'd even gotten to deliver the birds and the bees speech, sitting across from him at a kitchen table, saying, *There are things you need to know.* What had I gotten? Sleepless nights, dirty diapers, basket after basket of laundry. A shrieking bundle of bad temper who'd never even smiled.

I squeezed my eyes shut as I felt the world slide sideways and balled up my fists on my stupid Gloria Vanderbilt jeans. "Lisa?" asked the leader.

I shook my head. I was thinking of Becky nursing her daughter under the pink blanket. When Caleb nursed, his hands were never still. They would move from my breast to his head, exploring the texture of my skin. They would wave in the air. Sometimes, they would float against my chin or my cheek like leaves.

"Excuse me," I said, hoping my good manners would outweigh the fact that I'd gotten up so fast that my wheeled chair had whacked into the wall.

"Lisa," the leader called. But I didn't slow down until I was out the door, out of the elevator, out of the hospital, leaning against its sun-warmed brick wall, sucking in great gusts of air with my head dangling near my knees. The sky had gotten dark. I had to go somewhere, and Mas seemed as good a place as any.

"Hey!" Becky called, as I pushed through the door. "What are you doing here?"

"I'm . . . I thought I'd . . ." I looked around and remembered that it was Monday; Mas wasn't even open. The dining room was empty, swept clean, with all of the tables empty, except for one that was surrounded with three chairs and covered with appetizers. Ayinde was sitting in front of a plate of empanadas. Kelly's Kate Spade diaper bag was looped around another chair, and Kelly herself was standing in the corner talking into her cell phone headset.

I turned toward the door. "I'm sorry. I got confused, I guess."

"We're having Moms' Night Out," Becky explained. She pulled down another chair and motioned for me to sit.

I shook my head. "No, really, I shouldn't, I . . ."

Becky led me to the chair and handed me a glass. I looked around. "Where are the babies?"

"Ava is with Mimi," she said, "who showed up with a manicure kit and didn't believe me until I called Andrew to confirm that you can't put nail polish on a newborn. Julian's with . . ." She looked at Ayinde.

"Clara," Ayinde said. "She works for Richard and me."

"She's your maid," Becky teased.

"Household helper," Ayinde said. "And she loves the baby."

"Steve's taking care of Oliver," Becky said, pointing her chin toward Kelly, who was still talking into her cell phone.

"Honey, you have to pull his foreskin back gently—don't hurt him!—and then you just use the washcloth a little bit . . . okay, okay, don't panic, it won't fall off." Kelly hung up the phone, shaking her head. "When did I become the world's expert on penis cleaning?" she asked.

"Just be glad you don't have a girl," Becky said. "The first time Andrew had to give Ava a bath, he called me in the middle of the dinner rush to ask how he should—and I quote—'handle the area.' You'd think they'd have covered that in medical school." She looked at Ayinde. "How does Richard do with the baths?"

"Oh, Richard doesn't do baths," she said, sipping from a glass of what looked like sangria. "I'm the only one who does baths."

"In your Priscilla Prewitt–approved tub," Becky said.

"Actually, I take him into the tub with me," Ayinde said. "It's wonderful."

"I used to do that," I said. I ducked my head. Once, Sam had come into the bathroom to take pictures of the two of us in the tub together, and I'd been so self-conscious about my stretch marks that I'd thrown a bottle of shampoo at his head. But it had been wonderful. I remembered cradling Caleb's slippery body, the feel of his wet skin against mine, holding him under his armpits and swirling his legs through the water. What had happened to those pictures?

Becky handed me a napkin. "Are you okay?"

I nodded, blinking rapidly, determined not to cry and ruin their night. "Are you sure there's nothing I can do?" I asked. "I think we're low on chicken stock."

"Don't be silly." She handed me a plate. "What's going on?"

I took a sip of the sangria, feeling it warming my chest and belly. "I went to this group. This grief group. It . . ." Another swallow. "I kind of left abruptly."

"How come?" Kelly asked.

"Because it's just a bunch of sad people sitting around telling their sad stories, and I don't . . . I can't . . ."

Becky sat quietly, looking at me. "Do you think it would help to talk about it? It sounds like an okay idea to me. I mean . . ." She gave a nervous chuckle. "I don't know what it must be like for you, I can't even imagine, but I guess being around people who'd been through the same thing . . ."

"But they hadn't been through the same thing. That's the problem." I took another sip of sangria. And another. "The thing is . . ." I took a deep breath and stared at my hands. "I didn't even want to be pregnant in the first place." I wrapped both hands around my glass and spoke without looking at any of them. "The condom broke. I know how stupid that sounds. It's like the reproductive version of 'the dog ate my homework.' And we weren't married; we weren't even engaged." I remembered Sam's quick indrawn breath, my own gasp once he'd pulled out of me, still half hard, and the condom nowhere to be found. I'd fished it out later with my fingertips, counting the days since my last period, thinking, *This could be trouble.*

I'd been on the Pill before I'd moved to Los Angeles, eighteen years old, with my diploma from George Washington High, where I'd been voted Best Looking and Most Dramatic and Most Likely to Be Famous, and three thousand dollars I'd gotten for selling the ring that I'd inherited. After I started going on look-sees and auditions and noticing that all of the women around me were a little blonder, a little more busty, and fifteen pounds thinner, I stopped taking it, figuring it might help me lose weight.

"You're underweight already," the nurse at Planned Parenthood said while I stuffed my pockets with the free condoms laid out in cut-glass bowls like after-dinner mints.

"Not for this town," I replied. I smiled and told her not to worry, that I didn't even have a steady boyfriend. And I hadn't, not for years. There was just me and a series of roommates in a one-bedroom apartment in Studio City. I took acting classes. I joined an improv troupe. I worked in an office that sold real estate for a little while, and I did telemarketing at night, until, after ten years of plugging away, I met Sam and landed a starring role in a movie on Lifetime, and Sam got his razor commercial, then a six-week guest shot on *Friends*. All of a sudden, we were flush.

And expecting. "It was terrible timing," I told them. "Sam and I had only been dating for eight months. We were both trying so hard to make it, and things were happening for him—for both of us, I guess."

In my third year of being twenty-six, I'd finally gotten to the point where I'd been recognized as myself a few times, instead of being mistaken for some other, more famous actress . . . or simply stared at by a blinking tourist who clearly thought he should have known who I was but didn't. "It was a really good time. Before that, I was doing all of this direct-to-video stuff. Lots of sequels, lots of original cable movies. And then I had all of these possibilities. And I had Sam. I was so happy."

Ayinde twirled her glass in her fingers. "How old were you?" she asked. I looked at her across the table, leaning forward with her arms crossed, and got a glimpse of her in her previous life, using that same professional calm to tell Fort Worth viewers the news. Kelly was biting her lip with her pale-blond hair covering most of her face, and Becky's hands were in constant motion as she poured more sangria and passed around more salsa.

"Twenty-nine," I said. "Of course, according to my agent, I was twenty-six. Out there, there's always someone younger and prettier and probably more talented. It would have been better, career-wise, if we could have waited." Maybe in five years, I thought, after we'd established ourselves; when Sam was old enough to be cast as Concerned but Loving Father in the car-insurance ads, and I could gain my fifteen pounds back and guest-star as Hard-Charging District Attorney Who Used to Be a Babe.

I hadn't counted on Sam's delight when I told him the news, on how easily he took it. "Sure, let's have a baby," he said, lifting me into the air and swinging me around in a way that only made me feel more nauseous. "Let's have a bunch." When I'd talked about losing out on jobs, he'd soothed me, saying it would only be a year, that a baby wasn't a life sentence, that we had money, and we loved each other, and everything would be fine.

I toyed with a tortilla chip, bending my head over the table. Outside the high windows, the street was quiet and the sky was dark and still. The restaurant's pumpkin walls and gold lamps made it glow with mellow light, like the inside of a treasure chest. I was remembering the day we had our ultrasound and learned that we were having a boy, and Sam sang "My Boy Bill" loud enough for everyone in the waiting room to hear. His joy had been infectious; I'd been swept away with him.

Then came the baby. "It was so hard after he was born. I had no idea."

"Hah," said Becky, leaning over to top off our glasses again. "Do you think any of us had any idea? Do you think anyone would ever have a baby if they knew?"

"Amen," Kelly murmured, her hands clasped on the table, her pale lashes resting on her cheeks.

I set the chip down, wondering how things could have been different if I'd had friends out there, other new mothers who were going through the same things I was. But I didn't. "I was all by myself. Sam had to go back to work—he'd gotten cast on *Sex and the City* as a premature ejaculator."

Becky laughed. "I saw that one!" she said.

"He was starting to get famous." I looked down at my body, remembering how awful I'd felt—bloated and sweaty, my hands and feet still swollen, my hair falling out in handfuls. I'd spend all day in the same pair of underwear and T-shirt that I'd slept in because what was the point of getting dressed? Unlike my husband, I didn't have anywhere to go.

The world felt as though it was collapsing in on me, getting smaller and smaller until it was the size of Caleb's room, of his crib. The books said new babies ate every three hours. Caleb ate every half hour. The books promised that new babies slept for something like eighteen hours a day. But Caleb was a catnapper. Ten minutes after he'd closed his eyes, he would be awake again, screaming. It had taken me four weeks to even find time to unpack the suitcase I'd brought to the hospital when he was born. "I felt like I was going crazy. I had these dreams . . ." I drained my glass. "I used to think about just checking in to a really nice hotel with a big, clean room and a big, beautiful bed and ordering room service and reading a book and just being by myself. Even for an afternoon. I felt like I was never going to have any time or get to be by myself again."

"What about Sam?" Becky asked. I looked around the table for the judgment I was sure I'd see there, but all I saw was interest. Kindness. I saw that, too.

"He tried to help, but he was working really long hours." I folded my hands in my lap and told them the story of the laundry, which was also the story of Caleb's last day.

None of us had slept the night before. Caleb started whimpering at midnight, a half hour after I fed him, swaddled him tightly, and set him into his crib. The whimpers became sobs, the sobs became shrieks, and from midnight until 2 A.M. Caleb screamed nonstop, eyes screwed up, face tomato red, a V-shaped vein throbbing in the center of his forehead, pausing only to gather his breath before starting to shriek again. Sam and I tried everything—walking him, rocking him, patting his back, settling him into his stroller and his bouncy seat and his swing. I tried to nurse him. Caleb gasped and screamed and batted at me with his fists. We burped him. We changed him. Nothing worked until finally, inexplicably, the crying fit ended as suddenly as it had started, and Caleb passed out on his back in the center of our bed. He had a pacifier stuck under his chin, but I was too scared to move it.

Sam and I bent over him, blinking owlishly, my husband in boxer shorts and a spit-up-stained T-shirt, with an unprecedented, razor-ad-unfriendly two days' worth of stubble on his square jaw; me in a nightshirt with nothing underneath.

"What happened?" Sam whispered.

"Don't talk," I whispered back and flicked out the light. And the three of us slept together until Caleb woke us at eight o'clock, cooing like a baby in a diaper commercial.

"They always do that," Ayinde said. She patted her lips with a napkin. "It's like they know. They know exactly how much hell they can put you through before they have to give you something—a smile, or a few hours' sleep."

I nodded. "I felt better when I woke up," I told them. "And it was a Saturday, so Sam was going to be home." At 10 A.M., I asked him to fold the laundry. I'd thrown in a load of colored clothing the night before.

"No problem," he said cheerfully. I could hear him whistling as he shaved—he was upstairs in the bathroom, and I was downstairs on the couch with the baby in my arms, looking at the Hollywood sign through the window, trying to figure out exactly how long it had been since I'd been in the car. "I'm just going out for a quick run," he said.

I gritted my teeth and said nothing, while inwardly I was seething. A quick run. I'd kill to be able to leave the house for a quick run, a quick walk, a quick anything.

At 11:15, my husband bounded back into the house, glowing with sweat and good health. He gave me a large, smacking kiss on the cheek and bent to kiss Caleb, who was nursing. "I'm just going to take a shower," he said.

"The laundry," I said, hating the shrewish sound of my voice, hating the way I sounded like my mother, like everyone's mother. "Please, I don't want to nag you, but I can't . . ." And I shrugged, indicating the baby. Indicating everything and wishing I had four extra hands.

"Oh," said Sam, blinking. "Oh, right. Hey, I'm sorry." He headed upstairs. I could hear the door of the dryer open, then slam shut, and I felt myself relax incrementally.

"Folding now!" Sam called.

"Congratulations!" I called back.

A few minutes went by.

"Still folding!" yelled Sam.

I bit my lip and looked down at Caleb, a warm, milky-lipped weight in my arms, already with the same square jaw and dimpled chin as his daddy, hating the mean thoughts that turned in my head. *Like he deserves a trophy for folding a load of laundry.*

"I'd never been so mad at him," I said. This time it was Kelly who laughed and gave a knowing nod.

"Folding!" Sam had called again. I bit my lip even harder, closed my eyes, and counted backward from twenty. *I love my husband,* I reminded myself. I was just tired. We both were. *I love my baby. I love my husband. I love my baby.* I chanted it like a mantra with my eyes squeezed shut.

Twenty minutes later, Sam was back downstairs, his skin still pink from the shower. "I'll be back by three," he said. I nodded without opening my eyes, wondering how I was going to take a shower of my own. The baby would sleep, I thought, even though Caleb had shown no evidence of sleeping so far—just eating and crying and dozing for maybe ten minutes and waking the instant I attempted to set him down and starting to cry again. But he'd have to sleep. Babies couldn't stay awake forever. They just couldn't.

Sam knelt down and held my hands. "Hey," he said. "When I come back, why don't you go out for a while? Get a massage or have a coffee or something."

I shook my head, hearing the shrewish note in my voice again. "I can't, I can't go anywhere. You know I can't. What if he needs to eat?"

He blinked, nonplussed, at the question or the sound of my voice. I wasn't sure which. "Or you could just take a nap."

"A nap," I repeated. *The impossible dream,* I thought.

Sam walked jauntily out the door for a lunch meeting with his agent, a tall, bald guy who called everybody *baby* because, I was convinced, he never bothered to learn actual names. I held the baby close against my sweating chest and dragged myself upstairs to our bedroom.

"He folded the laundry," I told them. My tongue felt thick in my mouth. "All of it. It was all over the bed in little piles, with his wet towel on top."

Ayinde sighed. Becky shook her head. Kelly smoothed her blond hair back from her cheeks and whispered, "Been there, done that."

I had laid myself down on the bed, right on top of Sam's wet towel. It felt like some horrible joke, some *Twilight Zone*–style punchline—*he folded the laundry, but he didn't put it away!* I saw my life flashing before my eyes, the next days, the next weeks, the next eighteen years, an endless blur of nursing and sleeping and walking the floors with a screaming baby in my arms, picking up after Caleb and picking up after Sam, too.

"No," I said out loud. I set Caleb down in the center of the bed, snug between a pile of boxer shorts and one of unsorted socks. I pulled on a nursing bra, panties, two more pads, one of Sam's T-shirts, and a pair of elastic-waist leggings and sat there as Caleb woke up again and started to cry again.

"I was just so tired," I said, lifting my hands, then letting them fall onto the table. I could still remember that edgy, sand-in-your-eyes feeling of never getting enough sleep. I could feel Becky's hand on my shoulder. I remembered the woman—Merrill—in the hospital conference room, shaking her husband's hand away. "I thought if I pushed him around in his stroller he'd fall asleep. We ran into Tracy, our neighbor. She was maybe fifty, and she lived in the apartment down the hall from ours. She did hair and makeup for one of the game shows that taped out in Burbank. I only knew her to say hello to, and once, when Sam was in *People,* she came by to get his autograph."

Most days Tracy and I would just wave to each other as I wheeled my screaming baby past her door. But that day she stopped me. "Why don't you let me look after Caleb for an hour?" she asked. "I've raised three boys of my own. I've got seven grandkids, but they're all east." She looked wistfully down at my screaming son. "I'd be so happy to hold a baby for a little while."

"Then you can have him," I said. I handed him over, watching how easily Tracy settled Caleb into the crook of her arm, how his stiff body softened as he leaned against her, how she was about a hundred times better at this than I was. And then I left.

"I mean, I didn't just hand him over . . ."

"Of course not," Becky murmured, patting my hand. "Of course you'd never do that."

I bowed my head, even though what I wanted to do was lay it down on my folded arms right there on the table and sleep. I told them how I'd programmed my cell phone and Sam's cell phone numbers into Tracy's telephone. I left our pediatrician's phone number, and wipes and diaper rash ointment even though Caleb didn't have diaper rash. I brought over a spare outfit and the Boppy pillow and the Gymini, piling Tracy's patchwork quilt–covered bed with blankets. "Go," she said, laughing, shooing me out the door, with the baby still tucked against her body, looking at me with his big dark-gray eyes.

And I went. I kissed my boy, and I went. I took the elevator down to the parking garage, retrieved my little convertible, and drove down Sunset with the wind in my hair. I went to my oh-so-Hollywood hair salon, where they had a waterfall by the front door, where the shampoo girls would bring you water with lemon or a latte or copies of the latest tabloids with circles around the stars whose hair they styled. I got a manicure and a pedicure, and I will testify before the Lord and all of His angels that it felt wonderful, and when the women brushing polish onto my fingernails looked at my ring and asked if my husband and I had any children, I lied and told her, *No.*

"They say that mothers have a sixth sense about when something's wrong with their baby," I told them, "but I didn't." I started to cry. "There was an earthquake . . ."

"You feel that?" the girl painting my nails had asked, and I shook my head.

"Little earthquake," she told me and bent her head back over my feet. "They happen all the time. I hardly even feel them anymore."

That was the first sign, but I didn't see it. The second one was that the security gate in front of our driveway was wide open, and there were two police cars parked in front of the building. Two police cars and an ambulance. I walked right by it. I only started to hurry when I saw the cluster of men and women in blue uniforms in front of Tracy's door and Tracy herself out in the high-ceilinged hallway, standing at the center of them, wailing. Shrieking. That's when I started to run.

I remember a police officer catching me by the forearms and holding me still. I remember Tracy's face looking as if it had aged a fast twenty years, like a newspaper left out in the sun, and how she wailed an inhuman sound, like an animal being run down in the road. "Oh, God," was what she kept saying. "Oh, God, oh, no, oh GOD."

"Ma'am," said the policeman holding my arms. "Are you the baby's mother?"

I stared at him open-mouthed. "What happened?" I asked. "Where's Caleb?"

The officer nodded over my head, and another officer, a woman, took my other arm. The two of them led me inside to Tracy's living room, where there was a glass-topped coffee table and a cream-colored sectional couch. I remember thinking how strange this was, how I'd never been inside Tracy's place even once before in all the time we'd lived here and how now I'd been inside twice in one day. I remember thinking that I would never own a cream-colored couch in my whole life or at least not during the next few years of it. I remember looking down at my toenails and seeing that they hadn't smudged, even when I'd been running. "Is Caleb okay?" I asked. And that was when the officer who'd been holding one of my arms got up and left and was replaced by a lady officer in her forties, thick-hipped and tanned, who held both of my hands in hers and told me that he wasn't okay and that they weren't entirely sure what had happened but that Caleb had died.

"Died?" My voice was much too loud. Outside, I could still hear Tracy screaming. She'd abandoned words at that point and was just making this horrible keening noise. *Be quiet,* I thought. *Be quiet and let me listen.* "Died?"

"I'm so sorry," said the woman holding my hands.

I don't remember what happened next. I don't remember what I said. I know that I must have asked for the details, asked how, because the nice lady police officer told me, in her gentle, soothing voice, that as best they could guess it had been sudden infant death syndrome, that Caleb hadn't felt anything, that he'd just gone to sleep and stopped breathing. That he had gone to sleep and never woken up.

"There will be an autopsy," she said, and I remember thinking, *Autopsy? But that's for dead people. And my baby can't be dead, he's not even a person yet, he's not even eating real food, he hasn't learned to sit up or hold things, he hasn't even smiled at me . . .*

The nice lady police officer was looking at me and saying something. *A question,* I thought. She'd asked a question, and she was waiting for my answer. "I'm sorry," I said, politely, the way my mother had taught me, when I was still Lisa, when I lived in a ranch house in Northeast Philadelphia. *Manners don't cost anything,* she'd said over and over. *Good manners are free.* "I'm sorry, I didn't hear you."

"Who can we call for you?" she asked.

I gave her my husband's number. Then his name. I watched as her eyes got wider. "I'm so sorry," she said again and patted my forearm. I wondered whether his being sort of famous made her sorrier than she would have been if we were just regular people, if Caleb had been anyone's baby. *I should ask to see him,* I thought. That's what a grieving mother would do. The whole ten weeks of his life I'd frequently felt like I wasn't really a mother but that I was just impersonating one. Now I'd just have to impersonate a grieving mother.

They led me through the Spanish arches, down a tiled hall, past a shelf full of faceless, eyeless mannequins, each with a different wig. There were people crowding the bedroom, EMTs and policemen, but they parted, wordlessly, as I walked past. *Turn back, turn back, thou pretty bride . . .* Caleb lay on the patchwork quilt, in the blue-and-white shirt with the duck in the center and blue sweatpants I'd dressed him in that morning. His eyes were shut, his eyebrows drawn down as if he'd just thought of something sad. His mouth was pursed in a rosebud, and he looked perfect. Perfect and beautiful and peaceful, the way he'd hardly ever looked in his entire ten-week life.

I could feel the air getting heavier as I walked toward him, changing from gas to a liquid, something heavy and cold. My feet wanted to stop, to freeze in place in the middle of Tracy's beige carpet; my eyelids wanted to close. I wanted not to see this, not to be here; I wanted to rewind the clock, start the day over, the week, the month, the year over. I wanted this not to be true.

If I'd been a better mother, I thought. *If I'd wanted him more. If I hadn't been in such a hurry to leave.*

"No," I said softly. "No," I said again, louder, testing it out. I remembered Sam in the OB/GYN's waiting room, his arms around me as I laughed, pleased and embarrassed. *I'll teach him to wrestle! And dive through a wave! When we go in the mornings for our swim! His mother can teach him the way to behave, but she won't make a sissy out o' him. Not him!* Caleb lay there, so still, his face so still. One hand lay on his side, the other rested on his chest. I went to pick him up and hold him, but the police officers told me that I couldn't.

"I remember how long his nails were," I told my friends.

Becky had her face buried in a napkin. Ayinde was wiping her eyes. "I'm sorry," Kelly whispered. "So sorry."

I took another drink, hearing my words slurred together and not caring; thinking finally, finally, I have come to the end. "I'd been meaning to clip them, but my baby book said to do it when he was asleep, and it felt like he was never asleep. He was always waving his arms around, and then . . ."

I straightened my back and tried to compose my face. "And then I came home," I said, without looking up. "And then I came here."

In the silence I could hear each of them breathing. "It wasn't your fault," Becky finally said. "It could have happened even if he'd been sleeping at home. Even if you'd been holding him."

"I know." I took a deep breath. "I know in my head. But here . . ."

I laid my hand on my heart. I couldn't tell them the rest of it; my cell phone ringing and ringing while I was still in the room with Caleb, Sam's voice on the phone, high and tense, saying the police had called and was I all right? Was the baby all right? What was going on? I opened my mouth to tell him, but no words would come out. Not that night, not for twenty-four hours, not until the funeral when I'd stood there like a mannequin while people hugged me and squeezed my hands and said words that all sounded like radio static.

Later, after a few cups of strong café con leche and some almond cookies, I walked slowly down Walnut Street. It was after eleven, but the night had gotten noisy again. The sidewalks were crowded with people: older couples on their way home from fancy dinners; girls in tight jeans and high-heeled, pointy shoes. The Internet café was still open, all six computers unoccupied. I slipped behind one of the screens and typed my husband's name and his e-mail address. *I'm here,* I wrote. I thought that I would write, "I'm okay," but it wasn't true yet, so I added only one more line: *I'm home.*

October

KELLY

Lucky. If Kelly heard the word *lucky* one more time, she decided, she would have to murder someone. Her husband, most likely.

She walked into the apartment and out of her shoes before the door closed behind her. The lamps were off in the living room, but even in the dim light that filtered through the blinds she could make out the mess—a pair of Steve's sneakers underneath the table, one of his shirts balled in a corner on top of last Sunday's newspapers.

"What'd they say?" Steve's voice issued from the darkness. Kelly squinted into the gloom. He was sitting exactly where she'd left him at lunchtime, cross-legged on the floor in front of the laptop on the coffee table. Oliver was nowhere to be found. Napping. Probably. She hoped.

"They said great. I can start next week," she answered. In the bedroom, she shucked off her pantyhose, sighing as her stomach expanded, and threw them on top of the unmade bed. She looked at her skirt and jacket before determining they didn't need to be dry-cleaned, hung them up, and unhooked the underwire bra that had been digging into her for the entire afternoon. Then she pulled on sweats and a T-shirt, pulled her hair into a ponytail, and held her breath as she tiptoed past Oliver's crib, still hardly believing that she'd actually spent the afternoon reinterviewing for the job she hadn't planned on returning to until Oliver was a year old; if she ever went back at all. When she first raised the possibility of working again with Steve, she'd expected him to look at her like she was crazy and say, "Absolutely not!" She thought he'd be indignant, furious, outraged at even the hint that she had to work because he couldn't provide for his family. And she'd thought—dreamed, really—that the outrageous, infuriating notion that she was thinking of going back to work and bringing home a paycheck because he wouldn't—or couldn't—would light a fire underneath him, get him off his butt and off the couch and back into an office in a week's time.

That hadn't happened.

"If that's what you want," he'd said, shrugging, effectively calling her bluff. "You know you don't have to, but if that's what will make you happy, you should do it." *Happy,* she thought. The word pained her just as much as *lucky* did. But whatever hopes she harbored that her boss would be the one to tell her she was crazy to even think about working with a brand-new baby at home had been dashed the instant she'd stepped into the office.

"Oh, hallelujah, thank you God," Elizabeth, her boss at Eventives, said, flinging her arms into the air. Elizabeth was Philadelphia by way of Manhattan, with a boyfriend in New York who took the train down, she'd say, "just enough to keep my life interesting." She had a glossy black bob and a slick of hot-pink lipstick, and Kelly had never seen her in shoes that weren't high heels or carrying a purse that didn't match them. "We've been swamped. Drowning. Desperate! We've got more holiday parties than we can handle. We'd love to have you back."

"Great!" Kelly said, trying her hardest to sound enthusiastic.

"Thing is," said Elizabeth, perching on one hip on the corner of her desk, crossing her showy legs, dangling a lime-green snakeskin pump from her toe. "I have to really be able to depend on you. No poopy diaper emergencies, no my-baby-got-sick sick days."

"Fine!" Kelly had said. Elizabeth had never had children. She liked to joke that she could barely commit to a coffee mug, so how could she even think of babies? Elizabeth had no idea what new motherhood was like. Kelly wasn't sure she knew, either, although experience was showing her that there wasn't much sleep involved, and your house was always a mess.

"I'll start next week," Kelly said, as she walked back into the living room, picking up the piles of newspapers and magazines on the floor, Steve's sneakers and jacket, and his copy of *What Color Is Your Parachute?* "We'll have to hire someone."

"For what?"

"To take care of the baby."

"What, I'm not good enough?" Steve asked. His tone was light, but he didn't sound like he was kidding. Kelly felt her stomach clench.

"Of course you're good enough, but you need to devote your time to your job search!" *And I didn't marry Mr. Mom,* she thought. "I'll start making calls tomorrow."

"Fine, fine," said Steve, as Kelly restacked the magazines, threw the newspapers into the recycling bin, and started washing what appeared to be her husband's lunch dishes.

Elizabeth had agreed to let Kelly work from home—"as long as you're getting your work done, not watching *Barney* or whatever it is the kids are into these days"—so at least she wouldn't have to worry about buying a new work wardrobe in her new size. The truth was, she couldn't work from home. She'd given Steve her office, so that he could have a computer and a phone line and a fast Internet connection for the job search she'd assumed would only last a few weeks. She'd take the laptop to a coffee shop with wireless access. That, and her cell phone, would get her by. She was lucky they had a second computer. *Lucky,* she thought and bit down hard on the sob that wanted to make its way out of her mouth as she dumped the books and shoes and magazines into the closet. *Oh, lucky, lucky me.*

Oliver started to cry. "Want me to get him?" Steve called. "No," Kelly called back and hurried into the nursery, scooping Oliver into her arms.

The telephone rang once, twice, three times. Kelly picked up the phone, balanced the baby on her hip, tucked a fresh diaper under her chin, and carried everything into the bedroom. "Hello?"

It was her grandmother. "You are so lucky, honey, to have Steve home to help you! In my day, you know, there was no such thing as paternity leave." *Yeah, right,* Kelly thought sourly. Paternity leave was the fiction she'd insisted on. "No, we are not telling people you've been laid off!" she had told Steve. "How do you think that sounds?"

"Like I got laid off," Steve had said with a shrug. "It happens, Kelly," he'd said, with a crooked smile. "It's not the end of the world."

She pulled in a deep breath. "Laid off sounds like 'fired.' I just think we should put a more positive spin on this. We can just tell people that you've decided to make a career change and that you're on paternity leave while you're exploring new opportunities."

"Whatever you think," he'd said, shrugging again. She'd been repeating the lie since June. "Paternity leave," she'd said, with a sappy smile plastered to her face, as if it was the most wonderful thing that any girl could hope for. "Steve is taking paternity leave, and then he's going to start looking around for other opportunities." That's what she told her sisters and her grandmother and even Becky and Ayinde and Lia. Paternity leave.

The words were starting to taste like rotten meat in her mouth, but the lying felt strangely, even comfortingly, familiar. When she was a girl, she'd forged her mother's signature on Terry's report cards and answered the phone when the principal called. *My mother can't come to the phone right now,* she'd say. *Can I help? I'm sorry, she's not in right now,* she'd say, or *She's not feeling well.* When the truth was more along the lines of *At three o'clock she starts pouring bourbon into her cans of Tab and talking to the television set,* but that wasn't the kind of thing you could tell the principal or Terry's soccer coach who called wondering why her mother hadn't shown up with Gatorade and orange wedges at the last game. *I'm sorry,* Kelly would say. But she hadn't felt entirely sorry. She'd felt a strange thrill, an odd sort of excitement.

She'd felt important. She was ten years old or eleven or twelve, and her brothers and sisters all treated the house like a way station, like it was something unpleasant they had to endure only until they could escape. Kelly tried to make something out of the place. She kept the kitchen floor swept and the couch pillows fluffed while Mary and Doreen and Michael and even Maureen went in and out, grabbing things from the refrigerator, drinking milk or juice right from the carton, pulling school uniforms right from the dryer, always in a hurry to be gone again.

She was the one who had handled the phone calls, she'd forged the signatures, she'd pulled Aunt Kathleen's knitted brown-and-orange afghan over her mother at night, easing the last can of Tab out of her hand. She'd washed the dinner dishes and straightened up the living room while her mother snored on the couch, shushing her siblings as they came in. "Shh, Mom's sleeping."

"Mom's passed out," Terry would say, her cheeks flaming pink, smelling like cigarette smoke and filled with the righteous indignation of a fourteen-year-old hepped up on nicotine speaking truth to power.

"Be quiet," Kelly would tell her. "Go to sleep."

So she was used to shifting the truth into a more palatable lie. She'd spent her whole childhood magically turning *passed out* into *busy* or *sick* or *sleeping.* She'd be able to turn *laid off* into *paternity leave* if she tried hard enough.

"And how are you?" asked her grandmother. "Mary tells me you're going back to work." Kelly knew what Grandma Pat was thinking. It was what her whole family was probably thinking. What kind of woman goes back to work twelve weeks after her baby's born? *The kind of woman who needs to pay the rent, that's who,* she wanted to scream.

"I'm fine," she said. "I'm fine."

Steve traipsed into the bedroom while Kelly and her grandmother talked about the weather. Her husband was wearing an undershirt and the same stained pair of jeans he'd worn all week, the ones with the fly that seemed permanently stuck at half mast. His suits and ties appeared to be on permanent hiatus. After the sixth night in a row of staring at the crotch of his boxer shorts, she snapped. "Are you auditioning for the role of Al Bundy?" she'd demanded. He sat up straight from where he'd been slumped on the couch, channel surfing, one hand toying with the zipper tab, and blinked at Kelly. "What are you so mad about?" he'd asked. *Are you kidding?* she wanted to say. That and *How much time have you got?* "It looks sloppy," she said. And then she went back to what she'd been doing. Washing the dishes. Folding the laundry. Feeding the baby. Paying the bills.

"And how's that baby of yours?" her grandmother cooed.

"Oliver is wonderful," Kelly recited.

"And that handsome husband?"

"Very busy," she said, wishing it were true. "He's looking at all kinds of different opportunities." Steve didn't meet her eyes. He was anything but busy, and Kelly knew that she'd started to sound like a nagging mother in her ongoing efforts to prompt him toward action and then, she fervently hoped, employment. *Who did you call today? Did you send out any résumés? Did you make any calls? Did you visit that website I told you about?*

And if she was turning into a nagging mother, Steve could, at times, play the sullen teenager, given to monosyllables and grunts. *Yes. No. Fine. Okay.* After one particularly grueling day in August—a day when they were both staggering around like the living dead because Oliver had been up half the night—he'd yelled at her. "Nobody's hiring! It's summertime, and nobody's hiring! Would you lay off of me for ten minutes? Please?"

But she couldn't. She couldn't lay off, she couldn't relax, and she couldn't tell him the thought that terrified her and haunted her dreams—what if she'd married a loser? A loser, like her father? A man who didn't care if his kids went without vacations and wore hand-me-downs and drove around in a van the church had given them? Instead, she muttered an apology and went to give the baby a bath.

"We're all just fine," Kelly told her grandmother. She bru...
past her husband, walking into the bathroom, the phone tucked
under her chin and Oliver in her arms, and squatted down to gather
Steve's dirty socks and underwear and dump them into a laundry basket. "We'll talk to you soon."

She hung up the phone, changed Oliver's diaper, and kissed his
belly and his cheeks as he waved his hands in the air and chuckled at
her. In the living room, Steve was planted in front of the laptop with
his fly down and the ESPN website pulled up. Fantasy baseball.
Excellent. As he heard Kelly approach, he clicked guiltily over to
monster.com and hunched his shoulders as if he was afraid she was
going to hit him.

"How's your grandmother?" he asked, without turning around.

"Fine," she said, opening the refrigerator, where she was greeted
by the bleak vista of two-week-old orange juice, two withering apples, and bread that looked like a science experiment, with each slice
jacketed in blue-green fuzz.

"Want to order Chinese?" Steve called. Kelly closed her eyes. Chinese food was thirty dollars, which was nothing when Steve was
working, but now that he wasn't, the takeout dinners were adding
up. But the thought of defrosting one of the hearty, wholesome meals
she'd frozen back when she was still pregnant, back when Steve was
still employed, made her feel like crying.

"Sure," she said instead. "Get me chicken and broccoli, okay?"

They ate, as they did most nights, without much conversation.
Pass the duck sauce, Kelly would say. *Could I have more water?* Steve
would ask. It reminded her so painfully of her dinners at home, struggling to make conversation and not mention the most obvious and
wrong thing in the room—her mother, swaying almost impercepti-
bly in her chair at the foot of the table and her father, glaring at all of
them from the head.

Oliver blinked his long lashes at them from his bouncy seat. Underneath the table, Lemon rolled onto his back. Steve yawned and
stretched his arms over his head. "Ooh, big yawn! Daddy's sooo

_____r. *After another long day of doing nothing!* she

_____ Oliver smacked his lips, following their every

_____ eyes.

"_____ ungry, big guy?" Steve asked, beaming as he scooped

_____ his lap, letting him play with the chopsticks while Kelly

h__ ___ breath, hoping he wouldn't shove one of them up his nose or

into his eye. She got up to clear the dishes.

"Can I help?" Steve asked.

"No, no, I'll get them." This was the way it had always been; the way she'd once liked it. Steve worked long hours, and Kelly took care of the house. She hadn't felt burdened when she dropped off the dry-cleaning or picked up the groceries. It was only fair because he was making so much more money than she was. *And he would be again,* she told herself.

"Are you sure?" he asked.

"I'm fine," she told him. She shut the dishwasher, dried her hands, and carried the baby to his room to nurse him again and give him his bath. At eight-thirty, she began walking up and down the hall with Oliver in her arms, singing to him until he fell asleep. Then she cleared the table, tossing out paper napkins and chopsticks, casting baleful looks at the Ghetto Couch, which was still crouching, front and center, in their living room. "I'm going to take a shower," she said. Steve nodded. Kelly padded down the hall into Oliver's room. The baby was sprawled on his back, arms and legs akimbo, mouth open, eyes shut. She closed her own eyes and laid her hand on his chest, holding her breath until she felt its gentle rise and fall. How old would he be, she wondered, before she stopped sneaking into his room to make sure he was still breathing. One? Two? Eighteen? She tiptoed out of the room, then went to the office to enter Oliver's wet diapers and naps into his spreadsheet and write a cheery e-mail to the caterers and florists and musicians she'd gotten to know. *Dear colleagues!* she composed in her head. *I'm sure you weren't expecting to hear from me so soon, but I'm back to work, a little more quickly than ex-*

pected . . . The desktop computer flickered into brilliant life with just a quick tap at the mouse.

TEACH FOR AMERICA read the words on the screen, Huh? She scrolled down, thinking this had to be a mistake or a pop-up ad. *We call upon outstanding recent college graduates to commit two years to teach in low-income rural and urban communities to expand opportunities for children growing up there.*

Oh, God. Was Steve seriously thinking about relocating to some slum, with wife and baby in tow? Kelly swallowed hard, feeling suddenly light-headed and queasy, and flicked through the five other windows her husband had left open. BE A TEACHING ASSISTANT IN PHILADELPHIA'S PUBLIC SCHOOLS, one invited. And there was a page giving all the pertinent information about Temple University's one-year teacher certification program.

Teaching. Dear God. She remembered their wedding day, how he'd fought with the priest over the "for richer or poorer" part of the vows. He hadn't even wanted to say "poorer." "It's not in the realm of possibility," he told Father Frank calmly, as the priest stared at him, then at Kelly, bushy eyebrows raised as if to ask, *Is he kidding?*

Kelly sat in front of the computer, feeling her heart kicking against her rib cage. He couldn't be serious . . . could he? She thought about Mr. Dubeo, who'd had all eight of the O'Hara siblings in his American History class and who'd driven the same Chevy Nova for the fourteen years they'd been in school. Mr. Dubeo had worn thick plastic glasses and five different polyester ties, one for each day of the week. The same five ties for fourteen years, and he'd carried plastic-wrapped sandwiches in his briefcase and eaten them at his desk during fourth period. Steve couldn't be thinking of being a teacher. He couldn't.

Oliver started fussing in his crib. She shuffled down the hall, picked the baby up, and held him in her arms. Her little boy, her gorgeous, sweet, pinchable little guy. She blew kisses on his belly, changed his diaper, carried him back to the living room, and sat on the Ghetto Couch to nurse. She tried to ignore the dust in the air and the new set of newspapers on the floor as she cradled Oliver's head in her right hand. Instead of firing their once-a-week cleaning lady to save money, she should have cancelled the digital cable. She just bet that Steve would be looking harder for work if there weren't three hundred channels at his fingertips. She just bet that his suits wouldn't be hanging in the closet and that there wouldn't be an ass-shaped groove in the couch.

Once the baby was sleeping again, she pulled off her clothes and let them drop to the floor by the side of the bed, and then, wearing just panties and a bra, she crawled underneath the covers, with Lemon breathing dog breath into her face. Five minutes later, Steve was in bed, reaching for her. *He can't be serious,* she thought, squeezing her eyes shut before she realized that her husband wasn't trying to touch her breast or her leg. He was trying to hold her hand.

"Kelly?"

She kept breathing slowly and deeply.

"Kelly, are we going to talk about this?"

She ignored him. *No, we are not going to talk about this. There's nothing to discuss. You're going to get the kind of job you had when we got married and I'm going to stay home with our baby, the way we agreed I would.*

Steve sighed and flopped onto his back. "You don't have to go back to work if you don't want to," he said.

Kelly rolled over to face him. "Did you get a job?" she asked eagerly.

Steve pulled back. "Jesus, you scared me!"

"Did you get a job?" she asked again.

"No, Kelly, I didn't get a job in the last ten minutes, but there's no reason to panic. We've got savings."

True enough, she thought. Steve had sold his share of the online investing firm he'd helped get off the ground after graduate school for a decent sum—not the millions he and his partners had been worth on paper at one point, but they certainly had more in the bank than other couples their age. But she didn't want to touch their savings because what would happen when they were gone? "I don't want to use our savings," she said.

"Yeah, well . . ." She could see him shrug in the darkness. "Our circumstances have changed. We can use that while I look around."

"But I don't want to," Kelly said. "I'm not comfortable with that. I don't mind working." *Liar,* she thought. "But I want you to be working, too. I don't want us to just sit around spending money we were supposed to invest."

"I want to find a job I like, and that takes time," Steve said, now sounding whiny. Wimpy. Weak. Your W word here. "I wasn't happy in a big company, Kelly."

"Well, who ever said work's supposed to make you happy?" she asked. "That's why they call it a job, you know? Do you think my job makes me happy? I didn't grow up dreaming about organizing Christmas parties and summer picnics for a bunch of forty-year-old guys in suits. But I do it because it gets the bills paid."

Her husband blew out his breath in frustration.

"I'm going to sleep," Kelly said again. But she couldn't. When Steve started snoring, she crept back into the office and opened her Favorites folder. There was the oval commode and the Cubist bar stools, and the Donghia bed. She sat there, staring, her face bathed in the blue glow of the screen, for three hours, until her son's cries summoned her to the nursery again.

BECKY

"Oopsies! Oopsies! Spit-up in aisle five!" Mimi trilled.

Becky prayed, for what felt like the millionth time in the last three weeks, for the strength not to murder her mother-in-law. She looked at Ava, who seemed perfectly fine. "I think if you just wiped her off . . ."

"Oh, I'll just get her a fresh outfit." Which would be Ava's fourth fresh outfit that day—not bad, Becky thought. When she'd first arrived, Mimi had run through an astonishing seven outfits before lunchtime. Becky wouldn't have minded so much, except she was the one doing the laundry, and Mimi insisted on dressing Ava in what Becky had come to think of as slut-wear. At present, the baby was clad in a miniature pair of ripped jeans with a chain dangling from one of the pockets and a pink onesie that read GRANDMA'S LITTLE ANGEL. As a final touch, there was a pink-and-white-sequined lace headband wrapped around Ava's still-bald skull.

"Do you think her hair will come in soon?" Mimi asked, as she'd asked every day, while she carried the baby up the stairs, her own belly chain dangling, her own hot-pink high heels trip-trapping on the hardwood floors.

"I don't know," Becky said. *I don't care,* she thought.

"Soon you'll have hair," Mimi confided to Ava. "And then you'll be so beautiful! All the boys will want your number!"

"She's beautiful already," Becky called. "And smart! And nice!

And we don't care about boys yet! And . . . oh, fuck it," she muttered and sank onto the couch. This was awful. It was unbelievable. Unendurable. Unacceptable. But after twenty-six days in residence, Mimi was showing no signs of leaving, and, worse, Andrew was showing no willingness to make her.

"She's lonely, Becky. She likes being here. And isn't she helping you out?"

Becky said nothing. She didn't know how to tell Andrew that leaving Ava with Mimi while she went to work made her profoundly uncomfortable because, even though she couldn't prove it, she was positive that Mimi was ignoring every single one of her requests, suggestions, and out-and-out orders regarding Ava's care and feeding. *No people food,* Becky would tell Mimi, and she'd come home at eleven o'clock at night to find her daughter's tongue dyed purple and the cellophane torn off a pint of blueberries. *No bottles,* she'd say, but she was completely convinced that Mimi was slipping her daughter formula on the sly. *No television,* she'd requested, but just the day before, Mimi had started a breakfast conversation with the words, "When Ava and I were watching Oprah . . ." And she'd given up on the clothes. Pre-Mimi, Becky had stocked Ava's dresser with dozens of pretty, affordable, appropriate outfits from Old Navy and Baby Gap. It didn't matter. Every time she turned around, Mimi had put the baby into something more outlandish. Last night, Ava had been wearing a tiny pink tutu. *To sleep in!* Becky had whispered to Andrew as they lay uncomfortably on the pullout couch. *This has to stop!*

"All dressed!" Mimi announced, carrying Ava, now arrayed in a frilly yellow sundress and—*No,* Becky thought, blinking, *no way.* But there it was. A tiny yellow bow, somehow affixed to Ava's head.

"Mimi, how did you . . ."

"Cornstarch paste!" her mother-in-law said. "Works wonders! Now nobody will think you're a little boy," she cooed to Ava. "Isn't that right! We're ready for a nibble," she said to Becky, without looking at her.

Cornstarch, Becky thought, shaking her head as she walked down to the kitchen and called possibilities up the stairs. *Cashews?* Too fatty. *Cheese and crackers?* Didn't Andrew tell you I've got a wheat allergy? No? *An apple?* Is it organic? Can you cut it up? And take off the skin? And maybe if you've got a little cheese to put with it and maybe a few of those cashews after all and another glass of this wine.

Once Mimi's plate had been prepared and Ava had gone down for her second nap, Becky started on dinner. She snipped sprigs of rosemary from a pot on the windowsill, tuned the radio to the classical music station, and read a few recipes for clafouti to calm herself down.

At five-thirty, Ava started to cry. "I'll get her!" Mimi yelled. "Ewww, stinky!" Becky sighed, washed her hands, and went to change her daughter's dirty diaper, counting the minutes until Andrew would come home. It was so unfair. She'd actually had plans for the night. Somehow, in between working three nights a week, keeping the house, and toting Ava to music class and playgroup and yoga and walks in the park, she'd managed to take ten minutes online, during which she'd ordered three X-rated DVDs with which to celebrate her and Andrew's triumphant—and so far unscheduled—return to the marital bed.

The telephone rang, and, of course, Mimi picked it up. "Hayahhh. Oh." She held the phone pinched between her fingers as if it were a dead fish. "For you."

Becky looked at the caller ID and headed to the baby's room. "Hi, Mom," she said.

"She couldn't even say hello to me?" her mother asked indignantly. "And why is she still staying with you? How long has it been?"

"Don't even ask," Becky said.

"How are you doing?" Edith asked. "Are you holding up all right?"

Becky bit back the words she was dying to say. *Come get me! Or let me come home! I'm living with a crazy lady and I can't take it anymore!* "We're all right," she said instead. "We're hanging in there."

"Oh, honey. I wish I could be there to help."

"It's okay," Becky said. "I'll give you a call later. I've got to go."

She set the table with Ava cooing in her bouncy seat as Mimi flipped aimlessly through the channels and asked Becky if she had an emery board (no), a Diet Coke (ditto), or whether she could hold the baby (Mimi, let's just let her settle down a bit).

At seven o'clock, Becky heard Andrew's key in the door and had to restrain herself from hurling herself and the baby at him and begging to be taken to a hotel. Preferably one in another country.

"Hah, angel!" said Mimi, elbowing Becky out of the way and swooping in for a kiss.

"Hi, Mom," Andrew said, giving Mimi a perfunctory kiss on the cheek. "Hi, honey," he said, wrapping his arms around Becky and giving her a kiss of a very different kind. She thought of the three DVDs, stripped of their plastic and tucked between two of her cookbooks, with a pang of regret.

"We're having lamb," Mimi announced, as if Andrew couldn't see that for himself. "We never had lamb when Andrew was growing up," she told Becky. "I don't know why. It always seemed like, I don't know, the thing you got when you couldn't afford steak."

Well, that's just me and my low-class family, Becky thought. She stretched out the meal for as long as she could, half listening as Mimi ran down what sounded like the entire roster of Andrew's high school class ("And that nice Mark Askowitz rented a villa in Jamaica for his mother to use. Do you keep in touch with him?"). She spent half an hour bathing Ava, putting her into her pajamas, singing to her until she fell asleep. When Becky tiptoed out of Ava's room, Mimi was clomping down the hallway in her high heels, not making even the tiniest attempt to be quiet. "Sleep well!" she had the nerve to call over her shoulder as she disappeared into Andrew and Becky's bedroom.

When the bedroom door was closed, Becky slipped one of the DVDs out of the cookbook and into her pocket. She met Andrew back in the living room, where he was wrestling with the pullout couch. "Thanks for being such a good sport," he said.

"I brought us a present," Becky whispered, flicking off the lights and turning on the television set.

When she showed him the disc, his eyes lit up. "Nice!"

"Actually, naughty," she giggled. They waited, holding hands and kissing, until what seemed like a decent interval. Once Mimi's raspy exhalations began drifting down the stairs, it was playtime.

"I love you," Andrew whispered twenty minutes later, when they were both breathing normally.

"As well you should," said Becky. She closed her eyes and drifted into sleep to the music of her mother-in-law's snores.

The morning began with Mimi descending into the kitchen in suede pants and a fur-trimmed sweater, a face full of makeup and her usual barrage of requests. Did Becky have fresh orange juice? *No.* Flavored decaf coffee? *No.* Spelt bread? *Mimi, I don't even know what that is. Sorry.*

The instant Becky sat down at the table, Ava started to scream.

"Don't worry!" Mimi singsonged, grabbing Ava out of Becky's arms. "Let's just watch the video I brought over!"

"We don't watch videos with her!" Andrew called toward his mother's back. Mimi ignored him.

"Let Grandma just find the remote control." Becky heard the television set clicking on. Then she heard the noise of the DVD player powering up. Andrew and Becky looked at each other, frozen in disbelief. *Oh, shit,* Andrew mouthed. They turned at the same instant, slamming into each other. Becky slipped and fell. Andrew stepped over her without ceremony and galloped up the stairs. Too late. Even from her current location—curled on the floor, with her face a few inches from the bottom of the refrigerator—she could hear the grunts and moans, and, worse, oh, God, oh, no, the sound of slapping. "Yeah, you like that, baby?" a voice inquired. And there was the sleazy background music, *bomp-chicka-bomp-bomp.* And, inevitably, Mimi's scream.

"*What is this?*"

It would have been funny if it had happened to somebody else, Becky decided, picking herself slowly off the floor, as Andrew clicked the DVD player into silence. In fact, it was kind of funny anyhow.

"*What in God's name . . .*"

Oof. She got to her feet, hoping that Ava hadn't seen anything that would scar her for life, and headed up the stairs as Andrew stammered out an explanation that amounted to *I have no idea how that got in there.*

"I raised you better than this!" Mimi was shrieking, standing in front of the television set with her hands planted on her bony hips. Becky pressed her lips together, feeling her entire body shaking with laughter.

"I have never been so disgusted in my entire LIFE!"

Good thing it wasn't the anal scene, Becky thought. And that was it. She bent double, tears streaming from her eyes, as Andrew continued to blurt out apologies.

"You should be ashamed!" Mimi yelled, eyes flashing beneath their layers of eyeliner.

Becky wiped her eyes, thinking that no matter what else, this woman was never ever ever going to make her husband feel guilty about sex ever again. She squared her shoulders, flipped her hair over her shoulders, picked Ava up from the couch where she'd been unceremoniously abandoned, and said the one thing that she knew could save her husband's ass. "Actually, Mimi, it's mine."

"You . . . you . . ." Mimi's thinning black hair stood in a frizzy corona around her head. Even the fur on her sweater seemed to quiver.

"Mine," Becky repeated. She popped the disc out of the machine and stuck it in her back pocket. "Jessa Blake's a particular favorite of mine. I really enjoyed her work in *Up and Cummers Four.*"

"I . . . you . . . oh!" Mimi exclaimed. She shot Becky a poisonous look, stormed up the stairs, and slammed the door of their bedroom. Becky looked at Andrew, who looked back at her, a smile curling the corners of his mouth.

"Up and Cummers Four?"

"I'll rent it someday. Don't worry. You don't need to have seen *Up and Cummers One, Two,* or *Three* to appreciate it."

He tucked his hand under the back of her head, tilting her face toward his. "You're really something, you know that?"

"In a good way or a not-good way?"

"In an amazing way," he said and kissed her, before picking up his briefcase and heading out the door. Becky took Ava for a very long walk, and they spent another two hours loitering in a coffee shop, ignoring the evil looks of the counter staff. At four o'clock, the house was quiet, and the bedroom door was still closed. *Mimi must be sulking,* Becky thought. *Or recovering from the shock.* She'd just put Ava on the changing table when the telephone rang.

"Hello?"

It was Ayinde. And she was crying. "Becky?"

"What?" Becky asked. "What's wrong?"

"Something happened," she said. "Can you come over?"

Becky felt her heart stop. "Is it Julian? Is Julian okay?'

"Julian's fine," said Ayinde, "but please, can you just come?" And then she started to cry again.

"I'll be right there," Becky said, thinking fast—the diaper bag was packed with wipes, a fresh outfit, and the half dozen diapers that Ava could go through in a single afternoon.

"Don't listen to the radio," Ayinde said. "When you're driving. Please. Please, promise me you won't." Becky promised. She changed Ava's diaper and picked up her car seat. She checked her purse for her wallet and her keys and headed out the door. It wasn't until she was halfway to Gladwyne that she realized she hadn't even told her mother-in-law good-bye.

AYINDE

Her education had emphasized the classics—lots of Shakespeare, lots of Milton and Donne, the Bible as literature. Ayinde had studied the full complement of dead white men, thick volumes heavy on symbols and signs. Looking back, she would have expected a sign of her own: thunder, lightning, a hail of frogs, a plague of locusts. At least a flood in the basement. But there was nothing. The day her world cracked open was a day like any other day—better than most, in fact.

She and Julian had slept together, side by side, in the vast, Richard-less bed. At six in the morning, the baby woke up. Ayinde had opened the blinds and sat cross-legged, leaning against the slip-covered headboard, listening to the hiss of the blender as the cook whipped up Richard's protein shake; the soft ruffling of pages as she laid the newspapers out on the dining-room table; the sound of the florist's truck making its way up the driveway.

There was a gentle tap on the door. "Good morning," Ayinde called. Clara slipped in, nodded at Ayinde and the baby, set a tray with tea and toast and honey and the morning papers on the table at the foot of the bed, and slipped out again. Ayinde closed her eyes. She was sure the staff was wondering about her. She knew the other players' wives were. At the last unofficial team gathering—a barbecue in July at the coach's summer home at the Jersey Shore—the wives had showered Julian with gifts: a custom-made jersey with his father's number, miniature Nikes and Timberland boots, tiny ensembles in denim and leather, nylon Sixers warm-ups in size Newborn.

Then the questions had begun. One question, really: Have you found a nanny? All of the other wives had full-time help—live-in help, in most cases. And none of them worked. They spent their days shopping, lunching, working out, being wives, eternally available to their husbands for travel, for support, and for sex, Ayinde supposed. They couldn't believe she didn't want a nanny. Ayinde had kept quiet while she quoted a salient bit of *Baby Success!* to herself. *If your job only serves to give you a sense of purpose, a sense of meaning in the world, I want you to go over to that little darling (unless it's naptime, of course!) and hold Dumpling. All the meaning, all the purpose, everything you could ever want or hope for is right there in your arms. You have a job already. Your job is Mother. And there's no job in the world more important than that.*

The old, pre-Priscilla Ayinde would have dismissed the rhetoric as reactionary, antifeminist bullshit, and maybe tossed the book against the wall for good measure. Post-baby Ayinde—Ayinde with Julian in her arms, haunted by memories of the halfhearted parenting she'd received, determined to raise her baby perfectly or at least damn close to it and, if she was being honest, no job prospects on the horizon—had swallowed it whole. What could work give her that her own baby couldn't? Assuming she could even get hired in the first place? *My job is Mother,* she whispered to herself. She only said it to herself. She'd once made the mistake of saying it out loud to her friends, and Becky had laughed so hard that she'd almost choked on her latte.

There was another tap on the door, and Richard came through, smelling of aftershave and soap. Loose nylon shorts clung to his hips and drooped to his knees; a sleeveless T-shirt showed off his muscular arms. *He looks so good,* Ayinde thought, but it was a remote kind of appreciation, the same as she'd give to a statue in a museum. "Hey, baby," he said, kissing her head. "Hey, little man," he said and brushed Julian's head with his fingertips. They went over his schedule—he'd

be at Temple all day, leading a clinic for high school players, then
holed up with his business manager and publicist after dinner to go
over the specifics of a new credit-card endorsement deal. He cupped
Ayinde's chin and kissed her gently. Then he walked down to the
kitchen, where his shake and his newspapers were waiting, then, presumably, out the front door, where his car and driver were waiting,
and then on to Temple, where a few dozen awestruck high school players would be waiting, thrilled at the chance to breathe the same air as
her husband.

It was a beautiful fall morning, the sky crisp and blue, the leaves
of the maple trees just starting to turn. Ayinde pushed Julian's
stroller down the long driveway. She wondered if they'd get trick-or-
treaters; whether any intrepid neighborhood kids would brave the
hike up the driveway or whether Richard would simply station the
security guy in the Hummer in front of their mailbox and instruct
him to hand out candy.

At ten o'clock, she set the baby down for his Priscilla Prewitt–
prescribed nap and managed to shower, brush her teeth, and get
dressed. At two o'clock, she drove into town and met Kelly for lunch.
They ate grilled chicken and arugula salads at Fresh Fields, while the
babies sat in their strollers, ignoring each other. "How's work?" she
asked.

"Fine!" said Kelly, smoothing her lank blond hair. "We're still
looking for a nanny. Let me tell you, I have seen some head cases this
last week. So right now Steve's home with the baby while I work, but
it's fine!" Oliver started to fuss. Kelly lifted him up, sniffed his bottom, grimaced, and reached for her diaper bag. "Oh, God, oh, no. Do
you have a diaper? And some wipes? God, Steve always does this. He
uses everything up and then he doesn't replace it. I can't believe I left
the house without looking!"

Ayinde couldn't help herself from feeling the tiniest bit smug as
she gave Kelly her packet of organic recycled-cotton wipes and one of
her cloth diapers ("best for the environment and for Dumpling's soft

l'il bottom," said Priscilla Prewitt) and, after lunch, as she clicked Julian's car seat into place and deftly folded his stroller into the trunk. *My job is Mother,* she whispered, as she drove them both home. And she was good at it, too, she thought, even if it was boring and tedious, even if she felt time stretching like taffy, even if she found herself constantly looking at her watch, counting the hours, and even the minutes, until Julian's next nap or his bedtime, when she'd get a break. Her job was Mother, and she was doing just fine.

When she got home, there were six cars in the driveway, parked hastily, as if their owners had gotten as close to the front door as they could before running inside. Ayinde pulled up behind the last car, feeling the first tickle of unease at the base of her spine. Four strange cars and two that she recognized: the black Town Car, sleek and anonymous, which drove Richard where he needed to be driven, and the Audi whose license plate read COACH, a car the same distinguished silver as its owner's hair. *No ambulance, though,* she thought, thinking of Lia. She slipped her handbag over her shoulder, hefted Julian, still in his car seat, out of the car, and walked inside. The cook was slowly wiping a counter that looked clean already, and the business manager standing inside the door nodded hello without meeting Ayinde's eyes.

Richard was sitting in the dining room, slumped by himself at the head of a table that was made to seat eighteen. His mahogany skin had an ashy undertone, and his lips looked blue around the edges. "Richard?" She set Julian down on the table. "What's wrong?"

He raised his eyes to look at her, and there was an expression of such anguish on his face that she stumbled steps backward, catching her heel on the fringe of the antique Persian rug and almost falling. "What happened?"

"I have to tell you something," Richard said. His eyes were bloodshot. *Sick,* Ayinde thought wildly. *He's sick, he needs a doctor, he should be in a hospital, not here . . .* She looked around. Strangers were filing into the dining room. There was a man in khakis and a wrinkled Oxford shirt carrying an oversized FedEx envelope; a woman in a navy suit and a chignon stood behind him. Not a stethoscope or a white lab coat among them.

"What's going on?"

"Why don't we all sit down," the coach said. The tone of his voice, the gentleness there, reminded Ayinde of her own father—not in real life, of course, but the part he'd played on Broadway in *The Moon at Midnight* and the speech he'd given, telling his onstage daughter that her mother had died. He'd won the Tony for it, she thought dimly.

Julian had fallen asleep in his car seat. She lifted him into her arms anyhow, pillowing his sleeping face against her shoulder. Richard pushed himself slowly out of his chair and walked over to her, moving as if he'd aged a fast ten years or torn a tendon, a basketball player's worst fear. "Something happened in Phoenix," he said. His voice was so low that Ayinde could barely hear it.

Phoenix. Phoenix. Richard visited there frequently; it was where the soft-drink company he represented was headquartered. His last trip had been three weeks ago. "What happened?" She stared at Richard, trying to figure it out. Had he hurt himself there, playing pickup ball, working out in a substandard hotel gym?

"There was a girl," he mumbled. Ayinde felt her whole body go cold. *Perfume,* her mind whispered. She clutched Julian so tightly that he gasped in his sleep. *Perfume,* her mind said again. And then came three words, delivered in a voice that was unmistakably Lolo's: *Told you so.*

She raised her chin, determined not to break down in front of this crowd of strangers. "What happened?"

"She . . ." Richard's voice trailed off. He cleared his throat. "She's pregnant."

No, Ayinde thought. Not her Richard. Not that. "And you're the father?"

"That's for the courts to determine," said the woman in the blue suit.

"Who are you?" Ayinde asked coldly.

"This is Christina Crossley," said the coach. "She's a crisis communication manager." He ducked his head. "We've hired her for . . . for the duration. Until we get this straightened out."

Christina Crossley Crisis! Ayinde's mind sang.

"The woman has made allegations," Christina Crossley said. "Richard will have to fly back to Phoenix tomorrow and give a DNA sample. After that . . ." She lifted her shoulders. "We'll see." Christina Crossley pressed her lips together. "The problem is, she's already gone to the press. The tabloids. The *National Examiner* is planning on leading with the story on Wednesday, which means the legitimate media will treat it as fair game."

Fair game. Ayinde tried to puzzle out the phrase, to consider each word separately, but it still made no sense. It wasn't a game, and it certainly wasn't fair. Not to her. Not to Julian.

"We've scheduled a press conference," Christina Crossley continued. "For tomorrow night at five, so we'll be sure to make the nightly news cycle." She offered Ayinde a professionally compassionate smile. "We can take this afternoon to work on your statement."

Ayinde stared at the woman before she decided that there was only one statement she could conceivably make.

"Out," she said.

Christina Crossley looked at the coach, then at Ayinde. Her professional smile had cooled a few degrees. "Mrs. Towne, I'm not sure you appreciate the gravity of what we're facing here. In a very real sense, Richard's livelihood—his future—depends on how we're able to manage the story . . ."

"OUT!"

They moved fast—the coach, Christina Crossley, the whey-faced white guy whose name she hadn't been given, all of them hurrying over the waxed hardwood floors and the hand-knotted Persian rug. The crystals in the chandelier rattled with their footsteps. Richard, Ayinde, and the baby were alone at the table. Richard cleared his throat. Ayinde stared at him. He shuffled his feet. She said nothing. She felt iced over, frozen in place.

"I'm sorry," he finally blurted.

"How could you," she said. It wasn't a question but a statement. *How could you.*

"I'm sorry," he said again. "But Ayinde, it was nothing. It was a one-night stand. I don't even know her last name!"

"You think I believe that?" she demanded. "You came to me the night our son was born smelling like some other woman's perfume . . ."

"What?" He stared up at her, bewildered. "Baby, what are you talking about?"

"How many?" she yelled at him. "How many women, Richard? How long have you been cheating on me?"

"I don't know what kind of perfume you're talking about. It was just this once, Ayinde. I swear."

"I guess that's supposed to make me feel better—oh, you only cheated on me once," she ranted. "How could you have been so stupid! How could you not have . . ." Her voice caught in her throat. "How come you didn't use protection?"

"She said it was safe."

"Oh, Richard," Ayinde groaned. In all the years she'd known him, she thought her husband was many things—smart, kindhearted, a little vain. She'd never once thought he was stupid. Until right now.

"It was a mistake," he was saying, looking at her with his tormented eyes. "I swear to you."

"You swore to me once already," Ayinde said. She felt as if she'd left her body and was watching the scene unfold from a vast, airy distance. "You swore to love and honor me. Forsaking all others, right? Or am I not remembering it correctly?"

He glared at her. "Well, you promised the same things, and then you kicked me out of my own bed."

She was so stunned that she found it hard to breathe. "So this is my fault?"

He looked down at the table and said nothing.

"Richard, I had a baby . . ."

"You had a baby," he said, "but you had a husband, too. I needed you, and you pushed me away."

"So this is my fault," she repeated, thinking that this was another truth of Richard's life—there was always someone to blame. He could pin a loss on his teammates—a guard who couldn't shut down an opposing center, a forward who couldn't sink his foul shots. He could hang his personal failings on his upbringing—a teenage mother, a doting grandmother, neither one with an education, both of them with their hands open, ready to indulge Prince Richard with whatever their income would allow. And then the NBA, too much, too fast, cars and houses and money, all of it wrapped up with the built-in guarantee of someone there to take the fall and a Christina Crossley to swoop down and smooth over any manner of unpleasantness when you finally did stumble badly enough to warrant the world's attention.

"I'm sorry," he said. "If I could take it back . . ." His voice broke.

"You need to get tested for STDs. And AIDS," she said. He stared at her sullenly for a minute then shook his head. Ayinde thought once more of her mother. Lolo had hated Richard from the first time she'd heard his name. "Sportin' Life," she'd called him, after the drug pusher in *Porgy and Bess. How is Sportin' Life?* she'd ask when she called. *You don't marry a man like that,* Lolo instructed her daughter, as if Ayinde had asked for her advice. *No, not at all! You have your fun with him, baby girl. Get your picture in the papers. Then find yourself a man to marry.*

I love him, Ayinde told her mother. Lolo shrugged and went back to the painstaking application of her false eyelashes, the ones she wore every day, even when she was only going down to the lobby, where there was no audience except for the bored doorman to watch her pick up her mail.

Then it's your funeral, she'd said.

Ayinde narrowed her eyes and stared at Richard. *The whole world will be laughing at us,* she thought, and that thought slammed her back into her body, into this room, into the here and the now of what her husband had done. *Laughing at me. Laughing at Julian.* She lifted her chin even higher. "Get out," she said.

"They'll want to talk to you," Richard said. "About what we're going to do next."

"Get out," she said again, in a voice she barely recognized as her own. He got up with his shoulders hunched, slumping out of the room, and she was left by herself with Julian in her arms. She tucked her nose against his neck, breathing in his scent—milk, warmth, his sweet breath. Priscilla Prewitt had a chapter on divorce. *Marriage on the rocks? Keep your eyes on the prize. Remember what really matters. Remember who comes first. Study after study—as well as good ol' common sense—tell us what we know in our hearts. Babies do better with mommy and daddy both under the same roof.*

Ayinde squeezed her eyes shut, knowing that even though she'd told them to leave, there were still people in her house. If she listened closely enough, she would be able to hear all of them—the cook, the maids, the publicist, the business manager, the trainer, the masseuse, the gardener, the landscaper, the delivery men, assistants, interns, and secretaries—wandering in and out of her house just like Richard had wandered in and out of their marriage. She wondered whether everyone knew what had happened. She wondered whether Richard had ever brought women home when she was visiting her parents in New York or when she was out for the afternoon. She wondered whether the maid had smoothed the sheets and the cook had whipped up breakfast for two.

She slumped onto a love seat and groped for her cell phone. And then she called her friends and told them to meet her in the guest house and please not to listen to the radio as they drove.

Richard hadn't really left, Ayinde realized. He'd just locked himself in the guest room. Ayinde walked past the door half a dozen times, gathering sloppy armloads of her clothes and Julian's, carrying them down the stairs, past the kitchen where the cook and Clara kept their heads down, ostentatiously not looking at her, past the dining room where the coach and the lawyers and Christina Crossley sat, out the door, and into the guest-house bedroom. Then she stood in the driveway with her baby in her arms and waited.

Kelly's car pulled into the driveway first. "What happened?" she asked through the window. Her cheeks were pale. Her hair hung in wet tendrils against them, and she smelled like Ivory soap. "Are you all right?"

"I want to wait until Becky's here," Ayinde said.

Kelly nodded and got out of the car, and Lia got out of the passenger's seat. "I was helping with Oliver," Lia said. "I hope you don't mind . . . Here," she said, stretching out her arms. Ayinde looked down and saw that she was holding Julian as if he were a sack of flour, one arm wrapped haphazardly around his midsection. One of his socks had gone missing. And he was crying. *How long had he been crying?* she wondered, as she handed him over to Lia, who settled him against her shoulder.

"Shh, shh," she whispered. Julian hooked his thumb into his mouth, and his wails tapered off, as Becky's little Honda pulled up her driveway.

Ayinde led them into the guest house, which, per Richard's instructions, had been turned into an upscale clubhouse, all heavy leather furniture, wide-screen television set, a fully stocked bar at the back of the living room above which Richard's trophies stood on specially built glass shelves. *Everything but the NO GIRLS ALLOWED sign,* Ayinde thought. She should have gotten a sign like that. She should have stapled it to her husband's crotch.

Her friends sat in a row on the couch with their babies and her own in their laps. Then there was no more time to stall.

"Richard," Ayinde said. Her voice wobbled. "He went to Phoenix for business. He met . . . there was . . ." She realized she had no idea of how to say it. "A woman in Phoenix is saying she's having his baby." There. Simple and to the point.

The three of them stared at her. "Oh, I don't believe it," Kelly finally said. "Richard wouldn't do that."

"How do you know?" Ayinde asked harshly. Kelly dropped her eyes. "He did do it," Ayinde said. "He told me he did. And I trusted him." Then Ayinde bent over at the waist, clutching herself, breathless from the sudden pain that ripped through her belly. It was like being torn open. It hurt a hundred times worse than even labor had.

Becky's arms were warm around her. She helped Ayinde straighten up and led her to the couch. "Has he done this before?"

Perfume, Ayinde's mind whispered again. "I don't know," she said. *Oh, really?* she heard Lolo ask, in her arch, mocking way. *You don't know, or you don't want to know?* "Does it matter?" She could see snippets of the Gospel According to Priscilla Prewitt floating in front of her eyes. *Remember what really matters . . . the most important job in the world . . . mommy and daddy together under the same roof.* "I can't leave him. Not with a baby. I won't."

"So what are you going to do?" Becky asked.

Ayinde could guess at what came next. When she'd worked as a reporter, she'd covered a dozen scandals like it, read about a hundred more. She'd be trotted out like a show pony to stand by her man. She'd be photographed gazing at him with a Nancy Reagan look of idiot adoration on her face. Her job would be to hold his hand. The world's job would be to laugh at her. She'd be a punch line, a cautionary fable, a bad joke. And over what? Some groupie, some cheerleader, as disposable as one of those wax paper cups full of sports drink the players gulped and discarded during games? Some starfucker who'd hurried back to her girlfriends in triumph, bearing a trinket Richard had tossed her—an autographed cap, a T-shirt, a baby? She bent over, gasping, as the pain tore through her again.

Becky's voice was as kind as Ayinde had always wished her own mother's voice would be. "Maybe you should talk to Richard."

Julian started his stuttering *eh, eh, eh* that meant a full-blown cry would start soon. "Shh, honey," Lia whispered, rocking him against her chest, the brim of her baseball cap shadowing his face.

Ayinde felt her body moving without her volition, felt her hands smooth her hair and her feet start walking.

The guest-room door was closed but not locked. The doorknob slid under Ayinde's hand. Richard was lying in bed in the dark, dressed right down to his shoes, with his arms pressed tightly at his sides. *Corpse pose,* she thought. In yoga they call that corpse pose. She opened her mouth but found that she had nothing to say to her husband; nothing at all.

November

LIA

"Good-bye, good-bye, good-bye, babies," Kelly sang, enthusiastically and slightly off-key. Her ponytail bobbed as she pushed Oliver along the sidewalk. Kelly and Becky and Ayinde and I had met for coffee after the music class the three of them attended, and from what I could gather, the "Good-bye" song was how every class concluded. "Good-bye, good-bye, good-bye, mommies . . ."

"Oh, God, please stop that," Becky begged. "I'm never going to get it out of my head. It's worse than Rick Astley."

"All those girls named Emma," Ayinde murmured, "and not one Ayinde in the bunch." Her smile curved her lips but didn't touch her eyes. I wondered how music class was going for her since the Richard Towne miniscandal had erupted. I wondered if the other mothers stared or if they'd tried not to. That had been the worst part, I thought. When I had Caleb, there was a little park I used to go to, a few other mothers I'd developed a nodding acquaintance with. The one time I'd been back to the park afterward, I could feel the effort coming off of them like heat rising off the pavement in July as they tried not to stare and murmured the same handful of platitudes I just bet Ayinde was currently enduring: *We're so sorry* and *What a shame* and *Time heals all wounds*.

I fell into step with them—three mommies, three babies, and which of these things is not like the other? But they didn't seem discomfited by my being there, either. Maybe that was because we were all still feeling so strange around Ayinde.

"I love Julian's sweater," I told her. Her face brightened a bit.

"Thank you." The sweater was navy blue with red trim and felt barnyard animals cavorting on the front. Julian wore it with blue jeans, matching knit cap, and miniature Nikes. I was pretty certain that his outfit had cost more than any of the clothes I'd finally broken down and bought for myself. Nothing fancy, just basic jeans and khakis and T-shirts to supplement the jeans and sweatshirts I'd salvaged from my old high school wardrobe and my mother's blue coat, which I couldn't seem to let go.

"So listen," Kelly began. "Oliver only woke up twice last night. One and four-thirty." She looked at us hopefully. The skin underneath her eyes looked bruised and fragile. "That almost counts as sleeping through the night, doesn't it?"

"Absolutely," Becky said. "Hang in there." We walked, and I tried not to feel out of place without a stroller. Kelly, of course, had the hot, high-priced Bugaboo, as seen in *In Style* and on *Sex and the City.* Ayinde had effortlessly trumped her with a Silver Cross pram her mother had brought back from London. And Becky had Ava strapped into a secondhand Snap 'n Go that she told us she'd bought at a tag sale. When Kelly had asked whether it was up to the current safety standards, Becky had stared at her blandly and said, "More or less," before she'd started to laugh.

We worked in pairs to carry the strollers into Becky's hallway. Her house was warm, and it smelled like sage and cornbread and pumpkin pie.

"Are you having Thanksgiving dinner?" I asked.

"Nope. Mimi is. She called and invited us over for Thanksgiving dinner and then asked us to bring . . ." She paused. "Thanksgiving dinner."

"Are you kidding?"

"Would that I were. But I can't complain. At least she's gone." She rolled her eyes. "Did I tell you she got seventeen parking tickets while she was in residence? She shoved them all under the door on her way back to Merion." She made a face. "And guess who wound up paying them?"

"I thought she was rich," Kelly said.

"I think that's how the rich stay rich," Becky said. "They get the less fortunate to pay their parking tickets." Becky set Ava on the blanket on the kitchen floor, between Julian and Oliver. "Want to play?" she asked. "Lia and I have invented a new game."

I reached into a drawer, pulled out a fistful of yarmulkes, and pressed one into Kelly's hand. "Try to throw it on Oliver's head."

Kelly was sitting in Becky's rocking chair with an afghan wrapped around her shoulders and her eyes half shut. She wrinkled her nose, looking down at the yarmulke she had pinched between two fingers. "I don't know," she said. "It's not disrespectful?"

"It's a yarmulke, not the blood of the Redeemer," Becky said.

I watched Kelly turning the skullcap over in her hands, running a fingertip along the words ANDREW AND REBECCA embossed in gold thread, thinking that she was the most cheerful person I'd ever met in my life. Every time I'd seen her she was fine! Great! Terrific! Of course, once you got her talking, you'd learn that Oliver still wasn't sleeping more than three or four hours at a stretch and that she was working every day, plus running off to parties two or three nights a week after the baby was in bed. I wondered how Kelly would handle a crisis, and then I smiled, imagining the phone call. *Hi, it's Kelly! My leg's caught in a bear trap! Can you come help me? No? Well, that's fine! It's kind of a cute accessory!*

"The babies don't mind," Becky said. To prove it, she took a yarmulke of her own, aimed carefully, and tossed it onto Ava's head. "And seriously, how else are they going to entertain us?"

Kelly pressed her lips together. "I just don't think we should be throwing religious objects at our babies' heads."

"Christina Crossley wears a cross," Ayinde said from the corner of the kitchen, where she was thumbing halfheartedly through a copy of *Saveur.* "It sounds like a nursery rhyme, doesn't it?"

We sat for a minute, Becky and I standing in the corner of the kitchen where the babies lay on a quilt; Kelly in the rocking chair with her eyes half shut.

"Is she . . . very religious?" I finally asked.

"Don't know," Ayinde said, setting the magazine down. "Could be. She booked us on *60 Minutes* for next week, so maybe she does have an in with God. Or a deal with the devil. Either way, Richard and I get twelve minutes of prime time to hold hands and make goo-goo eyes at each other. Want to hear my statement?" Without waiting for an answer, she pulled a sheet of paper from her diaper bag, straightened her shoulders, and began to read. "I ask for the public to respect our privacy and our son's privacy as my husband and I work through this very difficult time." She refolded the sheet of paper and gave us a big, glossy smile as she straddled one of Becky's barstools. "So, what do you think? Do you give it five stars and two thumbs up? Does it have a good beat? Can you dance to it?"

"Oh, Ayinde," Kelly said softly. I looked away. I was thinking about my own husband, how during the short months of our marriage, when I'd been huge and miserable most of the time, he'd never been anything less than sweet and solicitous. I don't think he'd ever even looked at another woman, and he was surrounded by beautiful ones every day.

"Do you want to do it?" Becky asked, then looked abashed and quickly busied herself with the coffee pot. Ayinde put the statement back into her diaper bag.

"I don't want Richard's life to be ruined," she said with her back to her friends. "Because that means Julian's life is going to be ruined. Or not ruined but tainted. Forever." She put her hands in her pockets. "Other than that, I don't know." She blew out a frustrated breath, sending her braids dancing against her cheeks. "The logistics are insane. Christina Crossley took three hours yesterday videoconferencing with some image expert in Dallas, deciding on my outfit for the taping. In case you were wondering, I'm wearing a slate-gray Donna

Karan suit, which says I'm serious, and a long-sleeved powder-pink shirt underneath, which says I have a heart."

"You could've just borrowed my I'M WITH STUPID T-shirt," Becky said, earning a wan smile.

"The statement's very good!" Kelly said, perky as ever, even though she looked as though she wanted to pull the afghan over her head and sleep for several days. "It's very effective. Very succinct." She peeked over the edge of the afghan. "Can I have some coffee?"

"The girl was on *Dateline*," Ayinde said. None of us said anything. We already knew. The girl—Tiffany Something, a onetime spirit dancer for the expansion team out there—had been on *Dateline* and Ricki and Montel and on the cover of several magazines, always with her belly front and center and headlines that were some variation of the words LOVE CHILD. There was, it seemed, an endless appetite for the seamy details of what the tabloids called her NIGHT OF PASSION with SEXY SIXER Richard Towne, who had been above reproach for so long as the NBA's shining example of a family man. And because the tabloids had already run everyone's name and picture, the so-called legitimate newspapers felt completely justified in doing the same thing. The *Philadelphia Examiner* had even snapped a picture of Ayinde with Julian in a sling on her chest walking through the park. Becky and Kelly had been furious, but Ayinde had just given a weary shrug and said that the concept of the sins of the fathers not being visited on the sons hadn't made it to Philadelphia quite yet.

"It's worse that she's white," Ayinde said. She started flipping through *Mastering the Art of French Cooking*. "Because now there's not only the cheating thing, but there's the pissed-off sistas, too. The ones who take it personally every time a black man looks at a white woman."

"How did they feel when he married you?" I asked.

"Oh, I'm black enough for them," she said with a slanting smile. "They were fine with Richard being married to me. But now . . ." She shook her head. "The team's already talking about hiring extra security to get him in and out of the arenas. Some women at Madison Square Garden were throwing condoms at him." She closed the book and slid it back onto the shelf. "I wish I'd thought to throw a few condoms at him. Back when it would have made a difference."

She walked to the center of the kitchen where the babies were lined up and tossed her yarmulke at Julian. It hit his shoulder and fell off. "Five points," she said and sat back down.

Kelly's eyes widened. "You're playing for points?"

"For cash, actually," said Becky. "First one to a hundred points gets ten bucks. It's twenty points if you get it on his head and it stays there; ten points if you get it on his head but it falls off; five points for other body parts. Oh, and you win automatically if the baby's first words are Shabbat Shalom."

"Well, all right," Kelly said. She turned her yarmulke over in her hands, then looked over her shoulder as if she was expecting to see Jesus Himself there, wagging a finger in remonstration. She cocked her elbow back and let the beanie fly. It landed on Oliver's head and slipped forward. "Oh, no!" she cried, rushing to remove it. "It's getting all drooly!"

"Not to worry. I've got about five hundred more," Becky said. "Mimi overordered." She rolled her eyes. "We went to her house for brunch yesterday. Ava pulled off her hairpiece."

"Mimi wears a hairpiece?" I asked. I hadn't ever seen Mimi, but Becky had told me enough about her that I had a pretty good mental picture . . . to which I'd now be adding a wig.

"Yeah. It was news to me, too," Becky said. "She suffers from thinning hair, which has to do with her estrogen levels. She told me all about it later. Allllll about it."

"At least she calls. At least she babysits," said Ayinde. We looked at each other again. Ayinde's mother, the very glamorous Lolo Mbezi, had only made the two-hour trip from New York City to Philadelphia once, and Richard's mother had stopped by once, on her way to Atlantic City, with a gift-wrapped tricycle in the back of the Escalade Richard had bought her. She'd gotten sulky when Ayinde had explained that Julian couldn't hold his head up by himself, let alone sit on a tricycle.

"Has your mother called you since . . ." Kelly folded her yarmulke into halves, then quarters. "Has she called you lately?"

"She calls," Ayinde said. "She says she wants to be supportive. She hasn't said, 'I told you so' yet, but I know she's got to be thinking it. And, to tell you the truth, I think she's happy about it."

"Why would you think that?" Becky asked.

"She's gotten all this work since . . . well, since. All the newspapers are running that stupid picture we took and the one of her from the 1970s."

I knew the picture she was talking about. It featured a Studio 54–era Lolo in profile, wearing a dashiki, gold armbands, and about eighteen inches of Afro.

Ayinde sighed and wrapped her long fingers around a mug of coffee. "I wish I could stay here."

"In town?" asked Becky.

"No. In your kitchen." She looked around at the red walls, the battered dining-room table, the shelves full of thumbed-through, sauce-stained cookbooks, the crimson-and-blue quilt where the babies were resting.

"I want to stay, too," Kelly said, pushing off with her toes on the floor, rocking back and forth. She kept folding her yarmulke into eighths, then sixteenths, as if she was hoping it would disappear. With her chin down and her hair in its ponytail, she looked about twelve years old.

"What's your problem?" asked Becky.

"My husband," she said. "My husband is my problem."

"Wait, wait, don't tell me," said Ayinde. "He's been having an affair with a twenty-year-old?"

Kelly smoothed her ponytail over and over. "He got laid off." She got to her feet, grabbed Oliver under his armpits, and lifted him to her shoulder. "I know I told you that he was just investigating other opportunities and that he was on paternity leave, but he wasn't. He got laid off, and he hasn't been investigating anything except day-time television." Her lips quivered. She pressed them together hard.

"When did this happen?" Becky asked.

"In June. Six weeks before Oliver was born," Kelly said. She planted kisses on Oliver's pudgy cheeks while we did the math.

"Are you all right financially?" Ayinde finally asked.

Kelly gave a short laugh. "We are now that I've gone back to work. I mean, he keeps saying we should use our savings—he was in a dot-com start-up right out of graduate school, and he actually was one of the three people our age to make it out before the bubble burst—but I don't want to touch it; it's our nest egg. So I'm paying the bills." She was rocking back and forth, patting Oliver's overall-clad bottom, looking as if she was going to collapse under the chubby baby's weight. "I didn't want to go back to work. I always thought that I'd take a year off and stay home with the baby, only now . . ." She rocked back and forth faster. "I feel like I don't have a choice. And . . ." Her cheeks were flushing. "I like working. That's the bad part."

"Why is that bad?" Becky asked. "It's not a bad thing to like what you do."

Kelly settled the baby onto her hip and started pacing the length of the kitchen. "Maybe it's not that I like working. I like leaving. I like getting out of the house so I don't have to be with Steve twenty-four seven, but then I have to leave the baby with him, and I feel guilty about that because I know they're not doing anything educational, they're not going for walks or reading books or watching *Baby Einstein,* they're just lying on the couch watching *SportsCenter.*"

"Oh, Kelly," Becky murmured.

"And Steve . . ." Kelly dropped her eyes, pulling Oliver's face into her neck. "I don't know what's going on with him. I don't think he's even trying."

"What do you mean?" I asked.

"All he's been doing is seeing this career counselor. Some ass-hole," Kelly spat. I winced and wondered whether I'd ever heard her curse before. "They meet three times a week and do personality quizzes. *Are you an introvert or an extrovert? What's your emotional profile? What job would be your perfect fit?*" She shook her head. "I just wanted to shake him and say, 'Who cares about the perfect fit! Just go do something!' But he's just been sitting around all day, like it's been a weekend for months. No interviews. No nothing. And I'm working, and Steve's doing nothing. Nothing," she repeated, and she jumped to her feet. "I've got to go."

"Kelly," Becky said, stretching out her hand.

"No, no, I've got a bunch of phone calls to make," she said, picking up her diaper bag. "Florist, caterer, lighting company, and I've got to go to the drugstore, and our toilet's backed up, so I've got to track down the plumber. I'll call you guys later." And with that, she ran up the stairs.

Becky and Ayinde looked at the stairs, then down at their babies. "I'll go," I said, and hurried after her. "Kelly! Hey!"

She'd gotten Oliver into the stroller and was trying to pick up the whole thing and wrestle it out the door.

"Let me help." I opened the door and helped her lift the stroller down to the sidewalk. "Do you want me to walk you home?"

"Nnnooo," she said slowly. "No. I can't ask you to do that."

"Do you want me to stay with Oliver?"

I held my breath, half believing that she'd laugh at me or give me a cheerful brush-off, another version of *No, no, everything's fine.* Instead, she stopped in her tracks. "Could you?" she asked. "Could you do that?"

"Sure I could. I've got to work at the restaurant tonight, but this afternoon I'm free."

"Oh my God. You'd be saving my life. Steve could . . ." She rubbed her eyes with her fists, and I wondered how long it had been since she'd gotten a stretch of uninterrupted sleep. "I could tell him that he could take some time and get some work done, make some calls or something. We'd pay you, of course."

"Don't worry about it. Just let me go get my stuff."

"Thank you," she said. She grabbed my hand. Her eyes were gleaming. "Thank you so much."

"Oh, no. No, no. No, no, no," Becky said, shoving the yellow bandanna backward over her disheveled curls.

I looked up from the manchego cheese I was slivering to put on the salads. "What's wrong?" It was eight o'clock at night. I'd spent my afternoon at Kelly's, playing with Oliver while Steve closeted himself in the office, and I'd been working in the kitchen since six o'clock, with only a quick break to go back to my apartment to shower and exchange my Gloria Vanderbilts for a pair of high school Sassons. My apartment was no longer empty. The week before, Ayinde had asked whether I could use a few things. "I'm redecorating," she told me. The next morning, a truck bearing what appeared to be the entire contents of her guest house had arrived. I called Ayinde and said there was no way I could accept all of her things, but she'd insisted. "You'll be doing me a favor," she said. So now I had oversize leather couches and armchairs, lamps and a coffee table, a projection-screen TV, and several of Richard's framed MVP certificates, which I assumed I'd be returning at some point.

Becky retied her bandanna. "I have twenty-five hungry businessmen who are expecting Chilean sea bass with wild mushrooms and tamarind sauce, and . . ." She flung open the walk-in dramatically. "I have no wild mushrooms. I don't even have domestic mushrooms with bad-ass tendencies. I have no mushrooms at all."

I stole a glance toward the dining room, where the businessmen seemed quite happy with their sangria and seared tuna on tortilla chips, with Sarah shimmying around in high-heeled patent-leather boots, keeping their glasses full.

"Maybe you can give them extra arepas," I suggested.

The phone in the kitchen rang. "Becky," called Dash the dishwasher, waggling the receiver. "For you."

She took the phone. "Yes. What? No. No, I can't. No, I . . ." She shoved the bandanna backward again. "Oh, man."

"What?"

She shook her head, turning toward the deep fryer, where the arepas were bubbling away. "Day care's closing at nine, and I'm never going to get out of here by then, and Andrew's scrubbing in on an emergency pancreatic duodectomy—don't ask me what that is; I don't even want to know . . ." She groaned, flipped the arepas deftly out of the basket, and looked into the walk-in again, as if the mushrooms might have materialized during the phone call. "I'm going to have to call Mimi," she said, raising her eyes toward the ceiling. "Why, God, why?"

"I could get the mushrooms," I said.

"No, no, that's okay. I'll just send Sarah out with more booze. That doesn't look like a crowd that's going to get upset about missing their vegetables."

"Or I could get Ava."

Becky put her forefinger against her lips and pretended to think about it. "Hmm, the mushrooms or my daughter? I say, get the kid. I'll call the day care, so they don't think you're stealing her. Hang on, let me give you a key." She rummaged in her pocket. "You can take my car, the car seat's in the back, one of us should be home by midnight. Here, wait, let me give you money . . ."

"For what?"

Becky looked at me, then scratched her head beneath the bandanna. "Incidentals?"

"I'm fine," I said. "Where'd you park?"

"Twentieth and Sansom. You're saving my life, you know that? I'll be grateful to you forever. I'll name my second born after you." She handed me the keys and pointed toward the door. "Run like the wind!"

The hospital's day-care center was on the third floor of the hospital, and Ava was the last baby there, curled up in a crib in a corner of the room where the lights were turned down low. "Her father came in to see her about an hour ago," the day-care lady whispered after she'd perused my Los Angeles driver's license and waved away my offer to call Becky and have her reconfirm that I was okay to take the baby. She handed me Ava's bag with her bottle, a blanket, and a change of clothes. "She's been down about forty-five minutes, and Dr. Rabinowitz says she sometimes sleeps the whole way home."

"Hi, baby," I whispered. Ava sighed in her sleep. I lifted her gently into my arms, set her into her stroller, and went out to the car.

"Bye and bye, bye and bye, the moon's a slice of lemon pie," I sang down on the street as I eased her into the car seat and pulled a fuzzy pink cap over her bald head. She opened her eyes and looked at me curiously.

"Hi, Ava. Remember me? I'm your mother's friend. I'm going to take you home to sleep."

Ava blinked as if this information made some kind of sense.

"We're going to go to your house and have a nice bottle . . . well, actually, you're going to have a nice bottle. And then I'm going to change your diaper, and tuck you into your crib."

Ava yawned and closed her eyes. I looked all around us, down the street and then over my shoulder as I got behind the wheel, looking for homeless people, crazies, potentially noisy revelers. But Walnut Street was quiet. "You're very cute, do you know that?" I whispered toward the backseat. At Becky's house, I lifted the sleeping baby into my arms and tiptoed to the second floor. Ava's room was tiny, with hardly enough room for a crib and a rocker and a mobile of a cow jumping over the moon. It smelled like diaper cream and Johnson's Calming Body Wash, which I, personally, had found useless. "If there was really something that could calm your baby down," Sam had said, "wouldn't it cost a lot more than three ninety-nine?"

I fed the baby with the bottle labeled BREAST MILK, with a little skull and crossbones drawn beside it—for Mimi's benefit, I assumed. Ava sucked down four ounces with her eyes closed, making pleased little gulps as she drank. I patted her back until she burped. I changed her diaper, kissed her feet, wrapped her in her blanket again, and cradled her close to my chest. I imagined I could feel my milk letting down, that bittersweet tingling sensation I'd get before Caleb was ready to nurse. *What would Caleb have been like at her age?* I wondered. *Would he be calm, with Ava's wide, watchful eyes? Would he follow my fingers as I spider-walked them over his belly? Would he smile at me?* I sat in the rocker with Ava in my arms, breathing in her scent, the sound of her exhalations, feeling sad but somehow peaceful as I remembered my son.

"Ready for bed?" I finally asked. The baby's body seemed to melt against mine, her little head tucked against the side of my face, her belly against my shoulder. I could feel her breath against my cheek as I settled her into her crib.

I went downstairs and could hear the house settling around me. My mind did the math automatically. If it was ten o'clock here, it was seven in Los Angeles. I slipped my cell phone out of my pocket. I could call him, but what would I say? That I'd held two different babies and nothing had gone wrong? That I missed him? That I thought about him every minute I wasn't thinking about Caleb?

I took my shoes off and crept back up the stairs. Ava was snoring, and she'd turned herself over, planting her head on her arms with her bottom in the air. I couldn't keep from smiling as I padded past her into the bathroom. My face in the bathroom mirror looked different . . . or, rather, similar. I looked more like my own mother than I ever had in my whole life. It was in the eyes, I thought, and I lifted a lock of my hair. I'd dyed it brown for a part in a toothpaste commercial once, and Sam had looked at it, asking, "Is that your original color?"

"Who can remember?" I told him.

"I think it looks nice," he'd said.

I wondered how I'd look as a brunette again. I figured I'd have to do something, as the two-toned look had gone out with 1985-era Madonna. Brown might look good, I thought, listening to the baby monitor in case Ava woke up and needed me. It would be like coming home.

December

KELLY

At six A.M., a week after she'd told her friends the truth about her husband, Kelly lay in bed, body stiff, hands balled into fists, listening to Oliver gurgle and coo and babble to himself, hoping, as she did every morning, that Steve would wake up before she did. She glanced sideways. He was sprawled on his back, snoring, mouth gaping open. "Let me take him," he'd told her every morning for the first two weeks the baby was home. She hadn't let him. What was the point? He couldn't nurse the baby, and soon he'd be working again so he needed his rest.

Stupid, she thought, as Steve snored. Because now it was almost five months later, and he still wasn't working, and Oliver had gotten to the point where he wouldn't accept anyone but her first thing in the morning.

Kelly eased herself out of the warm bed and went to get the baby, who stopped chewing on the edge of his blanket and just looked at her before breaking into a broad grin that displayed his dimples. "Good morning, angel," she said, feeling her heart lift as she carried him to the changing table, nuzzling his brown hair that seemed to get thicker every day. Oliver hadn't been the best-looking new-born—he'd inherited Steve's nose which worked better on an adult than on a baby, and his face had looked like a puffy balloon over his scrawny limbs—but he'd turned into a gorgeous baby, pudgy and sweet-tempered, hardly ever crying. His thighs were Kelly's favorites. They were deliciously plump, soft and squishy as twin loaves of fresh-baked bread, and she couldn't keep herself from planting kisses up and down them before she pulled off his pajamas and wriggled him into a pair of overalls and a red-and-white-striped shirt.

Gorgeous but—she could admit it to herself only in these quiet morning hours—a little boring. She loved him, she would die for him, she couldn't imagine her life without him, but the truth was, after fifteen minutes playing with him under his Gymini or reading him one of his Sandra Boynton board books, her fingers started itching for the keyboard, for the BlackBerry and Palm Pilot, for the cell phone, the relics of a life where she'd had places to go, important things to take care of, even the occasional forty-five minutes to curl up in bed and page through *Metropolitan Home.*

Steve came up behind her, breathing his sour morning breath on the back of her neck, rubbing his stubble against her cheek until she moved away. He'd sometimes shaved twice a day when he was working; now he'd go two or three days without shaving at all. "Let me do it. You can go rest."

"We're fine," she said without turning around. *There was something wrong with her,* she thought. She wanted Steve to help, and then when he showed up, she was just irritated that he hadn't gotten there faster. She'd wanted a baby so desperately—the perfect baby to complete their perfect family—and now that she had one . . . She fastened Oliver's overalls as Steve shrugged and went back to the bedroom. She did want her baby. No matter how bad things got, she'd always believe that.

Kelly sat cross-legged on the bed, opened her nightgown, and pulled the baby against her. This was the happiest time of her day, sitting in the warm half darkness with Oliver in her arms, and afterward, when he was done, she would set him on the bed and then lay down beside him, slipping between the sheets to drift into a dream of how her life would have turned out differently if she'd married anyone but Steve.

Brett, she thought. Brett had flirted with her for a month during her junior year of college, and she'd thought he was sweet and funny but too odd looking for her taste—he was six and a half feet tall and beanpole skinny with a mullet and a weird *hyuk, hyuk, hyuk* of a laugh. She'd told him she just wanted to be friends, and he'd sighed and said, "That's what they all say." According to her alumni magazine, Brett had moved to Silicon Valley, started up a dot-com, and sold it for many millions of dollars before the crash. There'd been a half-page feature on him, complete with a head shot. He'd lost the bad haircut and acquired a wife and three children. The article didn't mention his laugh.

Or she could have ended up with Glen, her high school boyfriend, captain of the debate team. Mary had run into his mother in the beauty shop and learned that he was now a partner in a D.C. law firm. Glen hadn't been the most passionate guy in the world— Kelly could still vividly remember how he'd refused to make out with her the night before the SATs, saying they should conserve their energy for the test—but he'd had ambition to spare. If she'd married him, she wouldn't be the one running herself ragged.

At eight o'clock, Lemon started nosing at Kelly's palm, and Oliver opened his eyes. Kelly changed his diaper, then put him back in his crib, wailing, while she threw on the clothes she'd left lying on the floor the night before and took ten seconds to brush her teeth and slap cold water on her face. Then she put Oliver into his stroller, hooked Lemon up to his leash, pulled her hair into a ponytail, and left Steve still sleeping. She walked to the elevator, trying to keep the dog's leash from tangling in the stroller's wheels.

Lemon whined as the elevator carried them down to the lobby. He'd been a reasonably well-behaved dog in the prebaby days, but ever since Oliver's arrival, he'd been summarily demoted from his position of number-one most-loved nonverbal creature in the house. Pre-baby, Kelly had been able to take Lemon on long walks, to buy him fancy collars and matching leashes, to fuss over him, and scratch his belly. Post-baby, Lemon was lucky if he got fresh water and a pat on the head in passing. And he wasn't enjoying his new status as a second-class citizen.

"Lemon, shhh!" she hissed, as he started whining, then barking, and the baby gave a startled full-body jerk and began to cry. She slipped a pacifier between Oliver's lips, threw Lemon a dog treat, and made it onto the sidewalk, pushing the baby and pulling the dog.

They commenced the daily lurch-a-thon. She took five steps, then ten, then Lemon planted himself in the center of the sidewalk and refused to budge. "Lemon, come!" she said, as men in business suits and women in high heels gave her a wide berth. "Lemon, COME!" she said, tugging at his leash, hoping that nobody was watching her or speed-dialing the ASPCA and reporting her for dog abuse.

They made it around the block to the Promised Land, the neighborhood coffee shop. Kelly tied Lemon's leash to a parking meter, pushed the stroller with one hand and opened the door with the other.

"Triple espresso," the barista sang out as Kelly approached the counter.

"You know it," she said. She didn't think she was supposed to be drinking so much coffee while she was still nursing—poor Oliver would be a caffeine junkie before he hit nursery school—but she couldn't get through the day without it. She dumped skim milk and fake sugar into her cup, took her first gulp, then headed outside to collect the dog. Oliver's stroller had a cup holder, which bore the printed warning NO HOT BEVERAGES! DANGER TO BABY! In the past months, Kelly had gotten proficient at one-handed pushing, with Lemon's leash wrapped around one hand and her cup balanced in the other. The system worked perfectly most of the time. That morning, Lemon lunged playfully toward a skateboarder, and Kelly jerked her hand back, hissing as scalding coffee splashed her wrist and hand.

Finally, back in the apartment, Kelly left Oliver dozing in the stroller, dumped food and fresh water into Lemon's bowls, and powered up the laptop, drinking coffee and checking her e-mail as fast as she could. She'd gotten through half of her unread messages when the baby started to stir.

She looked toward the bedroom. The door was still shut. "Steve?"

The door popped open and Steve popped out, still in a T-shirt and underwear, with his flaccid pink penis wagging through the slit of his boxers. "Why didn't you wake me up? I could have taken the dog out."

"Just take the baby for a minute," she said.

"No problem," he said, scooping Oliver out of the stroller.

"He might need to burp!" Kelly called over her shoulder, knowing it was a lost cause. Steve would give the baby a few halfhearted whacks on the back, then determine that the baby didn't need to burp. Well, it wasn't that Oliver didn't need to burp, it was that Steve gave up too early. That was turning into quite the pattern, she thought, putting the computer on standby, parking herself in the rocker, and unfastening her bra.

Please, she whispered to herself, as she placed the plastic cups over her nipples and flicked the machine on. *Please let this end soon.* "Please," she muttered, looking at the plastic bottles attached to the cups and at her nipples, once a pretty carnation pink, now turned beige, cracked and ugly as an elephant's knees. There was maybe an eighth of an inch of milk in the right-hand bottle, only a few drops in the left. Pumping was tedious and uncomfortable, and it was impossible to do anything else while the machine was running. It took both hands and all of her coordination to keep the cups in place, and if she didn't relax, no milk. "Please," she said again and closed her eyes, rocking until the timer went off and fifteen minutes had elapsed. She unhooked herself gratefully and held the bottles to the light. Three ounces. Not enough for a full bottle. It'd be formula again.

The doorbell rang as she was pulling her shirt into place. Kelly gathered the bottles and ran to the foyer like she was hoping to see Santa Claus or Ed McMahon with an oversized check. She knew it would be Lia on the other side. And as far as she was concerned, Lia, who'd agreed to babysit three days a week, was better than Santa and Ed combined.

"Hi!" Lia said, sweeping into the apartment, her hair (newly dyed a shiny chestnut) gathered into a glossy ponytail, her white shirt (clean, unspotted) tucked into her khakis (ironed, this season's). Kelly could feel herself relaxing as Lia bent and plucked Oliver out of the exersaucer where Steve had deposited him. It was so nice to have a living human being in the house who'd actually help.

Kelly caught a flash of Steve's underpants and heard the bedroom door slam as Lia touched her nose to Oliver's. "Hi, Ollie-by-golly!" Kelly watched Lia hold her baby. The two of them—Oliver so smiley, Lia so beautiful—looked like one of the ads she'd seen in her parenting magazines, when she still had time to read them. Whereas she looked like the "before" photographs in any of the makeover stories. *I should have married Lia,* she thought. Lia never had to be asked twice to burp a baby. Lia knew instinctively, or from her own experience, that a wet diaper could still feel dry and would never pull one of Steve's favorite tricks, which was to hook his thumb underneath the legband, take a quick feel, and say, "Nope, he's dry," when the diaper in question was visibly soaked and you could practically see ammonia-scented stink lines coming off of it. Lia would never plop in front of the TV set with the baby in her arms and watch *SportsCenter* or surf the Net with the baby tucked haphazardly into the crook of her arm. She and Kelly could cook low-fat meals and take Oliver to the park, the zoo, the Please Touch museum. There would be no sex, of course. Kelly didn't think she'd miss it much.

She gave Lia the rundown—what time Oliver had gotten up, where they'd walked, what he'd eaten—as she packed up her laptop, cell phone, keys, Palm Pilot, and wallet. Steve ambled back to the table, dressed—more or less—in an ancient, threadbare T-shirt, bare feet, and jeans. "I'm going to be working at home today," he said, half defiantly, half apologetically. The little speech was for Lia's benefit, not Kelly's, because where else would he be quote-unquote working?

"Fine," Kelly said, trying to sound cheerful for the baby's benefit. She gathered her gear and returned to the coffee shop.

"Back so soon?" the barista called.

"Me again," said Kelly. She ordered another triple espresso, plugged in her laptop, and wondered what the staff at the coffee shop made of her, sitting there for five hours a day, five days a week, sucking down espresso and typing away. She wondered if they hated her for taking up the space, a prime table by the window. Maybe they thought she was a graduate student or a struggling poet, something grand and romantic or at least interesting.

She hit the Power button and slugged down scalding espresso in short little sips, tapping her toes until the sluggish, temperamental old laptop fired up. Her cell phone trilled. "Kelly Day!" she chirped and then closed her eyes, resting her head on her palm as she took notes on the Margolies wedding and the Drexel holiday party and the Pfizer Diversity Day celebration, for which she'd been tasked with procuring a jelly-bean rendering of Dr. Martin Luther King. She typed and took notes and asked the right questions, trying to time her calls to when nobody was ordering a frappuccino, so that her clients wouldn't hear the blender whirring in the background.

It was a joke. A sham. She felt like the Wizard of Oz, a fraud behind the coffee shop's green awning, working her ass off while her husband stayed home watching soap operas—he'd denied it hotly when she'd confronted him, but the TiVo to-do list still included recording the daily episodes of *As the World Turns*. She'd work, making calls, making notes, checking her watch, thinking about Oliver, wondering if he was napping; thinking about Steve, wondering if he was napping, too.

At five o'clock she speed-walked home. Lia was playing with Oliver on the living room floor, rattling stuffed animals in front of his face. Steve was nowhere to be found. *Probably visiting the career counselor again* she thought, hurrying to the bedroom and holding her breath as she inched the shaper brief and control-top pantyhose over her hips, and zipped up her long black velvet skirt as best she could.

"Oh, look how pretty!" Lia said to Oliver, as Kelly sat, legs splayed, on the ghetto couch and struggled into her high-heeled party shoes. "You really do look nice."

"Yeah, well . . ." She paused for five seconds in front of the mirror in the hallway, swiping lipstick over her lips, trying to smooth her flyaway hair. "I just hope this goes well. And thank you. Thank you so much."

She sat on the couch with the baby on her hip, jiggling him up and down. No Steve. She stabbed his number on her cell phone. "Where are you? You were supposed to be here at six, remember? Lia had to go to Mas, and I've got a party . . ."

She could hear the sounds of traffic in the background—engines and horns blaring. "There's, like, a five-car pileup just past Aramingo," Steve said. "I've been stuck here for forty-five minutes. Nothing's moving."

"Can't you get off and take back roads?"

"As soon as I get to the exit, I will, but I can't exactly drive through other people."

"What am I going to do?" she moaned. Lia was gone, she'd never be able to get a sitter on such short notice, she didn't know the neighbors well enough to leave Oliver with them, and if she didn't leave soon she'd be late for the party she was managing that night.

"Can you take him with you? It shouldn't be for very long. As soon as I get off the highway I'll meet you at the party and take him home."

"Fine, fine," she said, grabbing the diaper bag and her purse, giving Steve the address, hanging up the phone and running out the door.

The hostess's name was—Kelly flipped open her dayrunner as she got out of the cab—Dolores Wartz, and the event was a holiday party in an apartment building's function room for her sorority alums. Dolores Wartz was fortyish, a squat bulldoggy woman with heavy makeup caked in the grooves that ran from the corners of her mouth to her chin, and lipstick the color and consistency of strawberry jam caked on her lips.

"Kelly Day?" she said, beaming. Her smile evaporated as she caught sight of the baby. "What is that?"

"This is my son, Oliver," Kelly said. *And he's not a what, he's a who.* "I'm so sorry about this. My husband was supposed to be home but I guess there was a big accident on 95 . . ." Oliver squirmed in her grasp, and there was the unmistakable sound—not to mention smell—of a baby filling his diaper. *Shit,* Kelly thought. "I'm just going to run to the bathroom. My husband should be here any minute."

"I hope so," Dolores Wartz said, fingering the heavy gold sorority pin on her lapel. *Great,* Kelly thought. She hurried to the bathroom, where there was, of course, no changing table. She locked a stall, set the baby on the floor, trying not to think about the germs crawling on the tile, knelt, and changed him as fast as she could. She washed her hands and hurried back to the foyer, where Dolores Wartz was glaring at her and Marnie Kravitz, Elizabeth's assistant, was shifting her weight from foot to foot like a little kid who needs to use the bathroom and is afraid to ask permission.

"Kelly," Marnie said.

"Yes?" Kelly said, noticing that Marnie had taken their boss's "festive seasonal attire" directive very seriously. She was wearing a green skirt, red-and-white snowflake-patterned tights, and a red sweater with fluffy white reindeer cavorting across the bosom.

"We are having a *crisis,*" she said, laying her hand across Rudolph's blinking nose for emphasis. "We have no *napkins!*"

Kelly pulled her gaze away from Marnie's hypnotic reindeer. "Excuse me?"

"The tablecloths came, and the liquor, and the caterer's setting up, but they thought the florist was bringing the linens, and the florist said you only told her to bring tablecloths . . ."

Oh, no. Kelly grabbed for her Palm Pilot and saw its red light flashing. Dead battery. Just her luck. And Marnie was practically wringing her hands. Kelly saw she'd painted her fingernails in alternating red and green stripes.

"What are we going to do?" Marnie moaned.

She reached into her purse and handed Marnie her emergency fifty bucks. "Run down to the Seven-Eleven on JFK and buy some."

Marnie's eyes bulged. "But they'll only have paper! Kelly, we can't use paper napkins!"

"It's not the end of the world," Kelly said. She tried to keep her tone light, but Dolores Wartz was looking at her as if maggots were crawling out of her mouth. Oliver took the opportunity to swing his hand and bash her on the ear. Steve, she thought, goddamnit, as her ears rang, where was Steve?

"Couldn't you hire a sitter?" Dolores Wartz asked coldly.

Kelly took a deep breath. "As I said, my husband will be here as soon as he can."

"I have two children. Twelve and fourteen," Dolores Wartz said. She said nothing else. But then, Kelly thought, she didn't have to. The subtext was perfectly clear. *I had two children and I never had to bring either one of them to work with me. I had two children and I managed much better than you are.*

"I'm going to see how the caterer's doing," Kelly said. She settled Oliver against her hip and hurried through the first guests, past the bar set up in the corner, into the kitchen, where she slumped against the side of the ovens and closed her eyes.

"Wow, what a cutie!" one of the waitresses said.

"You want him?" Kelly asked. "I'm not kidding. Take him. He's yours." She looked around. Shrimp cocktail, crabcakes, cheese straws. Real creative, she thought, as the waitresses loaded silver platters and filed out the door.

She grabbed a cheese straw off a tray and ate it fast, realizing that she hadn't had anything all day except espresso. She was finishing a crabcake when a smiling woman in a lavender suit stuck her head into the kitchen. "Sorry to bother you, but do you know where I could find a napkin?" She pointed ruefully at a blob of cocktail sauce on her lapel, and beamed at Oliver. "Ooh, what a cutie!"

Kelly gave her a grateful smile and dug in her diaper bag for the packet of baby wipes. "This should work."

"Perfect!" said the woman. She blotted the sauce, squeezed Oliver's foot, and headed out the door just as the waitresses returned.

"Hey," said one of them, peering at Kelly's head. "You've got . . ." She reached out with two long fingernails and plucked something out of Kelly's hair. Kelly blinked at it. A Cheerio. She'd given some to Oliver the day before. Had she been going around for twenty-four hours with cereal stuck in her hair?

"New fashion," Kelly said crisply.

"Excuse me." Dolores Wartz had shoved through the door. "Kelly. Your husband is here."

Thank you, God, she thought. She managed to smile at Dolores before she race-walked to the door and shoved Oliver into his father's arms. "Go now!" she hissed.

"Why?" Steve asked. "Is something on fire?"

"Just go!" she said, trying to tuck the diaper bag under Steve's arms. "I've got work to do!"

Steve looked up. "Hey," he said. She followed his gaze. Mistletoe. Left over from someone else's party, she thought.

"Steve, I've got a million things to do . . ."

He leaned forward and pecked her cheek. "Go," he said. "I'll see you later."

She wiped her hands on her skirt and faced the crowd—sixty women, most of them with glasses of wine in their hands, nibbling cheese straws and swaying to the Christmas carols.

The bar was busy; Marnie had given some napkins to the waitresses and set out more on the cocktail tables. Under control, Kelly thought, and let herself relax.

At eleven o'clock the caterers were gone, the guests had departed, the last of the linens had been folded away, the last of the dishes replaced. Kelly said good night to Dolores Wartz, who grunted something in return. She slipped off her shoes in the elevator and limped onto the sidewalk. She'd finally managed to find a cab and had settled herself into the strawberry incense-reeking backseat when her cell phone rang.

"Kelly?" Elizabeth's voice was colder than Kelly had ever heard it. "I just got a very disturbing phone call from Dolores Wartz. Do you want to tell me what happened?"

"Well, that was fast," Kelly said. It looked like good old Dolores hadn't wasted a moment saying hello or good night to her kids. Just had to get right on the phone and tattle on me. "Look," she began, "there was an accident on 95. Steve was late, so I had to bring Oliver, but he was only there for, like, half an hour, and he wasn't bothering anyone."

"Dolores said that he was crying and that he was never taken out."

"He wasn't crying," Kelly said. "He was maybe making noise, but he wasn't crying. And Elizabeth, he's a baby. He's not a bag of trash!"

"She was very disappointed," Elizabeth continued. "She said you were paying more attention to the baby than you were to her party."

Well, the party didn't need its diaper changed, Kelly thought, but she bit her lip and said nothing.

"She's asking for her money back."

Kelly balled her hands into fists. It took her a moment to recognize the unfamiliar sensation that caused her eyelids to prickle with tears. It was something she hadn't felt since the fifth grade, when the principal had called her into the office and said that, while he admired Kelly's entrepreneurial spirit, it wasn't fair for her to charge admission to the jungle gym. She was in trouble. No. Worse. She'd screwed something up. "Fine," she said. "Whatever my commission was, you can send it to her. Tell her I'm very sorry she was so disappointed."

"Fine." Elizabeth paused. "Kelly, we had this conversation when you started working again. You need to learn to keep your personal and professional life separate."

"I'm sorry, Elizabeth," Kelly said, feeling somewhere between deeply ashamed and furious. "But I can't control the traffic!"

"You should have had a backup plan in place . . ."

"Well, clearly . . ." Kelly forced herself to be quiet. She took a deep breath. "I'm sorry," she said again. And she was—but not for the reasons Elizabeth probably thought. She was sorry for Oliver, sorry that she'd subjected him to spending even a minute in a room full of toxic bitches who couldn't bring themselves to be the least bit understanding or the least bit kind. "Send her my money," she said.

"Fine," Elizabeth said. Her voice was fractionally warmer. "Let's try and put this behind us, Kelly. You know you're one of my most valued employees."

Kelly knuckled her eyelids and willed herself not to cry.

"I'm sorry," she said again. "I'll call you in the morning." She flipped her phone shut, pressed her cheek against the cracked black vinyl of the backseat, and sobbed for the sixteen blocks home.

BECKY

The war started innocently enough, with a package in the mail addressed, in Mimi's scrawling hand, to A. RABINOWITZ. Mimi still had not let go of the idea that her granddaughter should have been named Anna Rabinowitz. *Like it would kill her to write Rothstein,* Becky thought, tucking the package under her arm. She tossed it on the kitchen counter and forgot about it for two days. When she finally got around to opening it, she wasn't sure what she was seeing when something satiny slithered out of the box. Something made of red and green diamonds, with Ava's name embroidered at the top.

"Is this what I think it is?" she asked Andrew, holding the offending item pinched between her fingertips.

Andrew glanced up briefly. "It's a Christmas stocking," he said.

"Andrew." Her husband looked up from his coffee cup. "This may come as a surprise, but as it turns out, we're Jews."

"Well, yes, but . . ." He shrugged and took another sip. "Mimi does Christmas. And now that she's in town, I guess she wants to do it with us."

"What do you mean, Mimi does Christmas? Is that like *Debbie Does Dallas?*" Becky turned the box over and groaned when a red-and-green BABY'S FIRST CHRISTMAS! bib fell out.

Andrew poured himself more coffee. "She just figured that just because we are Jewish is no reason for us to be deprived of Christmas."

"We don't believe in Jesus. That's a pretty good reason."

"Becky, please, let's not fight."

She folded the stocking back into its box. "So you had a Christmas tree?"

Andrew nodded.

"Hung up stockings?"

Another nod.

"Sang carols?"

"On occasion." He added milk to his cup. "She thought Christmas was more of a secular national holiday than a religious event."

"But . . ." Becky's mind was whirling. "So now she thinks that Ava's going to celebrate Christmas."

He shrugged, shifting his weight in his seat. "I never discussed it with her."

"Well, I think we should. We're not even going to be here on the twenty-fifth. Remember? We've got tickets to go see my mom."

"So I'll tell her," Andrew said. "It's not a big deal. Really, it's not. I'll call her tomorrow night."

But first thing the next morning, there was a knock on the door and seven feet of fir tree on the front steps.

"Thanks, but we don't need a tree," said Becky to the short man in jeans and an Eagles jacket all but obscured by the branches.

"Delivery," he grunted, shaking the tree at her. Pine needles drifted down around her feet. "Paid for already. Sign here, please."

"Just leave it on the curb," Becky said after she'd signed.

"You serious?" the man asked.

"You can have it, if you want."

The man looked at Becky, looked at the tree, shook his head, spat on the sidewalk, and left the tree leaning against her stairs. "Merry Christmas," he said.

"Happy Chanukah," Becky called and shut the door, vowing that she and Andrew were going to have a meaningful discussion about the true meaning of Christmas as it pertained to the Rothstein-Rabinowitz family as soon as he got back from work.

Twenty minutes later, the telephone rang. "Oh, you're home!" Mimi trilled. "Did the tree arrive?"

Becky drew herself up straight, tensing her muscles, readying herself for the inevitable fight. "Yes, Mimi, about that tree."

"Isn't it just heavenly?" her mother-in-law asked. "I do love the smell of a fresh fir tree!"

"Listen, Mimi, about the tree . . . we're not Christian."

"Well, I know that, silly!" Mimi giggled.

"So . . ." Becky was starting to feel as though she'd slipped into Wonderland, where up was down and down was up and even the simplest, most obvious facts in the world required elaborate explanation. "We aren't going to celebrate Christmas. We aren't even going to be here for Christmas. We're going to be in Florida. So we really don't want the tree."

When she spoke again, Mimi's voice was as cold as the December air. "You're not having Christmas?" she demanded.

Becky's hand tightened on the telephone. "Andrew and I have talked about it, and this is how we both feel. Of course, you're welcome to do whatever you like with Ava in your house. But no Christmas here. I'm sorry."

"You're canceling my granddaughter's first Christmas?" Mimi screeched.

God help me, Becky thought. "No. Of course not. And like I said, whatever you want to do in your house is fine, but . . ."

"But what about Christmas dinner? Who's going to make the HAM?"

Ham. Ham. Had Andrew mentioned a ham?

"I made plans," Mimi bleated. "I already invited my relatives. How will I ever hold up my head if you cancel? It's already bad enough that you couldn't even name your daughter Anna—a beautiful name, a classic name, my mother's name, in case you've forgotten . . ."

Becky bit her lip. Back to this again.

"But then you cancel my granddaughter's first CHRISTMAS!

I've got the recipes all picked out, and I've got presents for my grand-daughter to put under the tree, and you . . . you . . . GRINCH!"

Becky felt a fit of giggles coming on. "Okay, Mimi, let's not lose our tempers here."

"You have to have Christmas!" Mimi said.

"I don't have to do anything except be black and die!" Becky replied.

This shut Mimi up. For all of ten seconds. "WHAT DID YOU SAY TO ME?" she screamed.

"Who gave you the right to tell us what to do?" Becky asked. "Do I call you up and tell you who I'm bringing to your house and what holidays to celebrate and what to cook?"

"Don't you talk to me like that! You're out of line! Way out of line!"

"How am I out of line?" Becky asked. Her giggles were gone. Her last shred of patience had also vanished. "This is our house, and Andrew and I have every right to decide what to do here. We can name our baby what we want, we can celebrate what we want, we can invite who we want."

"I bet this was all your mother's idea," Mimi ranted. "I bet your MOTHER wanted you to cancel Ava's CHRISTMAS. She gets every-thing she wants, and I get left out in the cold! I get nothing! It's not fair!"

Becky took a deep breath, determined not to be baited or to quote any more movie dialogue at her mother-in-law. "If you want to cele-brate Christmas, that's up to you. What Andrew and I do in our house, with our daughter, is up to us."

Mimi's voice was deadly cold. "If you insist on going to visit your mother, I will never set foot in your house again."

Hallelujah, Becky thought. "Well, I'm sorry you feel that way," she said calmly. "But Andrew and I have discussed this. And our de-cision is final."

"You . . . you . . ." There was an outraged, wordless shriek. Then a dial tone. Mimi had hung up on her.

Becky stared at the phone. She didn't think anyone had hung up on her since sixth grade, when she and Lisa Yoseloff had gotten into a fight about whose turn it was to sit behind Robbie Marx on the bus. She clenched her shaking hands into fists and looked at Ava, who was sitting on the kitchen floor, happily clapping her plastic measuring cups together. "I hate to have to say this, but your grandmother is insane."

"Ehgah?" Ava said.

"If 'ehgah' is baby for insane, then yes. But not to worry." She picked up the phone. "We're going to call Daddy and get this whole thing straightened out."

"Can we change the tickets?" Andrew asked.

Becky pressed the phone against her ear. She must have heard him wrong. She'd told him the whole story, from the tree delivery right down to Mimi's threats, and this was his response?

"Andrew. Your mother called me a Grinch, hung up the phone on me, and she seems to be having some kind of psychotic fantasy in which I'll be preparing her holiday ham. She's out of control. I think skipping town is the smartest thing we could do."

She heard him sigh. "Mimi just called me. She's pretty upset." Another sigh.

"Yeah, I figured that out when she hung up on me. Look, Andrew, she's having a tantrum."

"You could call it that," Andrew allowed.

"And you know what you do when a little kid has a tantrum? You don't give him what he wants. You just walk away. You tell him he needs to calm down and that you won't talk to him until he does."

"I just think it would be easier if . . ."

" . . . we gave her what she wanted. I know. But look at the history! We always give her what she wants, and it never makes her happy. Not in the long term. Not even in the short term, really. We can't keep doing the same thing over and over and over, giving her what she wants and giving her what she wants and having her blow up at us anyhow. It's not working. Don't you see that?"

There was a pause. "Becky . . ." Andrew began.

. . . *she is my mother,* Becky concluded in her head. She felt her heart sinking. How could she not have seen this coming? Her husband, wonderful, handsome, sexy Andrew was a mama's boy of the first order. He wasn't even really married to her. He was married to Mimi. Mimi was the one whose wishes came first, whose screaming fits got her exactly what she wanted. Becky was just along for the ride.

"Why don't we just call and see if we can leave the day after Christmas instead of the day before," Andrew said. "It's not that big a deal. We'll still get to spend a whole week with your Mom. We'll give Mimi her day; we'll let her have her Christmas."

Becky shook her head. "No," she said. Her voice was quiet but firm. She wasn't going to pull a Mimi. She wasn't going to scream or threaten or slam down the phone. But she wasn't going to change her mind. "No."

"You're not even willing to do that?" Andrew asked. "To just give her one day?"

"It's not the day; it's the principle of the thing. We've got to take a stand somewhere, or else we're going to live the rest of our lives with Mimi running the show."

His voice was getting more indignant. "It's not like that."

Becky thought of all the examples she could give him; the dozens of tiny ways that Mimi manipulated and undermined them. The blueberry muffin she'd shoved down Ava's throat; the bow she'd cornstarched to her head, the parking tickets she shoved through their mail slot. The way there wasn't a single picture of Becky and Ava in her house; just pictures of Mimi and Ava, and Andrew and Ava, as if the two of them had grown the baby in a lab or picked her off a tree. The wedding dress that Mimi had worn to their wedding. "The Greatest Love of All." "Think about Ava," she said instead. "What do you think this is teaching her? She who screams loudest, who calls names and hangs up the phone on people, gets what she wants? That it's okay to tell your children how to live their lives? To never let them decide anything for themselves? To never let them grow up?"

"Mimi's not young anymore," he said. "She's not young, and she's all alone. I'm all she has."

"And you can be there for her," Becky said. "She's your mother. You're her son. I get all of that. But I'm your wife. Ava's your daughter. We should come first, don't you think? At least some of the time?"

There was a pause. "Did you really tell her that you didn't have to do anything except be black and die?" Andrew asked.

Becky twisted a curl around her finger. "It just popped out. I'm sorry."

She heard his sigh as if he was standing right there in the room with her. "I'll talk to her," he said quietly, as if he was talking to himself. "It'll be okay."

Andrew didn't come home until ten o'clock that night, and when he walked through the door his face was ashen and his eyes were red. Becky looked up from the floor, where she'd been playing with Ava, keeping her up way past her bedtime so that her father could see her before she went to sleep. "I take it things with Mimi didn't go well?"

Andrew shook his head. "She said we never told her we were going to Florida."

Becky felt her temper rising. "Do we have to clear it with her before we go anywhere? I'll double-check the ketubah, but I'm pretty sure it doesn't say anything about needing my mother-in-law's permission to go on vacation."

"And she's disappointed that she won't be having Christmas with her granddaughter."

"Well, you're the doctor, but I don't think anyone ever died of disappointment," Becky said, pulling a wooden block out of Ava's mouth, where she'd been working it over with the single tooth that had popped out the week before. "Easy there, Fang."

"Khhee!" said Ava and wriggled sideways in search of other prey.

"So you stuck to your guns?" Becky asked.

Andrew nodded. "She was crying."

"I'm sorry to hear that," she said. "But she'll get over it, won't she?"

Andrew slumped into an armchair. He picked up one of Ava's blocks and started twirling it. "I'm not sure."

"Oh, come on. This isn't going to kill her. She's just got to learn to compromise a little. You're married now. She can't have you at her beck and call, doing everything she wants. And like I told her, she can do whatever she wants in terms of holidays, religion, whatever, in her house. She just can't tell us what to do here."

Andrew buried his face in his hands. Becky got to her feet and wrapped her arms around his shoulders. "We're going to get through this. And then we're going to be in Florida. Fun and sun! Sand and surf! We'll put Ava in that little lobster bathing suit and let her float around the shallow end. Right, Ava?"

"Ish!" said Ava and popped another block into her mouth.

"Girlfriend, what have I told you about eating wood?" asked Becky. She replaced the block with a teething ring and kissed Andrew's ear. "It's going to be okay," she said. "She'll find someone else to cook her ham, and someday she'll get married again, and by the time we come back from Florida, she'll have forgotten all about it."

Andrew stared at her bleakly. "I hope you're right."

AYINDE

"Sorry I'm late," said Dr. Melendez, hurrying into the exam room. She stopped at the edge of the table and beamed at Julian, who gave her a gummy smile in return. "Oh, my," she said. "What an angel."

Ayinde felt her body relaxing, and she beamed down at her son. Her marriage might have been a mess, but at least she was succeeding as a mother. Well, more or less.

"Missed your six-month, huh?" the doctor chided. Ayinde looked down at her fur-lined boots.

"We were busy," she said. Dr. Melendez merely nodded. Was it possible she didn't know what was going on in Ayinde and Julian's life, or was she just being polite? "I'm very sorry. We're probably behind schedule on our shots."

"It's not a big deal," the doctor said, peering into Julian's ears. "I just don't want to make a habit of it. Tell me how things have been," she said, running her hands deftly over Julian's body as the two medical students behind her watched. She wiggled his feet, squeezed his knees in until they touched, then let them slip apart. "Is he on the move yet?"

"He's not crawling, but he's sitting up well and reaching for things. And babbling a lot, and trying to pull himself up on the edge of the couch." Ayinde paused for breath.

"Sounds just fine," said the doctor, slipping the stethoscope into her ears. She listened, glanced at Julian's chart, then slid the stethoscope's bell to another spot on his chest and frowned. "Hmm."

Ayinde's breath caught in her throat. "Is everything all right?"

Dr. Melendez held up a finger for silence. Ayinde watched the second hand sweep around the clock. Ten seconds, fifteen, twenty. She closed her eyes. "Is everything all right?" she asked again.

Dr. Melendez unhooked the stethoscope and looked at Julian's chart again. "Has Julian ever had any trouble breathing? Have you ever noticed him breathing rapidly?"

"No," Ayinde said, shaking her head. "No, never."

"Has anyone ever mentioned to you that Julian has a heart murmur?"

Ayinde sank onto the wheeled stool next to the examination table. "No," she said. "No. He was perfect. He was born a few weeks early, but other than that, he was perfect."

"Well, he's got a little murmur, and I'd like a cardiologist to take a listen. And probably a look."

Ayinde leaned over and lifted Julian, still clad only in a diaper, into her arms. "What's wrong?" she asked. Her voice was rising, and her own heart was banging against her ribs. "How bad is a heart murmur?"

"Lots of times, they're no big deal," Dr. Melendez said, squatting so she was at eye level with Ayinde. "The murmur by itself doesn't tell us much. Heart murmurs are very common, and frequently they're indicative of a problem that will correct itself over time. Julian's been healthy and thriving, as you've said, and his growth, well, as you can see, no problems there."

Ayinde found herself nodding rapidly. Julian had been in the ninety-fifth percentile for height and the eightieth for weight since he'd been born. *My big man,* Richard used to call him, when they'd still been speaking.

"There's a good chance that he might just have a condition that we'd watch as he grew or something that we can handle with medication."

"And if not?"

"Well, there are surgical options," Dr. Melendez said. "But let's not get ahead of ourselves. The first thing we need to do is find out what we're dealing with." She reached for her prescription pad and started writing. "I want you to see my colleague Dr. Myerson."

Ayinde felt dizzy. She tightened her grip on Julian. "So we should make an appointment?"

"Yes," said Dr. Melendez, handing over a prescription slip with a name, a telephone number, and an address. "He'll probably see you next week. And I want you to keep an eye on Julian. If you notice he's having trouble breathing—if he's gasping, if his lips turn blue—I want you to call us immediately and take him to the nearest emergency room. I don't think there's much chance of that happening," she continued, putting her hand on top of Ayinde's forearm. "If something was going to go wrong, it would have happened by now. The chances are good that he's fine. I just want us to be sure."

Ayinde nodded and said thank you. She fumbled Julian into his clothes and his stroller. She folded the prescription into her pocket, and walked to the parking garage where she strapped Julian into his car seat, collapsed behind the wheel, and called Becky.

"Does your husband know any pediatric cardiologists?"

"What's wrong?" Becky asked instantly.

"Julian has a heart murmur."

"Oh. Oh. Okay, don't panic. Lots of babies have them."

"I know, but we have to see this Dr. Myerson, and he might not have appointments until next week, and Richard's traveling— they've got games—and I don't think I can wait that long."

"Ayinde," Becky said. "The baby's not going to self-destruct. But let me see if Andrew can call in a favor."

"Thank you," Ayinde said. She stared at the phone in her hand for a long moment, her thoughts turning to the woman in Phoenix. She'd been forbidden from watching TV, forbidden from reading magazines—"Ignorance is bliss," Christina Crossley had told her. "Believe me, I've been through this enough to know that the less you

know, the better"——but Ayinde had seen the other woman's face gazing at her from a dozen newsstands, and once, she'd bought a copy of
the *National Examiner* and read it in the car while Julian dozed in his
car seat. The girl's name was Tiffany, and she'd been nothing but a
twenty-one-year-old junior college dropout and part-time spirit
dancer before Richard Towne's affections had elevated her to an object
of national scrutiny. Tiffany's baby's heart would be just fine.

Ayinde put her shaking hands in her pockets, willing them to be
still. Richard was in Boston, she thought——these days, she didn't
keep careful track of where he was going and who he was playing. She
dialed the number she hadn't called since she'd been in the hospital
herself, nine months before. *He better answer this time,* she thought and
felt relief course through her when the phone was picked up on the
first ring.

"Hello?"

It wasn't Richard. It was Christina Crossley, who'd comman-
deered the family's cell phones.

"Christina, this is Ayinde. I'm at the doctor's office with Julian. I
need to speak to Richard immediately."

"Why? Is something wrong?"

Ayinde could almost hear the other woman's mind clicking, running through possible problems, gauging their possible impact on
the campaign she was waging to save Richard's image and, by exten-
sion, his endorsement deals.

"I need to speak to Richard," Ayinde said. "Right now."

"Let me find him," Christina Crossley said. Seconds later, Richard
was on the line.

"Ayinde? That you?"

"I need you to come home," she managed to choke out. "There's
something wrong with the baby."

"Doctor, I don't understand," Ayinde said to Dr. Myerson, as he
weighed and measured Julian. Andrew had pulled God only knew

how many strings and gotten them the first appointment in the morning the next day. Richard had flown home from Boston, and they'd spent most of the night peering at Julian, who lay peacefully on the bed between them. They'd listened to his every inhalation, checking his lips to make sure they weren't blue, until at two in the morning, Richard had tucked a blanket around his wife's shoulders and said, "You go to sleep. I've got this." It was the first time she'd shared a bed with her husband in months.

"He was just fine when he was born, he's been fine ever since, he eats well, he's hit all of his developmental milestones . . ." She fumbled for the *Baby Success!* baby log she'd been keeping meticulously, a daily rendering of how long he'd nursed, what he'd eaten, wet diapers, dirty diapers, the time and duration of his naps.

"Sometimes these conditions don't present immediately," the doctor said. Dr. Myerson was in his fifties, balding, with dandyish glossy black wingtips and short, stubby fingers that Ayinde had already decided she didn't want anywhere near her baby's heart, even though Andrew had assured her that he was the best. Best or not, he lacked Dr. Melendez's nice bedside manner. Ayinde prayed that meant that he was good at his job. "Lots of surgeons are kind of arrogant," Becky had told her once. "What about Andrew?" Ayinde asked, and Becky had shrugged and said that she hoped her husband was going to be the rare exception.

Dr. Myerson listened to Julian's heart for twenty seconds before pulling off his stethoscope, handing the diaper-clad baby back to his mother, and turning to Richard and Ayinde. Richard reached for Ayinde's hand, and for the first time since the afternoon of Miss Phoenix, she let him take it. "Okay," said the doctor. His voice was high and scratchy. He sounded like a cartoon character. "From what I can tell by listening, I would bet that Julian has a ventricular septal defect—a hole between the right and left sides of his heart."

The world swam in front of her eyes. "What does that mean?" Ayinde asked.

"Why didn't anybody notice this before?" asked Richard. "He's had checkups—every month, right?"

"Every month for the first three months and then every three months," she said, leaving out how they'd been late for the six-month visit. "He's been perfect."

"As I said, these defects don't always present at birth. Now, to answer your question, Mrs. Towne, well, let me show you." He picked up something from the counter, a red-and-blue plastic model of a baby's heart. *So small,* Ayinde thought. "Now," he began, "the heart has four chambers, the left and right atria and the left and right ventricles. Normally, the left and right atria are separated by the atrial septum, and . . ." he pointed, "the left and right ventricles are separated by the ventricular septum."

"And Julian has a hole . . ." Ayinde tightened her grip on the baby, thinking, as she'd thought all through the night, that he looked completely healthy. Tall and long-limbed, with bright brown eyes and his father's smooth chestnut skin. Never had a cold. Not even the sniffles. Now this.

The doctor pointed again. "Here. Between the two ventricles. It's not an uncommon defect."

"You can tell that just by listening?" Richard asked.

The doctor preened and nodded.

"Does it . . ." Ayinde's breath caught in her throat. "Does it hurt him?"

The doctor shook his head. "He's not in any pain."

"How do we fix it?" Richard asked. "Does he need an operation?"

"It's too early to say," the doctor replied. "It could be that all we'll need to do is keep an eye on it, and it'll close up on its own, no muss, no fuss."

Richard cleared his throat. "Will he be able to run? To play sports?"

Ayinde stared at her husband in disbelief. Richard held her hand more tightly. "I just want to know that he'll be okay," Richard said.

The doctor was scribbling something on a sheet of paper. "Best-case scenario, he's completely fine, and the hole closes up by itself. As I've said, this kind of disorder isn't uncommon, and we'll just watch him. We'll listen to his heart every week, for starters, and then, if he remains asymptomatic, less frequently. He'll have to take antibiotics before he goes to the dentist, and that'll be about it. He'll have a long, happy life. Of course, there are other possibilities, but before we discuss them, I'd like to do some more diagnostic procedures."

Ayinde bent her head. "Why did this happen?" she asked.

"I wish that medicine had the answer to that, but we don't." The doctor's scratchy voice became incrementally more gentle. "It's a common birth defect. One out of every hundred babies has a problem with the heart. Sometimes it's poor nutrition or poor prenatal care, moms who use street drugs while they're pregnant . . ." He looked at Ayinde.

She shook her head before he could ask her. "Nothing. I might have had a glass of wine or two before we knew . . . before we were sure . . . but . . ."

"Don't blame yourself," he said. "No parent likes to hear this, but it's . . ." He shrugged, the starched shoulders of his lab coat rising. "Just one of those things."

Ayinde started to cry. Richard squeezed her hands. "It's going to be all right," he said.

She felt her own heart thundering in her chest. The dizziness was getting stronger. *I did something,* she thought . . . but what could it have been? What could she have done to have brought this on herself, on her baby?

She twisted away from him, moving toward the door. "I need to make some phone calls."

Richard tightened his grip. "Ayinde . . ."

"Why don't I give you a few minutes," Dr. Myerson said, and he was out the door almost before the words were out of his mouth. Ayinde wondered how he'd ended up in this line of work, giving bad news to families day in and day out, and how he handled it. Did he want to go home every night and cry?

She raised her face to her husband's. "I want to call my friends. I want them here with me. Becky's husband's a doctor, and her friend, Lia . . ." Her throat closed. "She had a baby . . ." And she ran out of words. She held Julian in her lap and pressed her face against her husband's chest and sobbed.

He cradled her head in his hands. "Shh . . . shhh, Ayinde, shh now, you'll scare the baby." He wrapped her body in his arms and rocked her and the baby, holding them both against his broad chest. "It's going to be all right," he said.

"How do you know?" she asked.

He gave her a crooked smile. "Because God isn't that cruel. You've been through enough."

She wondered what Lia would say to that. Lia knew better. God was, sometimes, that cruel.

"Let me do something for you," he said. "Let me take care of you. I know I've done a pretty poor job of it lately, but I want to do better, Ayinde. If you'll let me."

She found herself nodding.

"You stay with the baby." He reached out his hand for her cell phone. "Let me call your friends."

She nodded again and wiped her eyes. "Their names are . . ."

"Becky," Richard said. "And Kelly—that's the little one, right, whose husband isn't working? And who's this other one?"

"Lia," Ayinde said. She was feeling both dizzy and stunned. How was it that Richard knew the names of her friends? He'd only been introduced to Becky and Kelly once, in the hospital, in the whirlwind after Julian's arrival, and he'd never met Lia at all. "Becky will know how to reach her."

Richard paused. "Do you want me to call your mother?"

Ayinde shook her head. Lolo thought that her daughter had made a mess of her life, that she'd married badly and that nothing but sadness would result from that union, and Ayinde wasn't going to give her any ammunition or evidence to show that she was right.

"I'll be right back. Here." He found a paper cup, turned on the tap, and handed Ayinde a cup of water. Then he walked out the door, a tall, broad-shouldered man moving with an athlete's ease, drawing glances from nurses, from other worried mothers, even from other children. Ayinde lifted Julian onto the table and slowly, carefully, gently, started putting his clothes back on.

"Hey, Ayinde." Becky must have come right from Mas to Ayinde's house. She was carrying two plastic bags and wearing black-and-white-checked pants, a long-sleeved T-shirt, her hair twisted on top of her head, and an apron streaked with green. *Cilantro,* Ayinde thought. Kelly was right behind her, in jeans and a zippered hooded sweatshirt, her hair lank around her shoulders, circles under her eyes, and Oliver in her arms. Lia came into the kitchen last, dressed in fitted black pants and a black sweater. She'd gotten her hair colored since the last time Ayinde had seen her. The dark roots and blond ends had been replaced by a rich chestnut mane that fell in waves past her shoulders. *This is how she must have looked,* Ayinde thought fleetingly, *in her real life. Before . . .*

"I brought dinner," Becky said, setting the fragrant bags down on the countertop. "How are things?" she asked.

"They don't know yet. The electrocardiogram and the X rays were inconclusive," Ayinde recited. "Tomorrow morning he has to have something called a transesophageal echocardiogram." Richard told her he'd explained the basics—that Julian had a hole in his heart, that the doctors were running more tests. A hole in his heart. It was almost poetic. She'd been walking around for weeks feeling like someone had torn a hole in her own. "It's an outpatient procedure, but they do it under general anesthesia, and the doctor had an opening first thing in the morning. Where's Ava?"

"Day care," Becky said, as she started unpacking the food she'd brought, opening a series of steaming Styrofoam boxes, setting out napkins and silverware. "Where's Julian?"

"In his room. With his father. I'm sorry to take you away from work . . ."

"Don't be silly," Becky said. "Although you might have to apologize to Sarah. I think she almost fainted when Richard called. It was like God calling to see if He could get a table at seven-thirty." She passed Ayinde a plate filled with braised pork, black beans, and saffron rice. Ayinde pushed it away. "I can't eat anything. I can't eat, I can't sleep . . . I just kept thinking, you know, what if something happens, what if he stops breathing . . ." She buried her face in her hands.

"Oh, Ayinde," Becky said. Kelly covered her eyes with her hands. It was Lia who sat beside Ayinde, Lia who reached for her hands. Lia who sat quietly and let her cry.

"Hey, little man," Richard said.

He was sitting in a rocking chair in the hospital's waiting room, long legs bunched up uncomfortably, with Julian in his lap. Ayinde held her breath and paused in the hallway. She'd gone to the bathroom to splash water on her face, leaving Richard with the baby.

" . . . so you're gonna be asleep for a while," Richard said. Julian looked almost newborn-tiny again, leaning back in the crook of Richard's arm. "And when you wake up, you might have a little sore throat, and then we're gonna know what's going on with your ticker." He tapped the baby's chest with one thick finger. "Could be, you're just fine. Have to take it easy a little. Go on the inactive list. Or it could be you're going to have to have a little operation to fix you up right. But whatever happens, you're going to be just fine. Your momma loves you so much, and your daddy loves you, too. It's all going to be all right, little man. Everything's going to be fine."

He gathered the baby into his arms and rocked him. "So don't worry," he said. Ayinde saw that he was crying. "You don't have to play basketball. You don't have to do anything but just get through this all right. We're going to love you no matter what happens."

She cleared her throat. Her husband looked up. "Hey, baby," he said and wiped at his eyes.

"I'll take him now," she said. She held out her arms for the baby.

"Let me carry him for a little bit, all right?" Richard asked.

"Okay," she said. This time, she was the one who reached for his hand. "Okay."

The nurse came for Julian at nine o'clock sharp. "It'll take half an hour," she said, lifting him into her arms. Ayinde braced herself for the baby to cry, but Julian simply looked around, then opened and closed his hand in his baby version of a wave. "Try not to worry."

Ayinde walked the beige-painted halls. She felt as if she'd memorized each loop of the carpet, each name on each door. Sometimes Richard walked alongside her, not touching her, not saying anything, but walking closely enough that she could feel the warmth of his body. Then he would sit down, and her friends would flank her; Becky and Kelly on one side, Lia on the other. Becky was silent. Kelly murmured under her breath. "Hail Mary, full of grace, the Lord is with thee. Blessed art thou among women, and blessed is the fruit of Thy womb, Jesus. Holy Mary, Mother of God, pray for us sinners, now and in the hour of our death. Hail Mary, full of grace . . ."

Ayinde prayed her own prayer, one word long, one single syllable. *Please. Please, please, please, please, please,* she thought, walking down the hall and back again. She would endure anything—a cheating husband, a scornful mother, public humiliation. She'd swallow it all if only her son would be healthy. "Please," she said out loud. What would she do if she lost her baby? She'd probably end up like Lia; running like a kicked dog, trying to find some place where things felt better, some place that felt like home. But Philadelphia was her home now, she thought, as she turned at the end of the hallway and started back again. She had a life here, however messy it was at present. She'd had her baby in this hospital, she'd walked him on the sidewalks, sat with him in the shade of a weeping willow tree in the park. Her friends were here, and their babies were here, and Julian would grow up alongside them. If Julian got to grow up. *Please,* she prayed and walked with her head down, barely noticing when Lia took her hand. *Please, please, please . . .*

She heard Richard before she saw him, the familiar beat of his footfalls as he came down the narrow hall. She looked up from the carpet, and there was her husband in motion: Richard running, the way she'd seen him a thousand times on basketball courts the world over. Richard snagging a rebound, sinking a layup, Richard rising into the air as if he'd willed himself to float, winning the tip-off, sending the ball flying precisely into one of his teammates' hands while the crowd gasped in wonder. "Baby."

She turned and found that she could neither move nor breathe.

"It's okay," Richard said. He was beaming. And suddenly she was in his arms, pressed against him, holding on tight. "There's a hole, but it's a small one; it'll close up on its own. We just have to watch him closely, but he's going to be all right."

"All right," she repeated. She felt her knees buckling, but this time, Richard was there to catch her before her shoulders hit the beige wall. "Shh, shh," he whispered and kissed her cheek. Then he led her down the hall for the last time, back to the island of couches and coffee tables, the out-of-date magazines, and the parents with tense, fearful faces. Her friends were waiting for her, sitting side by side on a couch, Becky in her cook's black-and-white pants, Kelly twisting her rosary beads in her lap, Lia's face in profile so stern and lovely that it belonged in a painting or on a coin. They looked at her with their faces upturned like flowers, their hands linked, like sisters. "It's going to be all right."

January

LIA

"Hi," I said, smiling as I approached the two-top—an older couple, white-haired. Grandma and Grandpa out for a nice night on the town. "My name's Lia, and I'll be serving you this evening. Can I tell you about our specials?"

"Only if you tell us how much they cost," said the woman, narrowing her eyes at me as if I'd tried to make off with her purse. "I despise it when servers tell you the specials and don't tell you how much things cost. Then you're surprised when you get the bill. Usually unpleasantly."

I struggled to keep my smile in place. "Of course. Tonight, we have a ceviche—that's raw fish marinated in lime juice . . ."

"I know what ceviche is," the woman said, gesturing with her butter knife. "Don't patronize me, darling."

Whoa. Evil Granny. "Our ceviche tonight is salmon in a lime and blood-orange marinade, and it costs twelve dollars. We're also offering an ancho-rubbed veal chop, served with a savory chipotle flan, for eighteen dollars. Our whole fish of the night, which is prepared brushed with olive oil, kosher salt, and pepper, is dorado." I paused. The old woman raised her eyebrows. "Dorado is a firm-fleshed, mild . . ."

"I know."

"I'm sorry. It's served with plantains, and it's twenty-two."

"We'd like the pulled pork empanadas," said the man.

"I do hope they aren't greasy," said the woman.

"Well, they are deep-fried," I said.

Sarah slipped by me with a tray held aloft. I looked past her and saw the party at the table behind the one I was serving. My breath caught in my throat, and I reeled two steps backward without even thinking about it. "Excuse me," I murmured.

"Excuse *me*," said the old woman. "We weren't finished!"

"I'll be right back," I said, and then I brushed past the first-daters at table eight, the three girls gossiping at table nine, and fled to the kitchen, where I pressed my hands against the stainless-steel serving counter and tried to catch my breath.

"Hey, are you all right?" asked Becky, hurrying past with a bowl full of beaten eggs.

I nodded and held up one finger.

"Seen a ghost?" she asked.

It was something like that, I thought.

"Hey," I said to Dash the dishwasher. "Can I have some of your water?"

"Sure!" he said, handing me the bottle, looking dazzled. "Have it all!"

I took a long swallow. Then I poured some on a napkin and draped it over the back of my neck. My mother used to do that for me on hot summer days. *There, isn't that better?* she'd ask, with her hand resting between my shoulders.

I straightened up, retucked my white shirt into my black pants with red trim at the ankles—toreador pants, I'd thought when I'd bought them, just right for waitressing at Mas—and peeked through the door. I hadn't been wrong. It was Merrill, from Parents Together, the one who'd gone on and on about how the Make-a-Wish people had failed to provide her dying son with a visit from a porn star. She was with her husband, the man who'd patted her shoulder so ineffectually. Merrill and her husband and a little boy.

I dropped off the gossiping girls' check and returned to Grumpy Grandma.

"Well!" said the old lady. "Look who's here!" I was watching Merrill's table out of the corner of my eye, watching as she leaned toward the little boy, smiling at something he'd said.

"I'm sorry," I said. "Do you have any questions about the menu?"

The man shook his head. "I'd like the grilled shrimp, please."

The woman pointed at one of the entrées. "Is the chili-crusted rack of lamb spicy?"

"Yes. Yes, it is."

"Well, could they make it without the chili?"

Merrill's little boy was maybe two or three. He climbed out of his booster seat, and his father helped him pull on a red wool coat.

"I could ask," I said, knowing what Sarah would say—if they want plain old meat, let 'em go down the street to Smith & Wollensky.

"Do that for me, darling," the woman said. Merrill stood up, setting the check folder back onto the table, and guiding the boy to the door. At Parents Together, she'd worn jeans and a sweatshirt—the international uniform of the brokenhearted, I sometimes thought. But tonight she was all dressed up, hair straight and shiny, mouth painted and eyes lined, in black pants of her own, a white blouse and a belt of gold links, and red-and-gold Chinese slippers. You wouldn't look at her and think that anything was wrong. She looked like any other youngish mother, out for the night. I felt my knees start to sag, and I grabbed onto the back of the aged party's chair to keep myself and my new toreador pants from sliding to the floor.

"Is there a problem?" Grandma demanded.

"Sorry," I said. Merrill and her son and her husband pushed through the door and, without even thinking, I ran back to the kitchen. "Can you cover for me?" I asked Becky.

"What?"

"Cover for me," I said, pulling off my apron, handing her my checks. "I've got seven, eight, and nine. The people at seven are miserable. I'll be right back." I ran out of the kitchen, through the restaurant, and followed Merrill and her family onto the street. "Hey!" I called. "Merrill!"

She turned around, looking at me. "Oh God, did I leave my credit card? I'm always doing that . . ." Her voice trailed off.

"It's Lisa. From Parents Together." I smoothed out my apron. It was freezing outside. I wished I'd thought to grab my mother's blue coat. "I'm sorry to bother you, I just . . ."

"Honey." Her husband took her arm. "The movie's starting soon."

"You two go ahead," she told her husband, keeping her eyes on my face. "Lisa and I are going to get a cup of coffee."

"I don't want to keep you. I don't want to ruin your night . . ."

"It's okay," she said. Her breath came in silvery puffs. She opened the door to the coffee shop on Nineteenth Street. I followed her inside.

"Is that . . ." I swallowed hard. "That little boy. Is that . . ."

"My son," she said. "His name is Jared."

"And you had him after . . ."

She nodded, taking a seat at one of the back tables. "After." We both knew what After meant.

"How? That's what I wanted to ask you. Can you tell me how?"

She nodded, and in that gesture I caught a glimpse of the furious woman I'd seen in Grief Group, the one who would not let herself be comforted and who still seemed to be in so much pain. "I thought that we wouldn't. That we couldn't. I thought we'd be one of those couples everyone knows—oh, they lost their son and their marriage couldn't take it and they split up. But Ted—that's my husband—was so good through the whole thing with Daniel that sometimes . . ." She ducked her head. Her voice was almost inaudible. "I got to the point where I could almost see it as a kind of a blessing, what happened to Daniel, because it let my husband show me how much he loved me. How I'd never have to doubt it. I know how that sounds, but . . ."

I pressed my hands against the table to keep them from shaking.

I was remembering Sam—a glass passed across a bar, a straw wrapper slipped over my finger, a wedding dress lying on a hotel bed. *Let me be your family now.*

"Ted asked me if I wanted to try again six months after Daniel died," Merrill said. "I wasn't ready then. I thought if I had another baby, another little boy, I'd be holding my breath his whole life just waiting for the leukemia to come back and finish the job. Ruin my whole family. Take everything I had, instead of just Daniel. I thought that every time he sneezed or got a bruise I'd be dragging him to the doctor's . . . that I wouldn't be able to just let him be a kid. I was too scared."

"Is that how it was?"

"A little bit. Especially at first. I think mothers like us, mothers who've lost a child, we're always holding our breath a little bit. But they grow up anyhow, and no matter how careful you want to be, they just want to be kids and do kid things. Ride a bike, play soccer, go outside in the rain . . ." She rubbed her hands together. "I've got a good husband," she said. "That was probably three-quarters of it. The rest of it was just me. I decided that it was a choice. You know those people who say that happiness is a choice?"

I nodded. There'd been a great many of them in California.

"Hope is a choice, too. I know it sounds silly . . ."

I shook my head.

"I remember I was lying in bed the second night after Daniel died. Ted and I had to make the arrangements—that's what they called it, make the arrangements, and what it meant was we had to pick out his coffin. My mother was with us, and she kept saying, 'It's not God's plan for a parent to bury a child.' All I could think was that I never knew there were coffins so small and that he wouldn't have liked any of them. He had his whole room covered in posters and NASCAR stickers. He hated getting dressed up for church, and all the coffins were . . ." She shook her head. "They were just so wrong for an eleven-year-old boy. I went home that night and I was lying in bed. I hadn't even taken my shoes off. I was just lying there in the dark, and I remember thinking to myself, You can live or you can die."

"So you decided to live," I said.

Merrill nodded. "I decided to hope. It was the hardest thing I ever did. The first year, a lot of days, just getting out of bed and getting dressed felt like more than I could handle . . . and there were days when I couldn't even do that. But Ted was so good—he was so patient with me. Even my mother wasn't so bad, after a while. Eventually, it got to the point where Daniel's death wasn't the first thing I thought of when I woke up. And I could look at other children—other boys— and not feel jealous or sad. They were just part of the landscape. And what happened with Daniel was a part of my history. An important part, a terrible part, but not something I was obsessing over every minute. It turned into something that had happened to me, not something that was still happening." She tilted her head. "Does that make sense?"

I found that I couldn't say anything, so I nodded instead.

"I would have told you this at group, if you'd stayed. Did I scare you away?"

"Oh, no, it wasn't your fault," I said. "I just wasn't ready, I guess." I looked at my watch. Twenty minutes. Shit. "I should go. My job . . . I've got to get back to my tables. Thank you," I said, stumbling to my feet on shaky legs. "Thank you so much."

"Call me," Merrill said, writing down her number on a napkin. "Please. If you need anything, or if you just want to talk."

I folded the napkin and ran back to Mas. Sarah was standing at the bar. "Hey, are you okay? Becky's been taking care of your party at table seven, but you never entered their entrées. I've been sending out complimentary apps . . ."

Shit. "I'm so sorry," I said. I collected my checks and my apron and hurried back to the table.

"Well," said Grandma. "Look who's reemerged."

"I'm very, very sorry," I said. I touched the napkin in my pocket, the one with Merrill's phone number, hoping it would give me strength. The woman snorted.

"That's enough, Judith," said the old man.

The woman's jaw gaped open. "I beg your pardon?"

"She'd like more water," the man said.

I nodded. I went to the bar, poured the water, and went back to the kitchen again.

"Hey, if you're gonna cry, don't use a towel," Dash said over my shoulder. "Becky's all over me about the towels. Here." He handed me a fistful of toilet paper. "Are you going to be all right? Do you need to go home?"

I shook my head, blew my nose, dabbed carefully underneath my eyes, the way one of the makeup artists I'd known in my previous life had shown me. I freshened my lipstick, combed my newly brown hair, and counted out enough crumpled bills from my pocket to pay for Grumpy Grandma's lamb. *Hope,* I thought, remembering Ayinde's face when she'd told us that Julian was going to be all right. In the kitchen, Becky was arranging frizzled leeks on top of someone's steak. "Hey," I said.

She looked up at me, grinning. "You okay?"

"I'm okay," I said. I smoothed my hands along my apron. "I'm going to be outside for a minute. I'm not leaving or anything. I just need to make a phone call."

KELLY

The Wee Ones Music Class met in a big, historic church on Pine Street that had stained-glass renderings of Christ over the altar and Alcoholics Anonymous posters in the basement where class was held. On Tuesday morning, Kelly pulled off Oliver's snowsuit and hat and scarf and sat down on a carpet remnant with her husband beside her. Steve waved at Becky and Ayinde as Galina, the leader, started thumping on the elderly piano, launching into the opening chords of the "Welcome" song. "Hello, good morning, good morning to Nick. Hello, good morning, good morning to Oliver." They sang to Cody and Dylan and Emma and Emma, to Nicolette and Ava and Julian and Jackson. "Hello, good morning to the mommies. Hello, good morning to the nannies," Galina sang, pounding the keys. "Hello, good morning to the daddy . . ."

Steve bounced Oliver on his knee, waving his maraca to the beat as the group started singing. "If you're happy and you know it, clap your hands!" Kelly stifled the urge to look at her BlackBerry. "If you're happy and you know it, clap your hands!" She knew Elizabeth was still unhappy about the Wartz party. "If you're happy and you know it and you really want to show it . . ." She slumped against the wall, feeling conflicted and displaced, and tired. Above and underneath it all, tired.

"Hey," Steve whispered. "If you need to get going, the Big O and I are doing fine."

"No, I'll stay," she whispered back. There were daddies who took their sons and daughters to music class, including a fiftysomething fellow who brought a three-year-old (Kelly had never been able to figure out whether it was his grandson or his child). Andrew had taken Ava more than once. Even Richard Towne, with a baseball cap pulled low over his eyes, had shown up one Tuesday morning, steadfastly ignoring the stares of the other parents and the one mommy with a digital camera who'd surreptitiously snapped a shot of him with the baby in his arms, singing "The Farmer in the Dell." But those daddies had jobs to return to, not just a job search. A so-called job search, she thought sadly, as Steve arranged Oliver's fingers around a baby-sized tambourine and helped him to shake it.

Kelly looked at the poster and considered Step One of the Twelve Steps: We Realize That Our Lives Have Become Unmanageable, and We Turn Them Over to a Higher Power. Her life had become unmanageable. But where was the twelve-step group for overextended mothers married to men without jobs?

"Let's play!" said Galina, unzipping a gym bag, sending a dozen rubber balls bouncing into the circle. The big kids—the two- and three-year-olds, the ones who could walk—screamed with delight and toddled toward the balls. Oliver gave a hiccupy gasp and started to cry as Steve put a red ball in his lap. "Shh, shh, it's okay," he said, showing Oliver the ball.

Kelly straightened Oliver's sweater and thought of the phone call with her sisters the night before. "How's Mr. Perfect?" Doreen had asked.

"Fine!" said Kelly. "We're all fine! Everything's fine!" After she hung up the phone, she sat at the kitchen table, writing checks. Steve came over and sheepishly handed her his credit-card bill. Eleven hundred dollars. "For what?" she asked, a little more sharply than she meant to.

Steve shrugged. "Dinner. Clothes. Oh, my mom's birthday." Kelly looked at the bill. Steve had spent three hundred dollars, probably for something useless to gather dust on her mother-in-law's étagère. She'd felt sick as she'd written out the check.

"Why don't you let me cash in some of our bonds?" he'd asked.

She shuddered. What would happen if they ran through their savings and Steve still wasn't working? What would happen if they couldn't pay their health insurance and one of them got sick? She knew how that story ended—bill collectors on the phone at seven in the morning. Used cars and hand-me-downs. No way. She'd worked too hard for Oliver to have to endure any of that.

"A lion looking for her food is walking through the grass," Galina sang. Kelly sang, too. All of the mothers sang; all of the nannies sang. Steve sang, too, loudly enough so that Kelly couldn't help but hear him. "Who knows another animal?"

"Cow!" called a nanny.

"And what does a cow do?"

The nanny got onto all fours as her charge—one of the Emmas, Kelly thought—giggled, knowing what was coming. "Moooooo!" she sang out. The children laughed and clapped and mooed.

"Does Daddy know an animal?" Galina asked, looking at Steve.

"Um," he said, looking at Oliver. "Dog?"

"Dog! Doggie is good! And what noise does doggie make?"

Steve grinned gamely. "Ruff, ruff?"

"Bark louder, Daddy, louder!" Galina coaxed.

"Ruff, ruff," Steve barked.

"And what does doggie do?"

"Wags his tail!" chorused Emma One and Two, Cody, Nicolette, and Dylan.

"Let's see Daddy wag a tail!"

Across the circle, Ayinde was looking studiously down at the top of Julian's head, and Becky was biting her lip. She knew better than to laugh, Kelly thought; Becky had been on Galina's shit list ever since she'd used one of the toddler-sized xylophones to plink out the bass line of "Smoke on the Water" three weeks before.

"Wag, Daddy!" Galina instructed. Her Russian accent gave her the sound of a lesser Bond villain. "Wag!"

Steve laughed and shook his butt. Oliver giggled and tried to clap his hands. "Go, Steve!" Becky called.

"Nice work, Daddy. Okay, everyone. Let's put our balls away!"

I think he's done that already, Kelly thought, as the Good-bye song started. *Good-bye, good-bye, good-bye, mommies . . . good-bye, good-bye, good-bye, babies . . .* She worked a sleepy Oliver back into his snowsuit, pulled his hat snug over his ears, and she and Steve wheeled him through the crowd of AA attendees and the fog of cigarette smoke that surrounded them. Out in the lobby, Kelly glanced toward the chapel, the stained-glass Mary looking serene in her halo and white robes. *Probably because Joseph had a job.*

Back at home, Kelly changed Oliver's diaper, kissed his belly and his cheeks, and looked longingly at her bed. *Maybe just for a minute,* she thought, slipping off her shoes.

The next thing she felt was being shaken awake. She kept her eyes shut. She'd been having the most wonderful dream about Colin Reynolds, her eighth-grade crush, whom she'd French-kissed in the junior-high gymnasium. In her dream, Colin Reynolds was all grown up, and they were doing a lot more than kissing, and there wasn't a baby, or a husband, in sight.

Steve shook her again. "Kelly. Telephone."

"I'm sleeping."

"Oh," he said. "I didn't know." Kelly buried her face in the pillow, hearing a Becky-style wisecrack in her head—*Yeah, that lying in the dark with my eyes closed thing must have really had you fooled.*

"Take a message," she said, as the baby started to cry. Shit. She pushed herself upright and looked at the clock: 5:03? That had to be wrong.

"Have I been asleep all afternoon?" she asked, lifting Oliver out of his crib and onto the changing table, as Steve trailed behind her with the telephone.

"I guess you were tired," he said. *Five o'clock,* Kelly thought. She hadn't done any work, and the dog probably needed his walk, and she hadn't even looked at her in-box. Elizabeth was probably fuming.

She tucked the telephone under her chin. "Hello?"

"Kelly Day?"

"Yes."

"Hi, my name is Amy Mayhew. I'm a reporter for *Power* magazine, and I'm hoping you'd help me with a story I'm working on."

"A story about what?"

"Having it all," she said. "Women who've managed to succeed in the workplace while raising families."

Succeed. The word alone was almost enough to send Kelly into gales of laughter. Either that, or a crying jag. But if she could pull it off—if she could appear to the public like a woman who was managing to succeed in the workplace while raising a child—it might help her work her way back into Elizabeth's good graces.

"I've been doing a little research about you." Kelly could hear a keyboard clacking in the background. "You're with Eventives, right?"

"That's right," she said. "I was doing IT venture-capital consulting, and I sort of wandered into the event-planning business. Now I work with Eventives, which is considered the top operation in Philadelphia, and we're looking to branch out into New Jersey and New York. But I'm only working part-time right now."

Kelly could hear more typing. "You just had a baby, right?"

"July thirteenth," she said, unsnapping Oliver's jeans and whipping his diaper off one-handed. "So I'm just working twenty hours a week. Well, technically, that's all. But you know how it goes."

"Not really," Amy Mayhew said. "No kids for me yet." From her oh-so-serious tone and brittle little laugh, Kelly could picture Amy Mayhew—her sharp navy suit and a pair of just-right heels. On her desk there'd be a slim little mock croc clutch that managed to contain her keys, a wallet, a lipstick, and a few condoms and still be approximately one-sixteenth the size of the diaper bag that Kelly routinely lugged around town. Amy Mayhew would not have three inches of bangs hanging in her eyes because she hadn't been able to get to her hairdresser in four months, and her fingernails would be manicured, and she'd smell like some subtle perfume, instead of Kelly's signature scent of B.O., breast milk, and desperation.

"Hello?"

"I'm here," Kelly managed to say as she resnapped the baby's pants.

"So listen," she said, "I'd love to set up an interview. What does your month look like?"

"Well, I'm pretty flexible." Kelly hurried back to the bedroom, set Oliver in the middle of the empty, unmade bed, grabbed a pen from the bedside table, flipped to a fresh page in Oliver's baby book, which hadn't been updated in months, and started scribbling. *Hair. Manicure. New suit (?).* She still couldn't fit into her old ones. New shoes, too. She'd have to find her briefcase. She'd had a gorgeous briefcase once. Calfskin leather, gold handles. She thought she'd glimpsed it in the closet, wedged underneath the car seat Oliver had already outgrown.

"Is next Friday good? Maybe we can have lunch."

Lunch Fri, Kelly wrote. She used to have lunch. She used to take clients out for two-hour expense-account meals at the Capital Grille and Striped Bass. She'd have a glass of wine and a salad and grilled fish or roasted chicken. Lunch, back then, did not consist of peanut butter eaten while Oliver napped, scooped straight out of the jar and licked off her fingers because there weren't any clean knives because neither she nor Steve had run the dishwasher.

"We were thinking we'd want some photographs of you in the workplace, and then some of you at home, with your baby . . ."

Shit. Shit. Shit, shit, shit. She'd have to clean—the kitchen floors were way past nasty; Steve had spilled a bottle of formula in front of the refrigerator and hadn't done a very good job of cleaning it up. She'd need fresh flowers, she'd need to vacuum, she'd need to get Steve to clean up the office, and find someplace to stash the bags of zero-to-three-month baby clothes she'd been meaning to take to Goodwill . . . Furniture. She'd need that, too. Or maybe she could tell them that she had furniture that was being cleaned or something, or that they'd moved it because they were having the carpet replaced . . .

" . . . and your husband."

"Husband?" Kelly repeated.

"Right," Amy Mayhew said, laughing a little. "You know, the family unit."

"Um, my husband travels a lot for business."

"Remind me what he does again?"

"Consulting for Internet start-ups." The words flew out of her mouth like a flock of malevolent birds. *Oh, God,* she thought, *what if Amy Mayhew Googled Steve to check?* "He's just starting out . . . nothing official yet, no website or offices or anything, but he's on the road a lot. He's working with some of his business-school friends. *Shut up,* she told herself. This was always how she'd known when her sisters were lying. Instead of a simple answer, you'd get Hamlet's soliloquy. "So he might not be able to be in the pictures."

"Oh, well, how's this Friday?"

"Perfect!" Kelly said. They set a time. Amy Mayhew said she was looking forward to meeting her. Kelly said she was looking forward to it, too. Then she hung up the phone and carried the baby into the kitchen. Steve was lying on the couch.

"What was that about?" Steve asked.

"Some survey," Kelly said. "I'm going to take Lemon for a walk. Can you give Oliver his rice cereal?"

"Sure," said Steve.

"And can you maybe get dressed?"

Steve looked down at himself as if he was surprised to see that he was wearing only boxer shorts and a T-shirt. "Why?" he asked. "I'm not going anywhere."

She bit back the insults that wanted desperately to make their way out of her mouth. "I know you're not going anywhere, but it's five-thirty at night and it's a work day . . ." She let her voice trail off.

"Fine," he said, pulling a pair of jeans off the floor. "Pants," she heard him mutter. "Your mother's a stickler!" he called to Oliver. Kelly rubbed at her temples. She could feel her customary late-night headache making an early appearance. She swallowed two Tylenol, started a load of laundry, scraped her hair back into a ponytail, and jogged into the living room.

Lemon was sitting by the front door, with his tail wagging, and Oliver was sitting in his high chair with cereal dotting his face. Steve was in the kitchen, feeding the baby. "Once upon a time," Steve said, "there was a brave prince who lived in a castle." Oliver waved his hands in the air and made a pleased-sounding coo. "The prince was so brave that he could swim across moats full of sharks and alligators and Dallas Cowboy fans," Steve continued. "He could slay dragons with a single stroke of his terrible sword, and parallel park in even the tiniest parking space, and he could rescue the beautiful princess from spells and enchantments." Steve sighed. "And then he got laid off, and the beautiful princess didn't want to talk to him anymore."

Kelly's heart twisted. *I'm sorry,* she started to say—but sorry for what? Sorry that he'd gotten laid off? She'd told him that, and it hadn't made a difference. Sorry that he felt so terrible? Well, he wouldn't feel so terrible if he'd just find a job, and Kelly had told him that a few times too many already and if he'd do it, they'd be fine, and she could quit walking around fantasizing about killing him and making it look like a shaving accident so that his life insurance policy would pay off.

She cleared her throat. Steve looked up. "Hey," he said.

"Hey," she said back, fastening Lemon's leash. "How'd he do?"

"Half of the rice stuff, two bites of prune glop," Steve reported, sliding the high chair's tray off and carrying it to the sink.

"Good," she said, "I'm going to . . ." Her heart stopped as Oliver leaned forward. "Steve!" she screamed, and started forward. Not fast enough. The baby tumbled, face first, onto the floor. There was an audible thud and a second of silence. Then Kelly scooped the baby into her arms, and Oliver opened his mouth and started howling.

"Oh my God, oh my God!" Kelly said.

"Is he okay?" Steve asked, looking stricken.

"I don't know!" Kelly shouted over the baby's wails. "Why wasn't he strapped in?"

"I forgot!" Steve said. "Is he okay?"

Kelly gave him a scathing look and carried the baby past him to the kitchen to get the telephone, noticing on her way that Lemon had, indeed, peed on the floor again. She dialed the doctor's phone number that was written on the refrigerator, hitting 1 and 1 and 1 again until she was connected with the nurse on call. "Hi, this is Kelly Day. My baby is Oliver. He's five months old, and he just fell out of his high chair . . ."

Steve tapped her shoulder. "What can I do?" he whispered. "Does he need ice or something? Should we call an ambulance?"

Kelly pushed him aside. She knew that if she looked at his face for even a second longer someone in their house would need an ambulance, and it wouldn't be Oliver.

"Calm down," said the nurse. "Any baby who can scream like that doesn't sound too badly hurt. Did he fall on a hardwood floor?"

"No," Kelly said.

"And he didn't lose consciousness or stop breathing? Is he bleeding?"

"No," she said. Her knees had started to shake. She leaned against the wall. Oliver sobbed and buried his face in her neck. "He just fell. My husband didn't fasten the straps."

"These things happen," the nurse said. "And most of the time, the babies are just fine. If he's crying like that, and he didn't pass out or vomit, chances are he's fine. Try not to beat yourself up. Or your husband. Just keep an eye on him for the next few hours, and call us if anything changes."

"Okay," said Kelly. "Thank you." She hung up the phone and cradled the baby in her arms, saying, "Shhh, shhh," as she rocked him. "Poor guy, poor guy," she said, carrying him to the rocker, where she pulled up her shirt and guided his face to her breast. Oliver stared up at her, his lashes still heavy with tears, looking miserable and betrayed, then gave a resigned sigh and started nursing.

Steve reappeared. "He looks okay," he said.

Kelly ignored him.

"But we should take him to the doctor, right?"

Kelly said nothing.

"I'm really, really sorry . . ."

"You're sorry," she repeated. "Why wasn't he strapped in?"

"I told you, I forgot!"

"Yeah," she sneered. The dam broke, and the poison came pouring out. "Just like you forgot your deadline. Just like you forgot to run the dishwasher. Just like you forget to put on your goddamn pants unless I remind you."

Kelly adjusted her shirt and got to her feet, shoving past her husband, who stood as if paralyzed in the doorway. "I've got to take the dog out."

"I'll walk him."

"Don't do me any favors!" she said, plopping a once-more wailing Oliver into his stroller, buckling his straps with broad gestures, hitching Lemon to his leash, and hurrying the three of them into the elevator and onto the street.

She was halfway down the block when Steve caught up, looking sheepish and scared.

"Go away," she said, picking up her pace.

"I just thought you might need this," Steve said. He showed her the diaper bag that she'd forgotten. "I put a bottle in, just in case."

"Thanks," she said. She pushed the stroller to the corner and stopped at the red light.

"Let me walk with you. Please? I feel awful."

Kelly didn't tell him that he shouldn't, but she did move over enough to give him room to stand beside her. Steve stowed the diaper bag underneath the stroller and stepped behind the handlebars. When the light turned green, he started to push, and they walked for three blocks in silence. "So what was that survey about?"

The lie she'd told the reporter came slamming back into her brain. "Oh, nothing much," Kelly said, hoping that he wouldn't see her blushing in the darkness. "You know, what kinds of articles do I find interesting, and have I bought a new car in the last twelve months."

"Sorry I woke you up for that," Steve said. "Listen, if you need to get some work done, you can head home. I can walk him. I can watch him when we get home."

And let him fall again? Or get run over by a truck? Kelly thought. No way. She'd have to make something up to explain why she'd missed the conference call she'd scheduled with Elizabeth and a new client. A cold, a sprained ankle, female trouble. Something that pertained to her, and not the baby, because Elizabeth had made her feelings about the baby very clear.

"No, I've got it."

"Kelly, you're exhausted. Let me help," Steve said.

She shook her head wearily, wordlessly, and followed Steve as he pushed the baby back home.

LIA

My mother got to Mas before I did, and when I arrived she was already sitting at the table, facing the door. She carried a boxy black pocketbook, big enough for her to take home a class's worth of tests. It was sitting in front of her, between her fork and knife where the plate should have been, and her hands were curled around its handles, as if any minute she might pick it up and swing it at me. Or at someone. Swing it, and then run.

"Lisa." She sounded almost shy. Worried, too. She cleared her throat. "You look . . ." I could hear our history teetering in the balance of that pause. *You're not going out of the house like that. Take off that lipstick. Put on a coat.* I licked my lips, remembering the two weeks' worth of silence after I'd streaked my hair blond when I was thirteen—I'd buried the bottle of peroxide deep in the trash can in the garage and told her that lemon juice and sun had done the trick. I'd buried the receipts for every cosmetic purchase there, too, after my mother had *tsk-tsked* over a bottle of Chanel foundation and told me it must be nice to have money to throw around on nonsense. "You look well," she finally said, fiddling with her purse handles. "How are you?"

"Fine."

She looked around the dining room: sixteen tables, half of them full. "Is this where you work?"

"Yes," I said and sat down. I'd already figured out what we were going to eat. On Sunday afternoons, Mas served high tea, with chili-pepper scones, cinnamon-dusted chocolates, finger sandwiches with curried shrimp, egg salad, cucumber, and butter. I'd made up the tray myself, and I'd brewed a pot of plum-ginger tea. "Mostly in the kitchen. It turns out I'm not a very good waitress."

Her hands gripped the purse handles more tightly. I poured her a cup of tea, which she ignored. "I've been talking to your husband," she told me.

I almost dropped the teapot. "Sam?"

She nodded. "We've been talking for a few weeks."

"What . . ." I swallowed and licked my dry lips. "What did he say?"

Her face was expressionless. "Well, initially he was very surprised to learn that I was alive."

Oh, dear.

"He wants to know if you're coming home," she said. She took a single sip of tea and went back to holding her handbag. "He sounds like a nice young man."

Was it my imagination, or did she actually sound wistful? I set the teapot down carefully and wiped my hands on my napkin. "What did you tell him?"

"What could I tell him? What do I know?" she asked. Her back was ruler-straight; her words were clear and precise. She could have been talking to a class of fifth-graders instead of me. "I don't think you're all right. I don't know if you're coming home."

"But . . ." I shook my head. I'd arranged this meeting, I'd planned everything I was going to say to her, and now she'd turned the tables. "You knew I was married?"

"Lisa. I'm your mother. And I'm not stupid. You haven't exactly been invisible, you know."

I stared down at my plate. I thought I had been invisible, as far as my mother was concerned. She never went to movies, and I'd never been in anything that had appeared on ABC, so how could she know? Had she actually seen any of the direct-to-video movies I'd made? Or the infomercial that only aired in the wee hours of the morning, for a quote-unquote revolutionary hair-removal system? I'd been Girl with Moustache. Fake, of course, but Sam had never quite let me live it down.

"So you knew I was married."

"Lia Lane," she said. Her lips—with the lipstick already starting to wander up past her lipline—curved upward. "It sounds like a superhero. Much better than Lia Frederick."

"And you know about Caleb."

She swallowed hard. Once. Twice. When she spoke again, her voice sounded fragile and cracked as an antique mirror. "I didn't know his name."

I reached into my purse. They took pictures of all the babies in the hospital nursery, and one of the nurses had handed me Caleb's snapshot when we were on our way home. I'd tucked it into the diaper bag and forgotten about it until I came to Philadelphia and had found it again. Or it had found me. It was the only thing I'd never intended to give away; the one thing I couldn't let go. Caleb's face was tomatoey red in the picture, wrinkled and cross looking. He was wrapped in a hospital blanket, and he wore a pink-and-blue-striped cap.

I pulled it out, smoothed the edges, and passed it across the table into my mother's hand.

She took the picture and suddenly every part of her was shaking—her hands, her lips, the loose skin of her neck. "Oh," she whispered. "Oh."

I bent my head. My eyes were brimming. I thought I'd been ready for anything—her anger, her scorn, her cold dismissiveness, her eye-rolling questions of "What kind of drama did you get yourself into now?" But these little hurt baby-bird noises coming from her throat? No. "Mom. Hey, Mom, cut it out. It's okay."

Her grip on the picture was getting tighter. I could hear the paper start to crumple.

"Mom!"

I reached across the table, but she was too fast for me. She lifted the picture in the air. And then she started crying. The people at the table next to ours quickly averted their eyes. One of the other waiters showed up and looked at me. *Napkins,* I mouthed. He nodded and hurried back with a fresh stack of them.

My mother wiped her eyes with a napkin, her shoulders shaking as she cried without making a sound. When her grip loosened enough, I eased the picture out of her hands and put it back in my purse.

She looked at me. Her eyes red and watery, and her lips were trembling. I wondered if she'd ever tried to call me. I wondered what I would have said to her if she had.

"I wish I knew," she said. Her words were swallowed by a sob.

"Knew what?"

"I wish I knew what I'd done that made you hate me so much."

I felt the air rush out of me. "You hated me first," I told her. *Because he loved me more than he loved you,* I thought.

She blinked at me. "Is that really what you think?"

I shrugged, feeling suddenly uncertain. I had believed that, the way . . . well, the way a kid would believe in Santa Claus or the Tooth Fairy. It was the story I'd told myself, the one I'd constructed as a teenager and had never questioned in all the years I'd been away. And I'd called her and invited her here determined to forgive her, to open my hand and move forward. But . . . the possibility spun in my mind, like a leaf caught in a drain. What if I'd been wrong? What if there was nothing for me to forgive? What if I turned out to be just as much to blame as she was?

My mother pressed her lips together, speaking slowly, as if every word pained her. "I remember when you were a baby. I was the one who did the feedings, I was the one who changed your diaper, and rocked you, and sang you to sleep, but when your father came through the door . . ." She shut her eyes, shaking her head a little.

"Your face would just light up. It was hard for me, a little. I loved you so much, but it felt like you only smiled for him."

No, I thought. Oh, no. I don't want to hear this, I don't want to think about it, I don't want to remember . . . but I couldn't help myself. The pictures were coming, unbidden—me in the rocker in a stained nightgown, rocking and rocking while Caleb shrieked. Me wearing Sam's sweatpants because none of my prepregnancy clothes fit and I couldn't bear to pull on the maternity ones again, marching the too-short hall like a prisoner, back and forth, back and forth, as the hours piled on top of each other, all night long. Me holding Caleb as he screamed in the bathtub, me holding Caleb as he screamed on the changing table . . . and Sam taking Caleb in his arms for five minutes at the end of the night, lifting him into the air and singing him "Sweet Baby James," and Caleb not screaming at all.

"I forgave him a lot because you loved him so much."

"Forgave him what?"

She sighed again without meeting my eyes. "It's water under the bridge," she said. "It was so long ago."

I turned all of my memories of my father over in my mind—the zoo and the flower shows, the restaurant lunches and the ice-cream cones in the park. I wasn't much liking what I saw on their flip sides. When I was eight and nine and ten, some days I'd come home from school and he would be there. We'd sneak out of the house to matinees and fill up on licorice and fast-food hamburgers afterward. "Don't tell your mother," he'd say, smiling a conspirator's smile as he slid a twenty-dollar bill out of her wallet and into his own. "This is our secret." It had never occurred to me, at that age, to think about why he was home all the time, but now, I wondered.

And there'd been more. Sometimes there would be a woman who'd join us at the movies or at McDonald's or Friendly's or Nifty Fifties afterward. "This is Susan," he'd say. Or Jean or Vicki or Raquel. His hand would linger on the small of her back. "A friend of mine from work." Susan or Jean or Vicki or Raquel was always younger than my mother and prettier. Jean had had platinum-blond hair and a breathy giggle. Vicki had given me a lipstick that came in a ridged gold tube. Had I known what they were back then? Had I known all along? Had she?

"He had girlfriends," I said. I waited for her to say no, but she didn't say anything.

Her sigh moved across the table like a cold wind. "I hoped you didn't know that," she said. "I hoped he'd at least have the sense not to tell you."

"So why did you stay with him? Why did you stay, if you knew?"

She tightened her fingers on the handle of her purse. "It's different when you have a child." I thought about Ayinde and Richard and saw how that could be true, how a baby could make you forgive even the worst transgressions. "I didn't want to divorce him because I knew that if I did you'd never see him again. He'd just pick up and start all over someplace else, with someone else, and he'd tell you he'd visit, but he wouldn't. I knew him well enough to know that."

"But that's what happened."

"One of his girlfriends gave him an ultimatum," she said. Her voice was low and toneless. "Me or your wife. He . . ." She licked her lips and took another sip of tea. "Well. You know what he chose."

Not me, I thought. He hadn't chosen me. I remembered, with a hot flush of shame, how after Sam and I got married, I'd gone to a fancy stationery shop on Rodeo Drive that was known for its hand-calligraphied wedding invitations. They'd made me a proof, but I never went back to place my order. One was all I wanted. There was only one person I wanted to receive a piece of cream-colored paper announcing that Lia and Sam had become man and wife. I'd sent it to the last address I had for my father: an apartment complex in Arizona. Three weeks later, I'd gotten a letter in return, a note, really, on a ripped-out page of a legal pad. *Congratulations,* it read in his familiar back-slanting handwriting. *And now that you are a "big success" in Hollywood, maybe you can spare something for your "Old Man."* I'd never told

Sam about it. I'd never told anyone. *Well, that's that,* I had thought, and I'd tucked the note away. That's that.

"He loved you, in his way. Probably better than he ever loved anyone else." She gave me a small smile. "You were his girl. Remember how he used to say that? He'd come home . . ."

" . . . home from work and swing me in the air," I said. My voice sounded like it was coming from the end of a tunnel. "You're my girl."

"Well, work," my mother said. "Sometimes it was work, and sometimes . . ." Her voice faded. Her hands fluttered in the air. "I'm sorry," she said. "I'm sorry you had to learn this about him. I'm sorry about your . . ." She tripped over the words. "Your son."

"What about the quilt?"

She looked at me, her eyebrows drawn in puzzlement. It was the least of my questions, the least of what lay between us, but it was all I could think to ask her about.

"That quilt. The Strawberry Shortcake quilt. The one you wouldn't buy me. And then he got it for me and he left and you never got me a new one. You said we couldn't afford it."

She looked down at her hands, and in her face I could see the outline of how she'd look when she was an old lady. It was probably the way I'd end up looking, too. "That quilt was the only thing he ever gave you," she said. "I wanted you to keep it so you could remember your dad."

"That's not true. He gave me lots of things. My Barbie dolls . . . my tea set . . . my roller skates . . ."

My mother was shaking her head.

"But . . . but . . ." Oh, this hurt. I was remembering my father leaning over me as I lay in bed, setting a bag or a box beside my pillow, whispering, "Look what Daddy bought his number-one girl!"

"I'm sorry," she said. "I wanted him to be a better father—a better man, really—and when he couldn't, I guess I didn't see the harm in pretending. So I'd buy things for him to give you, and I'd wrap them up, and I was just happy to know that you liked them. I wanted to give you everything you wanted. Every mother wants that, I think." She wiped her eyes with her napkin. "I wanted to give you a better father, most of all, and when I couldn't give you that . . ."

I didn't know what to say to her. I didn't know if I could say anything.

"All those plays," I finally said. "All those plays in high school. *Bye Bye Birdie* and *Mame* and *Gypsy.* You never came . . ."

"You didn't want me to," she said. She smiled a little. "I believe your exact words were that you'd kill yourself if you saw my face in the audience."

I shrugged and managed a smile of my own. "Well, I was an actress." I remembered those fights. "Don't come," I'd told her, slamming my flimsy bedroom door. "Don't come, I don't want you there!"

"So you never saw my face. But I was there." My mother loosened her grip on her pocketbook long enough to reach inside. She pulled out a manila folder I'd have just bet she'd stolen from some supply closet at her school. She slid it across the table. I opened it and found a crumpled flyer, a leaflet for the first comedy troupe I'd joined. It was ten years old and had been folded and refolded, and the paper felt as soft as linen in my hands. "Where did you find this?"

"On eBay," she said. Underneath the flyer was a page cut out of *TV Guide.* It was a story about a series set in high school that had aired for half a season seven years ago. I'd been a featured extra, which meant you could see me in every episode that had aired. In the picture you could see the side of my face.

"That's not from eBay," she said. "I got a subscription. That and *Entertainment Weekly* and *People.* And all the tabloids, too." The same ghost of a smile revisited her face. "I bring them to the teachers' lounge when I'm done with them. It's made me pretty popular."

I flipped through the folder. There I was in an ad for a made-for-TV movie that had aired on a channel that my mother's cable system didn't even carry. There were pictures of me in dresses and jeans, in miniskirts and bikinis, and finally, one of me in my Las Vegas wedding dress. *Razor ad-man Sam Lane and his bride, actress Lia Frederick.* My Hollywood-blond hair was piled on top of my head in the updo I'd let the hotel's hairdresser talk me into. My stomach was still flat, and I could see, in the background, the brilliant bottle-green feathers of one of the birds in its cage in the lobby.

"Look," she said. Her hands were shaking. "Here." At the bottom of the folder was a stack of yellowing programs. She fanned them out in front of me. My name was on the cover, my old name, my high school name. Lisa Urick. "Every single one. Every single night."

I gripped the edges of the table tightly. "You didn't want me to go to L.A."

"I didn't want you to go when you were eighteen," she said. "I wanted you to go to college first. And I just didn't know how to talk to you. You were so angry at me, so angry all the time . . ."

I said nothing. I had been angry. Maybe I'd been angry at her because she was there, and I couldn't be angry at my father because he wasn't.

"I kept track, though," my mother said. "It got harder once you changed your name, but I think I've seen every single thing you've ever done. When you were on *The Price Is Right* . . ."

"Oh, God," I said, groaning as I remembered my five-day stint filling in for an ailing Barker's Beauty. "The actual retail value of this showcase . . ."

"But I guess you missed my television debut," she said with a sly smile.

"What? Not . . ."

She nodded. *"Jeopardy!"*

"Oh, Mom! Your dream come true! Did you win?"

"Three days in a row. Sixteen thousand dollars. Not enough to come back for the Tournament of Champions, but I got the roof fixed." She ducked her head. Typical, I thought. Give any other woman in America sixteen thousand dollars, and she'd splurge on jewelry or a spa vacation. Give it to my mother, and she'd fix her roof. "It was hard to come home afterward," she admitted. "Knowing I wouldn't have anything to look forward to. And I wondered . . . well, if maybe you'd see me, and think about getting in touch."

My eyes filled with tears again. I remembered how Sam had once flipped to *Jeopardy!*—this was on our honeymoon, at that enormous hotel in Las Vegas—and I'd threatened to throw the remote control into the toilet if he ever subjected me to any sort of game show. "As God as my witness," I'd told him, "I had to watch *Jeopardy!* five nights a week for eighteen years, and I'll never watch *Jeopardy!* again." He'd agreed in a hurry, although maybe the fact that I'd been wearing the white-lace merry widow, the one with cutouts over the nipples that one of my friends had given me as a joke, had something to do with that.

"Did you meet Alex Trebek?"

She giggled—actually giggled—as her cheeks turned pink, like a schoolgirl with a crush. I could see her history in her face then, the clear-eyed, smart, pretty girl who'd married Fred Urick and hoped for love for the rest of her life but wound up teaching fifth grade, with a husband who didn't work and who ran around and a daughter who'd disappeared.

"Mom," I said. "I'm sorry. I'm so sorry about everything."

She nodded. "I know," she said softly. "I'm sorry, too." *It was a start,* I thought. Maybe someday I'd be able to show her the other pictures I had of Caleb, the inked footprint I'd brought home from the hospital, the pictures Sam had taken of the two of us in the bathtub, the little knitted white hat I'd made him. *It was a start,* I thought again, as I reached across the table and took my mother's hand.

BECKY

Becky sat up in bed and was hit with a wave of dizziness that sent her reeling back to the mattress. *Food poisoning,* she thought, as the room spun. It was an occupational hazard. Typists got repetitive stress injuries, executives got ulcers, chefs got forty-eight hours of vomiting, shivering, diarrhetic misery. *Serves me right for eating those oysters,* she thought and closed her eyes, groaning. It would be rotten luck for her to get sick. Life was so good. She hadn't heard from Mimi since the Tragedy of the Christmas Ham. Neither had Andrew. Not a single phone call, not one e-mail, not one page, not a single slutty baby outfit in a package addressed to A. Rabinowitz. Sometimes Becky felt as if she were living under a radioactive cloud that would split open and rain down poison at a moment's notice, but most of the time it was wonderfully peaceful, blissfully quiet.

Andrew emerged from Ava's room with the baby, still in her pink pajamas, in his arms. "Not feeling good?"

"Ugh," she gasped, as another wave of dizziness rolled over her. "I think I'm sick," she said and flopped back down on the mattress. Andrew felt her forehead and the glands in her neck.

"No fever, but it could be a stomach bug. Want to call the doctor?"

Sure, Becky thought. And get lectured about the ten—no, fifteen—pounds she'd failed to shed since Ava's birth? "I'll be okay," she said. "Do we have any ginger ale?"

353

Andrew carried Ava down to the kitchen and came back up, five minutes later, with flat ginger ale and a plate of saltines. Becky sipped and munched. "Much better," she said. "Yum. You know, I don't think I've had a saltine since I was . . ." Her voice trailed off. She stared up at Andrew. "Oh, shit."

Andrew had the nerve to look pleased as he carried Ava into her room. "I think Grumbelina and I are going to take a walk," he said.

"Oh, shit," Becky repeated.

"Now, let's not get ahead of ourselves," Andrew said. He was beaming as he carried Ava out of the room. Becky heard him say, "Would you like a little brother or sister?"

Oh, shit, she thought again and pulled the quilt up over her head.

Fifteen minutes later, Andrew and Ava were back, with a bag from the drugstore.

"What is that child wearing?" Becky grumbled, taking in her daughter's ensemble of red-and-yellow-checked corduroy pants, a lime-green onesie, a pink sweater, and a blue ski cap. Andrew was a dear, sweet man, but he was also color-blind. At least he'd avoided the hot-pink fake-fur-trimmed leggings that Mimi had sent, along with matching marabou mules.

"Don't change the subject," Andrew said, as he helped her out of bed and steered her toward the bathroom.

"This is crazy," Becky said. "I've got a bug or the flu or something. Don't you think I'd know if I were pregnant?"

"Humor me," he said again. "Let's rule out horses before we go looking for zebras."

"No," she muttered, heading into the bathroom, where No became a bright blue Yes.

"How could this happen?" she demanded five minutes later, waving the dipstick in the air.

"Well, Becky," said Andrew, with a smug little smile on his face and Ava in his arms, "I think we know how it happened."

"But I'm still breast-feeding! And I used the diaphragm!" *Most of the time,* she thought, remembering the twenty-six nights they'd been stranded on the pullout couch and she hadn't always been motivated enough to tiptoe up the stairs and risk waking Mimi on her way to the bathroom.

"Well, nothing's foolproof," Andrew said.

"I can't believe it. How am I going to do this? How? I can barely handle one baby, and now I'm going to have two? Fifteen months apart?"

"What do you mean, you can barely handle one baby?" Andrew, to his eternal credit, looked nonplussed. "I think you're doing a great job."

"You don't know . . ." Becky flopped onto the bed and pulled the quilt up over her head. "I yelled at her one time. We were walking up from South Street. I had to go to Chef's Market, we ran out of saffron at the restaurant, and she started screaming at Fourth and Pine and she just wouldn't stop; she was screaming at the top of her lungs for eight blocks. And I did everything I could think of—I picked her up, I tried to nurse her in a coffee shop—she just wouldn't stop crying, and I yelled at her. I stuck my face right in her stroller, and I said, 'What do you want me to do?' People were staring."

"Nobody was staring."

"They were totally staring." Becky rolled over, pulling the quilt more tightly against her. "And I won't be able to work for a while. And Andrew . . ." She looked at him and wiped her eyes. "I like working. I love Ava . . . I mean, I totally love her almost all of the time, when she's not screaming for eight blocks, but I'm so happy when I drop her off at the hospital and I get to go to work. It feels like being paroled some days. Like I'm Sisyphus, and I finally get to quit pushing the rock." She twisted a lock of her hair. "I'm a terrible mother."

"Ah, yah," Ava chirped, as if in affirmation.

"Don't listen to her," said Andrew. "You are not a terrible mother."

She sighed again and sniffled. "I love the restaurant. I'm never going to be able to do it with two babies. I should probably see if Sarah wants to buy me out."

"Don't be silly," Andrew said. "It's not a life sentence. And there are things we can do."

Becky wiped her eyes with her sleeve. "I guess I might as well get it over with," she said. "I'll have—what? Another two or three years of diapers and nursing, and then that'll be it. Done. Over and out."

"Unless we have another one."

"Oh, no, sirree. You're getting snipped."

"What?"

"Snipped," she repeated. "I'm not running the risk of this happening again."

He set Ava down on the bed and bent his head against her belly. "Hello, baby," he whispered. Becky's eyes filled with tears. Instead of feeling thrilled the way she'd felt when she'd found out they were expecting Ava, she felt sad and confused and disloyal somehow. Ava was the baby. Now she'd be a big sister at fifteen months old. Becky hadn't wanted it that way. She figured that they'd have years together, just the three of them, years for Ava to be the center of their world, their little star. Now they'd be four. And she'd be exhausted.

"You have the most wonderful big sister," Andrew said, as he stroked Becky's hair with one hand and patted her tummy with the other. Becky put her hand on top of his head, stroking his hair. How could she love another baby as much as Ava? How would she even be able to manage another baby? *God,* she thought. She'd be one of those women with the double strollers, burdened like a Sherpa with backpacks and diaper bags, bowls full of Cheerios, pockets full of binkies and rattles and half-off coupons for Pampers.

"You have the most beautiful mommy," Andrew said. Becky shut her eyes, feeling a rush of dizziness and nausea and, worst of all, déjà vu. They'd done this all before. Andrew rubbed cocoa butter onto her skin, his hands moving in slow circles, and in her ninth month, he'd read *Goodnight Moon* to her belly. It had all been so special, so new. How would it feel this time around?

"Becky," he said. He wrapped his arms around her.

"Do you realize I'm going to have to wear those fugly maternity clothes again?" she asked. She leaned her forehead against his. "Promise me that this will be okay," she said. "Promise me it will."

"We can hire a nanny if we decide we need it," Andrew said. "Or we can have the cleaning ladies come twice a week. I know it's not perfect, but really, we're lucky, when you think about it."

Lucky. She mouthed the word against the warm skin of his neck and knew that it was true. If there was one lesson she'd learned from new motherhood and from her friends, it was that any bit of good fortune had to be counted as lucky . . . and that there was always, always someone worse off than you.

KELLY

The doorbell rang at ten o'clock Friday morning, an hour after her
husband had left, half an hour since she'd shucked her sweatpants and
T-shirt and scrambled into the perfectly pressed suit that she'd snuck
home from the dry cleaner's the day before. Kelly slipped on her
heels, laid a clean blanket over her shoulder, and laid Oliver, dressed
in Oshkosh overalls and a red-and-white-striped onesie, on top of it.
Then she checked her lipstick and opened the door.

"Hey, Kelly!"

Amy Mayhew was even younger than she'd sounded on the
phone. Twenty-four, tops, Kelly thought. She wore a knee-length
skirt, a navy sweater, and knee-high boots with kitten heels. The photographer was a bearish man of fifty or so in khakis and a baseball cap.
His hands were warm as he shook her hand and tickled Oliver under
the chin. "What a handsome fellow!"

"Thank you," she said, and led them inside, through the nearly
empty living room that she'd gotten up at six to clean. "Can I get either of you some coffee?"

Amy and the photographer, whose name was David, both said
they'd love a cup. Kelly set Oliver, who'd been fed, burped, diapered,
and slipped a good-behavior-ensuring dropperful of Infants' Tylenol
forty-five minutes previously, into his Ultrasaucer, and walked into
the sparkling kitchen, humming as she poured coffee and set the cups
on the tray Becky had come over that morning to arrange. There was

a bowlful of sugar cubes, a pitcherful of cream, a plate of half-moon-shaped cookies dusted with confectioners' sugar. *Perfect,* Kelly thought, carrying the tray into the living room, admiring the way the sunlight spilled across the freshly mopped floors, the way the air still smelled faintly of the pear-scented candles she'd lit the night before. You could hardly see how awful the Ghetto Couch was underneath the queen-sized cream-colored cashmere throw Ayinde had lent her, and the cardboard boxes covered with an antique lace tablecloth made a perfectly acceptable stand-in for the coffee table that Kelly did not, as yet, possess.

She sat on the couch and smiled at the reporter. "So," she said. "What can I tell you about my life?"

Amy Mayhew's laughter sounded admiring. Kelly wondered what she would have made of this cozy domestic scene when she'd been single herself. "Let me give you a little background. My piece is focusing on a new generation of women—the ones who've refused to accept the working woman/stay-at-home mom dichotomy and have found innovative ways to balance their families and their careers. Why don't we start with your biography?"

Kelly smiled as she recited her siblings' names, the town where she'd been born, the year she'd finished at Penn, the venture-capital consulting firm that had kept her on the road for two hundred days of the two years she'd worked there. Oliver bounced in his Ultrasaucer, occasionally yelling out, "Brr!" as Kelly told them about growing up in Ocean City and how she'd single-handedly started a gerbil craze in her school. Amy Mayhew laughed appreciatively as Kelly explained how she'd brought a gerbil of her own to class, petting and fussing over it, and when she'd built the demand, she'd purchased more gerbils at rock-bottom prices from the pet store and sold them to her classmates for five dollars apiece. And then she'd lucked into the purchase of a pregnant gerbil, and she'd earned more than a hundred dollars before her mother told her she was sick of living with cages full of furry rats and put a stop to Kelly's rodent cottage industry.

She told Amy how she'd planned her own birthday parties and

those of her siblings since she was five years old, leaving out that her early planning skills were largely a result of her mother being too drunk or disinterested to care. She covered her family history as fast as she could, lingering on Maureen, who was pursuing a Ph.D., and skipping over Doreen, who'd gotten laid off at the DMV. "And your parents?" Amy asked.

"My father works for the post office. My mother is deceased," Kelly said. The reporter made sympathetic noises and didn't ask, 'Of what,' which left Kelly from finding some fancy way to say *cirrhosis* or giving any indication that her death had been a relief.

"La la la, ga ga ga, da da da," Oliver said, waving his stuffed bear over his head.

"Dada?" asked the photographer with a smile.

She leaned toward Oliver, smiling at him, feeling her heart lift as he smiled back and the camera clicked just in time to capture it. "Dada's on a business trip!" she said brightly. Dada had actually been dispatched to Sam's Club with a shopping list as long as his arm, after Kelly had explained her daylong cleaning frenzy by saying she'd invited her girlfriends over for lunch, but the *Power* people didn't need to know that.

Oliver gurgled, displaying his gums and both of his two teeth. He reached for Kelly, and the camera clicked as she lifted him into the air. "Great," David murmured, as Kelly swooped him over her head. Just then there was an ominous gurgling noise. Oliver opened his mouth, and watery, pinkish vomit came pouring out, soaking Kelly's suit and puddling on the floor.

"Oh my God!" Amy Mayhew said, stepping backward so fast that she almost went crashing down on—and through—the cardboard box masquerading as actual furniture.

"Oh, dear," said Kelly, as she settled Oliver, who was shrieking, onto her shoulder. "Just give me a minute. We'll be right back."

Shit, she thought, hurrying down the hall. It must've been the Tylenol. She ran into the baby's room, yanked off his outfit, and looked around wildly for a replacement. *Sure, I'll do the baby's laundry,*

Steve had been telling her for the past three days. She opened the dryer. It was empty. She opened the washing machine and groaned as she saw all of Oliver's clothes, still soaking wet. She kept one hand on the wailing baby on his changing table and yanked drawers open one after another before she realized, with mounting fury, that the only clean things for the baby to wear were his christening gown or pajamas. Pajamas, she decided, pulling a clean navy-blue pair onto the baby's legs as he kicked and howled.

"Is everything all right in there?" Amy Mayhew called above the baby's shrieks.

"Just fine!" Kelly called back. She did the snaps, found a clean blanket, and carried Oliver into her bedroom and laid him on a blanket on the bed. She shucked off her sodden, sticky suit and pawed through the hangers in the closet, shoving Steve's abandoned suits aside until she found a clean skirt that she thought would fit. Oliver whimpered. She swabbed his cheeks and chin with a diaper wipe and dialed the phone with her free hand.

"Hi, this is Kelly Day. I'm calling about my son, Oliver . . ." She kicked off her shoes and yanked hard at her skirt's zipper, which didn't want to close, bending forward to press her forehead against Oliver's belly so that he wouldn't wiggle off the bed. "I gave him some Tylenol about an hour ago, and he just threw up . . ."

"Were you treating a fever?" *Thank God,* Kelly thought, *it was a different nurse than the one who'd answered after Oliver had fallen out of his high chair.*

"I'm sorry, what was that?"

"The Tylenol," said the nurse. "You mentioned you'd given him Tylenol."

"Oh, um, he's been teething . . ." A total lie, but what was she supposed to say? *I'm medicating my child so that he'll behave during a magazine interview?* Between this and the high-chair accident, she'd officially forfeited her shot at Mother of the Year. "You know what? He seems fine now. I'm going to try to nurse him, and I'll call back later." She hung up the phone before the nurse could say a word and rifled through the closet. Her favorite sweater was in the to-be-dry-cleaned pile, covered in dog hair. Her second-favorite sweater now fit her so tightly that it made her look like a Varga girl after a long weekend at the All-U-Can-Eat buffet. She ran her right hand over the dusty top shelf, finally hitting the Lord & Taylor box Doreen had sent her for Christmas. She grabbed it and flung it on the bed. The sweater inside was lavender. Low cut. Fuzzy angora. But at least it was clean. She yanked it over her head and hurried back to the living room with Oliver in her arms.

"Sorry about that!" she said, smiling brightly. "Everything's under control now."

The reporter and photographer gave each other a dubious look. Kelly stifled a sneeze as a bit of angora drifted into her nose.

"So, you went back to work when the baby was how old, exactly?"

"Sixteen weeks," she lied. It had actually been twelve, but she thought sixteen sounded better. "And it was only a few days a week, a few hours a day at first. My manager was great about letting me ease into things." Another lie. She'd jumped in with both feet, basically cramming forty hours' worth of work into a twenty-hour work week to prevent them from having to dip into their savings. And to give her a few hours a day away from the spectacle of her husband lounging around with his fly down, away from the baby who demanded all of her attention and both of her hands.

"And you've got a nanny while you work?"

"I had relatives filling in for a while, and now a friend of mine babysits," said Kelly. "I know how lucky I am to have her." That, at least, was true, as long as Steve counted as a relative. And she was lucky, compared with the majority of women in the country, who'd be lucky if they got six weeks off after having a baby, who'd have to put their babies into day care or hope there was a responsible and willing relative within driving distance. She was lucky that her family still had benefits (true, they'd only have them for six more months until Steve's COBRA ran out, and they were outrageously expensive, but it was better than nothing). She was lucky to have friends who, in a pinch, would watch Oliver if an emergency came up.

"And my boss lets me work from home, so I'm usually just right down the hall," she concluded, turning Oliver deftly before he could perform his latest trick, which involved grabbing onto the neckline of whatever she was wearing and trying to pull himself up—and, consequently, pull her top down. That was Lie Number Three, but she couldn't very well tell them that she worked on a laptop from a coffee shop because her husband had taken over her office, which he apparently needed to manage his ever-increasing number of fantasy football and baseball teams.

"Tell me how your clients have reacted," Amy asked. "Do they mind that you're not available eight hours a day?"

"Actually, I find that I'm able to be just as connected as I was when I worked at the office. I carry a cell phone, of course, and I've got a pager for emergencies."

"But what if you have something to deal with and your friend's not here? What do you do with . . ." Amy snuck a fast look down at her notebook. "Oliver?"

Kelly bit her lip. In cases like that, what she did was hand the baby off to Steve, along with a stack of board books and toys. "I take him for walks!" she said triumphantly. "He's always happy when he's in his stroller, and I talk on my headset, so I can use both hands to push . . ."

Amy was looking at her skeptically. "But what if you need to consult a document? Or a memo or something? Isn't it hard to work when you're not right in front of your computer?"

"Well, if there's something I really need, I can print it out, and, um, refer to it as we're walking . . ." Yeah. Right. She imagined herself walking up Walnut Street, Oliver in his stroller, cell phone in her ear, trying to read a crumpled-up printout folded against the handlebars. "Or when we're sitting at the park. Or I can wait until he's napping, or asleep, or . . . well, I've got friends, they're mothers, too, and we kind of cover for each other if there's a crisis. I could have one of them take him. If there was a fire I really needed to put out." There. That sounded nice. Cozy, even. Sort of *Little Women*–ish, all these nice new mommies swapping babies and homemade coffee cake across the white picket fence. She wiped her hands surreptitiously on her skirt as she heard the camera clicking away. Her heart was pounding. If faking Having It All was this hard, actually having it all must be impossible. "And a lot of my events are at night, after the baby's sleeping, and my husband's home, so that works out well."

"I think it's amazing," Amy said. "The idea of taking care of another person . . . most days I can barely take care of myself!"

You don't know the half of it, sister, Kelly thought. "Enjoy yourself now," she said. "You'll be here soon enough."

Amy Mayhew smiled, but Kelly could tell she didn't really believe her. Or maybe she thought that the world would have reinvented itself by the time she was ready to reproduce, that science and sociology would have yielded some perfect solution, allowing babies and jobs to exist in perfect harmony.

"So give me a day in your life," Amy said.

"Well, I wake up at six or so . . . ," Kelly began, running through her morning, leaving out the parts about dragging an unhappy golden retriever down the block.

David began unpacking boxes of equipment, setting up a light in one corner. "Is your life the way you pictured it?" Amy asked. "Like, when you were in college. Is this what you imagined things would look like?"

"Um. Well. Hmm." Kelly tried to remember exactly what she'd imagined. A husband who'd be earning at least as much as she was, for one thing. She'd envisioned a few years of fourteen-hour days, travel, all-nighters, weekends, whatever it took to establish herself. She'd imagined her wedding, of course, and then an apartment just like this one, only with more furniture, a perfectly decorated nursery with a perfect, silent baby lying at the center of a perfectly appointed crib. She'd pictured herself pushing a stroller, her hair shiny, nails polished, wearing the same size jeans she'd worn in high school, doing all the things she wouldn't have time for as a working woman—sipping a latte, browsing in bookstores and boutiques, meeting friends for lunches, during which the baby would lie like an angel in his stroller or, perhaps, sit on her lap so that her friends could admire him. She'd envisioned herself in the kitchen, preparing dinners from scratch while the baby napped. She'd dreamed of a candlelit bedroom, a husband she'd still want to sleep with, luxurious, inventive sex. She'd imagined all of the trappings of motherhood—the crib bumpers and bedsheets, the stroller she'd push—but not the reality of it. Not the reality of a baby who, in her fantasies, had appeared as little more than a kind of chic accessory, the thing to have this season. Not the reality of a husband who wasn't what she'd thought he was when she'd said her vows and made her promises.

"Kelly?"

I was wrong, she thought. So wrong. "It's much harder," she said. Her voice was flat. Amy Mayhew was staring at her. Kelly cleared her throat, dislodging another bit of lavender fluff. "This is so much harder than I ever thought it would be." She cleared her throat. "Because, the thing is, even if you're just working part-time, your boss is going to expect a full week's worth of work, no matter how understanding she is. That's just the nature of the working world—things have to get done, babies or not. And if you're like me—if you're like any woman who ever did well in school and did well at her job—you don't want to disappoint a boss. And you want to do a good job raising your baby." She shoved up her sleeves. "It's not like you think it's going to be."

Amy Mayhew looked professionally sympathetic. "How is it different?"

"Babies need you. They need you all the time, unless they're sleeping, and if you're lucky they'll nap for an hour, tops, and then you have to decide what you want to do with that time. Do you want to do work? Return phone calls? Empty the dishwasher? Take a shower? Pump breast milk for the feedings when you're not going to be home? You usually wind up doing five things at once."

"Multitasking," Amy Mayhew said with a nod.

"Yeah. Multitasking," she said. "So you wind up calling clients back while you're hooked up to the breast pump, only you can't take notes because you're using one arm to hold the phone and the other one to hold the cups in place. Or you sit your baby on your lap and read him event proposals in the same voice you use to read *One Fish, Two Fish, Red Fish, Blue Fish* and hope he doesn't notice the difference. And you eat a lot of take-out. And you don't get much sleep."

Kelly paused for breath, not much liking Amy Mayhew's expression, which was beginning to look a lot like pity.

"What about your husband?" Amy Mayhew asked. "Does he help?"

The word *husband* snapped Kelly back to reality . . . or, rather, back to the false reality she was trying to perpetrate upon the unsuspecting readers of *Power* magazine.

"Well, he's very busy," she began. "He travels . . ."

"Do you mind if I stick this in here? Just to get it out of the way for the pictures?" The photographer was holding his jacket and gesturing toward the closet, the one where Kelly had stuffed six months' worth of clutter: newspapers, magazines, a half-empty box of diapers that Oliver had outgrown, Steve's golf clubs, the sandals she hadn't worn in months, Lemon's dog food and chew toys, a garbage bag full of baby clothes, a shoebox full of unsorted photographs, library books, one single pathetic-looking half-deflated IT'S A BOY! balloon . . .

"Oh, wait!" In slow motion, Kelly saw him reaching for the handle. She set Oliver down on the floor and got to her feet, but she wasn't fast enough. There was a low rumble as the door slid open and then, in the blink of an eye, her life had avalanched down onto the freshly vacuumed floor.

"Oops," said the photographer, as the cascade continued (a six-month free trial disc from AOL, a rubber-banded stack of unpaid bills, a broken pair of sunglasses, a copy of Dr. Ferber's *Solve Your Child's Sleep Problems,* a copy of Dr. Sears's *The No-Cry Sleep Solution,* a copy of Dr. Mindell's *Sleeping Through the Night*). "Oh, man, I'm sorry," David said.

"Don't worry! No problem!" Kelly started shoving things back into the closet, but the more she pushed, the more stuff came pouring out (two copies of *Philadelphia Chickens,* three copies of *Where the Wild Things Are,* the ridiculously ugly knitted afghan from Mary that she didn't have the heart to chuck or give away, a box of breast pads, a can of powdered formula). She bent down, breathing hard, pushing with her feet, scooping with her arms. It wasn't doing any good. For every single thing she managed to put back onto the shelf or squeeze onto the floor, there were three more things waiting to take its place. And either she was imagining a loud clicking sound, or this whole thing—including her bent-over butt, encased, more or less, in a skirt with a gaping zipper—was being photographed for posterity. She finally straightened up, blowing wisps of hair off her sweaty face. "Let's just leave it."

Small potatoes, she told herself, walking away from the detritus of the last six months of her life. "It's small potatoes," she said out loud, thinking about her friends. A baby who died, a baby who was sick, a husband who was cheating, those were all big deals. A messy closet and an undermotivated spouse? No big deal.

Then Oliver started to cry again, and Lemon was barking, and the front door opened, and Steve walked in, dressed in a long-sleeved T-shirt, stubble on his chin, hair curling over his collar, with a puzzled look on his face and his arms full of discounted diapers.

"Kelly?"

No. Oh, no.

"You must be Steve!" Amy Mayhew said cheerfully.

He nodded, staring at the two of them. "And where's your baby?" he asked.

Amy laughed dismissively. "Oh, no, no, no baby for me!"

Steve's forehead furrowed as he looked at Kelly. "What's going on?"

Lie, lie, think of a lie. "You're back early!"

"Yeah, Sam's Club didn't have half the stuff you wanted, so I thought I'd just come home and say hi to everyone."

"We thought you were out of town!" said Amy.

"Huh?" said Steve. He looked at his wife. Kelly swallowed hard.

"This is Amy Mayhew and David Winters. They're from *Power* magazine."

Steve stared at them, his forehead wrinkled.

"They're here to talk to me," Kelly said.

"About what?" he asked.

She plastered her very best good-girl smile to her face and prayed with all her heart. *Cover for me,* she thought. *If you ever loved me at all, cover for me.* "Work and family," she said. "Having it all."

"Oh," he said, repeating it slowly. "Having it all."

"I told you, remember?" she said, feeling desperate. "I know I mentioned this. You must have forgotten. He's so busy," she explained to Amy and David.

"Well, he must be," Amy Mayhew said. "Consulting's hard work."

Steve stared at his wife. *Consulting?* she could practically hear him think. *Please,* she begged him telepathically. *Please just go away.*

"I'll be in the office," he said. He turned on his heel, stepped over the mess spilling out of the closet as if he didn't even see it, and stalked out of the room.

"Steve, wait!" Her fingertips brushed his sleeve as he moved past her. "Will you excuse me?" Kelly said to David and Amy, and then she ran down the hall, put the baby in his crib, and hurried to the bedroom. Steve was standing in front of the closet in the bedroom. There was already a suitcase open on the bed.

"What are you doing?"

"Oh, gee, I don't know. I guess I'm consulting. If that's what you're telling people these days," he said.

"Well, what was I supposed to say?" she hissed. "That you're un-employed? How do you think that would have looked in print?"

"You know what? I really don't care. You're the one who's so big on appearances," he said, gathering shirts and jeans from the floor where he'd left them.

"Steve . . ."

He glared at her, then crossed the room to the dresser, taking handfuls of underwear and undershirts, the ones Kelly picked up off the floor or fished out from underneath the sheets, the ones she washed, dried, folded, and replaced in the drawers. *What does he think?* she remembered asking Becky. *That there's a Boxer Fairy who flies around magically replacing his underwear every night?*

"All right, you know what? Go on, then," she said. "Call me when you've got a new number. Or, better yet, call me when you've got a new job. I don't think I'll hold my breath."

"Go back to your interview," he said, snatching more clothes off of the floor. "Why don't you just tell them you're a single mother?"

"I might as well be!" she yelled, pushing herself between his body and the bed. "For all the help I get from you, I might as well be a single mother! Do you think I wanted to go back to work twelve weeks after our baby was born?"

"For the hundredth time, Kelly, you didn't have to go back to work. You went back to work because you wanted to. And if you'd let me help—"

"If I let you help, you drop the baby!" she shouted. "If I let you help, you tell me his diaper's dry when it's wet, and you tell me he doesn't need to burp when he does, and I did need to go back to work!"

"No," he said, in a maddening singsong voice, as if he were speaking to a stupid child. "No, you didn't."

"I did because I didn't want to burn through all our savings!" she shouted. "Because, unlike you, I've got a problem with sitting on my ass all day long! You know what," she said, "I wish I were a single mother! Because single mothers don't have to pick up their husbands' dirty dishes and empty beer bottles every night. Single mothers don't have to wash anyone else's laundry, or pick up anyone's messes, or, or put the toilet seat down at night because their husbands can't be bothered to remember—"

"Keep your voice down," he hissed.

" . . . because they're too busy watching soap operas!"

He jerked as if she'd slapped him.

"Oh, yeah, I know all about that. Do you think I wouldn't notice that suddenly TiVo's taping every episode of *As the World Turns*?"

"That's not me!" he yelled. "I watched it once, and the stupid machine started taping on its own!"

"Yeah, right," Kelly said. "I'm out working, doing all the shopping, all the laundry, all the cooking, all the cleaning, all the everything . . ."

" . . . not because you had to."

She ignored him. "I'm raising our son single-handedly except for the ten minutes a day you stop surfing the Internet long enough to read him one lousy book, and I . . . DO . . . EVERYTHING! And I'm tired!" She yanked hard at the hem of her sweater, which was riding up over her midriff. "I'm so tired."

"So take a break!" he yelled. "Take a break! Take a nap! Quit your job! Or don't!" He threw his hands in the air. "You want to have it all, you go right ahead."

"I can't take a break," she said, as she started to cry. "You don't understand. I *can't*. Because then what? What if you never start working again? What happens when we don't have any money left? What happens to us then?"

"Kelly . . ." He was staring at her, his expression somewhere between puzzled and . . . what was that look? She knew it in an instant. It was the same look Scott Schiff, her once-upon-a-time boyfriend, had given her when they'd pulled into her driveway in Ocean City. Pity. "Nothing's going to happen to us." He reached for her and pulled her against him, and she let herself lean into him, she let herself close her eyes. "What are you talking about? We've got plenty of money. I've told you that a million times . . ."

"Not enough," she said and wiped her face again. "It's never enough."

"It's plenty."

"You don't understand." She pushed him away and wiped her face with one of the T-shirts on the bed. "You don't understand me at all."

"Then let me." He reached out his arms for her, fingers spread wide. "Tell me. Talk to me."

She shook her head. In high school, all eight of the O'Haras had been eligible for donated uniforms and free lunches. But to get your free lunch, you had to give the cafeteria lady a yellow ticket instead of the red one that kids paid for. On her first day of ninth grade, Mary had taken away her yellow ticket, torn it up, and shoved a can of Diet Coke into her hand. "Drink this," Mary had told her. "We don't need anybody's handouts." For years, she'd lived by that code, making her own way, paying her own fare. *We don't need anybody's handouts . . .* and she had ended up married to a man who was collecting unemployment, spending days on the couch, and proposing they live off their savings.

"I made a mistake," she whispered, wiping her eyes again. "I made a mistake with you."

"No," he said and shook his head, "no, Kelly, you didn't . . ."

"I made a mistake," she said again. "Please go." She wiped her eyes again and walked out the bedroom door, back toward her perfect living room, and the perfect nursery where her perfect baby waited, back into the life that looked almost exactly the way she'd pictured it and felt nothing like how she'd imagined.

She carried Oliver into the living room. Amy and David were sitting on her couch, their faces so carefully blank that she couldn't tell—and didn't care—whether they'd heard every word or nothing at all.

February

February

LIA

Sam had told me that I didn't have to meet him at the airport. "It's not a big deal. I can just take a cab."

"No," I said, feeling a sob rise in my throat at the sound of his familiar, faintly Texan voice. I just wanted to press the phone to my ear and listen to him forever. But I wanted to make a gesture, to give him a sign. I wanted to be there when he got to Philadelphia. I walked to Thirtieth Street Station, then took a train to the airport, an hour ahead of time. I paced back and forth in front of the baggage claim, thinking wistfully about the days before 9/11, when you could go right to the gate and greet someone you loved.

Time crawled by. I watched people walk by, old women in wheelchairs, students with backpacks, frazzled-looking families pushing metal carts with teetering stacks of luggage. One family went past me with twins in a stroller and a baby, a newborn, riding on his father's chest. When the mother caught me staring, I smiled at her. "Have a good trip," I said. I could see the dark circles under her eyes, the way her hair had been dragged into a haphazard ponytail, how she was moving like her bones ached. *I remember that,* I thought.

"I'll try," she said. And then they were gone, and I felt a tap on my shoulder, and there was Sam.

"Hey." At the sound of his voice, my blood felt warmer, my skin, too, as if I'd been cold and hadn't noticed and someone had finally come along and offered me a sweater.

"Sam!"

"Shh," he said, giving me a cockeyed smile. "Don't want to start a riot." He dropped his voice to a whisper. He held me out at arm's length, inspecting me. "So here you are."

"Here I am."

And here he was, taller than I'd remembered, broad shouldered in his fleece-lined jacket, a knitted cap pulled down low on his forehead, the star-shaped scar in the middle of his chin from where he'd wiped out on his Big Wheel when he was five. I looked at his forehead, where the homeless lady had thrown an apple, then down at his hands, which had helped ease our son out of my body. *Congratulations, Dad,* the nurses had said, and Sam had bent down to kiss my forehead, resting his lips against me without saying a word.

I felt weak-kneed as he lifted a lock of my hair between his fingers and studied it underneath the airport's bright lights.

"You changed your hair."

I shrugged. "Well, it kind of changed on me. That's what happens when you don't stay on top of your highlights."

"You mean . . ." He placed his hand against his heart. "You're not a natural blonde?"

I felt myself blushing—blushing over such a silly thing. And over all the other things I'd told him that hadn't been true. "Sorry to disappoint you."

"I'll get over it. Somehow. It's pretty." He shrugged and slung his bag over his shoulder. "There are enough blondes in Hollywood already."

"I . . ." My hands and knees were shaking. There were a million things I wanted to ask him. *Are you all right?* and *Do you forgive me?* and *Do you understand why I left, why I had to?* And, of course, *Do you want me back?* But all I could manage was. "There's a train back into the city."

"Nah. We ride in style. I ordered us a car."

"Really?" I wanted to link my arm through his, to hug him or hold his hand, but I wasn't sure whether I had the right to do it yet or whether I ever would again. I might have looked different, but, to me, Sam looked the way he always had, tanned and strong and sure of himself. "That was nice."

"Don't thank me, thank the network. I told them I'd stop by the affiliate and say hello, and they were only too happy to pay for the trip. Plane tickets, car and driver, hotel room at . . ." He paused to pull a folder of tickets out of his back pocket and consult a scrap of paper he'd tucked in there. "The Rittenhouse Hotel. Do you know where that is?"

I took a deep breath. "It's right down the street from my apartment."

"Ah," he said. That was all he said. I looked at his familiar face and tried to figure out what he was feeling. *Angry,* I thought, as my heart sank. *God, he must be so angry at me. To lose a son and a wife in less than a month . . .* "I'm sorry," I said, knowing how completely inadequate the words were.

He shrugged a little. His eyes were opaque, unreadable.

"Do you want to," I started to say. Then I stopped. I wondered about where he was living, whether he'd moved or whether he'd stayed in the place where Caleb had lived, right down the hall from where he died and I felt my heart breaking for him. For my son. For all of us.

The driver, in a cap and dark coat, held a clipboard with the words JAMES KIRK. Sam held the door for me, then slid in beside me, and we pulled away from the curb.

"Nice alias," I said.

He nodded. "Now, what were you trying to ask me?"

There were a lot of things I wanted to ask—will you stay with me had been on top of the list—but what came out of my mouth was, "Do you still love me?"

"Oh," he said. And then I was in his arms, tight against him, and the smell of his soap and his skin were all around me, and I could hear his heart. "Oh, Lia." I reached for his hands, wanting to hold them in mine . . . and wanting to answer a question. He was still wearing his wedding ring. I could feel it against my fingertips. So there was that, then. At least there was that.

"You're Caleb's mother," he said. "I'll always love you because of that." He stroked my head again. "And the new hair's pretty hot."

I kissed his cheeks, his lips, his forehead, his hair underneath the cap. He held me tight.

"So you disappear for nine months, then crook your finger and have me come running?" he muttered into my hair. "Is this some radical version of playing hard to get?"

Words came tumbling into my mouth, but I kept them there. I slid into his lap, and I kissed him some more.

He pulled away to stare at me. "You missed me, then, I guess." His voice was breathless, almost panting, and I could feel him tremble as he held me. We hadn't made love since Caleb had died. We'd tried, once, one night when neither one of us could sleep, but we'd both wound up crying and lost our good intentions.

"I missed you so much," I said, before bending my head to kiss him again. "So much."

He pressed a button, and a plate of smoked glass slid up between us and the driver. "Don't want to cause a scene," he said, fumbling at my jacket, my sweater, my scarf. "All these clothes. My goodness. These East Coast boys must have a terrible time."

"No East Coast boys," I whispered. "Only you." I leaned back, and with one swift motion pulled my jacket and my sweater off and over my head. I felt my heart race as he looked at me.

"Very helpful," he said. "Here, let me . . ." He unbuttoned his own shirt. His fingers were shaking. His skin was so hot. "Come here," he said, pulling me against him. "I need to feel you."

I lifted myself off of his lap and yanked my jeans and underwear down to my knees. I gasped as I felt his fingers against me. I wanted to say something about how I'd waited for him, how I'd thought about him, how there hadn't been anyone else, but then he was lifting me in his arms, holding me as if I weighed nothing until we fitted together like pieces of a puzzle. We rocked together, slowly at first, then faster and faster . . .

"Sir?" came the driver's voice over the intercom. I looked out the window, seeing the trees and storefronts and sidewalks.

"We're there," I whispered.

"Just keep driving!" Sam gasped. I couldn't help myself. I started laughing. "Just go . . . somewhere!"

The car stopped. Then the turn signal clicked and we were rolling again, and I rocked on top of him, my hands gripping his shoulders, looking into his eyes, slowly at first, and then faster, as our breath turned the windows gray. "Oh," said Sam. His eyelids fluttered. "Oh."

At the last moment, the last instant when he could find breath enough and control to ask, I heard him whisper the question in my ear. "Is it safe?"

I could have told him that nothing was safe and that no matter how careful you were and how hard you tried, there were still accidents, hidden traps, and snares. You could get killed on an airplane or crossing the street. Your marriage could fall apart when you weren't looking; your husband could lose his job; your baby could get sick or die. I could have said that nothing is safe, that the surface of the world is pretty and sane, but underneath it's all fault lines and earthquakes waiting to happen. Instead I just whispered the word "yes" into his ear. A minute later, he was groaning a word I couldn't make out. And then everything was quiet except for the sound of our breath.

AYINDE

Three weeks after Ayinde and Richard had brought Julian home from the cardiologist's office, Clara tapped on Ayinde's bedroom door. "Someone here to see you," she said.

Ayinde looked at her curiously. "Who?"

Clara shrugged. Then her hands sketched a belly in the air. "Embarazo," she said.

Pregnant. Ayinde felt the hair at the back of her neck prickle, as she lifted Julian into her arms and followed Clara down the stairs.

The woman was standing in the doorway in a pink-and-white wrap dress far too flimsy for the Philadelphia winter. Pale legs traced with bulging blue veins, high heels on her feet, and an expensive pink leather purse dangling from one wrist. Blond hair pulled back from the face Ayinde recognized from the tabloids. No winter coat because you wouldn't need a winter coat in Phoenix.

Ayinde's breath rushed out of her as if she were a punctured tire. "Clara, take the baby," she said, handing Julian over as the woman— the girl, really, Ayinde saw—stood there shivering on the porch.

"What do you want?" Ayinde asked, looking the girl up and down, seeing how uncomfortable she was in the cold and not caring. "Richard's not here."

"I know that." Tiffany's voice was soft and twangy, the vowels elongated. Her outfit and hair and makeup were too old for her, but her voice made her sound like she was twelve. "I came to see you.

Ayinde." She pronounced the name carefully, as if she'd been practicing.

"Why?"

She wrapped her arms around herself and tucked her chin into her chest. "I came to say I'm sorry for what I did."

Ayinde blinked. Whatever she'd been bracing herself for—some kind of lurid confession, a plea for more money—this wasn't it.

"I'm sorry," the girl said again.

"How did you get here?"

"The night I met Richard . . ." *Nicely put,* Ayinde thought. "He went to sleep, and I went through his cell phone. I found his home phone number, and I got the address from that. I thought, if I ever needed to get a hold of him."

"I'd say you got a hold of him just fine," Ayinde said.

The girl swallowed hard. "So I had his address, and then . . ." She shrugged, struggled with the zipper of her fancy bag, and pulled out a computer printout. "Mapquest."

"Aren't you clever," Ayinde said coolly. "Your parents must be so proud."

The girl was shivering. "No, ma'am, they're not." She lifted her chin. "I know you probably won't believe me, but they didn't raise me for . . ." She looked down at her belly. "For this. They're ashamed of me." She dropped her head again, and her words were almost lost in the wind. "I'm ashamed of myself."

Ayinde could barely believe what she was doing when she opened the door. "Come inside."

Tiffany walked as if her legs belonged to someone else and she'd just rented them for the day. Her belly swayed with each step she took as she followed Ayinde into the living room and sat perched on the edge of the couch. The cook edged into the room with a tray of tea and cookies, then hurried out with her head down.

"What do you really want?" Ayinde asked.

"I just wanted to tell you that I was sorry," she said. "I'm sorry for your troubles."

"What do you know about my troubles?" Ayinde asked.

"I read that your baby was sick," said the girl.

Ayinde closed her eyes. TOWNE TOT HEART TERROR, the tabloid headlines had read, and the hospital had written them a letter promising to get to the bottom of the incident and find out who'd violated patient confidentiality. "So some orderly loses his job," Ayinde told Richard wearily. The damage was done, and at least there weren't pictures. And Julian was fine.

"I just wanted to tell you," said the girl. She bent her head over her teacup, then set her saucer down and rubbed her hands against her legs, leaving pink streaks on her skin. "I know this sounds funny, coming from me, but your husband's a good man."

For what he's going to be paying you, you ought to be walking up and down Fifth Avenue with a sandwich board saying that, Ayinde thought.

"I asked if he wanted to see me again—you know, when he came to town for games—and he told me, 'No.' He said, 'I love my wife.' " She cleared her throat and looked up at Ayinde. "I just thought you should know that. And I'm sorry for what I did. I guess I wanted what you had, you know? How you looked in all the pictures, you and him. So happy."

Ayinde found that she couldn't speak.

"But he loves you, and that's the truth," Tiffany said.

"It didn't stop him from . . ." *Fucking,* she wanted to say. "Sleeping with you," she said.

"I don't think he meant to," said Tiffany.

Ayinde felt laughter, high and wild, rising in her throat. "So, what? He just fell in?"

"More or less," the girl said carefully. "And I'm sorry about it. I'm sorry I talked to the reporters, too. That was a mistake. I kind of got my head turned." She shook her head and rubbed her legs again. "My mother says that."

Mine does, too, Ayinde thought.

"And I'm sorry . . ." Tiffany wrapped her arms around herself and rocked back and forth. Ayinde looked at her, wondering how far

along she was and whether she was sleeping or whether she lay awake
at night, by herself, feeling the baby kick. "I know I made a mistake
with what I did. I've made a bunch of mistakes, and I want to do better, you know? For the baby?"

"For the baby," Ayinde repeated. She couldn't believe it, but she
felt—could it be?—sympathy for the woman who'd brought about
so much misery. Her baby wouldn't have an easy time of it—not
black, not white, not one or the other, with a single mother, too. The
world hadn't changed much since Ayinde's own parents had told her
that she was a pioneer. It hadn't improved fast enough.

Tiffany wiped her eyes. "I'm going back to school," she said in a
shaky little voice. "I don't think this dancing thing's going to work
out unless I go, you know, to New York or L.A., and now . . ." She
pressed an embroidered pillow into her lap. "I was thinking of maybe
sociology?" Her sentences tilted up like shallow bowls at the ends,
turning statements into questions. *Twenty-one,* Ayinde remembered.
She was only twenty-one.

"I think that's a fine major," she said.

"And I thought maybe . . ." Her words were coming quickly
now, tumbling over each other. "I don't know how you'd feel about
this, but I'd like my baby to know its father. And brother. Half-
brother, really. I want the baby to know that he has one."

Ayinde sucked in her breath.

"Would it be okay if I called you sometime? After the baby's
here? I don't want to bother you or your husband, but I just . . ."

Ayinde shut her eyes against the trembling vision in pink that
was Tiffany. It was too much. It was too much to ask of any woman,
too much to ask of her. What would Lolo say? Why, she'd arch one of
her pencil-thin eyebrows, tilt her cheekbones just so, and murmur
something that sounded pleasant on the surface but was devastating
underneath.

Ayinde could hear Tiffany breathing, could hear the sofa creaking
softly as she shifted her weight. She remembered her parents talking
to her when she lay in her canopied bed, bending their faces close to

hers, telling her what a lucky little girl she was to live so well, to go to such a fine school and travel to nice places for her vacations, and how it was her obligation, as a lucky girl, to be kind to those who weren't lucky. She remembered how they'd instructed her to always have a few dollars in her pocket for the homeless men who slept outside of her building, how if she didn't finish her dinner she was to have it boxed to go and leave the box beside a subway station because there was always someone poor and someone hungry who would need what she could spare. You have to be brave because you're lucky, Lolo had told her. She was still lucky . . . but could she be brave?

"I'm sorry," Tiffany said, after the pause had stretched out too long. "I guess I shouldn't have come. It's just . . . well, I'm scared a little, I guess, of having a baby . . . I know I should have probably thought of that before. . . ." Her voice trailed off. "My mother won't talk to me," she said softly. "She says I got myself into this mess, and I have to get myself out of it. She says it's my own fault for . . . you know. For what I did."

Ayinde could hear the click in the girl's throat as she swallowed. She could hear Julian babbling to Clara upstairs, making noises that sometimes sounded like actual words and sometimes sounded like Chinese and sometimes like a language all his own. His heart would eventually heal, the doctors had told them. Ayinde hadn't believed it. *You can live all right with a hole in your heart?* Dr. Myerson had given her a wry shrug. *You'd be surprised at what people can live with,* he said.

"Tiffany."

"Yes?" the other woman said eagerly.

"I don't think I'd feel comfortable with you coming here."

"I figured," she said sadly. "I guess I'd feel the same way."

"But maybe you could give me your number," Ayinde said. "I could call you."

"Really? You'd call me?"

"I'll call you," she said. "Take care of yourself, okay? Take care of the baby."

"Thank you!" said the girl. "Thank you so much!"

"You're welcome," said Ayinde. Once Tiffany was gone, she walked upstairs slowly. Clara was cradling the baby in her arms. She handed him over without a word, and Ayinde rocked him and kissed his cheeks. "You're going to have a half-brother or half-sister," she told him. He gurgled and grabbed at her earrings. She closed her eyes. *Lucky,* her parents had told her. She guessed it might even be true.

BECKY

In Becky and Andrew's years of marriage and parenthood, Mimi Breslow Levy et al. had never sent them a letter.

Phone calls, yes. E-mails—many of them marked URGENT and festooned with red exclamation points, certainly. Hundreds of faxes, packages by the dozen for A. Rabinowitz. But they'd never gotten an actual pen-and-ink missive until the Thursday afternoon Becky came home from work and found Andrew sitting on the couch staring glumly at a pair of handwritten pages.

"What's that?" she asked. *Bad news,* she thought, just from the look on his face.

"It's Mimi," he said dully. "She's disowning us. She says she doesn't ever want to see us again."

Through a mammoth effort, Becky was able to suppress her first instinct, which was to break into a joyous buck-and-wing while belting out "Happy Days Are Here Again."

"What do you mean?"

Wordlessly, he took Ava out of Becky's arms and handed her the letter. Becky sank onto the couch and started reading.

Andrew,

I don't know if I can find the words to express the way your actions of the past month have hurt me. Clearly, you and your wife have decided that you don't want me to have any part in your life or to have a relationship with my granddaughter. I can't imagine what I've done to make you feel this way . . .

"Oh, please," Becky murmured and snuck a glance sideways to where Andrew sat on the couch looking as though he'd lost a few quarts of blood.

. . . but ever since your marriage, and especially since my granddaughter was born, you have done nothing but treat me with a shameful lack of respect.

I have always tried to do what was best for you, even when it wasn't easy or when it came at my own expense. I sacrificed my own wishes so that you would always have everything you wanted and everything you needed.

Sacrificed what? Becky wondered. From what she'd seen of Mimi in action, there'd been precious little sacrificing and a whole lot of doing precisely what she wanted, garnished with a side of "I deserve respect" and a guilt trip for dessert.

She kept reading. *Your behavior has been nothing short of disgraceful. You are a disappointment as a son.*

"Andrew, this is ridiculous," she said. He pressed his lips together, saying nothing. "You're a wonderful son! You're so good to her. You're patient, and you're kind, and you're generous. You're so much better than any other man I know would be. You've been nice to her, you've included her . . ."

"Did you read the whole thing?" he asked.

Becky let her eyes skim the final paragraphs. *Disowning you . . . lawyers will be in touch . . . pushed me away . . . made a mockery of Christmas, which, you should know, is so important to me . . . I want nothing to do with either one of you ever again.* One phrase jumped off the page and practically slapped her in the face. *You have turned me away in favor of your wife and her family, who come from nothing and have no idea how to behave in decent company . . .*

Oy. Becky folded the pages. Andrew straightened up.

"You know what?" he said. "Maybe we should just let her go."

She blinked at him. Her mouth dropped open. "What?"

He got to his feet and ran his hands through his hair, pacing the length of the living room. "You're right. She's awful. She's awful to me, she's awful to you, and she's probably awful to Ava when we're not around." He took the letter out of her hand and shoved it back into the envelope so hard the paper ripped. "She wants to disown us? Fine. Good riddance. We'll be better off without her."

Becky closed her eyes. This was what she'd wished for, dreamed of, prayed about, and now here it was, handed to her on a silver platter. So why did it feel like such a hollow victory?

"Andrew," she said.

"What," he asked, folding up the envelope and shoving it into his pocket.

"Maybe we should think about this."

"What's to think about?" he asked. "She's manipulative, she's demanding, she's needy . . ."

"But she is Ava's grandmother," Becky said, hardly believing that those words were issuing from her mouth. "And the player-to-be-named later." She patted her belly. "She's this baby's grandmother, too."

Her husband stared at her as if she'd grown another head. "Are you sticking up for Mimi?"

"No, of course not. You're right. She's done terrible things, and as far as saying that you're a disappointment as a son, well, that's just beyond belief. But . . ." *Good God,* she thought, *what am I doing?* "I feel sorry for her," she said. "Imagine how lonely she'd be without us to harass."

Andrew narrowed his eyes. "Have you been taken over by the pod people?"

She handed him the phone. "Call her," she said. "We need to work this out."

Mimi had deigned to meet with them on a Sunday afternoon. Three days after her letter had arrived, Becky and Andrew left Ava with Lia and made the trip out to Merion, up the long, curving driveway that led to a teeny-tiny Tara. Mimi didn't answer the doorbell, and, after Andrew had opened the door with his key and led them inside, they found her sitting on a spindly gilt chair wearing a cashmere halter top with her head held high.

"I am not," she began, pointing at Becky and lifting her nose into the air as if she'd smelled something foul, "talking to her."

"My wife has a name," Andrew said.

Mimi glared at him as if she were observing him through a microscope. "I don't have anything to say to either one of you." *Eye-ther one of you.* Becky bit back a giggle. Queen Mimi, grande dame of a kingdom that only existed in her own imagination. "The only reason I agreed to this meeting is because I would like to see my granddaughter."

"Your granddaughter *Ava,*" Andrew said. Becky squeezed his knee.

"I have been insulted," Mimi said, stabbing upward with one fingertip. "I have been threatened. I have been ridiculed. I have been more than generous to the two of you—more than generous," she repeated, in case they'd missed it the first time. "And my generosity has been repaid with nothing. You're a disappointment as a son," she concluded. "And you," she said, raking Becky with her gaze, apparently forgetting that she had nothing to say to her. "The way you've spoken to me is unforgivable. You are beneath my contempt." With that, she got to her feet.

"I should have just cooked the freakin' ham," Becky murmured. Then she raised her voice. "Mimi, come back. Sit down," she said. Mimi's pace didn't slow. "If you don't want to do it for me or for Andrew, do it for Ava." Becky swallowed hard and forced herself to say the words. "Your granddaughter."

The pause seemed to stretch out forever. It ended with Mimi turning on her heel. "What," she said coldly.

Becky hadn't prepared a speech. She hadn't prepared to do anything except sit quietly by Andrew's side "Let me do the talking," her husband had said, and she'd agreed because if one thing had become clear in the course of her marriage, it was that she had absolutely no idea what was going on in Mimi's head or how to make any sense of it, and Andrew, at least, could handle her, even if his bag of tricks amounted to a single shopworn strategy—*Give her what she wants.* But Andrew either wouldn't talk or couldn't. Which left Becky with the floor.

She looked at Mimi, who'd resumed her seat and was glaring at the both of them. The woman who'd ruined her wedding, insulted her and her family, snubbed her mother, guilt-tripped her husband, and dressed her daughter as the world's littlest streetwalker. She breathed in deeply through her nose. *Feel your connection to every living, growing thing,* she remembered Theresa telling them in yoga class, back when she and her friends were mothers-to-be. She forced herself to breathe slowly and not see the woman in front of her, with her bird bones and brittle black hair, her threats and demands and pretension. She forced herself instead to imagine Mimi as a baby, an Ava-sized Mimi, standing in her crib, crying, with her little hands wrapped around the bars. Crying and crying with nobody coming to lift her up, nobody coming to help her.

The vision grew so clear that Becky could almost reach out and touch it—the soaked diaper and wet pajamas, the tears on the baby's face. And she could hear the baby's cries, the same indignant, self-righteous tone she'd gotten used to from Mimi . . . only imagining those cries from a baby made her hear them differently. She imagined baby Mimi's wet face, the trembling bow of her lips, the way her breath would catch in a hiccup in her throat before she'd start crying again. Crying and crying and nobody coming to help.

"I'm sorry," she said softly. And she was sorry for the baby in the picture. Where were her parents? Andrew hadn't told her much about Mimi's mother and father. They'd died before he was born, when Mimi was a teenager, a year before she'd embarked on her series of marriages. Mimi's father had been briefly, tremendously successful and then lost everything—bad investments, a partner who cheated him, something about embezzlement. And jail time. For the grandfather or the partner? Andrew wasn't sure. Mimi's mother had been strange. "Strange how?" Becky had asked, and Andrew had shaken his head, shrugging, telling her that Mimi wasn't what you'd call a reliable narrator, and he'd probably never know what the story there really was. All they had to go on was the evidence in front of them, and that evidence suggested damage. What had Lia told her, all those months ago? *She's the way she is because she got hurt.*

Becky raised her eyes. "I'm sorry," she said again.

Mimi glared at her, looking ready to spit. "What did you say?" she asked shrilly.

Becky looked at her without seeing her. She was still seeing that baby girl, abandoned in her crib. *Come here, baby,* she would say and scoop her into her arms, the way she'd done with Ava a thousand times. She would change her diaper, put her in clean clothes, feed her, soothe her, and sing her to sleep. *Bye and bye, bye and bye, the moon is half a lemon pie.*

Andrew's fingers were gripping her knee so hard she was sure they'd leave bruises. Becky tried to imagine birds with broken wings, dogs with crushed paws, and the baby in the crib, wailing away, crying for parents who wouldn't come. She thought of what it would be like to grow up without the one certainty that every baby deserved— *when I'm hurt or cold or scared, someone will come and care for me*—and how that absence could warp you so that you'd lash out at the people you loved, driving them away when all you wanted to do was pull them closer. And, at that moment, she meant every word of her apology.

"I'm sorry if I overreacted about Christmas," she said. "I can see now how much it meant to you."

Mimi's lips were opening and closing like a fish's.

"I don't think I'd ever be comfortable with having a tree in my house, but next year, I'd be happy to help you have a holiday dinner here," Becky said. "You've got more room, anyhow. And two ovens."

"I . . . you . . . we've already missed my granddaughter's first Christmas," Mimi said. Her manicured hands were clutching the arms of her chair convulsively. She looked confused, small and old and desperately unhappy. "You were visiting your mother!"

"Yes," Becky said calmly. "But just because we visit my mother doesn't mean we don't care for you. Ava can have her first Christmas next year," she said. She curled her toes in her shoes and tried desperately to keep the image of baby Mimi in mind, trying to remember how badly Mimi must have been hurt, instead of remembering the ways that Mimi had hurt them. "Andrew and I know how much you love Ava," she said. "She's lucky to have a grandmother like you."

Mimi bowed her head. Becky watched the other woman grip the arms of her chair. And then she got to see a sight she could never even have imagined. Mimi's eyelashes were fluttering rapidly. She raised one thin hand to her face and pulled it back, staring at the moisture on her fingertips as if she'd started leaking. Becky wondered how long it had been since Mimi had cried anything that weren't crocodile tears.

"I've got to fix my face," she said and bolted.

"Okay," Becky called to her back. "Happy New Year!" And then, not wanting to push her luck, she tugged Andrew to his feet and hurried him out the door.

It was cold but sunny, and the wind blew hard against Becky's cheeks as they walked along the icy veranda to their car. "What was that about?" Andrew asked, looking as bewildered as a man who's been bound and gagged to await the executioner's machine gun, only to find out it fired bubble-gum bullets.

"I don't know. Milk of human kindness?" She smiled. That was Sarah's joke about the tres leches cake they served at Mas. When customers asked what the three milks were, she'd say, "Evaporated, condensed, and the milk of human kindness."

"Milk of human kindness," Andrew repeated.

"You don't have to look so shocked. I do feel sorry for her, you know." She clutched Andrew's arm as she edged her way around a patch of ice. "She must be so lonely. And she probably doesn't have any idea of what little girls are like, or what they want, so maybe that's why she keeps buying Ava all that slut-wear . . ."

"All that what?"

Oh, dear. "Well, you know, all those things that say SEXY or HOTTIE or whatever."

"She probably just thinks it's fashionable."

"I feel sorry for her. I do," Becky said. Andrew held the door for her and helped her into the passenger's seat. "And I guess I was thinking about my friends. If Ayinde can forgive Richard and talk with that girl from Phoenix. And if Lia . . ." She sighed and bent her head. "We've got it pretty good, you know?" She yawned and stretched in the seat. "Of course, you should feel free to remind me of this the next time she does something outrageous." But even as she said it, she wasn't sure there'd be a next time. She suspected—or maybe just hoped—that all of the fight had been knocked out of her mother-in-law.

Or maybe that was too much to hope for. Maybe she would have to take it one day, one week, one holiday at a time, lurching from one crisis and blowup to the next in an endless loop of recrimination and rage. Maybe Mimi would be a misery to them until the day she died. But with so much joy in her life, perhaps, Becky decided, a little misery was in order. It was like the horseradish on the Passover plate— the bitterness that reminded you of how sweet life was.

Andrew pulled onto the highway. "So you're going to cook Christmas dinner next year?"

"Why not?" Becky said. "It won't kill me to cook a ham, if it matters so much to her. And as for the things that matter to us—like where we go on vacations or where we live or what we spend our money on or what we name our children . . ."

"We'll what?" he asked. "Lie to her?"

"We'll tell her what she needs to know," she said. "And then we'll do what we want. What's best for us and for Ava." She patted her belly with his hand. "And for the niblet."

"Ah. The niblet." He beamed at Becky. "When are we going to tell Mimi about the impending arrival?"

"Let's wait awhile, okay?" No matter how warm and fuzzy she was feeling toward Mimi, she knew that five and a half months of being quizzed about diet and weight gain and why she was still breast-feeding because surely that couldn't be healthy would be more than she could take.

"I think you're incredible," Andrew said. He cleared his throat. "The day Ava was born, I thought I could never love you more than that, but I do." He leaned close, touching her face, and kissed her softly. "You amaze me."

"I love you, too," she whispered. She tilted her seat back, adjusting the vent so that warm air blew over her knees. "I'm so tired," she said, yawning.

"Take a nap," he said and cleared his throat. "And thank you. If I forget to tell you later. Thank you so much."

"Ain't no thing," said Becky. She laced her hands over her belly and closed her eyes. At some point, she dozed, and when she woke up Andrew was backing into a parking spot.

"Andrew?"

"Hmm?" he asked, looking over his shoulder as he steered.

"Do you think we'll be good parents?"

He put the car in park and turned toward his wife. "I think we already are."

KELLY

On the twenty-third day of her separation, Kelly opened the mailbox to find two bills, an overdue notice from the library, and a large manila envelope containing a copy of *Power* magazine.

Kelly went upstairs and sat with the envelope in her lap for a while as Oliver crawled around the floor with his squeaky monkey toy caught in his undercarriage. "Bah!" he yelled. "Bah!" Then he turned around to look at her, and she gave him an encouraging wave and tried to smile. He yelled "Bah!" again and kept crawling forward. Finally, she pulled the flaps of the envelope open. The magazine slid into her lap. And there she was, on the cover, in her horrible lavender sweater with a burp cloth slung over her shoulder, standing in front of the closet, knee-deep in the ruins of her life. The look on her face, underneath the blow-dried hair and careful makeup, could only be described as bewildered. Bewildered and beaten down. *Having It All?* asked the cover. *Why a Working Girl Can't Win.*

She shut her eyes, and the magazine slid onto the floor. Oliver scooched himself over and reached for it with one chubby fist. She captured it in her own hands, guided it away, pulled the subscription card out of Oliver's mouth, and flipped to the page that Amy Mayhew had paper-clipped open. There was a note attached. *Dear Kelly. Thank you so much for your help with the story. As you can imagine, it didn't turn into quite the celebration my editors had imagined, but I think that what I wound up writing is much more honest—and may be more helpful to the generation of women who come next.*

"Helpful," she said and gave a rusty laugh. She set the baby in his high chair and opened a jar of oatmeal with peaches for his dinner and one for her own. Then she dropped her eyes to the magazine and read the opening sentences, beneath boldfaced words in quotation marks. It took her a minute to recognize the words as her own: "THIS IS SO MUCH HARDER THAN I EVER THOUGHT IT WOULD BE."

Kelly felt her eyes move almost inadvertently to the third cabinet in the kitchen, the one where they kept the Scotch and the vodka. A nice juice glass full of either one—topped off, perhaps, with one of the leftover Percocets from her C-section—and none of this would hurt so much. She'd done that the first night Steve was gone, when she couldn't reach Becky or Ayinde or Lia and she couldn't stop crying. But it was only one step from vodka and prescription painkillers to bourbon and Tab. She was determined not to go down that road, but she was beginning to understand how her mother could have. When your life turned into one big disappointment, a frantic hamster-wheel blur of work and baby with no one to love you or tell you that you were doing it well, bourbon and Tab did start to take on a certain allure.

She sighed and started to read.

By all rights, Kelly O'Hara Day should have the world at her feet.

"Yes, she should," Kelly murmured, spooning a bite of sweet goop into her mouth.

"Ghee!" cried Oliver. She fed him a bite of his own and kept reading.

Magna cum laude in economics from the University of Pennsylvania. A promising career in venture capital, followed by success in high-end event planning. Marriage to a Wharton whiz kid. But Baby made trouble.

"Oh, you did not," Kelly said, slipping another spoonful of oatmeal and peaches into Oliver's mouth. "It wasn't your fault. Don't even read this, sweetie. The media lies."

O'Hara Day went back to work after a scant twelve weeks of maternity leave. Initially, everyone was excited—the boss, the clients, Day herself, who'd get to keep a foot in the working world while she raised her son, Oliver.

But in the three months since O'Hara Day has been back on the job, nothing's gone according to plan. Colleagues and clients complain that O'Hara Day, twenty-seven, is distracted and ditzy, absentminded and hard to reach.

Ouch. Kelly squeezed her eyes shut. She knew her work hadn't been perfect and that there'd been one too many conference calls she'd missed or conducted from home with Oliver in his Ultrasaucer (which frequently turned into Oliver on her lap or Oliver screaming in her ear or Oliver trying to chew the telephone or pull her hair or do both at the same time). There had also, of course, been the ill-fated Dolores Wartz party, and Oliver's not-so-festive dirty diaper. But still, there was nothing quite like the pain of seeing what your coworkers really thought of you, spelled out in black and white.

In person, O'Hara Day, a tiny, peppy blonde, is friendly and outgoing, and in ten minutes' time, we're chatting away like girlfriends. But up close she looks like a woman on the verge of the proverbial nervous breakdown— overextended and frazzled, dependent on a fragile webwork of a babysitter and a husband who works from home to make her working days possible. "This is so much harder than I thought it would be," she says, sitting in a living room that's picture perfect only because a few months' worth of clutter has been shoved behind closet doors. And if O'Hara Day, with her smarts and her savvy and her Ivy League degree, can't successfully integrate a career and a family, it doesn't suggest that things for other working mothers are much different—or that thirty-some years after the feminists waged a so-called revolution, the workplace is likely to become a kinder, gentler place for the women who will follow in her footsteps.

Kelly wiped Oliver's chin. She found that she didn't care much about the women who would follow in her footsteps. Nor did she care how foolish she looked in the magazine, how ridiculous she appeared in the picture, what unkind things her coworkers had whispered into Amy Mayhew's ear. She was too spent, too overworked, and too tired to care about any of it anymore. "You know what the women who follow in my footsteps should worry about?" she asked Oliver. "Their husbands losing their jobs." And what was this bullshit about "a tiny, peppy blonde"? As if any man in the history of recorded time had ever been described that way in print. And "chatting away like girl-friends?" *In your dreams, Amy Mayhew,* she thought. *My girlfriends don't stab me in the back.*

She went through the next hour and a half in a fog—bathing the baby, putting on his pajamas, reading him *Curious George* while he batted at the pages and tried to chew the back cover, nursing him, rocking him, easing him into his crib while he arched his back and held himself rigid and screamed for what had become his customary ten minutes before finally dropping off. Then she went back to the rocker and sat there with her feet on the Peter Rabbit rug, the red-and-white-checked gingham sheets matching the red-and-white quilt, the lampshade and the wall hanging painted with her son's name, his blankets and sweaters all folded and tucked away. It all looked perfect. The way she'd imagined it, sitting here rocking, when she was pregnant. What a joke.

She couldn't keep working at Eventives. That much was clear. Not after they'd called her—what was it? "Distracted and ditzy." Anonymously, of course. The cowards didn't even have the guts to affix their names to their insults. But if she didn't keep working, there was no way they could keep the apartment. Even if Elizabeth was willing to pay her severance and give her cash for the vacation days she'd never taken, between the health insurance and the car pay-ments, it would be a matter of months before she couldn't pay the rent.

So they'd move. She could find somewhere cheaper. Then she'd have to find another job. Full-time, most likely, because it was clear that she wasn't constitutionally cut out for the balancing act of part-time work, and if she was going to be Oliver's sole support, part-time wouldn't pay well enough.

Maybe Becky would hire her, now that Lia was going back to Los Angeles. Or help her find something. Maybe she could be a restaurant consultant, helping them with their business plans, figuring out what neighborhoods would be receptive to what kind of establishment. Kelly started to get up out of the rocker, to reach for a notebook, to start making a list, and found that she couldn't. No energy. No motivation. She felt like a toy with the batteries yanked out.

She groped for the telephone with her eyes closed, dialing the numbers by heart.

"Hello?" said Mary. "Kelly, is that you? Is something wrong?"

Kelly rocked herself back and forth. "Something is."

"I'll get the girls," Mary said. There was a click as she put Kelly on hold. A minute later, she was back with Doreen in New Jersey, Maureen in San Diego, and Terry in Vermont on the line.

"What's up?" asked Terry.

"It's Steve," said Kelly. "Well, actually, it's everything."

For once, none of her sisters were laughing at her. "What's going on?" Mary asked.

"Steve left." Horrified silence. "He lost his job."

"I knew it!" Terry crowed.

"Terry, that's not helping," said Doreen.

"When?" asked Terry.

"Before Oliver was born," Kelly said.

The sisters gasped identically.

"It's been hard," Kelly said. "I've been working and taking care of the baby, and Steve's been just . . . well, I don't know what Steve's been doing."

"Steve's a loser," said Mary.

"Let's kill him!" said Terry.

"Terry, shut up," said Maureen.

"He's not a loser," Kelly said. She rocked back and forth faster, knowing that this would be the hard part. "He just wasn't cut out to work for a big company, I guess. He wanted to be a teacher, I think, and I didn't want to let him." She felt her throat tightening. "And he wanted to help with Oliver, and I wouldn't let him do that, either. I just thought I was the only one who could do it right."

"No way," Mary said sarcastically. "Not you."

"Please don't make fun of me," Kelly said, wiping her eyes. "Please don't."

"Sorry," Mary said, laughing her rumbling laugh. "Sorry."

Kelly held the telephone tightly, picturing her sisters' faces. "It's been awful. I was so angry at Steve, and I've been so tired, and . . ." She closed her eyes. "I just thought I had it all figured out."

"You always did," said Mary, but she didn't sound judgmental. Just sad. "Do you need money? Or a place to stay, just to give yourself a break? We've got the guest room."

"Where's Steve?" asked Doreen.

"He left," Kelly said. "He's gone."

"So we'll find him! And kill him!" Terry said.

"Not helping, Terry. Oliver needs a father," said Doreen.

Mary murmured in agreement. "You should call him," she said.

"I know," said Kelly. She hadn't wanted to hear it, but she knew that it was true. "Call him and then what?"

"Tell him you're sorry," said Maureen. Kelly felt her temper flare—*Sorry for what? Sorry for supporting us? For paying the bills?*

"You have to let people be who they want," Terry said. "Even if it's not what you want them to be."

"Terry, that's profound," said Kelly.

"I know!" said Terry, sounding pleased with herself. "Like, remember the summer you wanted me to work at Scoops with you, only I wanted to be a camp counselor? It's just like that!"

"Well, more or less," said Mary.

"We're here if you need us," Maureen said. "And you don't have to be perfect for us." She paused. "It's not all happily-ever-after, Kay-Kay. It's only that easy in fairy tales."

"But I have to try," Kelly said, knowing that she was talking to herself as much as to her sisters. And it was Terry, the youngest sister, who answered for all of them.

"Yes," she said. "You have to try."

• • •

Mary agreed to take care of the baby on Saturday afternoon. Steve was waiting at the door of the coffee shop where she used to sweat and swear over her crappy laptop, and Kelly was jolted back to the first time she'd seen him, wearing that incongruous suit and tie, bending over her at a bar. No suit today, she saw. Steve wore a blue sweater that she didn't recognize, khaki pants, and boots with snow dripping from the soles.

"Hi," she said.

He looked up. His face was unreadable. "Hi, Kelly." He cleared his throat. "You look good."

I'm not, she wanted to say. *I'm not good at all.* It had been five weeks since he'd left, and she'd missed him so intensely that it felt as if she'd had a headache every moment she was awake. For months and months, she'd been wishing him gone when she wasn't day-dreaming about ways to murder him and make it look like a shaving accident. No more dirty dishes to pick up, no more shoes to pick up and put back in the closet, no more messes to clean that weren't made by Lemon or Oliver. She hadn't thought about the silence, the way, after Oliver fell asleep, that the apartment was so quiet she could hear the rustle as she turned the pages of the Bible her mother had left her.

Try, she remembered her sisters telling her. *You have to try.*

"Come on in. It's cold," he said, holding the door open.

She stood on the sidewalk. Steve looked at her with his eyebrows raised.

"No," she said. "I have to show you something first."

"Show me . . ."

"We have to go for a ride."

Steve had met her whole family only once before their wedding, on the day of Kelly's graduation. She'd planned the day meticulously, making the reservation at Hikaru months in advance, buying her father a new jacket and tie for Christmas, taking Terry and Doreen out for sushi when they visited her on campus that spring. She'd made a half dozen phone calls the week of graduation, drilling her siblings on what they were going to wear, reminding Terry and Doreen to practice with their chopsticks, thinking that she'd learned her lesson with Scott Schiff and her family was going to behave like upstanding, middle-class citizens and not Coors-swilling, chain-smokers from some crummy seaside town in New Jersey.

Of course, the day had been a disaster. Her father had poked at his sashimi with the tip of one chopstick, lifting the slices of eel and fluke as if they were evidence at a crime scene. Her sisters had giggled and whispered to each other over bowls of teriyaki chicken, then slipped outside to sneak cigarettes by the Dumpster, and her brother Charlie had gotten drunk on the sake Kelly had ordered for the table and hadn't quite made it to the bathroom before he threw up. Steven's parents looked at them like they were a pack of rats, while Kelly sat at the head of the table wearing the pearls Steve had bought her as a graduation gift, smiling and nodding until she felt like a bobble-head doll. *And what do you do?* Kenneth Day had asked her father, and Kelly held her breath until her father recited what she'd advised him to say. *I work for the government.*

"He delivers the mail," Kelly said, as she drove toward the turn-pike.

"What?"

"My father," she said. Her hands tightened on the steering wheel. She hadn't told Steve much about her family, and she'd certainly never taken him to the house where she'd grown up, but if they were going to go on as husband and wife, he had to understand. The truth, the whole truth, and nothing but the truth.

"Kelly? Where are we going?"

"Home," she said, her foot pressing down hard on the gas pedal. "We're going home."

An hour and fifteen minutes later, they pulled up to the dingy Cape Cod house at the end of a cul-de-sac. She let Steve take it in through the car window: the patchy lawn, the peeling paint, the half-assembled pickup truck in the driveway, and the fading black-and-gold stickers that spelled out O'HARA on the green mailbox.

She looked straight ahead with her hands on the steering wheel. "I was never a Girl Scout," she said. "You know why? Because you needed a uniform to be a Girl Scout, and my parents didn't have enough money to buy one, and they didn't want to take charity."

"Oh." His voice was quiet in their too-big car.

"Whenever we got invited to other kids' birthday parties, we'd bring something from the dollar store wrapped in the comics from the Sunday paper, so eventually we'd make excuses about why we couldn't go. And every Christmas . . ." Her voice caught in her throat. "The ladies from the church would bring a basket with a turkey in it and whatever toys we'd asked for. Anything we wanted, they'd bring us, and they'd wrap it, too. And the cards would say 'From Santa,' but we figured out who they were really from, and we stopped asking because we all knew that taking charity was even worse than being poor."

Her voice was flat. Her hands looked horrible; the nails ragged and bitten, the cuticles cracked and bleeding. "I hated this house. I hated everything about it. I hated wearing my sister's hand-me-downs. I hated how everything smelled like cigarette smoke and how there was never anything nice or new and how . . ." She wiped her eyes. "When we got married, I promised myself that if I had a baby, I was going to be able to buy him everything he needed. He'd always feel safe. He'd never have to feel like he was growing up in a house like a leaky boat where the bottom could just fall out." She turned and looked at her husband in the eyes. "That was why I wanted you to go get a job. That was why it mattered so much. It made me crazy to think that we were going to go through our savings because . . ." She lifted her hands in the air. "Then what?" She looked past him, through the window, toward the house. "This?"

"Kelly." He reached for her hands. "I never had any idea. If you'd told me . . ."

"But I couldn't." She bit back a sob. "I didn't want you to know, I didn't want you to see . . ." She wiped her eyes and looked at him again. "I thought you wouldn't love me anymore."

"Hey." He reached for her, pulling her head to his shoulder. "I will love you forever. I'll take care of you. And Oliver. I just . . ." He exhaled. "I figured, we had the money, there wasn't any rush, I could stay home and be with the baby." He shook his head ruefully. "I couldn't figure out why you were so frantic." He rubbed one hand up and down his cheek. "Now I think I get it. And in spite of what you were thinking, it was never my intention to lie around on the couch forever."

"But that's what you were doing."

"For six months, yeah," Steve said. He started jiggling his leg. "I didn't take the whole layoff thing very well. It really threw me. And I just figured I'd take a break, take some time, spend time with the baby, get back on my feet." He paused, looking out the window. "My father was never around," Steve said. "I wanted to be a different kind of dad." He gave her a crooked smile. "If I'd known that—if you'd told me—I would have started working again. Even if it meant I wasn't seeing Oliver." His voice dropped. "If that's what it took to keep you."

She rested her cheek against him. She could hear the ticks of the engine cooling and, somewhere, not far off, a mother calling her child inside. "I thought I told you. I know I tried. I . . ." But even as she spoke, a part of her wondered. What had she said, exactly? What had she said out loud, and what had she only thought?

He wrapped his arm around her. "We made mistakes," he said. "Both of us did. But we've got a little boy now, Kelly. We have to work things out."

She sniffled. "I wish I'd known," she said. "I wish I'd known how it was going to turn out. I wish I'd known what was going to happen . . ."

"Hey," he said. "We didn't register for a crystal ball. But I know this. I'm not Scott Schiff, and I'm not your father." He gestured at himself, grinning his crooked grin. She remembered looking up at him, half drunk in a pile of leaves. He'd brought her french fries. He'd told her she was beautiful. And she'd believed him.

"See?" he asked, pointing. "No mailbag. Fly zipped . . ." He paused to check. "Most of the time. Whether I wind up teaching, or whatever, I will always take care of you and Oliver."

"Do you promise?" she asked. Her voice wobbled. He bent his head close, brushing her cheek with his lips.

"Will you believe me if I do?"

She nodded. "I want things to be different," she whispered, half to herself.

"Things can be however you want them," Steve said. She leaned into his body with her eyes closed, letting him support her weight, letting him stroke her hair, letting herself be held.

March

LIA

I sat in the park with my mother's blue suitcase and the lunch Sarah had packed at my feet. My friends were gathered around me—Kelly, who'd pulled Oliver over in a new red wagon; Becky, with Ava in a backpack; and Ayinde, tall and stern and beautiful, as if she'd been sculpted, her face a clay mask finished in the heat of a kiln, holding Julian in her arms. The sky was slate gray, the temperature in the forties, but the wind had a hint of softness to it, and I could see the buds on the dogwood and cherry trees, tight little knots of red and pink, the sign of spring to come. Sam had flown back to California two weeks ago to start furnishing the house he'd picked out, and I'd stayed behind in Philadelphia to pack, to close up the apartment, and to say my good-byes. Sam was returning in the afternoon to take me home.

"You do realize that you're breaking Dash the dishwasher's heart?" Becky asked.

"He'll get over it," I said.

"We'll miss you," Kelly said, sounding small and forlorn. "Do you really have to go live there?"

"It's where Sam is," I said. "And work, if I ever work again. And . . ." I wasn't sure I'd be able to trust my voice. "It's where Caleb is buried. I think I'd always like to live close enough so that I could go visit."

All three of them nodded. Becky cleared her throat. "I have news."

"Good news?" Kelly asked.

"I think so. I hope so." She lifted Ava, in a pink fleece coat and pink sweatpants, in her arms and stood up straight. "I'm. Um. A little bit pregnant."

"Oh my God, are you serious?" Kelly shrieked. "You had sex, didn't you?"

"Can't get anything by you," Becky said with a smile.

"You had sex, and now you're pregnant!"

"What are you, my eighth-grade health teacher?" Becky grumbled, but she was smiling. Glowing, actually. "It's a little overwhelming, but we're happy about it. Most of the time." She looked at Ava, who wrinkled her nose and giggled. "I don't know how this one's going to feel."

"What did Mimi say?" Kelly asked.

Becky rolled her eyes. "We haven't told her yet. And the truce is still holding, although at this point I've had to bite my tongue so many times I'm surprised it's still attached." She shrugged. "I've got to do it, though, if I want my marriage to work."

All three of us turned unconsciously toward Kelly, and, just as fast, all three of us turned away. She'd noticed, though. "I think," she said, in a small voice, with her head bent over the wagon. "I think we're going to be okay." She sat on the bench, pushing Oliver back and forth in his little red wagon. "I think Steve and I both had a picture in our heads when we got married, a picture of how it was going to be."

"Didn't we all," Ayinde said softly.

"So it's going to be different now. We're moving into a smaller place," she said and smiled. "With actual furniture. Steve's going to start substitute teaching and interviewing for full-time jobs for the fall, and . . ." She cleared her throat. "I'm going back to school for interior design at Drexel. They've got a great program." She looked at us shyly. "You guys liked Oliver's nursery, right?"

"Oh, it's so cute," Becky said. "That's going to be perfect for you!"

Kelly scooped Oliver into her arms and planted a kiss on the top of his head. "I don't care about perfect anymore. I just want good enough."

"Oh, Kelly," I said. I put my hand on her arm and squeezed, and then, unable to help myself, I reached out and grabbed one of Oliver's thighs. "Hey, Oliver." There were the rolls I'd gotten used to—for the time I'd known him, Oliver had legs like squished loaves of Wonder Bread—but it felt as if one or two of them might have gone missing. I inspected the baby carefully. He'd gotten taller, and his face had gotten leaner. He'd grown more hair, too. And suddenly I realized: He was growing out of his babyness, turning into a little boy.

I blinked to keep the tears back. They'd all changed so much. Ava had six teeth and, much to Mimi's relief, some hair at last. At ten months, Julian was tall and watchful, with a serious look about him, like a banker evaluating a mortgage application. I couldn't stop myself from thinking about Caleb and how I wouldn't get to see this, the growing up, filling out, the changing, the progression from bottles to baby food to real food, from rolling to crawling to walking to running.

"Check him out," said Kelly, her tone a mixture of pride and regret. "He's getting thinner."

"He's growing up."

"It's so unbelievable," said Kelly. "I guess that when it was really bad—you know, when Steve was home all day and I was just scrambling—I thought it would always be that way. That he'd always be a little guy. Well, a big little guy. But he's changing," she said, holding the baby against her chest. "And I am, too."

"We all did," said Becky. "The miracle of motherhood." She rolled her eyes.

Kelly looked at me. "You'll come back in July, won't you? For Oliver's and Ava's birthdays?"

"And then you'll have to come back again in the fall," said Becky. "For my birth day."

"Sure I will," I said.

Ayinde cleared her throat. "Lia," she said. "I think your mother has arrived."

I saw Sam and my mother, walking toward me from Walnut Street, arm in arm. *Wonders never do cease,* I thought, as I got to my feet. "I'm really bad at good-byes," I began.

"Oh, bullshit," said Becky, wrapping her arms around me. "We'll miss you."

"I'll miss you, too," I said, and now I wasn't even bothering to pretend I wasn't crying. "You guys . . . you don't even know, but you saved my life."

"I think we all saved each other," Becky said.

I held all of them in my arms for a moment—Becky and Kelly and Ayinde, Oliver and Julian and Ava. "Good-bye, good-bye, good-bye, mommies," I sang.

"Cut it out with that goddamn song," said Becky, wiping her eyes with her sleeve.

"Good-bye, good-bye, good-bye, babies," I said.

Ava stared. Oliver chewed solemnly on his thumb. "Bye!" said Julian, opening and closing his fist. "Bye bye bye bye bye."

"Oh my God," said Kelly, her eyes widening, "did you all hear that?"

"His first word!" said Becky. "Quick, Ayinde, did you bring your *Baby Success! Success Stories* book to write it down?"

"No, it's at home, I . . . oh, never mind."

"Ladies," said Sam, greeting my friends. "And gentlemen, of course," he said to Oliver and Julian.

"Bye bye bye bye bye," Julian babbled and waved his fist in the air.

"Come on," I said, "before I lose it." And I took my husband's arm.

"Lia?"

"Mmm," I said. Sam had given me the window seat, and I was

snuggled beside him, with a blanket pulled up to my waist and my cheek resting against the cool glass. We were somewhere over the middle of America. The sky was dark with clouds, and I was half asleep.

"Do you want something to drink?"

I shook my head, closed my eyes, and fell, almost instantly, into the old dream, the one I'd been having since I'd come home to Philadelphia. I was standing in the nursery that had been my son's, white carpet and cream-colored walls and a sheer curtain blowing in front of an open window. My feet were bare as I walked across the floor, and I could feel the wind blowing the curtain against my cheek—warm and soft, like the promise of something wonderful, the kind of wind you only got at night in California.

Only this time, the dream was different. This time, there was noise coming from the crib. Not crying, which would have been true to life, but soft cooing, nonsense syllables that were almost words, *La la la* and *Ba ba ba.* Noises I'd heard Ava and Oliver and Julian making as I'd watched them.

"Shh, baby," I said, walking faster. "Shh, I'm here." *Now I'll look down and the crib will be empty,* I thought, as I bent over the railings the way I had a hundred times in a hundred dreams. Now I'll look down and he'll be gone.

But the crib wasn't empty. I leaned and looked, and there was Caleb, wearing his blue pajamas with a duck on the front, Caleb as he would have been at this age, his eyes bright, his skin pink and flushed, cheeks and legs and arms plump and sturdy, reddish-brown hair on his head, no longer looking like an angry, malnourished old man but like a baby. My baby.

"Caleb," I whispered, lifting him into my arms, where he fit like a key in an oiled lock. He felt familiar, like Ava, like Oliver, like Julian, but not like any of them. Like his own thing. My own thing. My baby. My boy.

At that moment, I was both inside of the dream and outside of it; in the nursery and on the airplane, and I could see everything, could feel everything—my husband beside me, his hand warm on my knee, the window against my cheek cool from the air rushing against it, beaded with raindrops, the weight of the baby in my arms.

> *Bye and bye, bye and bye,*
> *My darling baby, don't you cry.*
> *The moon is still above the hill.*
> *The soft clouds gather in the sky.*

"Caleb," I said. The country spread itself beneath me like a lady's skirt, patches of brown and green stitched together with forgiveness, with hope, with love. I heard the wind blow through the open nursery window. Beside me, I felt my husband turning his body toward me, his breath gentle against my cheek, his hand warm over mine. In my dream, in my arms, my baby opened his eyes and smiled.

ACKNOWLEDGMENTS

Little Earthquakes is a work of fiction but, like Becky, Kelly and Ayinde, I was lucky enough to join a prenatal yoga class with a group of wonderful women who've been my friends and lifeline throughout the nine months of my own daughter's life, and who were generous enough to share their own stories of labor and delivery, marriage and new motherhood with me, and support me as I made the journey myself. Thanks to Gail Silver, Debbie Bilder and baby Max, Alexa Hymowitz and Zach, Carrie Coleman and James Rufus, Jeanette Andersson and Filippa, Kate Mackey and Jackson and Andrea Cipriani Mecchi and Anthony and Lucia.

I am awed and humbled by the hard work of Joanna Pulcini, whose efforts on behalf of this book included poring over the manuscript in coffee shops and hotel rooms from Los Angeles to New York. Her diligent, thoughtful, rigorous editing, and occasional babysitting were invaluable. I am lucky to have her as my agent and even luckier to have her as my friend.

My editor Greer Kessel Hendricks is worth a price above rubies for her skillful, compassionate reading, and hundred kindnesses, large and small. I'm also very thankful to her assistant Suzanne ONeill and everyone at Atria, especially Seale Ballenger, Ben Bruton, Tommy Semosh, Holly Bemiss, Shannon McKenna, Karen Mender and Judith Curr, the best publisher any writer could wish for.

Kyra Ryan gave me an insightful read and invaluable edits of an early draft, and Alison Kolani helped smooth out the final product. I owe a debt of gratitude to both of them, and to Ann Marie Mendlow, whose generosity to Planned Parenthood of Southeastern Pennsylvania has earned her a place in posterity (insofar as this books constitute posterity).

I'm grateful to friends near and far: Susan Abrams Krevsky and Ben Krevsky, Alan Promer and Sharon Fenick, Charlie and Abby Glassenberg, Eric and Becky Spratford, Clare Epstein and Phil DiGennaro, Kim and Paul Niehaus, Steve and Andrea Hasegawa, Ginny Durham, Lisa Maslankowski and Robert DiCicco, Craig, Elizabeth, Alice and Arthur LaBan, and most especially Melinda McKibben Pedersen, one of the best and bravest women I know.

The mothers of the Hall-Mercer playgroup shared their stories and listened to mine. I'm so glad that Lucy and I get to hang out with Linda Derbyshire, Jamie Cohen and Mia; Amy Schildt and Natalie, Shane Siegel and Carly, and Emily Birknes and Madeline.

Thanks to the lactation consultants at Pennsylvania Hospital for helping with both my in-print and real-time babies, and to the staff at the Society Hill Cosi for the free coffee, and for never begrudging me and my laptop one of the tables near the window, and the power outlet.

A special shout-out to Jamie Seibert, who came into my life like a gift from heaven and takes wonderful care of Lucy when I'm writing.

None of this would have been possible without of my family My husband Adam, my mother Fran Frumin and my Nanna Faye Frumin, Jake, April, Olivia, Molly and Joe Weiner, and Warren Bonin, Ebbie Bonin, and Todd Bonin gave me love, support and material (and, in Olivia's case, hand-me-downs). My daughter Lucy Jane made this book possible, and made my life wonderful.

And I will always be grateful for the support and love of one of my first editors, my friend Liza Nelligan, who died last spring.

I don't think I'll ever be able to express how much Liza's faith in me made my writing life possible, but I believe that her spirit and her love of laughter, and good stories, lives on in this story, and in every other story I'll tell. The lullabye that Lia sings is from *The Rainbabies*, one of the books that Liza sent to Lucy a few days after she was born. I've used it in this book in tribute to Liza.

POCKET
BOOKS

GOOD IN BED
Jennifer Weiner

Cannie Shapiro never wanted to be famous. The smart, sharp,
plus-sized reporter was perfectly happy writing about other
people's lives for her local newspaper. And for the past twenty-
eight years, things have been tripping along nicely for Cannie.
Sure, her mother has come charging out of the closet, and her
father has long since dropped out of her world. But she loves her
job, her friends, her dog and her life. She loves her apartment
and her commodious, quilt-lined bed. She has made a tenuous
peace with her body and she even felt okay about ending her
relationship with her boyfriend Bruce. But now this . . .

'Loving a larger woman is an act of courage in our world,' Bruce
has written in a national woman's magazine. And Cannie – who
never knew that Bruce saw her as a larger woman, or thought
that loving her was an act of courage – is plunged into misery,
and the most amazing year of her life.

'Wildly funny and surprisingly tender' COSMOPOLITAN

PRICE £6.99
ISBN 0 7434 1528 0

POCKET
BOOKS

IN HER SHOES
Jennifer Weiner

Rose Feller is thirty; a successful lawyer with high hopes of a relationship with Jim, Mr Not-Quite-Right, a senior partner in her firm. The last thing she needs is her messed-up, only occasionally employed sister Maggie moving in: drinking, smoking, stealing her money – and her shoes – and spoiling her chance of romance. If only Maggie would grow up and settle down with a nice guy and a steady job.

Maggie is drop dead gorgeous and irresistible to men. She's going to make it big as a TV presenter, or a singer . . . or an actress. All she needs is a lucky break. What she doesn't need is her uptight sister Rose interfering in her life. If only Rose would lighten-up, have some fun – and learn how to use a pair of tweezers.

Rose and Maggie think they have nothing in common but a childhood tragedy, shared DNA and the same size feet, but they are about to find out that they're more alike than they'd ever believe.

'A seriously smart and classy read' HEAT

PRICE £6.99
ISBN 0 7434 1566 3

POCKET
BOOKS

These books and other titles are available from your bookshop or can be ordered direct from the publisher.

0 7434 6893 7	**LITTLE EARTHQUAKES**	£6.99
0 7434 1566 3	**IN HER SHOES**	£6.99
0 7434 1528 0	**GOOD IN BED**	£6.99

Please send cheque or postal order for the value of the book, free postage and packing within the UK; OVERSEAS including Republic of Ireland £2 per book.

OR: Please debit this amount from my

VISA/ACCESS/MASTERCARD:

CARD NO:. . . . .

EXPIRY DATE: . . . .

AMOUNT: £. . . . .

NAME:. . . . .

ADDRESS:. . . . .

. . . .

SIGNATURE: . . . .

Send orders to SIMON & SCHUSTER CASH SALES
PO Box 29, Douglas Isle of Man, IM99 1BQ
Tel: 01624 677237, Fax: 01624 670923
Email: bookshop@enterprise.net
www.bookpost.co.uk
Please allow 14 days for delivery. Prices and availability
subject to change without notice